Sonata

Book Two of the Rhapsody Quartet

by A. M. Hodgson

Sonata

Copyright © 2014 by A.M. Hodgson
Cover Artwork by Alexis Orellana

First Publication: April, 2014
First Paperback Printing: January, 2016

www.amhodgson.com

For Lynne & Darin,
who have taught me that
love makes anything possible.

Contents

Prologue

Her eyes surveyed the wretched landscape with disdain.

"It's degraded further," she said aloud. Not so long ago, the corruption would have brought her to her knees in grief. There was nothing here but tepid pools, dusty brown earth, and withered, twisted trees.

She snapped a shoot from a branch of a once mighty giant, inspecting it. A fine residue lined the pads of her fingertips. She narrowed her eyes. An experiment: the twig fell apart into ash with the tiniest pressure of her thumb.

It was even worse than she'd suspected.

She smeared the powder on the silk of her dress. The Broken did not provoke tears anymore. She was stronger now.

A few feet ahead of her, a stagnant pool rippled forebodingly. A bubble popped, belching out a foul stench.

Where was he? This was the agreed hour and day. She wouldn't wait forever. If he did not arrive soon, she would leave. After all, she was a busy woman.

More minutes passed.

She threw her hands up impatiently, turning to leave.

The earth shuddered and groaned, the space crackling with magic. He'd arrived at last.

"You're late," she said, keeping her tone impassive.

He was dark, and he made her feel uncomfortable. Not *afraid*— she was not so easily intimidated by such trivialities— but unsettled. His very nature upset even this dismal place. From

1

beneath the wrecked trees, she watched small spider-like shapes scuttle amongst the shadows.

He glided over with movements as fluid as mercury. Like mercury, he was poisonous, but not without his uses.

He smiled darkly, "Did I keep you waiting?"

She narrowed her eyes. He knew her schedule was demanding. His tardiness would disrupt the rest of her day. Yet arguing with such a creature was like arguing with the wind: a pointless endeavor.

"Have you made any progress?"

He shrugged casually, but the movement was contrived. This was a creature of *certainty*, of black and white. He was attempting to control the interaction. "I've done as you've asked, if that's what you mean." He moved nearer to her, closing the gap between them.

It took every scrap of her willpower to stay put and allow the intimacy. "And?"

"And… things are going as expected. Everything's in motion. All your sources have been accurate, if *that's* your question. Isn't that what's important to you? So long as you keep your end of the deal, I'll *cheerfully* keep mine…" he paused, smiling broadly. Yet his eyes were calculating. "Unless you've changed your mind?"

She forced her shoulders to remain squared. "Everything should progress naturally, then. You needn't worry. I will honor our arrangement." She paused. "The siren must die soon. I have suffered her existence far too long."

"It's not like we haven't *tried.* It's surprising she's survived this long." He sounded almost admiring of the girl. It was infuriating.

"Your order is rarely surprised," she said with irritation.

He shook his head, chuckling. "No, we're not. We usually make it our business to know exactly what's going on in the Realm and Overworld… a fair difference from *your* kind."

She wrinkled her nose. His presumptions regarding her species were rude.

"Honestly," he continued, hands in his pockets, "it seems like a waste of resources. There *is* a simple and elegant solution to this…" he dragged a finger across his throat slowly, dramatically. "I could just streamline it. I'd even do it myself."

"Absolutely not!" she rebuked. "That's only a final resort. She's the last of her kind; I don't want to make her a martyr!"

"Still playing the politics?" he mused. He cocked his head, "Would you answer a question, Lady?"

She nodded.

He took a quick look around the landscape— the still water, the dead trees.

"Why meet here, in this forsaken place?"

She exhaled slowly, taking a fleeting glance around. *Why, indeed.*

"To remind us of what is at stake."

Part One
The Map

"Golden lads and girls all must,
As chimney sweepers, come to dust."

- William Shakespeare, *Cymbeline*

Chapter One

Brews

I lay sprawled across my bed in Marin's house, books littered before me. I was *attempting* to demystify the siren language. After Aldan's tome on my kind hadn't been any help, I'd asked Marin to check out some linguistic books from the school library on the off chance Siren had any relation to a human language. I pored over them, but I couldn't find anything like the delicate script. I groaned, collapsing into the mattress.

There were too many variables. I'd barely heard it aloud, and I had no basis for comparison. I didn't have an aptitude for this. Last year I dropped out of my Spanish class when it was too challenging, and Siren appeared infinitely more complex.

I slammed the book shut with a loud thump, frustrated.

From the corner of my room, I heard Glenn sigh. I didn't care. I was still mad at him.

Three weeks ago, an entire army of extras attacked me, determined to see the siren race eliminated. He'd risked his life for me, but in the end I saved him. Of course, Glenn was only in danger because of me. To keep him safe, I'd planned on leaving Whitecrest forever.

I wasn't going to go alone, though. I squeezed my eyes shut.

Score.

He was the closest I'd ever had to a boyfriend, and the only other siren in the world— as far as we knew. But Score was better at being a siren than I was. I'd been floundering since my transition, advertising my siren heritage to anyone with a slight inkling of magic. In contrast, Score blended in beautifully. The other extras didn't even know he existed.

He could've spent his entire life like that, but instead Score went out of his way to find and befriend me. It was his knowledge, not mine, that saved Glenn's life when the hostile extras attacked.

I'd missed Score these past three weeks. My feelings for him were unclear, but I did share a bond with him. Maybe it was just because we were the last of our race, but it felt like something more. After I'd abandoned him on the beach, he was probably long gone from Whitecrest.

I buried my head in the comforter. If Score was here, the writing wouldn't be a barrier. He spoke and read the siren language fluently.

When we'd last seen each other, Score had tossed me his mother's ring: a pretty band with a large oval opal flanked by two smaller, triangular white diamonds. It seemed like a promise at the time, a promise to find each other again. So far, I'd been under house arrest and hadn't heard a peep from him. It felt pretty hopeless— we'd only known each other a few weeks before my confinement.

I still wore the ring on my finger.

It really irritated Glenn.

What Score hadn't known, what I'd discovered later that day, was that the ring was a key— or rather, half a key. My father's ring, part of my own inheritance, was the second half. When I fit them into the slots of my family music box, a small compartment opened containing a map… written in Siren. Despite my efforts, I couldn't decipher it.

If Glenn hadn't been so diligent as my jailer, I'd have just called Score and invited him to read it. But my bodyguard had confiscated my mobile phone, and I doubted I'd be able to arrange such a rendezvous with him watching me like a hawk.

I made a frustrated grunt into the covers.

A feminine voice mumbled something in the corner. Marin.

Glenn didn't bother to speak quietly, "Don't ask *me* what's going on with her. She's still throwing her tantrum. Apparently, I'm not presently worthy of recognition."

I pulled myself up, groaning, but Marin was already bounding towards my bedside. Her blonde curls swung around her hips cheerfully, her blue-green eyes sparkling.

"Sarah!" she chirped, using my human name. "What's been with you the last few weeks? You've hardly left this room."

I shrugged. The official word at school was that I was sick with mono, giving me lots of time to recover at home. I spent my days trying to figure out everything I could about the siren language. So far I hadn't found anything useful.

"I get it, that attack was *scary*," she continued. "But you have to get over it. If I had a pearl for every time someone tried to kill me and failed—" She grinned, "Okay, so actually I'd still have fewer pearls than I do now. Poor use of the expression, sorry."

I smiled half-heartedly at the joke. Marin had become a surprising friend to me these past couple months. Despite being the class bully, she took me under her wing when she discovered the changes I was experiencing. Marin was well-versed in magic, so she immediately recognized me as an extraordinary. I was shocked when I'd learned she was a mermaid princess.

I rolled to the edge of the bed, sitting next to her. "It's not the attack, especially," I said, shaking my head. I wondered if I should tell her everything.

Her eyes were hungry, "Then what is it?" She grinned, "Ooh, I know! You broke up with Will!"

I nodded tightly. She didn't know that 'Will' was actually 'Score'. She assumed our relationship was as superficial as every human fling she blew through— a fun diversion, but just that: a diversion. What Score and I shared wasn't frivolous— though I really didn't know what I felt. Some days, it seemed crystal clear, but other times I was sure we were just friends.

The last time I'd seen him, we'd shared a kiss. My stomach flipped thinking about it. But emotions had been running high, and I had no idea if it meant anything. Probably not. But... maybe.

I heard Glenn make a "humph!" sort of noise from the corner. Clearly, my bodyguard's opinion on Score hadn't changed since learning he was a siren. Glenn was still unfairly prejudiced. I took a moment to glare at him, but he just ignored me.

Marin rolled her eyes, "Well, if it's bothering you *that* much, just go see him! He's been totally moping around school since you broke up. He asks about you all the time."

It felt like I'd been jolted with electricity. "You've seen him?!" I'd hoped to meet with Score again, but assumed he

6

would've left following our failed escape attempt. He wasn't keen on being around a lot of extras. I couldn't blame him. Not after what I'd been through.

"Look, you broke his heart, but that doesn't mean he's just dropped off the face of the earth!" She rolled her eyes, "He was here every single day that week you broke up."

"*What*?" Then it dawned on me. Glenn had chased him away before I'd even known he was here. I whipped my head towards him, "Why... *why* would you do that?!"

Glenn's face remained neutral, a single eyebrow raising, "So you're speaking to me again?"

I glared at him, "Why are you trying to ruin my life?!"

"Because it's better for him if he moves on," he said. "You *know* that."

"You had *no right!*"

"Yes, *I did,*" he sighed, pulling his willowy frame up. The normally impressive elf was subdued today. He gazed at me like I was a child throwing a tantrum. His green and brown flecked eyes were tired, his long features drawn, his silver hair less lustrous than normal. "You're finished with him, right? You can't have a," the tiniest pause, "*human* pining away for you forever. Especially not with who knows what out there trying to get you." He gestured to the door, "It's the whole reason I've been assigned to you. *I* can handle it. Your fragile little boyfriend can't."

I glared at him. Glenn was the only other person in the world who knew Score was a siren. Score had siren magic, and Glenn was underestimating it. He seemed to think the fortress I'd built from nothing but three notes was a fluke, something that only happened because I was under extreme stress. I knew better. Score's magic had saved my life, crafted a private beach, summoned flames from thin air.

I didn't respond because I'd been learning to guard the secrets of my species. The more other extras knew, the more frightened they'd become, the more incentive they'd have to end me.

"Honestly, Glenn," Marin turned to him, "you're taking this way too seriously. You have to let her have some fun! If she's attached," she shrugged, "that's fine. Eventually she'll move on, leaving Will a dried up husk on the side of the road." She examined her fingernails, "And you can't tell me you have ethical problems with *that*. I mean, human boys have used girls over and over and over for centuries!"

I frowned. While I didn't disagree with her exactly, I wanted to point out that human girls had done the same thing for centuries, too. But it was beside the point, because no one in this scenario *was* human. Unfortunately, Marin didn't know that.

Glenn shrugged, stalking back to the little reading nook he'd claimed as his space. "Whatever. If she wants to *talk* to him again, that's her call," he said, propping his feet up on the side table. "But I'll be with her."

I scowled. The likelihood of Score and I ever being alone again was looking bleak indeed.

The last time the three of us had been together, Glenn had trained an arrow at Score's head until I agreed to return home. I doubted Score would be enthusiastic about being in the same place as my elf guard again. The whole thing was giving me a headache, and aggravating my already foul mood.

I hopped up. "I'm going to take a shower and go to bed," I announced. It was only about 4:30, but I was tired of arguing. Maybe I'd watch a movie tonight and take my mind off all this nonsense.

Marin shook her head, "Nuh-uh. You're going to go out with me on the town, *just the two of us*."

Glenn's eyebrows lifted a notch, but he didn't say anything.

My heart quickened. It was true he used to let Marin and I do things alone, but all that had changed after the last attack. Was I truly going to get a reprieve from being babysat for an hour or two? I looked at him excitedly. "Can we really go somewhere alone?!"

He shrugged, uncrossing his ankles and bringing his legs back to the floor. "Why not?"

I stared at him.

Yeah, why not? I thought.

I'd been a shut-in the past three weeks.

"Seriously?" I asked, unable to contain my grin. Getting out of Marin's house— though it wasn't exactly cramped— sounded amazing.

He nodded, a small smile playing on his lips, "Yeah, *seriously*. It's reassuring to see cheer on your features again. Marin can handle herself. You can't get far in Whitecrest, and she can stall if there's trouble. Besides, the extras who attacked you have disbanded. The past three weeks have been quiet… I don't see any problem with it."

I let out an excited squeal, racing over to him, squeezing him tightly in spite of myself. He looked surprised but laughed, hugging me back for a moment before pulling away. "Just promise me," he said, "that you won't do anything that's *asking* for trouble, little bird."

I nodded, grabbing my coat from the wardrobe. I wrapped a scarf around my neck, "Thank you, thank you, thank you."

He chuckled, waving me on, "Just go before I change my mind!"

Grabbing Marin's hand, I raced down the stairs and out the door, giggling.

She laughed, "See, all you needed was some backbone." She looped her arm through the crook of my elbow. "Let's walk," she suggested. "It'll take longer."

I stretched out, inhaling the clean autumn air. It was clear, rain and mist-free. The setting sunshine peeked through the trees— a rare day in Whitecrest this time of year. I'd almost forgotten how good the ocean could smell.

"I've been worried about you," she said as we walked.

I turned to her, but she didn't look at me as she spoke. Marin had trouble with serious talks like this and usually avoided them. I shifted my gaze towards my feet.

"You've been practically catatonic these past weeks. I get that you're upset about the attack, but it's been *resolved*. The council stripped Aristos of his title. They were livid that so many extras would go against their orders. The Lady of Flowers was just about foaming at the mouth. The new centaur council member is a mare, too, so that's a huge upset. There's never been a female from them before."

I kicked at the wet pavement beneath my feet, "Honestly, that's just part of it. I'm still adjusting to magic, that's all."

Marin nodded, "I get it…" She peeked over at me, trying to be discreet and failing. "You've been really mad at Glenn, too. I could probably count on one hand the number of words I've heard you say to him in the last three weeks, not counting the last couple minutes."

"Yeah," I said, "we… had a fight. I was mad at him for

9

jumping into that group, that's all." It was only partially a lie. I *was* angry about that, but I was also mad at him for threatening Score and imprisoning me.

"Well," Marin said softly, "you need to forgive him for that." She paused. "He's very fond of you, Sarah."

"I know."

We'd reached the main drag of Whitecrest, which was only a half-mile long. Closed shops were crowded together. They'd open again when the tourists rolled into town for spring break, but for now they'd remain dark. Further down the block were the year-round businesses: the movie theater, the used bookstore, a couple of restaurants, a small coffee shop.

"Want to catch a movie?" I asked, pointing at the tiny cinema.

Marin crinkled her nose, "The last time I watched a movie with *you*, you complained about the soundtrack the whole time. No way. Let's head to the café," she suggested. "It's where all the cool kids hang out."

"*You'd* know."

"Damn straight, I'd know," she replied with a haughty toss of her blonde waves.

We tugged the door open. The smell of roasting coffee wafted towards us, making my mouth water. The lights were dim in here, but the ambiance was cozy. As we slid into a tiny booth, a waitress with short spiky purple hair and a barbell through her nose approached us.

"You guys want anything?"

Marin ordered a caramel latte. I took my time speaking, focusing my intention to only order a drink— not gain a new fan. I carefully asked for a white chocolate pumpkin latte with extra syrup. I liked my coffee sweet.

A crowd was gathering in my peripherals. I glanced towards them. The tiny stage was set for a band to perform— a guitar, a drum set, a microphone. I rolled my eyes, "Maybe we should leave. It looks like they're going to play." Humans performing music live sounded like torture to my siren ears.

"Oh *come on*," Marin said, "I get that your musical tastes are better than anyone else's in the world because you're all sireny and stuff. But seriously, can you just let your hair down and forget about being so above everyone for a second? Just enjoy that you're outside of the house!"

"If you think I was bad about soundtracks—" Marin gave me an exasperated look. I laughed, "Fine." I made a pained expression at her, batting my eyes, "But you don't know how much of a sacrifice this is." She really didn't, but I'd at least finish my coffee before insisting we left.

Marin smirked. A couple guys swaggered through a side door that led from outside and hopped onto the stage. Whitecrest being so tiny, I immediately recognized them: a couple seniors from school. Ryan Anderson, a boy with dyed jet-black hair and a couple tattoos peeking from beneath the collar of his shirt, strode to the microphone and adjusted it. A boy named Tim Howard settled at the drum set, twirling his sticks. Tim was known for being the class clown— I wondered why I'd never heard that he was a drummer before.

The outside door swung open again, and my heart leapt into my throat.

Trudging to the stage, grabbing the acoustic guitar, was Score.

The crowd was thick around the stage, but Marin and I remained in our little booth. My eyes fluttered to her. She grinned diabolically, "They've played here every night for a week, packing the house the past two nights. If you can believe it, there are *groupies*— for Will, mostly." She took a sip of her coffee, "He's pretty good. I mean, not *siren* good I'm sure, but good."

I stared down at my latte, trying hard not to laugh. Score was *exactly* siren good. I inhaled twice before looking up. The guitar started.

They were playing a cover of *Everlong* by the Foo Fighters. Score had his eyes closed, getting into it, but not playing to his potential. He only deviated from the set chords a couple times, playing with notes and rhythm to improve it. At calculated moments, he'd intentionally choose the wrong timing or note to make the playing seem less perfect, more human.

Tim kept the beat reasonably, but was hardly accomplished. Ryan had a decent voice, but it wobbled a little uncertainly on some notes. Score's playing helped to ride out the errors and guided the other guys. To a human, it probably sounded flawless. To me it felt like an assault. It would've been completely unbearable without Score's playing.

I smiled wistfully, considering how much better it'd be if Score was singing. On the other hand, it would've been Armageddon to the rest of the audience.

I leaned forward, settling my head in my hand, watching him. He looked tired. Purple shadows rested below his eyes. Score somehow made it fashionable, as though he was a tormented artist. His hair was a little messier than before, but it was still the same chestnut color, cut stylishly. Even from the back of the room, I could see the line of long, dark lashes resting against his cheekbones as he closed his eyes and played. I noticed for the first time he had the slightest dimple on his chin.

Score's hands flew confidently over the strings. I wondered if this guitar was his. Probably— he had at least twenty of them. It wasn't his siren-made instrument, but I knew he wouldn't play that in public.

He finished the last chord. As the final vibrations reverberated into the audience, he opened his eyes, sighing and looking up. His gaze fell upon me, flat brown eyes widening in recognition.

I think the band expected to keep playing, but Score stood as soon as the song was over and tapped Ryan on the shoulder, speaking with him. The chatter in the room made it impossible to hear what he was saying. After a couple seconds, he hopped off the stage and wove through the crowd towards me.

Ryan leaned into the microphone, "We're apparently taking a short break."

The crowd grumbled, annoyed they'd only had one measly song.

"Hi," Score said breathlessly to me.

I looked pointedly at Marin.

She rolled her eyes, "Whatever, losers." Waving an arm, she called, "Hey, Ryan!" The singer turned around to see Marin gesturing to him, "I'm sure you've always wanted to buy me a drink."

Ryan looked a little confused. The girls gathered near the stage were visibly perturbed, but Marin plowed through the crowd until she reached her prey, looping her arm around his and dragging him towards the baristas.

Score slid into the booth. The same pierced waitress asked if he wanted anything during the break. "Just some black coffee."

I made a face, "Yuck."

He raised a brow and gestured towards my drink, "And what concoction are you drinking? *I* prefer simplicity."

I smiled and stared into the foam of my latte, wondering what to say. A million things came to mind, but they all fell flat. I sighed, slumping down into the booth.

"So," he said, as lightly as possible, "where's the elf?"

I shrugged, "Home. He let me go out with Stacie tonight." I always used Marin's human name around Score. It was simpler.

"That's a bit of a miracle, isn't it?" he said with a bitter laugh. "I thought you were pretty much a prisoner."

I took a sip of the latte, "These days, I kind of am." I tapped my fingertips along the cup, "Look, Score, I'm sorry about… the last time we were together."

He shook his head, "I don't blame you. I blame that jerk."

"He's not a jerk," I said, frowning. Even though I'd been mad at him for weeks, I owed Glenn my life.

"He threatened to kill me," Score pointed out, "then banned me from seeing you."

I sighed and leaned against my hand. "I just heard about that today. I'm sorry. I didn't even know you'd been over."

"Whatever," he said, glancing towards his bandmates. Ryan was suitably distracted by Marin, but Tim looked like he wanted to get on with the show. He gestured with one drumstick towards Score.

"Look, Lyra," he said, "he can threaten all he wants. But unless he murders me, I'm not going to stop seeing you until *you* say that's what you want. Tell him that." He stood, downing his coffee like a shot.

Score grinned, noticing the sparkle on my hand.

"You're wearing it."

I nodded, feeling my face flush. I'd completely forgotten about the map.

"Actually, I have to tell you something else—"

Tim whistled impatiently. Score waved at him before turning back, apologetic. He leaned forward, brushing his thumb along my jaw, cupping my face in his hand. "I have to finish the set. I'm committed."

I nodded, feeling my heart sink.

He leaned across the table, hesitating just a moment before

his lips brushed against mine. I could almost feel every other girls' hackles raise.

"If you're around, I don't know if I can hold back," he said with a soft smile on his face. He settled back into the booth, "It'd be irresponsible for you to stay here now."

"Oh... okay," I said, disappointed.

He shook his head, laughing, "Come *on*, you're only missing Ryan's singing."

I giggled, though the few people who caught the line threw us incredulous glances like it was a ridiculous thing to say. Maybe it was, to a human. I grinned, feeling like I was in my own private club with Score.

"I'll see you soon... right?" he asked hopefully.

"I— yeah. Of course. As soon as I'm able."

He smiled again, slipping out of the booth. Weaving his way to Ryan, he pulled the singer from a laughing Marin who didn't seem to care a bit that she'd lost her latest arm candy.

I waved her down, standing. I returned my attention to Score. He and Ryan were already hopping back onto the stage. A couple girls cat-called, "Take it off, Will!"

I bit my lip, an odd streak of jealousy blooming within my stomach. The music started again, a song I didn't recognize. It was probably another cover.

"Hey!" Marin chirped, noticing I'd dropped a few dollars on the table. "You don't want to stay until the show's over?" She waggled her eyebrows, "Hottie McHothot should be available later."

"No," I said, "he asked me to leave."

"Huh..." Marin cocked her head towards the stage, looking a little pensive. She turned back to me, "I guess we can go."

We wove through the crowd, pushing our way out the door. The air was crisp and cold. Twilight had arrived, and with it the clouds and mist rolled in. I wrapped my scarf around my neck, shivering.

"So," Marin said when we'd gotten about twenty feet from the building, "you want to tell me why you're being so weird?"

I laughed, trying to play it off. "What do you mean?"

"You're acting super suspicious. For one thing, the way you've been carrying on this last week, I thought you'd be all over staying out as long as possible." She checked her cell phone, "We spent less than twenty minutes in Brews."

"Yeah," I said, considering it. Marin wasn't stupid, and I was tired of lying. I stopped walking, folding my arms close to my body. "Marin?"

She looked at me, expectant, "Yes?"

"Can you keep a secret?"

She rolled her eyes, *"Finally."*

Chapter Two

Confessions

We sat on the beach next to a bonfire, staring at the ocean tide. Marin was a surprisingly good listener. I spilled my guts to her about almost everything: Will's true identity, that he was another siren, that we were going to run away, that Glenn had stopped us, that my bodyguard already knew everything. The only parts I left out were the map, my alteration magic, and the secret behind my eye colors.

When I'd finished, she stared at me with a solemn expression, whistling beneath her breath. "No wonder you were so angry with Glenn! He broke you up!"

I sighed, digging my bare feet into the sand, "Yeah, I guess."

"So what was Will's— I mean, Score's— deal tonight?"

"He told me that it would be too hard to hold back if I was there. It's safer for us to be apart in that kind of situation." My eyes began to fill with tears, frustrated.

Marin slung an arm around my shoulder and squeezed tightly, "Hey, now! Everything's gonna be okay in the end. With me on your side, how could it not?"

~~~~~~~~~~~~~~~~~

When we arrived home, Glenn was carving notches into long sticks, creating spaces to run fletching for new arrows. Every few seconds, he'd pick up a long feather and check to make sure his measurements were accurate. He held it against the primitive arrow before setting it down to continue his work. He seemed involved in his task. He didn't even bother looking up at us when we entered.

"Goodnight, Lyra," Marin said, rushing down the stairs before I could chide her for starting an awkward conversation.

"So, it's *Lyra*, yeah?" Glenn said, still not taking his eyes from his work. The current arrow was almost finished, feathers cut and inserted. All it needed was an arrowhead to complete it. He moved on to a new one, "Decided to tell the mermaid all your woes?"

I sighed, kicking my shoes off. There was still sand between my toes— I'd need to rinse them before heading to bed. I crossed my arms awkwardly, "I needed to talk to someone sympathetic."

He let out a frustrated grunt, setting the crude arrow on the side table. "It's not that I don't sympathize." He glanced at me, "You haven't seemed like you've *wanted* to talk about it. Or *anything*." Glenn stood, making his way to me. He settled on the edge of the bed, leaving two feet between us.

"It's not that I haven't wanted to talk," I explained, "I've just been so angry with you." I peered at him, giving him a moment to respond. He was silent, willing to listen. I mustered my courage, "I don't think you did the right thing."

He sighed, his hands balled up into fists, "I know you don't. I'm sorry." The apology was clearly not because he thought he was in the wrong. It was only an apology for upsetting me. He relaxed his hands, "The truth is, regardless of how you feel, I wouldn't have forgiven myself if your plan had worked." He turned his head towards me, "It'd be easier than you think, finding you two out. It's a bloody miracle Score's remained hidden as long as he has."

"He's really good at blending in," I said a little lamely. "He was going to teach me."

"Do you know, Lyra, how I knew he was an extra that night?" Glenn asked. I shook my head. I *had* wondered. "I could feel the magic he was using in the air. I knew it wasn't yours. Everyone's energy has a different pattern, and his was prickly, like a cactus."

I turned to him, staring into his eyes. "And what does mine

17

feel like?"

He tugged me closer to him. Using the back of his fingers, he stroked my arm gently. It gave me goosebumps. "*Your* magic feels like a caress, little bird. I knew it wasn't you." He dropped my wrist, allowing it to fall back to my side. "The days before, I'd felt something, but nothing substantial. I don't know how he hid it."

I looked away. I knew. Score had a small ritual when we met, humming a simple song to help hide us. The day we tried to run, I'd been so wound up that I interrupted his song impatiently. I'd kissed him, assuming we were leaving soon, anyway. We'd been caught because of me. My shoulders slumped. Maybe I was a danger to Score, too.

Glenn stood. "I'm not confident in his abilities to protect you, Lyra. There's more to this world than you know yet, and I don't trust Score's knowledge. I've had the training. I can do this. What's more, I *want* to do this." His eyes flashed with determination, "I promise you, no one else will try so hard to keep you alive. I don't want to keep you under lock and key, but if I must, I will."

My face prickled as I gathered my nerve, but I needed to say it. It was better to be honest with Glenn. The more I tried to fight him, the bigger my problems grew. I couldn't look at his eyes, so I stared at the comforter, "I saw Score tonight."

His eyebrows raised, "Really?"

I nodded. *Go on*, I urged myself. "He said… he said you can't keep him from me. That unless *I* want him out of my life, he'll be around."

"I don't think that's a good idea. It's just going to draw attention to him if he's hanging around you." He shrugged, "But it's his choice." Glenn stared into my eyes, "I wasn't kidding before. I'll be present when he's here. I don't trust him. He's liable to try something stupid— like running away again."

I nodded, happy to be honest with him again. I stared at my sand covered feet. "Glenn… can I tell you a secret?"

He smiled wryly. "I'm already keeping one big secret for you, little bird. I may as well *thoroughly* not do my job. What's up?"

I stood, making a beeline for the wardrobe. I grabbed the music box my parents had left me.

Pulling the ring from my finger, I retrieved the second from inside the box. I pressed both into the lid. The inner mechanisms clacked as the little trap door opened, revealing the secret compartment.

I pulled out the map, unfolding it and laying it on the bed.

The top half was a typical world map, but below that was a map of a landscape barely familiar to me: the Realm. Scattered in tiny writing were symbols. All of them repeated several times on both worlds.

I flipped the map over, tracing for the fourth time the siren script on it. It looked like three verses of a song or poem. Below that was one smaller symbol. I sighed, picking up the map again, feeling hopeless.

He stroked the edge of the paper, "This is why you've been focused on the language these past couple weeks?"

I nodded.

"I'll keep it a secret, but..." His eyes were sympathetic, "This has magic in it."

"Does it?" I asked coyly. I'd noticed it myself the first moment I pulled it from the box. The paper hummed with energy.

"If we don't know what it does," he stated, "we need to destroy it."

I cringed, pulling the map close to my body. "Why?!"

"One of the five principles of magic— it requires form and function. Obviously there's a form, but the function is unknown. Magic's unstable when it's not channeled through a person. Enchanted objects need to be closely monitored to ensure they don't create..." Glenn looked into my eyes, "complications."

"What complications?"

"It can act like a poison if it contacts you for too long. It can combust, or distort reality— it's unpredictable. People who discover these sort of artifacts often find themselves turning into frogs," he said with a tiny bit of humor in his voice.

"But this isn't dangerous."

"How do you know?"

"It's from my parents."

"Perhaps," Glenn agreed, "or perhaps someone else planted it within that box."

"But the rings—" I started. Glenn just stared at me, the same determined look I saw when he caught me trying to run with

Score. "It has siren writing," I argued.

"That you *can't read*," he reminded me. "We don't know enough about your race to determine their intentions. It could make you disappear from this plane, or channel dead souls within your body, or— just trust me, it's dangerous untranslated."

"Well…" I began, "maybe *I* can't read it… but I know someone who can."

He groaned, understanding immediately. "You don't mean…?"

I nodded sheepishly.

Glenn dropped backward onto the carpet. He stared at the ceiling, sighing, "Whatever. Tell him to come over tomorrow."

I folded the map, replacing it within the hidden compartment of the music box. I turned my attention back to my bodyguard. Glenn was still lying on the floor.

"Thank you," I said. "For the chance, at least."

"Yeah."

I crawled next to him, lying on my stomach. "You're the best bodyguard ever."

He tried to keep his face hard, but failed, cracking a smile and chuckling. "Really? Yet you've got me breaking all sorts of rules…"

I propped my face in my hands. "The *very* best," I elaborated, batting my eyes.

He shook his head, laughing, "How *do* you do that?"

"Do what?" I asked, grinning.

"Take me from being so frustrated with you to… well, this. Even a few weeks ago…" He trailed off, face getting serious again.

He'd piqued my curiosity. "Even a few weeks ago, what, Glenn?"

He sighed, sitting up with his legs sprawled out in front of him. He turned to me, "You were so enraged with me. But by that next day, I couldn't be angry with you anymore." He cocked his head, smiling just a little bit, "It was your reaction. You were so upset and intent on me knowing it. Pouting. Somewhat adorable."

My pulse quickened. I didn't know if I felt flattered or insulted.

Glenn's hand brushed against my arm for just a moment, but he pulled away as quickly as he connected.

I couldn't explain the disappointment I felt.

When I dialed Score's number the next morning, I thought he might start whooping with excitement.

"Lyra! Is it really you?"

"No, it's another awkward siren girl!" I teased.

He laughed into the receiver— it sounded relieved.

"So you escaped from your ivory tower?"

"Hmm…" I said, looking up at Glenn. "Not exactly."

"Then what's up?" he asked with a bit more reservation in his tone.

"Could you come over?" I asked. "I have something I need to show you."

A pause. "I can be there by eleven." I glanced at the clock; it was 10:41 now.

"See you soon, then," I whispered.

~~~~~~~~~~~~~~~

I headed downstairs and began pacing as soon as I'd hung up. Glenn propped himself against one wall of the front parlor, watching me.

"I'm not going to *hurt* him," he muttered almost regretfully. "You may as well settle yourself upstairs to wait."

Marin wasn't even awake yet, staying up until god only knew which hour last night. I shook my head, continuing to pace. I didn't trust Glenn to greet Score civilly without me present. The thought of having both men in the same place terrified me.

The door finally rapped. I nearly jumped out of my skin, yanking it open and dragging Score inside. His guitar was slung over his back, his eyes filled with determination. Today they were a brown so dark it was almost black. The subtle shifts proved to me he'd abandoned his contacts for this visit. He eyed Glenn coldly, but the elf just rolled his eyes and gestured to the stairs.

I slid my hand into Score's, trying to reassure him.

Glenn sank into his usual chair. I loosed my hand from Score's, sitting on the bed. I stared at him, twisting my fingers together. Score was doing his best to remain patient, his arms folded across his chest. His eyes shifted colors to bright yellow, the edges tinged with pink. It was close to the happy gold I'd seen him wear before, but not quite— a different emotion, I was sure. I wondered what it meant.

After a few moments, he sighed. "You needed to show me something?"

I bit my lip. Glenn looked amused by our discomfort, but when I caught his eye, he cast his gaze to the floor.

"The night we were going to leave together—" I started. Score shot a poisonous glance at Glenn. The elf kept his face impassive, unimpressed. "That night," I continued, "I found this." I pulled out my music box, pressing the rings into the slots. The compartment popped open.

Score's eyes grew wide as he studied the carved box. "I didn't know you had another siren heirloom," he said. He stroked the sides.

"I never got that far," I muttered. "We didn't have much time to talk together, even less time to show you my own inheritance." I pulled out the map and unfolded it onto the bed.

"This is…" his eyes lit up, examining the precise lettering, "This is really amazing."

"I kept it to myself these weeks, trying to figure out how to read it."

Score grinned at me, "You ever get it?"

"No! What's the big secret, anyway? How do you do it?"

He shrugged, "I don't know. Like I said before, it's easier than reading English to me."

"The map's magic, mate," Glenn said in the corner. "It's a use it or lose it situation, I'm afraid. What does it do?"

Score looked at me, "You don't know?"

"There's no way *to* know," I said. "Not without a siren Rosetta Stone, anyway." I flipped the map over. "There's writing on this side." I pointed to the scrawled verses.

His eyes treaded over the symbols carefully but quickly. His irises shifted to turquoise. "The top is a poem, or a riddle… it's instructions to find siren cities! But *this*," he pointed at the three symbols below the verses, "is a *chord*."

"Which chord?" I asked.

"An 'A'," he answered. "Like this." He hummed, three notes harmonizing together to create the sound. I'd only done it once myself, and hearing Score do it now gave me goosebumps.

22

The map didn't change, but Glenn announced, "That unlocked some magic. I can feel it in the air."

I flipped the map again, checking to see if it'd transformed. It remained unchanged. I sighed, flicking the page impatiently. My fingertip brushed against one of the small symbols on the familiar world map. At my touch, the symbol illuminated to a soft glow. On the lower Realm map, a matching symbol pulsed.

Glenn closed the gap between us quickly, staring at the map. "Oh my," he breathed, "that's... that's brilliant."

"What is it?" I asked him.

He tapped the first symbol again. It stopped blinking. Glenn grinned, brushing his finger on a new one. It illuminated, along with another matching one on the opposite map. He laughed, "This is a *working, magical,* Realm map. Do you know how rare that is?"

"The magic Realm? The one I read about?" I asked.

He nodded, "Yes, exactly. There are gates everywhere." He pointed towards the tiny symbol near Whitecrest, "For instance, here's the gate that you used to attend the council meeting, where we met." He tapped a symbol that looked like two small squiggles with a slash running through it. On the bottom map the same symbol lit up on the southern edge of the Realm.

"Our scholars have been trying for *years* to create a map of gates to the Realm. The main issue everyone has is keeping track of it all. A numerical system doesn't work, because it's difficult to match corresponding numbers due to the sheer *amount* we'd need. It's too much information to convey easily. Yet this is elegant," he said. He looked to Score, "What does the symbol I just activated mean?"

"It means water. The gate would be in water."

"See?" Glenn said, laughing. "Amazing." He shook his head, "Most of us have incomplete maps, or no map at all. We memorize a handful of major gates, but you can see those are marked here, too." He pointed to a symbol that vaguely looked like a cursive L, "These are the main extraordinary thoroughfares. There's around 40, spread out. Traveling anywhere out of the way is more difficult. Every local knows their own tricks, of course, but none of the races are especially forthcoming with that information. Most gates are only known to keepers, like Aldan, and the council members." He stared down at the map, a look of admiration on his face, "Whatever else sirens were, they were innovative. They've managed to convey all the information on one map in a way that is easily read."

"So I can keep it?" I asked hopefully.

Glenn shrugged, "Honestly, if the council knew about it, they'd take it from you. They wouldn't *call* it stealing, but it may as well be." He stroked his chin, "I suspect it's harmless enough."

That statement surprised me. Glenn didn't usually say anything negative about the council. This implied they weren't perfect in his eyes either. I glanced at Score, "What do you think?"

He flipped the map over, looking at the printed verses. He stared into my eyes, his own conflicted. At the moment they were a bright blue.

"The truth is, this tells us where to start looking." He sighed, the edges of his eyes tinged with a misty gray. "I *think*, anyway. Like I said, it's written out like a riddle. But it tells us where to begin searching."

"Score, even if this gives us a clue, the council would find out. You'd be in danger, too."

Glenn nodded in the corner, "Almost certainly. They'd never let you take the map with you if petitioned."

I sighed. Score grabbed one of my hands, staring earnestly into my eyes, "My offer still stands. We could run. We have a starting point now."

Glenn leaned against the door, shaking his head. "I'm not leaving Lyra," he announced. "While I'm in favor of her discovering her heritage, I want her to be smart about it. She's already garnered hostility from someone, maybe several someones. If she runs into the wrong extra, she'll die."

Score's eyes narrowed. "So you're going to hold her back?"

Glenn glared at him, standing up straight. I noted with surprise that Glenn was an inch or two taller than Score.

"Let me make one thing clear," he said, his green eyes steely. "If you don't believe anything else, believe this: everything I do, *everything*, is for her sake."

"Really?" Score asked, "Does Lyra think that?"

I stared at the floor. I didn't want to be brought into this argument.

Glenn laughed harshly, "Maybe not. But here's an

example— the only reason I'm not throwing you out that window right now is because of her."

"Too bad," said Score coldly, "I'd love to show you what I've got."

I leapt to my feet, shutting the map back into the music box with a snap. "Thank you for the lovely time," I said shortly. I strode purposefully to the exit.

Glenn blocked the door before I got to it, his brows raising apologetically, "I'm sorry…"

"Move."

"Where are you going?"

I rolled my eyes, "Downstairs. I'm going to talk to Marin about her all-nighter of partying and irresponsibility. You know. *Mature* conversation." I pushed past him, stomping down the stairs.

"Looks like you're in trouble," I heard behind me. Score.

My back went rigid. I scowled, continuing my descent.

Glenn whistled softly, "I doubt I'm the only one."

Chapter Three

Mermaid Problems

I'd only seen Marin's room a few times, though 'room' was the wrong term. She had an entire wing. The space consisted of her bedchamber, spa, and something she called a 'boutique'— an enormous closet and dressing room.

I rapped timidly on the door.

"Ugh," I heard her groan from within, "go away!"

I knocked a little bit harder, "Marin?"

"Oh, gods, it's you," she moaned. "Fine, come in."

I opened the door, surprised by the amount of light. I'd only been in Marin's room at night, or when it was so cloud-covered I didn't realize the impact all the windows made. Two walls were solid glass, forming a sun-room on one side.

The wall across from her bed was also flanked by large windows. Between them a pair of French doors opened to a private patio that led to the beach. Right off the patio, a small stream wound through a lavish garden. How the staff had managed to grow such lush vegetation in the sand, I didn't know, but they'd achieved it.

The walls were a soft satin pink with crisp white borders. Her bedding was all white and a gauzy net canopy billowed from the posts like an aura. Expensive cream colored furniture dotted the room. Scattered across the tops were coral and seashells and the largest pearls I'd ever seen.

Marin sat on her bed in lacy pajamas, looking miserable. Her eyes were red and puffy. She clutched a tissue in one hand.

"Are you okay?"

She rolled her eyes, "Dinner with my father last night."

"At midnight?" I raised my eyebrows. We didn't even get home until eleven.

"Actually, around one. He was busy, but I expected it to be late." She grabbed her pillow, squeezing it to her chest. "We have dinner once a month together, to talk about… things."

Marin's relationship with her father was what I'd call rocky at best. The first time I saw them together, he was rude to her— borderline bullying. Marin had responded with as much venom herself. When I'd asked her about it, she refused to give me a straight answer. I wasn't sure what to say, so I sat on the couch in a far corner of the room.

Marin sighed, composing herself. The door rapped sharply.

"Miss Marin?" a maid called.

Marin crinkled her nose, "Come in, come in…" The maid stepped inside, handing her a letter in a thick envelope that shimmered slightly. The back was sealed with crimson wax. In the time I'd been staying in her home, I'd seen her receive at least five others like it. "Thank you. You're dismissed."

The maid bowed and exited, shutting the door behind her.

Marin rubbed her forehead, giving the letter an exhausted look. She tossed the parcel to the foot of the bed.

"You've been getting those pretty regularly. The last month, at least."

She laughed thickly, "I've actually been getting them for the past *decade*." My brows raised, but she just smiled. "You're an unexpectedly good friend, Lyra." She patted the edge of the bed, "Come on, sit with me. I know all your secrets now. I guess it's time you learned some of mine."

I settled next to her on the bed. There was so much I had to tell her, but at the moment Marin had her own problems. I looked at her expectantly. She leaned over and collected the shimmering envelope, setting it in my hands. "Go ahead," she urged.

It felt awkward, reading someone else's private correspondence. I looked into her eyes, "Marin… are you sure?"

She laughed, "You *should* know. Go ahead, read it."

I flipped the envelope over, staring at the crimson seal. It was formal, an imprinted fish circled by bold letters spelling a single word: Longfin. I sighed and tore it open, removing the letter.

To Her Royal Highness Princess Marin Ocean Adamaris Whitecrest, First of her Name;

From the deepest fathoms of sincerity, we would like to express our interest in your future visit to the North Atlantic and cordially invite you to Nauticus's Grand Palace to visit with your betrothed, Prince Dylan. The courtesans are most anxious to meet their future queen and discuss your impending nuptials with utmost seriousness. We assure you that such a visit will not be trivialized, and a ball will certainly be held in your honor— an event lavish enough to befit your station as Crown Princess.

As you have not responded to any of our previous requests, we must assume you are quite busy and will attend if you can. Should that be the case, we humbly offer a secondary option that may be more flexible for your bustling schedule: Prince Dylan and his honorable mother, the Lady Longfin, would cheerfully travel all the way to the Pacific to meet formally.

If either of these options are satisfactory to you, please respond via the usual methods within a fortnight so we may properly make suitable arrangements to transport Oceanids of our station.

The Prince is exceptionally anxious to acquaint himself with his bride at last.

Yours,
The Longfin Estate

I chewed on the inside of my cheek, "You're engaged?"

She stretched her legs out, leaning back into the bed, "Yes. I've been betrothed since before I was born. I've never met him, and I don't want to. It'll be one step closer to the throne if I do, one step closer to a life I don't want." She frowned, "Our dinners always end in a fight, but my father," she sighed. "Well, gods love him if he doesn't *try*. Every time we have dinner, he asks me to begin my royal duties. Sometimes he's subtle, but this time he flat out demanded that I grow up. I tried to walk out. I usually do, but this time…" she trailed off, her eyes drifting towards the windows, towards the ocean. "This time he was prepared. Blocked my way." She smiled, "You have no idea why I wouldn't want to take over, do you?"

I shook my head. 'Stacie' loved ruling the school, though she never seemed to take it seriously. I always assumed she'd love to take over the world. The mermaid world seemed a pretty good start.

She sighed, "How can I explain it without sounding… terrible? The truth is, the mermaids have been dealing with a huge problem for the past 4,000 years. There's probably close to ten million Oceanids— I mean, mermaids— in our population, in all the oceans."

I nodded, "Yeah?" The number didn't surprise me. If anything, it seemed like too few given the sheer size of the sea.

Marin leaned forward, "But for all those mermaids, out of the whole population, there's just *seven* men."

My brows raised. That *was* a problem. But then… "How can there possibly be so many mermaids if—"

She laughed, waggling her brows suggestively. "Human men, seduced into our watery temptress lairs. The child from such a union is mer, without fail." She took the paper from my hands, balling it up and stuffing it into the trash. "The thing is, I don't want anything to do with that idiot prince."

"Why are you so sure he's an idiot if you haven't met him?"

She groaned, "Because he's a *merman*. It's pretty much a given. They're *all* idiots. And arrogant. And self-absorbed. And not a single one is faithful! In fact, it's encouraged for them to—" she paused. "I'm getting carried away. Just… trust me on this one. He'll be everything I've imagined. But when I *do* meet him… well, that'll be the day my life basically ends."

The sentence was exceptionally dramatic, but Marin stated it like it was a simple fact— the same way she might note that the sky was blue.

"Do you *have* to meet with him?"

She laughed, shaking her head, "Mercifully, no. I'm spared that trauma for another day. But that doesn't mean he'll stop asking." She gestured to the wastebasket next to her nightstand. It was full to the brim with the softly shimmering letters, all still sealed with crimson wax. "And my father is getting impatient, too. The point is, these guys are born and raised arrogant assholes. My father's probably the best of the bunch, and his marriage with my mother…" she trailed off. "It didn't end well for her. There's so few mermen out there. They're expected to take many mates, and they're all perfectly willing to oblige.

"There's a line of things I have to do before taking the throne. One is marrying a merman. Another is moving to the capital— it isn't far, but it's in the Pacific, underwater. I'd complete a long apprenticeship with my father before…" She glanced up into my eyes, "Before I eventually killed him to take the crown."

My eyebrows lifted unintentionally. It explained the hostility. Even if her father wanted her to succeed, he probably wasn't anxious to die.

"I spent a sizable portion of my night crying as a result," Marin said, "I'm not even sure why. Normally I can roll with it. I mean, I always expect my father to say *something* to me, but last night he seemed almost vindictive about it."

"Huh." I didn't know what to say, so I stared at the floor for a few seconds before turning to her, "Sorry, Marin."

She leaned over, wrapping her arms around me and gave me a squeeze, "I'm glad, for the record, to know you."

"Me, too."

She cocked her head, "But you don't come to my room very often. What did you need?"

I laced my fingers together. "Things have gotten a little crazy."

"Oh," her brows raised in concern. "Did Score freak out when he found out I knew? I'm not going to tell anyone," she added hastily.

I shook my head, "No." I sighed, feeling a pang of guilt, "I haven't even mentioned it. There hasn't been time. When I spoke to you before— I guess I didn't tell you one detail. Inside my music box, my parents left me a map. But it could only be opened with both my ring, and Score's."

Marin whistled, "The plot thickens. What kind of map?"

I gripped her shoulders, "It's really important that no one finds out about this. It has a riddle on the back, written in Siren. Score said he thought it led to information about our species, but I'm not even sure what it says. I didn't get a chance to ask him to translate for me," I said miserably.

She looped an arm around me, "There will be time for

30

that."

"Yeah, maybe. Glenn seemed pretty impressed with it—it's a map of different Realm gates."

"Really? How many are listed?"

"Hundreds? Maybe thousands? I haven't had enough time to look at it."

"Whoa," she said, flopping back onto the bed again.

"I think my parents wanted to lead us somewhere."

"So you're leaving?" she asked, sounding panicked.

I shook my head, "Not any time soon. Glenn and Score got into an argument. Score wanted me to run with him, this time following the map. Glenn wouldn't allow it. They were practically going to blows discussing what was better for me. Neither cared about my opinion on the matter. So I decided to see you instead, rather than listen to them bicker."

She hummed sympathetically, "I think you made the right choice." She stretched, yawning. Her eyes sparkled as she broke into a huge grin, pulling herself from the bed. She wandered to her enormous closet, flicking through clothes. "So details. How much tension was between Score and Glenn?" She passed a shirt to me, and I draped it over one of my arms and trailed after her.

"It was a little weird," I admitted. I curled my toes into my boots, "I can't blame them. Poor Score had his life threatened, and Glenn was just trying to do his job."

"Yeah," Marin said, nodding sarcastically, "'just trying to do his job'." She flipped a second shirt over my arm. She pursed her lips, browsing through her skirts.

"What do you mean?" I asked nervously. I had a feeling I knew what she was implying.

"Puh-lease," she said, rolling her eyes. She tossed a black skirt onto my arms, "Glenn goes a little above and beyond with the whole bodyguard act. If you'd have run off? He'd get reprimanded, sure— but I bet the council would've called it a wash." She shrugged, "They don't devote resources to business that isn't pressing. A single missing siren? Not exactly a high priority..." She stood before her wall of shoes, hands on her hips, trying to decide. "Especially," she continued, "since they didn't seem to care when the whole species disappeared."

A blush crawled up my cheeks, but Marin was absorbed, retrieving a pair of red flats from the shelf. Glenn told me that he

31

cared for me, but we were just friends. Right?

"It's not like that," I said defensively. "Glenn is just vigilant, he's conscientious of—"

Marin snorted, "He's *conscientious* of your curves! If you could see the way he looks at you when you're not looking at him—" She shook her head, stripping from her pajamas and tossing them on the floor. "Trust me. I've been alive for a long time. I know when a guy has it bad. I *usually* take advantage of it." She slithered into a camisole before layering a cardigan over it, pulling the black skirt over her hips.

The door rapped, startling me. My face flushed.

"Princess?"

Glenn. I hoped he hadn't heard what we were talking about.

Marin bounded to the door, flinging it open.

"Good, you're here," Glenn said, his eyes finding mine. If he'd heard us, he didn't give any indication. I chewed on my lip as he said, "I'm sorry, Lyra."

"Whatever," I muttered, folding my arms across my chest. "Where's Score?"

"He returned home." Glenn's hands formed fists. He stared at the floor, "I told him you'd call tomorrow sometime."

That was a surprise. Glenn was obviously trying to make peace with me. "Fine," I muttered. "You're forgiven."

His shoulders slumped a little, "Well… good…" He sighed. "But I'm here because the council has requested our presence at the scrying pool."

My eyebrows shot up, adrenaline coursing through my veins. "Did they find out about Score, or the map, or—"

He shrugged, "I don't know, Lyra. I didn't tell them anything, if that's what you're asking. It's probably just their routine check up. It's about that time again."

"Oh," I said, relaxing.

Glenn placed a hand lightly on my shoulder, cocked his head and gestured behind him, "Ready?"

I nodded stiffly. We headed up to the tower that contained the scrying pool. When we arrived, Glenn closed the door behind us and locked it with a solid click.

It was as private as it could be in this house.

We gazed into the water. It remained black. Glenn cleared his throat, "Member of Her Majesty's guard, Glenn, checking in with the council in regards to the siren." The water rippled for a moment, and the darkness brightened just a tiny bit.

There they were, looking exactly as we'd seen them before, nine council members seated in a ring.

"Ah!" Lady Amaranthe said, "There you are. We were wondering if we'd hear from you at all."

"We were delayed," Glenn said apologetically. "Sarah was speaking with Princess Marin."

"Alone?" the Lady said, her brow arching sharply.

"The Princess is adequate at defensive magic," Glenn explained, "and they were within King Dorian's estate."

The Lady's shoulders relaxed marginally, "I do hope you are not shirking your duties, Glenn," she reprimanded. "Especially with that horrid attack at the commencement of Auct."

Glenn's mouth hardened, but he didn't say anything for a moment. Finally he sighed, "You're right. I will keep closer contact."

"Unnecessary, but we appreciate it nonetheless," Marin's father said. He grinned boyishly, his gaze moving to me. "We have fantastic news. A family of naga in Florida have accepted guardianship of you. You'll be departing in the morning."

My heart thudded dully in my chest. I was leaving Whitecrest.

"I'm…" I said slowly, "grateful for the thought, council members, but with all due respect—"

"Right now," reminded the vampire councilman carefully, "you are under the protection of this council and, in particular, His Majesty King Dorian," he gestured towards Marin's father. "We feel that his generosity has gone far enough. The naga have been kind enough to take you."

The Lady of Flowers nodded. "Indeed," she said, smiling widely. "In fact, this allows you to return home to the Amaranth Guard, Glenn."

He frowned, "With the attack three weeks ago, I hardly think it's prudent to—"

She raised one hand, silencing him, "The attack has been handled by the council, and those responsible are no longer a threat. Those who wish harm on the siren have been suitably disbanded. The menace is eliminated. The naga will provide adequate protection." Her eyes hardened, "You may *come home*,

Glenn."

"I…" he said slowly, "I understand." He bowed his head.

King Dorian smiled, "Good. Then it's settled. You'll be leaving tomorrow."

Chapter Four

Gone

I stumbled from the secret room, my legs sluggish. Glenn stared at the wall. Neither of us moved for several moments, but after a while he sighed loudly, steadying me by the arm and leading me down the stairs to my room.

I landed hard on the edge of my bed, my eyes fixed on the floor. I was leaving Whitecrest. Not only that, but I was losing every friend I had in the process. No Marin, no Score, not even my bodyguard could follow me.

My head felt heavy but I lifted my gaze to Glenn, my chest aching. He looked lost in thought. One hand rested on his chin; he stared vacantly ahead.

"Glenn?" I asked with a quaking voice.

His eyes snapped back into focus. "Yes?"

"What's a naga?"

"They're— they're snake people, Lyra. Human torsos, snake tails. Prefer swamps over other terrain. Capable of adequate defense. Threat level low, so long as they aren't offended." He said it as though he was reading from a dossier.

I twisted the comforter in my hands. *Snake people?*

The day got a little worse.

The door exploded inward as Marin burst through. "I just heard!"

Glenn turned to me. "Perhaps you should spend some time with the Princess, say your goodbyes, Lyra. I— I must prepare for tomorrow."

Marin tugged my arm, "Come on, I've got something for you."

I felt dazed, but allowed her to drag me down the stairs to her room. I sat down hard on her bed, staring into my hands.

"It isn't fair they didn't give you any warning! But naga aren't bad people, Lyra. They're mostly just shy."

"Yeah…"

"I don't want to lose my friend," Marin sputtered. "I have something for you." She dug in her nightstand drawer, producing a small vial with a clear liquid in it. She unscrewed it, setting the black plastic top on the dresser.

"What does it do?"

"Nothing yet," she admitted. "But…" she brought her gaze up, staring at the bright chandelier dangling from the ceiling. Her eyes watered, and Marin caught a single tear as it slipped down her face. She snapped the lid back on the vial, wrapping a bandana around the whole thing, "There."

She offered the small container to me. I took it, rolling it between my fingers before giving her a puzzled look.

"It's an eye scale of mine," she explained. "A mermaid's tear. So we can talk. When you want to communicate with me, remove the cloth— that's how I'll know you're calling. Then pour it into something shallow, and you'll be able to see me."

I clutched the vial closer to me, realizing how precious it was. "Thank you," I choked out. At least I could still visit with Marin. Maybe this goodbye didn't have to be permanent.

"Hey!" she chirped, "There's something else I can give you! For when I visit. We can go for a swim together." She opened the drawer again, retrieving a larger sea green bottle with a small silver cork protruding from it. A thick liquid languidly sloshed inside, like molasses. She tapped the bottle, "This is kind of rare, but I wasn't using it for anything." She uncorked it. The liquid inside was metallic silver. Fat drops fell like syrup from the cork into the bottle's opening.

I sniffed it suspiciously. It smelled like butterscotch. "What does it do?"

"It's a mermaid tincture— aquaspira. Something to help us when we seduce human men to our deadly lairs." She waggled her brows up and down. I had to laugh. "A spoonful of the stuff lets you breathe underwater. No gills necessary. Just that much lasts a full day. If you take more, the effect is exponential— a shot glass of aquaspira would probably last *weeks*. I mean, you couldn't talk, but you'd survive below."

I corked the bottle, smiling at her gratefully. "I'd love to swim with you sometime."

"You…" Marin stared down at the bedspread, uncomfortable. She was getting serious again. "You're my best friend, Lyra."

I wrapped my arms around her, squeezing her tightly. It still felt strange to me, even after so long, that I was taller than her. Before I'd turned, I was probably three inches shorter than she was— and Marin is barely five feet even. Now I towered over her.

"Thank you. Are you *sure* you want to give up the tincture?"

She rolled her eyes, "It's been sitting in my drawer for over thirty years. I'm not using it anytime soon. I could commission more if I needed. Besides, it just means I have to visit, right?"

A lump formed in my throat at the sentiment. I'd moved cities many times in my life, but no one ever cared enough to visit.

"I'd like that."

~~~~~~~~~~~~~~~~~~

Marin and I chatted for most of the evening, the time slipping away faster than I'd have liked. When I glanced at the clock and realized it was after nine, a pang of panic hit me square in the heart. I'd had every intention of calling Score, of telling him I was leaving, of saying goodbye. I'd wanted to spend time with Glenn, too, but it looked like that wasn't going to happen.

Marin gave me a tight hug, "I'll see you in the morning."

I nodded, brushing away a stray tear. "See you in the morning."

If I stayed any longer, both of us would be sobbing. Sighing, I trudged up the stairs with a heavy heart.

Pressing the door to my room open, I noted that Glenn had been busy while I was having my visit. His utility belt laid flat across the bed, two fully stocked bags looped through it. In addition, a small leather bag next to his chair nearly burst at the seams, and his quiver had been restocked.

He was business-like, noticing that I'd arrived. He retrieved the belt and clasped it across his waist, tying the bags to their appropriate loops.

"Glenn, are you already—"

"Lyra..." the sound was muted, but it brought my heart to my throat.

I whipped my body around, searching out the sound. Score stepped from the bathroom, his guitar slung across his back, a backpack in his fist. My own book bag was in his other hand. It didn't make any sense.

"What's going on?"

"We're leaving," Glenn said shortly. "*Now*."

Score tossed my bag in my direction. I caught it, frowning. It was stuffed. I'd planned to attend to that in the morning. "But I'm supposed to—"

"Shh," Score said. "We're leaving."

"Why?!"

"Head start," Glenn grunted. "You want to find out about your people? Now's your chance."

"What?!" I felt dizzy, trying to keep track of it.

"I have a basic idea of where to start, once we're out of Whitecrest," Score said as he slung his own backpack on his shoulder. With the guitar on the other side, it looked pretty awkward, but he seemed used to it.

My heart beat hard in my ears, but the boys clearly meant business. I fumbled with the drawstring on my bag, stuffing the gifts from Marin on top of whatever they'd packed for me.

Glenn grabbed my hand. Score's eyes narrowed, but he trailed behind us as Glenn pulled me down the stairs and out the front door.

When we'd reached town limits, I wrenched my hand back from the elf's grip.

"Will you two tell me what's going on?" I asked, shifting my bag on my shoulders, "When did the plan change?"

"Keep moving," Glenn grunted, pushing on my back.

I dug my heels into the ground, "No! I asked you a question!"

Score shook his head, rubbing his forehead with his fingertips. "He called me tonight, Lyra. On your phone. He said you were going to move away if we didn't leave immediately."

"But—"

Glenn cut me off, "It's one thing to find you a guardian, but to have Amaranthe withdraw my protection—" He shook his head, "You need me, Lyra. I didn't agree with the council's decision, so I made a choice."

I glared at him, "And my input was unnecessary?"

"You were busy." He jerked his head, motioning for us to continue forward. I grudgingly kept pace with the two boys flanking me. "Honestly," he continued, "I decided before the meeting was through this afternoon. Truth is, I had no intentions of leaving you."

I glanced at Score, "You're actually okay with this?"

He just sighed, gripping the strap of his bag. He stared at the ground, keeping the brisk pace Glenn had set. After a long time he said, "I've been ready to leave at a moment's notice, these past three weeks. Ever since before, ever since—" he glanced at Glenn, but the elf just rolled his eyes. "I promised myself if I ever got the chance again, I wouldn't waste it."

I looked to Glenn, then to Score, then back to Glenn. It was difficult to believe they really agreed on anything, let alone anything to do with *me*.

"Where are we heading?" I pressed.

"There's a gate outside of town, about five miles," Glenn explained. "Most likely abandoned. A good place to slip away."

"Why would it be abandoned?"

"Because," he answered, "it leads into the Broken."

"What's the Broken?" Score asked.

"Lyra?" Glenn said, having me field this one.

I tried to remember. "A while back, some sort of cataclysm happened. The Broken used to be an area of the Realm called the Borderlands, but... the magic is gone from it."

I looked over at Glenn, making sure I was remembering correctly. His mouth formed a line, "It's been almost 700 years since it first started. But the magic is vanishing and unstable. In some parts, it's twisted. It's incredibly unpredictable, and extremely dangerous."

"Is there a good reason for us to go through it?" Score asked him harshly.

Glenn just shrugged, "Necessity."

Chapter Five

The Broken

The gate was little more than a hole in the ground. We made our way off the path, through the trees. A wire fence with cautionary signs roped off this section of earth, but Glenn held it up, urging me forward. Twenty yards from the fence was the fissure itself. We stood at the edge of the pit, staring into the blackness.

"Are you sure this is the gate?" Score asked Glenn. His voice wavered.

Glenn smiled at Score's discomfort. "Yes, I'm sure. You're welcome to check the map again."

I craned my head over the hole, my heart speeding up. I couldn't make out much in the darkness, but the sides looked jagged and menacing. I took two big steps backward. I looked into Score's eyes, "Maybe double checking wouldn't hurt."

I tugged at the drawstring on my bag. One of the boys had hastily packed it, burying the music box. I pulled out wad after wad of clothes. Half were completely unpractical for the trip— yoga pants and tank tops. I was glad I'd been wearing my comfortable leather boots today. I shoved the bundle of clothes into Score's hands, finally retrieving the music box.

It took less than a second to click the rings in place and bring the map to eye level. Our location had a marking on it, as expected. I tapped the symbol, watching the corresponding one light up within the Realm. We'd be transported to the Broken, the northeastern most section.

I turned to Score, "What does the symbol mean?"

"Cave… I guess this is close enough."

I frowned, "Do we even know where we're going? What does it say?" I flipped the map over to the enigmatic writing.

Score pointed to the first little section, reciting:

"In ancient times, our legend sprang
From Muses' lips, a place we came.
Great libraries inside this space,
Forgotten tomes of our great race,
In labyrinth's depths you'll find us there,
Within the dread minotaur's lair.

"Without giving it much thought, I figure it means Greece." He returned the wadded clothing to me, and I stuffed it into the bag haphazardly. "That's the first concrete siren references."

"Where in Greece, though?"

"We don't have time to figure that out now!" Glenn snapped. "We need to enter the Realm as soon as possible! It'll be harder to find us there. The last thing we want is to be apprehended by the council."

I folded the map into the box, cramming it into my bag. I tightened the drawstring, staring into the chasm doubtfully.

Glenn extended his hand, "Trust me, Lyra."

I squeezed my eyes shut, taking his offered hand. Three steps forward, then a leap.

We plunged into the darkness of the pit.

The descent was like a shot, pulling my heart into my throat like a roller coaster ride. It was far faster than I'd expected, quicker than the fall from the strange water gateway I'd used before. Mid-way through I felt myself spinning, and suddenly I wasn't sure if I was falling down or up. Everything was pitch black— all definition to the world had vanished. Eventually, a light appeared near my feet. I tightened my sweaty grip on Glenn's hand as the spot of illumination grew bigger and bigger.

We broke through the darkness, and I realized at once we were moving *forward* across the landscape. A pale fluorescent light engulfed us as we were propelled from the gate. On this side it was an actual cave, not a hole. The terrain came upon us quickly, our momentum launching us. I cringed, scraping across the ground painfully. My arms and back gained a harsh rash from the pebbles scattered across the dust.

When we shuddered to a stop, I sat up, dazed and panting. I dropped Glenn's hand from mine. From behind us, I could hear Score come to a halt and groan.

I peered at my surroundings. It wasn't nighttime here, but the weedy light wasn't what I'd call day either. It felt artificial. The sky and ground were a tepid beige. A few vagrant bits of grass grew in tufts, the same flat color as the sky and ground. The most conspicuous piece of scenery was the craggy cave where we'd emerged.

"This looks a lot like where I met the council," I said. I rubbed my hand along the scrapes on my ribs. They stung, making me wince.

Glenn nodded, gracefully leaping to his feet, "That meeting space used to be in the Borderlands." He brushed his pants off and offered me a hand, heaving me up painfully.

I turned to Score, checking his wounds. He'd been less lucky than me— a gash along his jawline dripped with blood. He grimaced, shaking his head in a daze.

Glenn paced, "It used to be meadow, ringed by trees in the eastern area of the Borderlands. The council's seats were in the midst of one of the great forests, chosen thousands of years ago because of the hundreds of gates connecting there."

"So what happened to it? What was this cataclysm?" Score asked, taking my offered arm and hauling himself up. He rubbed along his jaw and cheek, swearing. It made me blush. "Sorry," he mumbled.

"No one knows," Glenn answered. "It just happened one day. The magic disappeared." He stood motionless, cocking his head to the side. After a long moment he declared, "I can't hear anyone or anything following us. I think we've made it. At least this far."

I folded my arms across my chest, "What now?"

Score gestured to my bag, "Check the map for a gate nearby?"

Glenn pulled his bow from his back, inspecting it for damage. A moment later he slung it over his shoulders, satisfied. "The closest gate will likely be leagues from here, but we're safe enough for the moment. We have time." He drew his quiver down from his shoulder and began to systematically check his arrows.

I pulled the map out, pursing my lips. Despite how easy it was to read, plotting the best routes would be mind boggling. I suspected there were going to be a lot of stops on the way.

Score studied the map. He pointed to a small symbol that was relatively close to our current location, in an area just beyond the Broken. He turned to Glenn. "There's a gate that will send us to Europe. It's a start, but we'd have to go through a section called the 'Azure Plains'."

Glenn nodded and continued to rifle through his arrows. "The Azure Plains is mostly unpopulated, if we can avoid centaur herds." He sighed, adding under his breath, "Which is the last group we'd want to encounter." He slung his quiver over his shoulder. The weapons were intact.

"But the symbol means it's a main thoroughfare," Score added with a frown.

Glenn kicked the ground and hissed, "*Arashk.* Are there any other gates nearby?"

Score stared at the map, considering it. He tapped several symbols, but after studying one for a few seconds, he'd get frustrated and jab a new one, dissatisfied. "There are, but they're all near extra cities. The closest one is still a couple days' walk. Everything viable still crosses the plains."

Glenn squinted at the horizon, "We'll sort it out later. For now, we'll head to the plains. Have you recovered? We need to put distance between ourselves and the Broken. The less time we spend here, the better."

I glanced at Score. He looked a bit worse for wear from the fall. A couple dark shadows had appeared under his eyes, and the scrape along his jaw had barely scabbed. I wondered if he'd ask to rest. He just squared his shoulders, saying, "Good idea. The sooner we leave, the sooner we'll get there."

I, for one, was pretty tired. I closed my eyes, finally nodding. "Alright. Let's get some distance."

~~~~~~~~~~~~~~~~

The terrain was barren, flat, and wretched. We trudged through an empty expanse of dust and brown earth. The dull light gave me a headache. Something about the Broken felt completely wrong, like it was the setting of a nightmare. I hitched my bag over my shoulder, already tiring. It felt like miles passed before anything about the scenery changed. Eventually I saw several small, murky pools and a few twisted trees dotting the horizon.

Glenn zigzagged through the gnarled forest with one hand resting on the handle of his dagger.

I somewhat understood the increased caution. The Broken was supposed to be a nasty place. Predators could leap out at you in an instant. Despite the general unease, I didn't feel a heightened sense of danger. The quiet hardly warranted being so ready with a weapon.

The setting was eerie, but what made it disturbing was what it was missing: life. No sound broke the landscape aside from the soft scuttling of our own footsteps— no wind, no birds, no insects, nothing. I shivered at how uncanny it felt.

Score took my hand in his. I turned around, smiling gratefully. I hadn't had a proper chance to think about our escape, but I was flattered he'd drop everything for me in an instant.

The trees were thicker now. We were still within the Broken, but I suspected we were getting closer to the borders of the strange terrain. I hoped so. The light gave me a constant dull ache between my brows, making it difficult to concentrate.

As the roots and branches entwined, the path became more narrow. Glenn seemed reluctant to touch any of the flora, so I followed his example and avoided the trees as much as possible.

We took a sharp bend. The path was less than a foot wide. Trees walled my left, and a stagnant puddle blocked the right. As a result, we walked single file. I reached behind my back, keeping my fingers locked with Score's.

Glenn directed us through a break in the trees. The forest looked thinner ahead— we were definitely nearing the end of the Broken. Relieved, I pressed forward, turning the corner from the narrow path.

As I stepped from the edge of the pool, a ropey grip wrapped around my ankle. With a sharp tug, it dragged me towards the tepid liquid. Instinctively, I screamed, thrashing my limbs and clawing at the taupe earth.

Emerging from the water was a vile creature. A vaguely human torso attached to a writhing mass of tentacles where its legs should have been. It had webbed hands at the end of a pair of strong arms that reached for me. The creature was hairless and smooth— as beige as the surroundings, but a paler shade. The monster had no eyes at all, only a smooth forehead. Two vertical slits crossed the center of its face instead of a nose. A gaping maw with sharp, twisted teeth opened, dripping with thick black sludge. It screeched, the sound worse than nails on a chalkboard.

Score tightened his grip on me, pulling frantically on my arm. An ache spread through my shoulder, but it wasn't my primary concern. I kicked at the monster with my free leg, but it wasn't fazed by my foot striking its tentacle. The creature had a hard grasp on me. It dragged me another six inches into the pool. The beast was winning this tug-of-war.

The cuffs of my boots became submerged in the lukewarm water, invading them. The moisture increased my panic. I jerked desperately, clawing at the ground with my free hand, thrashing my torso and unbound leg against the rocky earth, praying to find traction.

Score hummed a few notes. I stared into his eyes, which were a beautiful, reassuring light blue. They shifted, black and dark green snuffing out the light within them. Pure panic crossed his features, and he screamed, "Lyra!" He began to pull with renewed energy.

Glenn had been ahead of us, but he returned to my side swiftly. He let out a snarl, lunging forward towards the pool. His silver knife plunged into the appendage of the beast.

The creature let out another hissing squeal and splashed forward. In an instant, an arrow lodged in its skull, precisely between where its eyes should have been.

Score was already pulling me from the puddle. He untangled the tentacle from my ankle, tossing it aside in disgust. Now that the danger had passed, I began to feel the pain from the attack. I winced as I rolled up the cuff of my jeans, nearly crying as I peeled off my boot. A bruise colored the entire joint, so dark it looked black. My foot and ankle were swelled to at least twice their usual size.

Glenn stared at the injury, his mouth forming a grim line.

"What the hell *was* that?!" Score demanded, pointing at the corpse of the monster.

"A grog," Glenn answered soberly. "I don't know what it used to be, but when we met it, a grog."

45

"What exactly is a grog?" Score asked, kicking one of the lifeless tentacles with the toe of his tennis shoe.

Glenn squatted next to me, searching his pouch of herbal remedies. He produced a small vial of liquid. As he poured a couple drops on my ankle, a cooling sensation blushed out on impact. It spread down my foot and up to my knee. The edge of the pain was gone. I sighed in relief.

"A grog," Glenn explained, "is a creature twisted by decaying magic. *Anything* that's alive in this place is one, understand? That's why we have to move! Why we need to get out of the Broken."

Score glared, folding his arms across his chest, "What about Lyra?" He nodded to my ankle.

Glenn brushed his fingers gently across my jaw, bringing my eyes level to his. "Can you walk, little bird?"

I considered it. My ankle felt stiff and uncomfortable, but the actual pain had vanished. I nodded, "I think so."

"Good girl," Glenn said, pulling me upright. I hobbled along until the path widened and I could balance between the two boys.

I glanced at my protectors. Glenn was staring forward, determined to get us to safety before we could rest. On the other side, Score wore a troubled expression. Both looked deep in thought.

It was another hour before we reached the end of the beige nightmare. If I'd been able to keep a normal pace, we probably would've arrived within fifteen minutes. The border was obvious: a cheerful wood shattered the dull beige with a vibrant belt of color.

Glenn left my side as we crossed the tree line, scouting for danger. He swept his gaze to the left and right before nodding. Score helped me hobble across. In an instant, the buzzing dull light changed to something more natural, but dusky. I took a fleeting look back at the Broken and frowned at the dull landscape that was over the line— never changing, a fluorescent hell-hole.

"This is an elvish forest," Glenn announced. "Arathal. No clans will be near the borders. We can rest soundly tonight; we'll be safe."

My shoulders slumped in relief. I was exhausted. My ankle had begun to throb sometime in the past half hour. The brunt of the walk had taken its toll, seeping through the medicinal haze to the raw nerves below.

I descended slowly, leaning against one of the nearby trees for support. The bark against my back was smooth and silver. It was soft and pliant, like beeswax. The branches reached towards the sky, the limbs twining together like a braid, ending in soft lavender leaves.

I unceremoniously dropped the boot I'd been carrying, shaking my hand out. Pin pricks settled into my fingertips as fresh blood flow finally entered my joints. My ankle had been too swelled to wear the boot, and I'd been clutching it more tightly than I'd realized.

I closed my eyes, tilting my head back, feeling numbed by the day. Maybe I'd reached a point where my body and mind couldn't handle any new sensations, being too assaulted at once. I shook my good foot from its boot. Score retrieved it, placing the shoe with its mate.

Glenn turned to us. "I think you'll be okay for a little while. If there's trouble, use this." He tossed his knife— sheathed— towards Score. "I'm going to scout ahead and double check our security for the night. I'll bring back firewood, too."

Score narrowed his eyes, but accepted the offered weapon. "I'm surprised you trust me alone with her."

Glenn grinned, gesturing to my swelled foot. "She's not going very fast or far tonight, mate. I'm not worried." With that, he turned away, disappearing into the trees like a ghost.

Score descended, propping himself against the tree trunk next to me. He studied my face, "How are you?"

"I'm exhausted... otherwise..." I considered it, "Befuddled might be the right word."

Score's hand wove through my own. It was comforting. I slumped a little further down, relaxing. I brought my own gaze to him. I'd noticed earlier that his eyes were not obscured, but this was the first time I recognized the significance of it. He wasn't bothering to hide what he was.

"It's a lot to take in," he agreed.

"I think," I said carefully, "I'm glad you guys did what you did... I just wish you'd have given me some warning beforehand."

Score brought his knees to his chest, keeping his fingers locked through my own. His free hand settled on his guitar case protectively. Frowning, his eyes shifted to black and orange, but the edges remained rose pink.

"Lyra, I'm worried," he whispered.

"What's wrong?" I asked. I wondered if he was having second thoughts. Maybe Score wanted to return to Whitecrest and his parents and a more normal life. Score did okay for himself without me.

He paused, glancing into my eyes. He rubbed the back of his neck, "I couldn't use my magic."

My first impulse was to laugh. It was a valid concern, but mostly I was relieved. I was happy he didn't want to leave. I squeezed his hand, "It was probably just the Broken. It's a space without magic, or that twists magic."

He drummed his fingers on the guitar case, "Maybe you're right. I'll try again." He hummed a soft melody— only a few notes— then paused, waiting. His hand shook as the seconds ticked away, and nothing happened. "It didn't work, Lyra."

"Maybe it just—"

Score shook his head adamantly, "It's this place. It's this *Realm*, I can't use my magic here. You have to try!"

I shrugged. I never liked using my siren abilities, but to ease Score's mind now, I'd indulge him. I hummed softly, wishing for something simple— the wind to pick up. Nothing happened. My eyes widened. It'd been easy the times I'd done it before, but now… I tried again, opening my mouth this time, actually singing the notes.

Nothing.

Score groaned, leaning against the tree. "Great."

I turned to him. "It'll be okay. Glenn has it under control. We're completely safe."

He shook his head, "I couldn't protect you, Lyra. I thought I'd be the one to save you from that monster, but in the end…" He stared through the trees where Glenn had disappeared.

I tried to be reassuring, "Glenn's been saving me for a long time. I'm waiting for the day when he presents me with a bill and tells me how much I owe him."

Score shook his head bitterly, "So am I. I'm worried about what he'll want in return."

The inflections within his voice were strange. The undercurrents suggested that Glenn would ask for something I wasn't willing to give. "What do you mean?"

"I mean he's got feelings for you. Bad." Score snorted, "'Little bird'…"

A flush crawled up my neck, towards my face. I inhaled sharply, and my scraped ribs complained with the effort. I winced. "Glenn would never ask me to—" I couldn't finish it.

"Nothing crude…" Score sighed, squeezing my hand, "I just think he'll use whatever leverage he can to take you from me."

I snatched my hand away, my heart pounding hard in my ears. "*Take me from you?* First of all, I'm not a *thing* that can be stolen! And second, we're not a couple!" We'd never even been on a proper date, and he was implying that we were somehow committed to each other.

His brow raised. "Aren't we, Lyra? You have to know we're *supposed* to be together…"

I bit my lip. I didn't know anything except that I didn't want to lose either man from my life. Glenn was one of my best friends, but Score… We *did* have a connection, it was true. I couldn't imagine never seeing him again. There was a sense of rightness and comfort when I was with him that surprised me to admit to myself.

"But you're right, maybe I—" Score stopped speaking, interrupted by a rustling in the trees. He tensed, gripping the handle of the dagger. The light had almost faded from the sky. I hoped this wasn't an attack.

Glenn stepped through the brush, his arms loaded with fallen branches. His eyes barely flickered to Score before he dropped the bundle in front of me. He set to work looping stones in a ring, creating a makeshift fire pit. He piled the wood methodically, striking a spark from a flint and blade he retrieved from his boot.

When the fire was hearty, he turned to us. "Any trouble?"
Score shook his head, "No."

Glenn nodded, striding past the flames, and knelt before me. "And how are you holding up, little bird?"

I flushed at the nickname. "I'm fine, Glenn. A little sore, but I'll survive."

He smiled, rolling my jeans up to expose my wounded leg clear to the knee. "I didn't have this in my belt— it doesn't keep well— but it'll help your ankle. I found it growing about a mile from here." He opened his hand. Three golden flowers laid in his palm. They looked like minuscule bells. He crushed them with the tip of his index finger, then pressed the golden mash into my ankle. I winced at the pressure, though I could tell he was being gentle. This time there was no instant effect. I stared at the pulpy mess with furrowed brows.

Glenn just smiled, wrapping a huge leaf around the herb. "Give it time," he murmured, practically reading my mind. "Not all magic works like… well, magic."

I leaned forward towards the fire, enjoying the warmth on my skin.

"Glenn," I asked, "why did you go against the council?"

He stood, prodding the flames before answering. "I told you. I thought it was wrong to separate us. You need me."

"But why?" I asked, "You told me the danger had passed, that the extras who wanted me dead had disbanded, that—"

Glenn laughed, "I guess I did. But I lied." He threw another branch on the fire, which hissed and popped in response. "Truth is, I've had a terrible feeling lately— like the danger hasn't passed, only shifted." He paused. "I've learned to trust my instincts, Lyra."

"Then why tell me otherwise?" I demanded.

He stirred the fire with a stick. Sparks drifted lazily up in the air. "I didn't want to worry you. You seemed stressed enough as it was."

"I could've handled it," I protested, though I couldn't really blame him. I wasn't even speaking with him for the past three weeks. Of course he wouldn't want to upset me more.

Score settled against the tree next to me, tugging off his tennis shoes and sighing. It looked like he was going to spend the night by my side. Some of the tension in my shoulders dissipated. The idea made me feel oddly safe.

I turned my attention back to Glenn. The elf was looking at me with a smirk.

"Admit it," he said. "You'd have been mental if I'd told you there was more danger coming."

I shook my head adamantly before breaking into laughter. "Okay. Maybe I'd have been a *tiny* bit worried."

Glenn shook his head, grinning and resting his chin in his hand. His eyes fell on Score beside me. "This is the first time either of you've been to an elvish forest. We're in Arathal, which

50

belongs to the Foraeis clans. Not home, but they're all similar." He addressed Score, "You'll want to see this, too." He pointed upward, to the evening sky.

"Oh!" I gasped.

Though night had descended, the sky was so filled with stars that the areas between them looked dark blue and purple, not black. In some places, I could see the spirals of galaxies, in others, cloudy bursts of supernovas. It was like a painting of space.

Score let out a soft sound next to me. "That's... amazing."

Glenn smiled, poking at the fire again. "When I was a child, this was always my favorite time of day: when the heavens reveal themselves. It makes you feel like no matter what happens, no matter how terrible, everything'll be okay."

I stared into the twinkling collage above me, smiling.

Yes. Everything is going to be okay, I thought. I brought my dulcimer close to my chest, letting sleep overtake me.

~~~~~~~~~~~~~~~~~

We awoke as the sun broke through the trees, sending a wash of brilliant golden light across our faces.

I was pleased to find that the flowers Glenn had applied to my ankle had done their job in the night. It was completely mended. In fact, of all my injuries, it was the one that bothered me least.

Glenn offered dried meat and crackers to Score and me as a ration for breakfast, but it wasn't especially satisfying. The day was mapped out: a lengthy trek skirting the forest to reach the plains by evening to rest.

It was taking the long route, but the safer one. Both boys agreed it was best, though I'd have rather traveled more quickly. The more the day stretched, the more my body complained. It didn't feel like the few hours of sleep in the forest were adequate.

At dusk, we finally reached the tree line where the Azure Plains began and Arathal ended. The field lived up to its name— tall blue grass bent gently in the breeze, creating the illusion of rippling water. The sky was almost the exact same color. Aside from a few rolling hills, it was devoid of anything except grass and sky. Further away, I could make out sections where the grass was lower, cut down like a field that had been harvested.

51

"We'll set up camp in the plains tonight," Glenn announced as we entered the blue. "It'll give us a head start tomorrow. Perhaps we can get through two gates instead of one. That will move us closer to answers."

Score and I nodded wordlessly, exhausted. We stumbled forward with difficulty. The grass hit us near my shoulders, forcing us to struggle with every step.

"Better than I'd hoped," Glenn said, grinning. "This field hasn't been harvested yet. It'll help hide us. No fire tonight, though."

I almost groaned as a breeze picked up. Even with the grass sheltering us, no fire meant a cold night ahead. I shivered, letting my gaze wander upward. Maybe the phenomenal display of stars would lift my spirits.

To my disappointment, the sky was less spectacular on the Azure Plains than it'd been in the forest. It was similar to a night in Whitecrest— though perhaps fewer clouds. A swollen moon hung overhead, lighting the grass around us.

When Glenn could see that we couldn't walk any further, he nodded at us to stop. I threw my bag down, my arms aching from the load. I rubbed at my scraped back, hoping my ribs would ache less tomorrow. I doubted it. Between the long walk and the uncomfortable night of camping ahead, I'd probably only compound my injuries.

I rolled my shoulders, closing my eyes and listening to the stillness. The plains were peaceful. I could hear a soft breeze and my own harsh breaths, but I'd sleep soundly tonight.

I exhaled, opening my eyes and sitting. The pale blue grass tickled my face as I settled, leaning back on my palms. Score looked as exhausted as I felt. We shared an incredulous glance. Glenn seemed like a machine compared to us.

A wolf howled in the distance, shattering the silence.

Glenn sat up alertly, whipping his head to the sky. He shot us both a glance, barking, "Run. For the trees. *Now!*"

Chapter Six

Treetop

The urgency in his voice demanded haste despite our aching limbs. We were up and running through the grass in less than a second, our bags abandoned. My lungs began to burn. I turned to Glenn, who'd dropped back to keep pace with us.

"What—" I stammered, "are we— running— from?"

Glenn nodded upwards, towards the moon. "I was stupid to take you anywhere so open tonight. It was careless… I'm sorry, Lyra…" He looked into my questioning eyes, "It's Wolf's Time. They aren't supposed to be in the Realm beyond their own lands during the full moon. But there are rebels, and accidents happen. Because of my negligence, one is tracking us."

A werewolf? I pushed my legs to move even faster.

Score kept pace just behind me, then stumbled, crashing into the hard ground. I heard the commotion, whipping my head back to watch him roll forward, his limbs flying about.

I lurched to a stop, "Score!" I cried, "Score!"

I wanted to run to him, but Glenn caught me by the shoulders. The elf darted in front of me, racing back to our companion. "You okay, mate?"

Score looked dazed, grabbing his right leg. Even from this distance, even through his jeans, I could see the unnatural angle of the limb. But his face was determined. He pulled himself up, taking a shuffling step forward. His body buckled. Score cried out in pain, grimacing.

Another howl split through the silence. It sounded closer.

"*Arashk!*" Glenn swore. He took a quick sweep of the area, nodding, then pulled his dagger from its sheath. He drew the blade across his palm and darted into the grass, shaking his wounded hand violently.

He returned in a blur, moving faster than I'd ever seen him. "I'll lead it from you," he said to Score. "Just lay low; keep yourself hidden within the grass. We'll find you tomorrow."

I felt dazed. I placed a hand on my forehead, collecting myself. The wolf howled again. It sounded like it was right behind us. "Wait, just a—"

But Glenn didn't wait. Instead he threw me over one shoulder and ran, far faster than I could've on my own. His right arm was securely wrapped around my torso, his left was outstretched, hand open. His blood splattered into the blue stalks as he ran. He strode in a lurching, weaving pattern— a zigzag.

In front of my face, the grass twitched. I could make out a silver blur as the wolf pursued us, following the bloody trail Glenn was leaving in our wake. He carried me back to the elvish forest. When we reached the tree line, Glenn smeared his bloody palm across the trunk of a stalwart deciduous.

He shifted my weight squarely across his shoulders.

"Glenn?!"

"Shh!"

He bounced on the balls of his feet twice before nodding assertively, pressing his hands against the bark.

Then he began to climb, branch by branch.

The ground swayed before my eyes as it moved further from me. Though Glenn was surefooted, the ascent felt jumbled and jerky. I closed my eyes, trying to ignore the height and the tumbling of my stomach.

The wolf darted from the grass, snapping at Glenn's toes but falling a few inches short. Glenn continued to make his way up the tree. I thought I was going to throw up.

The were itself was huge— at least six feet from end to end. It stalked below the tree, pacing. The monster had gray bristly hair that was raised up into sharp hackles. It growled low, its jaw a gaping maw, no longer attempting to jump at us. Instead, it began to circle the tree, eyeing the natural structure for weaknesses before it sat. It watched us with glittering golden eyes.

When we reached the tallest branch that would support our

combined weight, Glenn balanced himself into a seated position. He straddled the branch, his back against the trunk. He gently shifted my body in his arms until I sat across from him on the limb. Panicking, I grappled for the branch, holding onto it for dear life.

"Relax," Glenn soothed, stroking my hand with his fingertips, "you're safe up here."

I glanced at the wolf prowling below us. A sliver of doubt lodged itself into my heart. "What if I fall?" I asked in a shrill, reedy voice.

"You won't fall. I'd catch you before you had the chance."

He sounded so sure, but I was dizzy with vertigo. I clutched at the branch even tighter, my hands beginning to ache, and squeezed my eyes shut.

I heard him sigh. Carefully, he pried my fingers from the branch. I was shaking, but Glenn was gentle with me, grasping me firmly by the waist and turning me around. I wasn't sure how he managed it so smoothly, but before I knew it, I was leaning with my back against his chest. He folded his arms over my stomach.

"There, now, little bird. Safe and sound."

I shuddered against him. He squeezed my midsection once, reassuring me. Despite my acrophobia, I did feel safer. I focused on my breathing: inhaling through my nose, exhaling from my mouth. After a few moments, the beating of my heart slowed to a frantic but reasonable pace.

I leaned into him. "What about Score?"

He shifted, gesturing to the wolf below. It was seated on its hind legs, observing us. "It's a lone wolf," Glenn explained. "That's why I used the blood. He'd assume I was wounded, the easiest prey, and pick up my trail. Now that we're treed, I doubt he'll leave us tonight. Once the moon has set, he'll just be a man."

I glanced up at the orb. With a start, I realized it was also more impressive than I'd ever seen it, the craters all clearly visible. We were back in elvish territory, back where the night sky was brilliant.

Glenn squeezed me again. My stomach knotted as I remembered the conversation I'd had with Score yesterday, about Glenn's feelings for me. Marin had told me the same thing before I'd even left Whitecrest. This was the first time I'd been alone with my bodyguard since.

I stared up at the stars, the swirling galaxies, the explosions of supernovas. After a few moments, I'd finally gathered my courage. "Glenn?"

"Hmm?"

My heart began to race again. I shook, staring up at him. He angled his head down, looking into my eyes.

"Score said," I began, taking another deep breath, "he thinks that— that is, he says that— you want to be with me. You have *feelings* for me." The statement felt flat, wrong, imperfect, but it did the job.

Glenn's brows raised. He tilted his head back, looking to the sky for a long moment before shrugging. "He's both wrong and right."

"What does *that* mean?"

The elf shifted beneath me. My heart was thundering in my ears. I wasn't sure if I was more nervous about his response or the height.

"It means I'm wrong for you, Lyra," he said regretfully, staring through the trees. "I'm not good enough for you. Not even close."

"Why do you say that?"

He didn't answer. Below us, the crickets had begun to chirp, settling from the commotion we'd caused on our arrival to the forest. A breeze rustled through the trees, making me shiver again. Glenn wrapped his arms around me protectively.

"Why?" I repeated.

A sigh. A pause. No answer.

Looking at him, I could see he was lost in thought, his gaze fixed on the forest before him.

I wondered if I really wanted to press it. Glenn promised me honest answers to three questions of my choice, and I still had two left. After considering it for a few seconds, I decided I needed to know.

"It's— It's my second question."

He closed his eyes, letting out a loud breath and squeezing me tightly. "Alright," he said softly, "I promised."

He gently picked me up, turning me again so I could face him. Glenn took a few moments to collect his thoughts, looking into my eyes but seeming to stare through them.

Finally, he said, "You don't realize my Lady wants you dead, do you?"

"What?! Why?!"

I gripped the branch again, my heart racing. I felt like I was going to fall. My mind raced, struggling to accept it. The Lady of Flowers hadn't shown any hostility towards me during the council meetings— if anything, she'd been more helpful than anyone else. She'd taken an active interest in my plight. The only other council member who seemed to care was Marin's father, and he practically *had* to because I'd been living in his estate. Lady Amaranthe had assigned Glenn to guard me, after all. But he had no reason to lie to me.

He shrugged, pulling my hands from their iron grip around the branch. He folded them within his own.

"I don't know why," he said. "I just know she does."

My lip trembled. I wondered what this meant about Glenn, about our time together. I bit down, stopping the quiver, taking a deep breath.

"Are you going to kill me?"

He laughed harshly, as if the question was completely absurd.

"No! Are you daft?" He pulled me closer to him, squeezing me. My body went rigid at the contact, unsure how I should respond. He pulled back, shaking his head, "*I* was never supposed to kill you, Lyra."

"Then why bother sending you at all?" I demanded.

Glenn leaned back against the tree, looking thoughtful and a little sad. "Appearances. That's what she told me, anyway. So it'd eliminate suspicions directed at the elves. So that it would look to be a total accident when— the attacks were her doing. At least, in part. Stirring trouble, starting rumors, pressing the centaurs, and goddesses knows what else. She instructed me clearly." His forehead creased, "I was to save you until she'd created so much animosity that there'd be no doubt— nothing could've been done to prevent your death. When that army came…" He paused a moment, brushing his fingertips along my hair, "I was *supposed to die*, and so were you, my little bird." I took a sharp breath. My ribs ached, but my chest felt heavy. "You saved us *both* that day, Lyra. That was the day—" He hesitated, closing his eyes, "That was the day everything changed. At least for me."

I considered the possibilities. "Did you tell her about Score? Or the map, or—"

He held his hand up, cutting me off. "No. You needn't concern yourself. As I said, when you saved me— I couldn't believe it," he laughed, rubbing his face wearily. "No one's ever shown so much devotion to me. I've always been expendable. My own queen didn't hesitate to send me to my death."

"Why would she bother telling you, then?" I asked. "Why not just let you think you were supposed to guard me?"

"Because in a *real* charge I'd never have taken on an army alone. I'd have escaped with you through Marin's Realm gate. We'd have run for one of the hundreds that connect there. I'd have submitted a thousand reports earlier, would've insisted on spells and enchantments to keep you safer, would've done a million things differently, a million things *better*. I needed to be convincing, Lyra, not perfect.

"Also, My Lady assumed it'd be a kindness if I could perform the proper rituals. I'd expected to head to the next life."

Despite the horrible confession he was making, I felt sorry for him. He'd saved me, appearances or not, and now he was saving me against his orders.

He's saving Score, too, I thought, my face prickling.

"So to answer your original question, little bird: *yes*. Yes, I have feelings for you. But you can see now— you *have* to see now, I'm not the one for you." He leaned into the tree, staring into my eyes. My heart beat erratically. "It pains me to admit it, but the boy in the field down there, the only other of your kind… He's the one you should be with right now."

"Then why did you take me with you tonight?" I asked, "Why not just leave me with Score in that field?"

"Because I'm selfish," he said, glancing down at the wolf. He brought his gaze back to my face, my heart thundering in my ears. I wondered what color my eyes were right now, what emotion this *was* exactly. "Had I lost you… I don't know what I'd do. I couldn't leave you behind, just in case my plan failed. The same reason I couldn't let you leave with him three weeks ago. I tell myself it's because you attract trouble, but…" He sighed, his gaze turning up to the stars above us. "That's a lie. It's because I can't bear to part from you. Selfish."

His brows turned up. He looked so lost, almost like he was pleading with me. "I'm hoping we'll find answers out here. Perhaps we'll discover why Lady Amaranthe is trying to end you when it seems you've done nothing to provoke her. There *must* be a reason, my Lady is usually rational."

I shifted on the branch, staring down at my hands shyly. I was beginning to feel more comfortable up here, with him. I looked at him, twining my fingers together. "Glenn, you've saved me a dozen times at least…"

He sighed, leaning his head back into the tree. "That's kind of you to say, Lyra, to try and make me feel better about what I've done."

"I guess," I said, "I don't know why you're so insistent that you're not good enough for me."

His eyes fell on mine, "I'm *right*. And you're with Score, and—"

I cut him off, irritated. It was the second time in as many days I'd been told that. I was tired of it, especially after three weeks apart. "Score and I are *friends!* And if we *are* something more, it's never been defined!" I was exasperated. I folded my arms across my chest stubbornly, "I don't know why you both insist on telling me what to do, how to feel, who to—" I was getting worked up in my rant. I shifted on the branch, beginning to slip. My heart leapt to my throat.

Glenn caught me fluidly. I flushed, suddenly in his arms, my face inches from his.

"Who to…?" he breathed, his eyes locked on mine.

I whispered, "You can't tell me who to be with any more than he can."

His eyes searched mine. He looked lost for a moment, conflicted, but then he took a breath. "Sod it," he murmured. "For this one moment…"

His lips fell on mine.

I could hear my heart beating frantically in my chest, surprise overtaking me. He was strong, but gentle. He guided my body closer to him, pulling me in as we sat precariously perched on a branch 80 feet above the ground.

The tension in my shoulders relaxed. I could feel one of his hands running up my back, one on the nape of my neck, gliding through my hair. He smelled sweet and earthy, like freshly cut grass after a rainstorm. It reminded me of summers and sunshine and running through a field barefoot. I pressed my body against him, my hands searching for his silver hair. I gripped it tightly, returning his kiss with more affection than I knew I had for him.

He curled one leg around me, sweeping me even closer to himself. My hands pressed against his chest, clawing at the coarse fibers of his tunic. His lips left mine, and I was grateful— almost dizzy, needing air. He continued to kiss along my jaw and up my cheekbones, following the line of my face until I could feel his hot breath on my ear.

He trailed kisses across my neck in a line that blazed like fire, breathing in my hair. I gripped at his grass armor, bunching it in my hands, moaning in surprise at his intensity.

The sound snapped Glenn back to reality. He pulled back hastily, breathing hard, his eyes wide and green and glittering in the full moonlight. He unwound himself from me, pushing me away from him, giving us space between our bodies. The distance was only a few inches, but it felt like a canyon dividing us.

I was shaking, dazed from the passion of the moment. I gazed at him with heated cheeks, my breathing shallow and quick.

He smiled at me wistfully, tucking a stray hair behind my ear. "I'll only say it *once* more, little bird. I'm not good enough for you. And that's the last time I'll entertain the thought."

Chapter Seven

La Rue

I woke up before sunrise the next morning to Glenn shaking me. The moon had gone down, eliminating the threat of the night. He silently held me in his arms, descending from our perch. He gracefully stepped over the werewolf curled beneath the tree, asleep.

He didn't look impressive now. He was a small, thin man with long scraggly hair— naked as a jay bird, covered in dirt. We were quiet, careful not to disturb him.

Glenn and I made our way back to the tall grass as quietly as we could. We only relaxed when we'd made it a hundred yards within the blue.

Glenn nodded, gesturing to where we'd left Score behind. I was grateful for the elf's good sense of direction and his keen eyes. To my relief, Score was fine. But he looked frazzled, lying on the ground. His knee was swollen. A yellow and purple bruise had developed around the whole joint. Unfortunately, it would be slow going today.

Glenn moved with purpose. He collected our abandoned bags and loaded himself with the majority of the luggage. Score refused to part with his guitar, but grudgingly allowed Glenn to take his backpack. I draped Score's arm over my shoulder, letting him use me as a crutch. We shuffled forward at a crawl. At this rate, we'd never make it to Greece. Everyday brought a new delay.

"We need to *at least* move for a half-day," Glenn announced, frowning. "But I doubt either of you will make it any

61

longer."

In honesty, hiking for half a day was optimistic given Score's current state. But the boy was determined despite his injury. He nodded, "Yeah," he agreed, wiping at his brow, "we need to get some distance."

I trudged forward, my brow furrowing as I contemplated our current predicament. In the span of two days, I'd been attacked and saved by Glenn as many times. Given what I'd learned last night, I needed to become more self-sufficient. I shifted Score's weight on my shoulder as we hobbled along, considering it. I didn't have any survival skills, and certainly no combat training. I hated the thought that I was *that* girl, the girl who always needed rescuing.

Glenn kept pace ahead of us, pressing the grass down to make it easier for Score and me to shuffle forward. The elf moved haltingly, repeatedly whipping his head back, his face screwed up in irritation. Though we continued to trudge along, I could tell he was distracted. Finally, he stopped, holding up one hand. "We're being pursued."

We paused behind him. Score sighed, "The longer we're in the Realm, the more I feel like it was a mistake to go this route."

Glenn glared at him, "Even with the dangers we're facing now, the Overworld would be far worse. It's much easier to disappear here."

"We've had at least one *major* problem every day we've been here!" Score barked. "You said you would keep her safe!"

I bristled at Score's comment, frowning and shifting his weight so I was a bit further from him. "Glenn's really good at his job," I protested, "and—"

Score cut me off, "Lyra, he's led us into the mouth of hell! The grog, the werewolf, whatever is after us now, rough terrain, injuries, never ending hikes—"

I narrowed my eyes, wondering if Score was more upset that we'd been placed in danger or that he couldn't use his magic here. "*I* trust him," I said shortly.

Score rolled his eyes, muttering under his breath, "I doubt our parents intended for this to be such a chore…"

I exploded, "If our parents had wanted us to find things easily, they'd have written instructions down in plain English rather than leaving riddles!"

62

The grass behind us rustled. Glenn sighed, "We have bigger things to worry about than the intentions of a dead race."

Emerging from the wake of the quivering stalks was the werewolf— still naked, still dirty. He didn't appear embarrassed by his nudity, however. He stood brazenly with his hands on his hips. I'd hadn't seen his face clearly before. He had a scraggly beard and a long, thin nose. His eyes were the same tawny gold as his wolf-form.

Glenn had already notched an arrow, knocking it back and aiming it at the wolf's head.

The man's hands flew up, "Let's not be hasty, yes?" He had a thick French accent.

Glenn was unimpressed. "Why are you following us? You can't be *that* hungry, wolf."

"Please," he pleaded, "I need your help. You're the only people around for miles." He tapped the side of his nose as he said it, as if he could smell it.

"We aren't offering help," Glenn said. "Leave us alone."

"Come now," the werewolf said, gesturing to us, "I can be of use, hmm? I can carry your things, help you hunt, or..." His eyes fell on Score, "Or I *could* be this beautiful young man's personal crutch."

Score looked like he didn't quite know how to take that. Glenn just snorted, "We don't need any help. If we did, we wouldn't want yours."

"You'd be leaving me to die!" the man said desperately. "I have nothing with me, no one to help me, no—"

"You should've considered that before illegally turning within the Realm!" Glenn snarled at him. "Leave. Us. Be!"

"Please!" the wolf cried again, but Glenn jerked his head, urging us to continue forward.

I glanced sympathetically at the naked man, shifting Score's weight over my shoulder. We hobbled along. The wolf didn't follow this time.

"You can't leave me here!" he called from behind us. "Mademoiselle! Surely you can see it! You're leaving me a dead man!"

I went rigid, my heart pounding in my ears. My steps faltered, then completely stopped.

"Keep going, Lyra," Glenn muttered.

I glanced back at the naked werewolf, hesitating. "Will he survive, Glenn?"

The elf sighed, rubbing his forehead. "I don't know. In truth? Probably not. But who cares?" he added. "He tried to kill us last night. The universe has a funny way of creating karmic balance."

I chewed on my lip, taking another fleeting look at the wolf. His eyes were desperate, pleading with mine. I couldn't do it. I couldn't leave him to die.

I gently slipped from beneath Score's arm. When I was sure he was steady on his own, I sank down to sit in the grass.

"What are you doing?!" Glenn demanded, "Get up! We need to keep moving, we need to—"

"I'm not in the habit of abandoning people, Glenn." I stretched my legs out. It was good to be seated. I hadn't slept much in the tree last night.

Glenn paced, his jaw hardening. "You're being ridiculous!"

"Lyra," Score whispered, "I understand you want to do the right thing, but that guy— we don't know anything about him. We need to be discreet."

I looked up at him. "A couple months ago, I didn't know anything about *you*. You asked me for a chance. I give people the benefit of the doubt." I leaned back on my palms, relaxing into the grass.

From across the sea of blue stalks, the wolf watched the scene unfold with hopeful eyes.

Glenn let out a snarl, kicking the grass. He squatted across from me, glaring as he growled, "Infuriating, stubborn, *willful* little bird! If I had more space upon my back and arms, I'd pick you up and haul you away, regardless of your intentions."

My nostrils flared, "Then I suppose I'm lucky, aren't I?! If you want to leave, then *leave*, Glenn! You don't have any problem deserting one person, another can't be that big of a deal to you."

He stood, tugging at his silver hair, squeezing his eyes shut. He paced back and forth, batting the grass away impatiently. He snarled again. "Risky, stupid, selfish—"

"It's more selfish to leave someone to die in the middle of nowhere!"

"Fine!" he barked. Glenn pointed at me, crouching down again. "I hope you're satisfied, Lyra." He jerked his head to the wolf, "I know you heard the whole thing, old man! The lady has saved your life. You should be grateful."

The wolf darted forward. I blushed at his nudity, picking myself up and keeping my gaze fixed on the ground. He gripped my hands in his own, "Thank you, mademoiselle! Thank you, thank you, thank you!"

"Please just— don't make me regret it," I sighed.

"No, no, no, of course not! May I introduce myself, then? My name is LaRue," he said with a flourish of his arms and a bow, "and I am at your service."

~~~~~~~~~~~~~~~~~~~~~

We didn't last much longer. Score's leg pained him as we shuffled through the thick tangle of grass. He didn't complain, but it was obvious from his labored movements how much the injury bothered him.

Glenn had offered LaRue a tee and jeans from within Score's backpack. The wolf took the articles with a grin and pulled them over his body. He reminded me of a child wearing his father's clothes; they hung on him. Despite the ill-fit, LaRue seemed quite happy with the apparel.

He twitched one eyebrow at Score, "Monsieur, may I ask your name?"

Score sighed, shuffling forward, "Why?"

"Because in polite company, this is how it's done," LaRue explained. "One asks for a name, makes small talk, then ascertains if he has the hopes of becoming one's lover."

Score's face went scarlet. "Then we can skip it. I'm not interested."

"That is a *damn* shame," the wolf said, linking his arm in mine to create a chain of the three of us. "But one must try, yes?"

I almost laughed— Score looked so uncomfortable. Finally, he responded, "I appreciate the compliment, but—"

"You're barking up the wrong tree, mate!" Glenn snapped from ahead of us. He swept his gaze around. "I doubt you'll get much further," he said, nodding towards Score. "We'll never make progress with you shuffling about. I'll run back to the forest and retrieve more mending blooms for that knee of yours." He sighed, "More delays."

Score looked grateful, "Sorry, I—"

Glenn just rolled his eyes, "Whatever. Cut his throat if there's trouble." He tossed his dagger to Score.

I frowned, but Glenn ignored me, disappearing into the sea of grass. I helped Score descend into a seated position, and he winced.

"Your leg is pretty bad, huh?" I said, feeling guilty.

"It's not great," he admitted, "but I'll survive." He leaned back on his palms. "I feel like we've made a lot of mistakes already, and we've barely started."

"If this is about LaRue—"

"Lyra, I'm not crazy about us picking up a stray werewolf—"

"Hey!" LaRue said, offended.

Score ignored him, continuing, "But that's not the real issue. It's this labored process, the way we're going about this journey." He looked thoughtful, finally saying, "I think it's wrong to rely so much on Glenn's judgment. I know you trust him, and I'm glad he's saved our lives, but—" He shook his head, "I just don't think this is the way we should approach our expedition."

"What would you have done differently?" I asked, tugging at one of the stalks of tall blue grass.

Score shook his head, glancing past me to the horizon. "I don't know. I probably wouldn't have left the human world."

"Why would my parents leave a map with all the Realm gates listed if we weren't supposed to use them?"

"To warn us," he answered. "To let us know which spaces we needed to *avoid*, and to give us an idea of what to expect. And for emergencies. I feel like this would've been a lot simpler if we'd just boarded a plane for Greece."

"You're going to Greece?" LaRue interjected.

Score rolled his eyes, not answering. It felt extremely rude, so I turned to the werewolf, explaining, "Yes. We're looking for a minotaur, I guess."

His eyes glittered, "Then surely mademoiselle means Crete, hmm?"

Score's brows lifted, "What are you talking about?"

"There's only one minotaur, and he lives on Crete," LaRue said, shrugging. "At least, that's what he's always *said*. But I've only seen him at a tavern, Realm-side."

"You know where to find him?" I asked excitedly, leaning forward.

LaRue just laughed, "Certainly! He and old LaRue go way back. Great friends."

Score and I exchanged a long look. Finally, he said, "Can you— can you help us get in contact with him?"

"But of course!" the wolf said, grinning. "Leave it all to LaRue!"

~~~~~~~~~~~~~~~~~

Glenn returned about two hours later with more of the small golden flowers.

"With the mending blooms in place," he said, wrapping Score's knee, "we can leave at daybreak and make some real progress."

Score sighed. "Our direction has changed. We're going to the Jungle of Moranth."

Glenn's eyes narrowed, "We discussed heading towards—"

Score shook his head, nodding to LaRue. "He knows where to contact the minotaur."

"And you trust him?" Glenn scoffed.

I leaned back, glancing at the wolf. He appeared harmless enough, now— as if all his menace had drained with the setting of the moon.

"I say we give him a chance," I announced, leaning forward. "We don't have much to lose, and it's the first solid lead we've had."

Glenn shook his head but didn't say anything, moving from Score to settle at my side. "You shouldn't trust so easily, little bird," he murmured. "It makes me worry for you."

I sighed. It was nice that Glenn cared for me, but the tone reminded me of my earlier thoughts. I frowned sharply.

"Lyra?" he asked, his brows lifting as my expression changed.

"It's nothing," I muttered.

"It isn't *nothing!*" Glenn protested. "Tell me. If something or *someone* is making you uncomfortable—"

I shook my head, staring up at the blue sky. A few fluffy clouds drifted overhead, the edges lined in a pale gold. "I just hate needing protection, that's all."

"You're not at fault, Lyra," Glenn said. "Most everything we've encountered in the Realm has just been bad luck."

I gripped at the tall grass surrounding me. "You don't understand, Glenn. I want to take care of *myself*. I'm sick of being the damsel in distress, of always needing rescue. I guess... I guess I'd like to train," I added.

His brows knitted together, and he gave me a look like I'd just grown a second head. "*Why*, Lyra?!"

I leaned forward, chewing my lip. He obviously didn't understand. I was tired of placing others in danger for my benefit. I was tired of letting others fight my battles for me. But most of all, I was tired of feeling so helpless.

"I want to be capable," I said slowly, finding the proper wording. "Right now I'm not. I'm so dependent on you."

Glenn smiled, eyes twinkling, "And I'm fine with that."

I ripped out a hunk of the blue grass. "But *I'm* not. I want to be strong, and fast, and—"

"You're serious, aren't you?!" he asked me with incredulous eyes. "You really want to— to *fight*, to feel the agony of training, to brutally, violently attack, to—"

"I just want to take care of myself."

His mouth twitched, and he watched me for several moments before saying, "As usual, I'm useless against your wishes. If you'd like, I can train you a bit, teach you a few things, help you to—"

I threw my arms around him, excited, "Really?!"

He just laughed, "Yes. Of course." He addressed Score, "I'm going to go show Lyra how to handle a bow." He said, "Will you be fine here, with him?"

Score's gaze flickered to the wolf. Even wounded, I suspected Score was more than a match for him physically— though he looked uncomfortable at the prospect of being left alone with the man. After a couple moments, he nodded, "Yeah. I need to plan a new route, anyway." He set to work unfolding the Realm map, puzzling over it. Glenn picked himself up, offering me a hand.

I smiled, a flurry of nerves striking my core. Glenn led me about a quarter of a mile away, to a space where the grass had been harvested. It was more open, and much easier to move through.

"We'll be able to practice here," he said, pulling his bow from his shoulders. "And the bales are decent targets." His eyes met mine. "Do you *really* want to learn?" he asked again, fiddling with the bowstring.

I took a breath, nodding, "Yes. I think I need to learn *something.*"

"Okay, then. Okay."

Glenn handed me his weapon. I held the bow awkwardly, staring at it. I had no idea what I was doing.

"So," he began, "you have your grip, here." He brushed his fingers near mine, "Hold it like this." He moved my hand up. "Not too tight. It should be gentle, like the caress of a lover."

I blushed at that, "What— what do you mean?"

Glenn just smiled, pulling my other hand over. "Balance it right..." he traced the arch of skin between my thumb and hand with his fingertip, "*there.*"

My heart sped up. I looked at him, adjusting my grip on the bow. He pursed his lips appraisingly. "Better. Now then, the fundamentals." He laughed, "And I know some of this will be condescending, so bear with me."

"Okay. It's the basics, right?"

"Exactly," he agreed. "String, arrow rest," he said, pointing out a small notch above the grip. "The top half is the upper limb, the bottom the lower limb." He laughed, "Easy enough, right?"

"Yes, but—"

"Patience, little bird, patience." He grinned, pulling out an arrow and gesturing to the pointy end. "Arrowhead. I use ironwood broadheads. This is sharp— I only carry arrows I intend to use, Lyra. You need to be careful when we practice." His eyes met mine, concerned, and I nodded. He looked satisfied, moving on. His finger traced over the center of the arrow, "Shaft. Made of sanctified wood." He bent the tiny follicles of the feathers on the butt, "Fletching. From feathers, obviously. There's more, of course, but that's a good starting point." He was standing close to me now, handing me the arrow. I accepted it nervously.

A soft breeze carried the scent of the strange blue grass. The smell was almost peppery in the waning light of day.

"Notch your arrow," he instructed. "Like this..." He stood with his body pressed against mine, one arm curled over my own. I did as he asked, my knees beginning to feel weak. I wasn't sure if I was nervous for the training, or if it was something else entirely.

"Draw…" he whispered in my ear. Glenn was rarely so close to me. His breath smelled like peppermint and herbs. I took a deep breath, following his instruction.

I fumbled a little, my hands trembling, and he sighed. "No, no, no… like this." His hand was over mine now. He split my index and middle fingers apart, sliding the end of the arrow between them. "Draw the string. Nice and smooth…" I pulled it back, wondering how far was too far. But he said, "Keep going, Lyra. Pull it so it sits right here." His fingertips danced on my right cheek, below my eye. I almost shivered at the sensation.

He took a step back, looking me up and down. "Your form needs work, but we can improve that later," he said. "For now, shoot."

"Where should I aim?" I asked. The space between my shoulders was beginning to burn with exertion, but only a little.

"The bale."

"Yeah, but where on the—"

Glenn laughed, "*Anywhere* is fine, Lyra."

I let the arrow go. It flew off to the left, missing the bale of the blue grass by a wide margin. I flushed, staring at the ground.

"No one gets it on the first try," Glenn said confidently, pulling out a second arrow. "The important thing is to learn from your mistakes. Try again."

I drew the string back, adjusting my aim. Another failure, not any closer.

Glenn sighed, pulling the bow from my hands. He looked thoughtful. "Are you sure you want to pursue this?"

I nodded, though I could feel prickles of heat on my face, "Yes. It'll just take practice, that's all."

Glenn shrugged, "Perhaps if you had a more concrete target…" He tilted his head, nodding, "Yes." He drew an arrow quickly, embedding it in the center of the hay bale.

I jumped. He'd made it look so simple, but I knew it was anything but easy. "So I'm aiming for near the arrow?"

Glenn just smiled, looking amused. "A perfect shot would split the shaft."

I frowned, feeling like I'd been set up to fail. "That's impossible!" I protested. "You see that on cartoons, maybe, or read it in Robin Hood, but no one can *actually*—"

Crack! A second arrow was notched and released, faster than I could make out clearly. My eyes followed the trajectory of the blur, my face feeling even hotter. Sure enough, Glenn had split the first arrow with the second.

"See? Possible," he said, shoving the bow into my hands.

I stared at the ground, flushing. My pride had been wounded a little. "But you're an elf, Glenn," I protested weakly. "You have magical reflexes, or—"

"No, I don't," he said simply. His arms folded across his chest, and he smiled. "And for your information, I'm only *half* elf."

I stared up at him. He looked like a full elf to me. I wondered what else he was. His mouth began to twitch, and his eyes sparkled. I wanted to ask him, I really did, but I was sure Glenn would count it as my last question. I hated to use it. So instead I sighed, "Okay. Try to split the shaft."

"That's the spirit," he said, handing me a new arrow. "Alright, little bird, aim for me."

I took a few deep breaths, drawing the string back. I took my time to aim. I let the string go, and—

"Ahh!" I cried, tears stinging my eyes instantly. The string had slapped my forearm, and the arrow *still* wasn't close to the bale.

Glenn laughed next to me. I whipped my head to him, glaring, "It's not funny!"

"It's a *little* funny." My nostrils flared. I rubbed my wounded forearm bitterly. Glenn just shook his head, "You're the one who wanted to do this." His mouth formed a lopsided grin. "You could still call it quits, little bird. No one will judge you."

I glared at him, snatching a new arrow from the quiver hanging on his back. I notched it, ignoring my throbbing arm. A welt had raised— red and angry— but I took a few steadying breaths, trying to remember Glenn's instructions.

I let the arrow fly, careful to keep my left elbow bent. This time, it arced smoothly, sticking into the left-most edge of the blue grass bale. I squealed, "I did it!" jumping up and down.

Glenn just laughed again, "So excited for one small victory... hmm..." His head tilted a little as he watched me.

I flushed, feeling self-conscious. "I— I'm— I mean—"

"No," he said, stepping forward, brushing his thumb across

my cheek, "I wish I had such enthusiasm." He slid a new arrow from behind his head, holding it between us. "Can you do it again?"

My heart pounded in my ears as I watched him, staring into his eyes. I took a breath, taking the arrow from him, drawing the string back and trying to focus. If I couldn't at least get the arrow into the blue bale again, I'd feel like a colossal failure.

Glenn slid his body behind mine, so he was standing unnervingly close again. He leaned in, placing his palm across my midsection. "Keep your core tight, Lyra," he murmured, pressing firmly on my stomach. I straightened my body. "And always learn from your mistakes. Try to keep your gaze on the same spot relative to the bow while you aim."

I released, sending the arrow in a straight line. It embedded within a foot of Glenn's target arrow. I couldn't help but grin, "That's better!"

"Yes," Glenn agreed, "it is." He handed me a fresh arrow. "Now do it a hundred more times."

Chapter Eight

Tension

Score had successfully plotted a new route that would take us through no less than four Realm gates to reach the Jungle and find the minotaur. By the next morning, his knee had healed as miraculously as my ankle. We set off, determined to finally make some real progress.

LaRue was a cheerful companion. He decorated his clothing with feathers and flora he collected from our surroundings. He also had the habit of relentlessly flirting with Score, though even he seemed aware that it wouldn't lead to anything.

For a solid week we trekked. The days were monotonous and exhausting, but thankfully without incident. For his part, Score seemed distant. In the private moments we had together, he insisted that we were going about the journey the wrong way. In the afternoons— after we'd settled, but before the sun had dipped down— Glenn and I continued our archery practice.

I'd improved marginally, but my successes were slow. I was frustrated at the pace.

Glenn had me repeat the same moves over and over, hours on end. I often asked if we could accelerate the lessons. He'd just chuckle, "Patience, little bird, patience." It was difficult to wait. So far, my training didn't yield much progress.

As we traveled through the Realm, I was privileged to see strange landscapes. Utilizing a fey-ring gate— a ring of mushrooms in the midst of the Azure Plains— we were transported across the Realm to a new location: the Dragon's Backbone, a mountain range amidst an arid landscape. The long row of jagged peaks ranged from hilly to monstrous, dwarfing everything around us. The highest summit was wreathed in so much cloud and smog, it was impossible to see the peak. The land smelled harsh, like smoke. We trekked over one of the mountain's slopes, near a valley between the peaks. The brown terrain was dotted with scrubby yellow grass and strange red-orange trees shaped like evergreens, but bearing leaves like deciduous.

We exited the Backbone through another cave gate, emerging in the Overworld amongst a frozen section of Canada's Yukon. It was surreal, darting from the heat of the Realm to the cold reality of the human world.

I was grateful when we arrived at the tree that would return us to the warmth of the Realm again. A crackle of magic spread across my skin as we entered the trunk, emerging from a hollowed log. The new location was a winding forest of pink and fuchsia: the Dew Groves. It wasn't exactly marshy, but the Groves were made up of shallow purple pools of water bound by little bridges of land. It was beautiful, quiet, and still— disturbed only by a few hummingbirds zipping between the dewy branches.

That evening, I sat with aching shoulders, leaning against my hands miserably. I was uncomfortable and still too cold. Glenn had left to collect firewood ten minutes ago. I sat hunched with my arms wrapped around my knees. Score was a few feet from me, looking similarly uncomfortable. A drop of water fell from the trees and slid down my neck, invading my clothes. I groaned, swiping at my numb nose. Everything was so damp, I wondered if Glenn would even find viable firewood.

Score stared at me, as I so often caught him doing, with soft rose pink eyes.

I turned to him, exasperated, "*What?!*"

He blinked, taken aback, mumbling, "Nothing…"

"If you have something to say, Score, just say it." I looked at him, to the maddening pink of his eyes. LaRue was curled into the fetal position on the outskirts of our camp, sleeping despite the chill in the misty air.

"I—" Score began, gazing into my eyes earnestly.

My jaw tensed in irritation. Once again, I had the feeling that Score was keeping something from me. "What?!" I hissed.

"Nothing, Lyra," he sighed. "It's nothing."

I frowned, rolling my eyes. "One of these days, you're going to have to come clean to me," I muttered. I'd told him before of my suspicions, and he'd pretty much confirmed them then. He just flushed, staring down at his feet.

"I still think we should stick to the Overworld," Score insisted.

I glared at him. "And I think of all of us, *Glenn* is the best equipped to know what to do."

"You place a lot of stock in his opinion," Score said, frowning. His eyes shifted to dark violet with bright green on the edges.

"He's saved my life dozens of times, and he's got a ton of experience. He was trained for combat and survival. He's—"

"Not a siren," Score finished with a sigh, leaning back. "There's no way he was intended to undertake this journey."

"You need to get over your grudge!" I snapped back, infuriated. "Or your jealousy, or— or whatever!"

"This isn't just— he could have all the experience in the world, but he's never dealt with siren needs before! I know he's got the best intentions for *you*, but I don't trust him as much as my own instincts."

"Well, *I* trust him more!" I retorted, frowning.

Score just shook his head. "Fine. I hope you're right. Both our lives are in your hands."

I nearly snarled at that declaration. "No! Don't, Score! Don't try and push that responsibility on me. It was *your* choice to leave Whitecrest! It was *your* choice to find me, it was—"

Score sighed, pained. "I guess I'm just saying I really hope— for both of our sakes— you're right about Glenn. That's all." He looked thoughtful, "I think—"

Glenn reappeared, slipping into camp silently with full arms loaded with branches. I was relieved to see him, tired of the chill. I flicked my gaze to the bundle— there was far less firewood than usual. Even with the flames, this night would be cold.

He addressed Score, "Any troubles?"

Score shook his head, staring at his feet, throwing the sheathed dagger back to the half-elf. "No."

Glenn's brow raised. "Is everything okay? Did I interrupt something?"

I sighed. "Not at all."

Score cleared his throat, "Actually, I was just saying I thought maybe— after we find the minotaur— we should travel by Overworld."

Glenn frowned, kneeling down to begin working on the fire. "Absolutely not. Do you know how simple it is to track someone up there? Extras stand out like sore thumbs in the Overworld."

"I managed for a long time on my own," Score said thoughtfully, "I don't think we'd have much trouble."

Glenn just rolled his eyes, striking some sparks on the pile of wood. It took additional coaxing, but he managed to persuade a small tongue of flame to appear. He turned to Score, "You got *lucky*, mate."

Score glared at him. "You don't know what you're talking about. I had to be careful, I had to—"

I was tired of hearing it. I interrupted him, snapping, "Enough! We can discuss our route later! It doesn't even matter right now— we've already got a plan to find this stupid minotaur!" I turned to Score, infuriated though I didn't know why, "Stop trying to be difficult!"

He bristled at my tone, "Are you *kidding* me, Lyra?! I've done my best to be amiable this entire trip!" He jerked a thumb towards Glenn, "He's said jump, I've asked 'how high?'— and I sure as *hell* haven't done any of it for *him!*"

My hands balled into tight fists, and my nostrils flared. I was about to tell him he could go, that he could leave if he wanted to, but I didn't get the chance.

From the edge of the fuchsia trees sprang a woman with wild hair and eyes. She landed atop LaRue's still form, straddling him, pinning his arms down. She was fearsome to behold, dressed in dirty black leather armor. All manner of weapons were attached to her body like appendages. Her hair was ebony, a wild and frizzy tangle of curls that stuck out in a huge poof. Her skin was caramel colored, her teeth jagged and menacing. But it was her eyes that were most unnerving— dark maroon, the pupils slitted like a cat's.

"You thought you could escape me, dog, but you were wrong…" she hissed.

LaRue's eyes popped open, his expression one of complete panic. "Birkita…"

She slammed her fist against his jaw. I winced at the cracking sound it made. "Where's my money, LaRue?!"

"Now, see," he said carefully, "the funny thing about that—"

She struck him again, this time in the nose— I could see it bend, already beginning to turn purple. "Where is it?!"

"I don't— that is to say— I—"

She pulled a knife from her belt. It was a dull silver, but the tip was a wicked sharp point. She shoved the end inside his nose. "Don't make me ask you again."

"Lost!" he moaned. "Gambled away at the casino in Delphine!"

The woman grimaced, "Then your life is worthless, you flea-ridden damned mutt! I could just *scream.*" She slid the flat of the blade across his cheek.

LaRue began to quiver, "No, no, no, let's not be hasty Birkita! I'll get you new money, yes?"

Birkita laughed, "Oh, you'll get me plenty of new money *after*, LaRue... do you know how much a were-pelt goes for these days?"

He blanched, struggling a little, but Birkita just dragged the tip of the blade along the edge of one nostril. A thin line of blood drizzled from it.

Glenn's hand found mine. I turned my gaze to him. "If we leave now, perhaps we can lose them both," he whispered.

I stared at him, horrified. "We can't leave him with her! She'll kill him!"

"I agree with Glenn," Score said next to me.

My jaw tightened. *That's convenient*, I thought.

"Lyra!" Glenn hissed, "Trust me, we don't want to get involved. That woman is a *banshee.*"

I snatched my hand from him, standing and striding over to LaRue.

"Lyra!" Glenn hissed. He sprang up with his hand on his bow, knocking an arrow back.

I squared my shoulders and moved forward. Maybe this *was* a mistake, but I wasn't about to stand by and let someone die in front of me.

"Excuse me," I said quietly to the woman.

The banshee became rigid, her face annoyed, "This doesn't

concern you, girl. I offer my condolences if the dog is indebted to you as well, but I promise you I have precedent." She turned her attention back to LaRue, grinning nastily.

"There has to be something that'll solve this," I said, holding my hands up. "You can't seriously intend on killing him."

The woman threw her head back, cackling. "You're a strange one, aren't you?" She brought her attention back to LaRue. "He deserves little more than death. He's a scoundrel, and though he's slippery, this time he's been caught."

LaRue's eyes were pleading.

I pressed her, "How much does he owe you?"

The banshee laughed again, grinning at me with her sharp teeth. "Far more than you likely have." She appraised me, glancing up and down my form. "What *are* you, girl? You're nothing I've seen before— which is a stretch, as I've seen it all."

"Well, I'm a—"

"*Lyra!*" Score snapped.

I turned to him. His eyes were frantic. He shook his head sharply, but I frowned, twisting my fingers together. "I'm a siren," I finished.

I could hear Score groaning.

She raised a brow almost imperceptibly, "I thought that species died off."

"Not completely." Score sighed loudly behind me. "What would it take? What would it take to buy his life?"

The woman stood, and I could see now she was tall— at least as tall as Score was. She regarded me carefully with her hands on her hips. LaRue began to push himself upright, but Birkita slammed her heel into his throat. The werewolf made a strangled sound, falling back to the ground.

"What do you have to offer, girl?"

Honestly, I didn't have much at all to give the woman. I was at a loss. "I don't—"

Score sighed again, stepping forward. "We're searching for siren ruins. If we find anything valuable, we'll give it to you, okay?" His arms were folded across his chest, his expression irritated but businesslike. My stomach fluttered. It was quick thinking, and I was grateful for it.

Birkita narrowed her eyes, considering carefully before she answered. "Honestly, I could get my money far faster by killing the dog. Then again…" She eyed me up and down, then turned her gaze to Score. "Traveling with two members of a presumed extinct species— that is an enticing diversion. Why not, siren?" She sheathed her knife, pulling her boot from LaRue's neck.

The werewolf tentatively stood, his eyes glassy. He rubbed his throat gingerly, swiping the blood that dripped from his nose. "Thank you, *chaton*," he mumbled to me.

"You *should* thank her," Birkita said, "because if you run, if you move to betray me, dog, I'll take her life instead."

At that, Glenn cleared his throat. "Make no mistake, wolf," he said coldly, "if you *ever* try to escape, I will hear you, and I will have an arrow within you before you've moved further than a meter."

LaRue looked offended, "Surely, monsieur doesn't think I'm the type to—"

"I know *exactly* what type of person you are. But you're playing with *her* life, now."

LaRue sobered, nodding. Next to him, the banshee grinned wickedly. "Well, then, it's settled!" She slapped the wolf on the shoulder, hard, and LaRue winced.

I shuffled back to the fire, settling next to Glenn on the ground.

"That wasn't the smartest move, Lyra," he said, prodding the flames with a stick.

"I don't leave people to die."

He rubbed at his forehead wearily. "So I'm learning. So I'm learning."

Score sat on my other side, not looking any happier than Glenn. I turned to him, feeling awkward. "I'm— thanks, Score. For thinking on your feet like that."

He shook his head, his eyes cast on the pink foliage below us. "I doubt I'd like you half as well, Lyra, if you didn't care so much. I just wish—" he sighed, "I just wish you'd think things through more carefully."

"Cheers to that," muttered Glenn.

I smiled, looking to my left, then my right. I wasn't sure how I'd managed to be lucky enough to have them both in my life, but I was, somehow. Even when they drove me crazy, they were both good men.

Chapter Nine

The Minotaur

We exited the Dew Groves two days later, entering the jungle through a gate formed by two trees twining together to create an archway. Birkita was quiet and observant. She watched the party like a hawk, but mostly kept her attention fixed on LaRue.

We continued on routinely. Glenn had been true to his word. He kept one eye on LaRue at all times. The wolf (and therefore Birkita) even accompanied us to our archery practices—Glenn insisted on it.

LaRue seemed less cheerful than he'd been in earlier days. He was quiet and moody. He'd been so silent, I was surprised that he approached me as we hiked through the foliage.

"Mademoiselle, I feel deeply indebted to you," he mumbled.

I shrugged. The ground was so covered with plants, it was slower going than it'd been on the other terrain we'd crossed. I had to pick my feet up to step over vines, bushes, and fallen branches. "Forget it," I replied, tucking a stray hair behind my ear.

The wolf frowned, looking at the ground. "I feel as though—"

He didn't finish the statement.

"You feel as though?" I pressed. I stepped carefully up and over a tree stump so encapsulated in flora that it looked like a tiny hill.

"May I ask you a question?" he said, his voice shifting to

something a little lighter.

"Sure."

"When I first saw you, when I was unfortunately dealing with my… time of the month…" He grinned, "I saw you up in that tree, with the elf, hmm?"

A blush began to crawl up my cheeks. "What… what about it?"

"But," he continued, "it's clear to me that the siren-boy also has feelings for you. So I'm just trying to ascertain, mademoiselle, which of them, exactly, is your beau?" My face prickled in embarrassment, but LaRue just laughed with sparkling eyes. "Oh ho! So I'm to presume you have choices? How delicious!"

I chewed my lip. "I'm not— they're not—"

"Take my advice," he said with a wolfish grin. He gestured expressively with one hand, "*Enjoy* the decision-making process…" He sighed wistfully, "But if it were *me…*"

I picked up the pace. Maybe if I caught up to Glenn or Score, LaRue would be less personal with his chatter. The boys were only about ten feet ahead of me.

"If it were *me*," LaRue continued, "I'd choose the siren-boy. He's beautiful."

I stared at the ground, moving as quickly as I dared. "He's a siren, LaRue. Like me. It's how we're built. We're attractive creatures— we're supposed to appeal to humanity."

"Oh, and let no man say you aren't a thing of beauty, mademoiselle!" He agreed, pursing his lips appraisingly. "But that boy… he's a masterpiece."

I flushed again, staring at my feet. Mercifully, the land was beginning to flatten out. I darted forward, catching up to Score.

I glanced at him, my heart beating in my ears in spite of myself. Of course he was attractive. He had to be; it was part of his magic. But LaRue had a point. From the first minute I'd seen Score, I'd felt an instant desire for him.

He was distracted as we moved forward. Noticing that I'd fallen into step next to him, he reached out, entwining his fingers through mine. I felt a soft tug of longing hit me in my stomach. A warm glow blushed from my core.

Ahead of us, Glenn stopped, pointing. "There's a building in the distance."

I squinted. All I could see were trees and darkness.

"That's the place," LaRue agreed behind me. "He'll be there. He's there every night for karaoke."

A minotaur singing karaoke? I almost laughed.

Score's nose crinkled, "*Karaoke…*" he muttered under his breath. I had to agree. Worse than human music was *live* human music intoned by the drunk and tone-deaf.

"Maybe we'll catch him before it starts," I said optimistically.

"Karaoke or not, we need to find him." Score's brows raised as his gaze fell on our interlocked hands. "Did I… I'm sorry, Lyra. I didn't even notice. If you don't want to hold hands—"

I shrugged, keeping our fingers laced together. "No," I said, surprising myself, "it's fine. I… it's kind of nice, actually."

He blinked, "Oh… okay."

After ten minutes, I could see the dark building. The trees had been thinned out to accommodate for the structure— a squat building with chipped paint. A faded sign swung above the door with words carved in a language I'd never seen. The door was covered with graffiti in a variety of writing systems, some little more than symbols. The boldest mark was along the door jam: a crudely scratched representation of male anatomy and the words 'Puck Wuz Heyre' scrawled in jagged Old English lettering. Every few seconds it glowed, drawing the eye.

Glenn tugged on the heavy wooden door, gesturing inside.

It was a dive in the truest sense of the word— dank, dingy, with patrons who looked as though they were one bad day away from suicide.

From behind the bar, an elongated figure stood. Its skin was knotted and bark-like, as if it was made from a tree. It had beady black eyes, a tiny nose, and thin lips. From its head grew twisted horns, sprouting green leaves at the tips. It had slender fingers and legs that bent unnaturally, ending in wooden hooves.

The creature nodded at us.

"Dragonfire brandy," Birkita requested, striding forward.

The figure pulled out a dirty shot glass, filling it with a liquid that sparked in blue and red. Birkita downed it then slapped the counter, "Another!"

"She's enthusiastic," Glenn muttered next to me. His gaze swept the dim, dusty tavern. He frowned, "I don't see a minotaur."

"Straton?" hissed the bartender. "He'll be here in a couple hours, after his 'shift'."

I sat on one of the stools, moaning a little. It was nice to get off of my feet. I rolled my neck, enjoying the reprieve.

Score slid onto the empty stool on my right. Glenn leaned against the bar on my left.

I turned to Score, "What are we looking for, anyway?" I asked, settling against the counter. I was tired, more tired than I'd realized. It'd been a long couple weeks of trekking.

"A clue," Score answered, his eyes darting to Glenn. "Just a clue."

~~~~~~~~~~~~~~~~

The minotaur arrived after another two hours, sitting wearily on a stool. I couldn't help but stare at him. He had a bull's head, but human-looking eyes. He dipped his muzzle in a bucket of milky looking alcohol, leaving a coat of cream on his nose. Below the fur of his cow's head, he had the physique of a bodybuilder. He wore a gold chain and a pair of brown leather pants, but nothing else.

I bolstered my courage, striding over to him. I tapped on his shoulder, "Excuse me."

He turned his great head, eyeballing me up and down before sighing. "Great. Well, that explains it."

"That explains what?" I asked.

He rolled his great eyes, slumping his enormous head in one hand. "Why I can't just *leave*," he wailed. It was closer to a bawl than a yell of anger.

I flinched. "I'm sorry, but I don't understand."

He gripped his horns with his human hands in frustration. "Of course you don't. Of *course* you don't," he muttered. He turned to me. If bulls could glare, that was the expression I saw. "Figures they wouldn't have told you anything, either." He took another long draught from the bucket. I shifted my weight from foot to foot.

My little group stood silently, watching the spectacle but doing nothing. I didn't know what to say. The minotaur didn't seem happy to see me, and I doubted he wanted to help us.

Birkita sighed, rolling her eyes and striding forward. She

tapped the minotaur on the shoulder. "Oy! We need answers."

"Answers? I'm supposed to be guarding the stupid, ridiculous, *empty*…" he ranted. "You want answers? Ask *her*." He jerked his enormous head towards me.

"Please," I said, looking at the floor, "I'm just looking for any siren cities, or… a library?"

His ear twitched at the word. Finally, he heaved a long snort from his nostrils. "I have the evenings *off*, you know. I negotiated it."

"Negotiated what?"

Ignoring me, he finished the last of the bucket's contents and stood. He towered over our group— he was at least ten feet tall. "Guess I'm not getting tonight off, after all. Fine. But I'm taking tomorrow instead. Follow me," he said tiredly.

Stooping low, gesturing for us to follow, he ducked out the door.

I hesitated a moment, but trailed after him. From behind me, I could hear the shuffling of my companions. When we were twenty feet from the building, the minotaur stopped.

"I'd have expected to see you in Crete. That's where sirens used to meet me— in the Overworld. I've never met one within the Realm."

Score glanced at me. "That's not surprising."

"Another one?" the minotaur asked, sighing again. "Well, you're not dead. *Great*." He didn't sound especially happy.

"You were glad the sirens vanished?" I asked.

He held his hands up. "Look— I've nothing against sirens as a whole. They did me a solid about a thousand years back. That's why we created our arrangement."

"What arrangement is that, exactly?" Score inquired.

The minotaur folded his massive arms across his chest. "I don't want to go into the details of what they did for me— but I guard their library, and guide sirens when they land on Crete. I know when they set foot on the island, I can feel their kind's presence there. Of course," he added bitterly, "there hasn't been much need for me the past thirteen years. I thought our negotiation would've dissolved when the sirens disappeared, yet I still couldn't leave the island— except my nights off. I've been stuck guarding nothing."

That didn't sound fair.

"Well," I said, "maybe we can make a new arrangement."

His eyes narrowed, "What do you mean, Matriarch?"

"If the sirens really *have* all died, that means Score and I are it. That means we're in charge, right?"

"It means *you're* in charge, my Matriarch," he corrected. "The male is worthless in siren dealings."

Score looked mildly offended but didn't say anything, just tensed next to me. I closed my eyes, considering my response. "How about this— help us out now, and your obligation will be fulfilled."

"Really?" he eyed me suspiciously. "What do you want in return? I'm already sworn to assist you."

"Just live your life! Score and I don't need a minotaur. If you want to go, once we're safely out of the library… why not?" I turned to Score— we were in this together, after all.

He looked thoughtful before saying, "Yeah. If there's still another siren, the contract wouldn't be valid, anyway."

The minotaur scrutinized us. "You're not like your relations— but you smell like sirens. I'll accept your kindness, if you're sincere." He reached up, unhooking the golden chain from his neck. He snapped his hands, pulling on it. The links stretched out to an impossibly huge hoop. He draped it around two large branches. "Step through the chain to enter my labyrinth," he instructed. "If you're truly siren-blood, your path will illuminate. Do not move away from the lights!" he warned us. "That's a good way to find yourselves dead."

Glenn stepped closer to me. "We're *all* going," he said.

The minotaur's eyes narrowed. "That would be unwise. The labyrinth will shift, and you'll lose your way."

"I'm capable," Glenn asserted, staring up into his eyes.

"It doesn't matter how capable you are," the minotaur responded. "No one can navigate the path but sirens. I *could* allow you entry, but it'd be unwise. You'll die. Painfully. It's foolish."

"Then I'll stick with the siren," he dismissed, gripping my hand tightly in his.

The minotaur let out a laugh that sounded closer to a bleat. "And you'll find yourself clutching ghosts and shadows when you enter! It's your choice, but it's folly."

I pulled my hand from Glenn's. "I don't want to put you in more danger. I can go with Score. We'll be back soon."

Glenn's mouth puckered. He stared into the loop.

"You could let him go alone," he suggested.

I shook my head adamantly, "I can't leave this to Score. We're supposed to do it together." As soon as I said it, I knew it was true.

Beyond the ring of gold didn't look like anything special— I could see the jungle through the hole. Glenn turned to Score, "She returns safe."

"I wouldn't let something happen to her," Score told him. "Trust me."

"Only if I must. Fine. Get going."

Score's eyes met my own. They were a beautiful pink, an anxious orange, and an excited turquoise. His look was a question.

Are you ready?

I took a deep breath and nodded. We stepped hand in hand through the hoop.

Chapter Ten

The Library

It was dark for a moment. My heart rate started to quicken, nervous that we'd fallen into a trap. I squeezed Score's hand nervously, but after a few seconds a dim light shuttered on— then another, and another. A clear path illuminated before us. As we walked the empty hall, the space continued to brighten.

Stone surrounded us, carved with strange designs and images of terrifying monsters. On either side, numerous halls branched from the main path, all dark and foreboding. I shivered. Score gave my hand a reassuring squeeze.

"You okay, Lyra?"

I nodded, "I think so. It's just strange, that's all."

He cocked his head towards the bleak offshoots, looking curious. "It *is* strange. I wonder what's down there…"

I tugged on his hand, prompting him forward. "I don't want to find out."

The minotaur had made it clear we needed to keep to this path and this path alone. The only safe course was to follow where the lights directed. The illumination was comforting. Whatever was beyond the path was dangerous— I could feel it in my gut.

It took us ten minutes, walking at our slow pace, to reach the library entrance. A pair of large stone doors greeted us. They were at least fifteen feet tall, with siren writing etched over them.

"What does it say?" I asked Score.

His eyes hovered over the markings, "'For those who seek enlightenment, wisdom, or attunement, you will attain what you require within.'"

"Attunement?"

"An approximation. It doesn't translate well to English, and I don't know the precise context." He ran a hand through his hair.

I touched the door experimentally with my fingertips. The stone shuddered, sinking down into the floor. The path was open before us.

It felt *too* convenient. "That was easy…"

Score just chuckled, "It's because you're a siren, Lyra. I bet the doors wouldn't have opened otherwise."

I squeezed his hand, stepping forward.

The library was massive. Above us, a large glass-domed ceiling allowed bright sunlight to stream down. I wondered if it was really daylight beyond the library, or if it was illusion. Surrounding us were bookshelves that shaped the room into curved rows. The shelves were crowded together, making it difficult to see beyond them.

Score stopped in his tracks. His eyes treaded over the features of the room, taking in every detail.

A long moment passed.

"Score?" I prompted.

"I've been here before," he said with certainty.

My gaze swept the space again. It wasn't impossible that he'd been here before, but *I* definitely had no recollection of this place. "Are you sure?"

He nodded, "Positive. I was here before my biological parents died. I *know* it."

I tilted my head, studying the room, trying to find some sort of familiarity within the bookshelves. It was completely foreign. I shrugged, examining the tomes crammed into the shelves. Everything here was written in that precise, scrolling siren language— useless to me. Maybe Score would find something helpful.

He paced next to me, his fingers running over the spines of the books solemnly.

"What do they say?" I asked him.

He shrugged, not removing his eyes from the books, "They're varied, Lyra. As varied as books in a human library." He gestured around, "But everything out *here* is just music. And it's labeled." He tapped the edge of the shelf, which was marked with a small silver sign written in that same indecipherable script.

I glanced at the shelves in disbelief. A million— maybe more— combinations of notes, pauses, and rhythms, all bound and lining the walls. I tugged on Score's hand, impatient. "Come on," I urged, "there has to be a reason we were sent here. Let's find it."

We made our way through the breaks in the shelves. Score told me this ring consisted of plays— mysteries, dramas, comedies, tragedies, adventures, and romances. The shelves were covered in a thick layer of dust— at least thirteen years' worth. I watched scattered flecks sparkle as they settled in the streams of sunlight, stirred from our visit.

Score stopped at the next set of shelves, fascinated. "This is siren history— all reference volumes. Everything about how we emerged, how we ruled, how our society worked." He thumbed through a volume, frowning, "But I don't see anything recent. There's probably nothing that'd tell us how the others vanished, or even who pursued them. I wish we knew who was attacking you, Lyra."

I chewed on my lip, my heart beating hard in my chest. I felt guilty I hadn't told him earlier. "Actually, Score... It's the elf queen, Amaranthe."

He spun to face me, "*What?!* How—"

"Glenn told me," I admitted. "He was originally sent to keep appearances, not to actually help me, but—"

"That damn elf!" Score barked, balling his hands into tight fists.

I bristled.

"He still saved us!" I protested, "And I trust him, Score!"

His nostrils flared, "I'm really glad you trust him, Lyra, I am! But you couldn't have told me this *before,* let me decide for myself if I wanted to trust him with *my* life?"

"I didn't know until after we'd left Whitecrest! And you didn't seem to care about my choice in *that* matter!"

His jaw tensed. "I didn't exactly withhold information from you."

"Are you kidding?! You still haven't told me what you're keeping from me!"

He turned crimson, shaking his head, "I've told you everything important, Lyra."

His eyes were orange— anxious, nervous. He was lying to

my face, and I knew it.

"Sure you have," I growled.

Score had nothing to say to that, but I felt justified when he turned a deeper shade of red.

I was soured by this expedition. Without the ability to read the language, the library had little to offer me.

"Let's hurry and find whatever we're looking for, so we can get back to Glenn," I muttered.

He shook his head, looking bitter. His eyes shifted, a bright green edging its way into orange flecked with violet. "Fine, Lyra. Why don't you move on, see if you can find anything. I'll keep looking out here."

I frowned, folding my arms across my chest. I stormed deeper into the library. I was almost useless here, and now I was angry.

I stomped to the last ring of shelves, hoping I'd find something obviously meant for us— something that'd hint at why we were being pursued.

As I rounded the corner, I was met with enough light that I had to shade my eyes.

Reflecting the sunlight, in the center of the library, was a golden chair. It was beneath the skylight, and was difficult to look at directly until I changed my angle. Embedded within the high back was an opal the size of a softball, surrounded by a jeweled structure. In the brilliant light, it flashed, scattering multiple colors onto the shelves surrounding it.

Next to the chair was a small table with a stone face. I brushed my fingertips across the dusty granite, revealing a golden symbol in the stone: a bird with open wings and a sun behind it. I'd seen similar designs on my inheritance. Several crystals lay scattered near a silver plaque bearing more siren writing. A single book sat next to them. Ignoring the trinkets, I stepped to the chair. I placed one palm on the armrest. It felt powerful, humming beneath my hand.

The tension drained from my shoulders. I called, "Score?"

He stepped beyond the bookshelves, a volume in his hands. "What now, Ly—" He stopped, noticing the chair, staring at it.

"This is important, right?" I asked, gesturing to it.

He gently moved me aside, keeping his gaze fixed on the throne. His hands brushed against it. "This… *this* is why I was here before. I turned four, so I had to learn to read; I was going to start school soon."

"What?" It was confusing. "So you were sent here to learn Siren? Like a class?"

Score nodded, "Yes— no, I mean. Not exactly, Lyra. It was instantaneous."

My brows furrowed. That was impossible.

"Are you sure?"

"Positive." He ran his index finger over the back of it, shivering. Score closed his eyes, taking a few deep breaths, collecting his thoughts. "If this is here, Lyra…" His eyes snapped open. Turquoise: he was excited. "If it's intact, we can— you can—" He raced to the table with the bird etched on it, flipping through the book next to the crystals. "We can do it to you!"

"Do *what* to me?"

"*Attune* you, Lyra," he answered with a grin. He thumbed eagerly through the book, his eyes skimming across the words. "So it looks like all I'd have to do is arrange the crystals in a certain way, then they'll reverberate through the light and react with your siren blood to crystallize the knowledge. But… transfers… hmm…" He paused, reading ahead before nodding, "It specifies a song in here, too, to help seal it in. *But…* there needs to be a second person…" He frowned, paging ahead again before grinning, relieved. "The second person just needs to already understand the language. It works by passing along the knowledge inside of them. And I could do it, Lyra!"

His eyes met mine, and my limbs began to shake with adrenaline. He was serious.

"How would we do it?" I asked.

"Basically, you'll just take a seat and hold onto some crystals," Score told me, smiling. "I'll take care of the rest. Easy."

"But what if— what if we mess it up?"

He grinned, picking up one of the gems, turning it in his hands. It caught the light; the inside was cloudy. "To be honest, I think it's pretty harmless. It shouldn't take too long, either, once I've read through the song."

"How do you *know?!*" I demanded, bunching the fabric of my shirt in my hands.

"Well… I kind of remember it. Being back here has jogged my memory." He glanced up at me, through his lashes, "I mean, I *was* a little older than you were, Lyra. That's why I could have it done. I remember thinking at the time it was a big deal, a big step, a big milestone. I felt so grown up that day."

"What did it feel like?"

"It didn't hurt," he said hastily. "Honestly, I don't remember the process itself much, or even the day— except right afterward. There was an intensity to that moment, sensory overload." He shook his head, smiling, "I can't believe I forgot about it until now."

"You were living a very human life until lately," I pointed out.

"Yeah, but this was such a big deal…" He shook his head, rapping his fingertips on the table top. "Do you want to try it?"

I looked at the chair nervously, biting my lip. This would probably be my only chance to learn siren-language— my only chance to see the map the same way Score did. I took a deep breath, squaring my shoulders.

"Yeah. Let's do it."

"Alright!" Score picked up the book, flipping through it. He studied every word carefully. It was comforting. Despite how thorough he was, it was only about ten minutes before he announced, "I'm ready." He smiled reassuringly, gesturing to the throne. "Take a seat."

My hands began to shake. I wondered if I had the courage for this after all.

"Score, I…"

He raised one of his perfect brows, "You can't tell me you're too nervous, Lyra."

He was right. I was being ridiculous. I straightened my back, sitting hard on the golden chair. The sunlight had warmed it slightly, but not uncomfortably. The light hum I'd felt earlier intensified as I sat. It felt like a vibration spreading from my spine through my limbs. The sensation didn't hurt, but it was uncomfortable.

My heart sped up, and I had to focus to keep my breathing normal.

If Score had been attuned at age four, I doubted anything bad would happen. After all, he'd never shown signs of wanting to harm me. I calmed slightly.

Score snapped two of the crystals into the arms of the chair, placing a third into my hands. He kept a fourth crystal between his own palms, then began to sing: first one note, then a second, then a third until he was making a chord. He held it for what felt like an impossibly long time, though I knew logically I could've done the same thing easily.

The energy in the room shifted. The crystal in my hand began to heat. It vibrated at a different frequency than the chair, starting slow and soft, building steadily until it made a sound in response to Score's chord.

A warmth rushed over my body, like stepping into a sauna. The heat was nice at first, but eventually it became stifling— a thick steam that built inside my brain. When it began to feel suffocating, the pressure released— like someone had cracked open my skull, freeing my spirit from my body.

I was in the whole room, everywhere at once, looking down at myself seated. I appeared terrified, clutching at the crystal, perched on the golden throne. Score looked steady and reassuring. I was aware of every volume on the shelf, of every detail in the room— the fact that the skylight above me was split into several sections that I hadn't noticed before, that the shelves in the room were arranged in perfect circles like a bullseye, that Score had the tiniest whorl in his hair at the top of his head.

I snapped back into my body, staring into Score's piercing forest green eyes.

It was like waking from a long dream— as if the knowledge had always been there, just buried somewhere within my subconscious.

I glanced at the text surrounding me. All the nonsense from before made perfect sense now. Most of the siren language was based on tones, pitches, and inflections more than the words themselves. A single phrase could have a hundred different meanings depending on how it was sounded out. The written language was a whole other beast, relying both on symbolism and phonetics to confer meaning. A complex series of brush strokes described the vocal inflections. I couldn't imagine trying to explain it to someone, or trying to learn it from scratch.

I placed my hand on my forehead, dropping the crystal in my lap, steadying myself. I was dizzy. Everything felt overwhelming.

Score crouched next to the chair instantly, so his eyes were level to mine. "Are you okay, Lyra? Did it work?"

I blinked a few times, trying to clear my head. I took a few deep breaths before nodding, pushing myself up to stand.

"Yes," I said finally. "It was— it worked. It's amazing."

He looked relieved, his shoulders slumping as he watched me circle the room, studying the volumes with more interest now that I could read them.

"I'm glad," he said, chuckling. "I was a little worried, towards the end there."

I slid a finger down the spine of one of the books, tilting my head. I was happy I could read it now. "You did everything right," I assured him, "and you weren't kidding before. It's a lot to take in."

He looked far more shaken up than I felt. I smiled gratefully, wrapping my arms around his waist and squeezing him. I hoped I reassured him.

"After that," he said with a chuckle, "you feel like you have to comfort *me*."

I pulled from him, digging through my backpack to pull the map from its compartment. I unfolded it onto the table.

Score peered over my shoulder, "That's probably more interesting to you now."

I nodded, running my fingers over the verses printed on the back. The chord below was so obvious now, too. An A, just as Score had said.

> *"In ancient times our legend sprang*
> *From Muses' lips a place we came.*
> *Great libraries inside this space,*
> *Forgotten tomes of our great race,*
> *In labyrinth's depths you'll find us there,*
> *Within the dread minotaur's lair.*
>
> *From library to meeting hall,*
> *Take the path scribed in Siren's Call.*
> *Do not despair the flight of death,*
> *And trust in every single step.*
> *Ascend the clouds as pilgrims did,*
> *Make haste to find that which we hid.*

Once inside our private chambers,
You can relax, free from danger.
Seek out the words of our great Bard.
Finding sense from each broken shard.
Use it and illuminate this
Make your way home to Atlantis."

I looked up from the map, meeting Score's eyes.

"Our goal is to find *Atlantis?* As in, lost underwater city of Atlantis?"

He shrugged, "That's what it says."

"And you didn't feel the need to mention that detail?"

It seemed like a pretty major omission. Score just looked past me, towards the golden chair before he answered. "Would you have believed me if I did? It sounded pretty far fetched when I read it the first time."

"What else are you keeping from me, Score?" I demanded, my hands balling into fists.

He closed his eyes, exasperated, "Lyra…"

I crossed my arms in front of myself, frowning.

I thought it was a fair question, but after a minute he just sighed, "I don't know what to tell you. I've been doing the best I can to be honest with you."

He was clearly done speaking. That was the most explanation I'd get. I sighed. I supposed it didn't matter anyway.

I tapped the second verse, "What do they mean by 'scribed in the *Siren's Call*'?"

"It's probably a book. What else *could* it be, here?"

He had a point.

"Well, let's find it and get out of here," I snapped, feeling cranky. I wasn't sure why Score brought this out in me. It seemed like I didn't know if I wanted to kiss him or kill him most of the time.

He looked a little dejected, his eyes shifting to violet. "You want to leave already? But there's so much we could learn…"

I glared at him. "We need to get back to Glenn, to the surface! We have two more of these stupid places to find!"

"This isn't stupid, Lyra!" he sputtered, leaning into his hand. "It's— this is *important!*"

"Yeah, well," I snorted, sitting on the edge of the table and folding the map, "it would've been better if they'd have left us instructions in plain writing. I get being cautious, but really, it's already in siren writing! Why the secrets? Why the riddles? Why not just tell us how to get exactly where we need to go? Did you see anything around here that would tell us why the sirens were hunted in the first place? Anything that'd help?"

Score shook his head, "No. Most of this is just the day-to-day, basic records on siren life. There's nothing here talking about relationships with other species. Those records are probably somewhere else. Maybe Atlantis."

"Then why are we even here?!" I demanded.

"So you could learn to read?!" he countered, glaring back at me.

My face heated. "Let's just find this stupid book and leave," I hissed.

"Fine. I'll start at the back, where the music is. You check the inner ring, and we'll meet in the middle. Hopefully, between the two of us we'll get through it pretty quickly— then we can get back to that elf you love so much."

My face prickled again. I wanted to yell at him, to tell him he didn't know what he was talking about. How I felt for Glenn wasn't the point. By the time I had my bearings, Score had already disappeared into the stacks, rows of bookshelves separating us.

I turned to the shelf nearest me and began to read titles quickly. I scanned each one before moving to the next.

I didn't see a '*Siren's Call*' here, though I did pull out a couple tomes to examine them more thoroughly. Everything in this tiny center ring was fiction: novels, stories, poems— even human volumes that'd been translated into siren writing. I tugged out a book of fairy tales, amused to see it contained familiar favorites like Cinderella and Rumpelstiltskin, despite being written in the delicate script.

I kept going, my fingers barely brushing the books as I moved on. After about half an hour, Score called, "Found it! We can leave."

I wove through the shelves to meet him. He was frowning, staring at the floor and clutching a blue bound book in one hand. "What does it say?"

He handed the volume to me. "Would you even trust me to tell you, Lyra? See for yourself."

I flipped it open, my brows raising marginally. There was a hand-written inscription on the first page of the book in that same specific scrolling writing.

For Lyra and Score: may you find what you seek.

I turned the page, reading:

"Many have been to the firmament chamber of the sirens to receive audience, but it has been years since it has been utilized in that capacity. Still, when mortal or extraordinary find themselves seeking out siren council or song, they will apply themselves upon a pilgrimage to ascend the steps at the edge of the world..."

Score pointed ahead, saying shortly, "It's located off the coast of Ireland."

I closed the book, stuffing it into my bag. "Then we have a destination. Do we need to find something for Birkita, to clear LaRue's debt?"

"I know just the thing..."

He wove through the stacks and returned with the enormous opal from the chair in his hands. It was still surrounded by the strange gold and jeweled setting. It was probably worth a small fortune.

"What do you think?" he asked, holding it up.

I smiled, feeling my tension dissolve away. "I think it's perfect, Score."

He returned the grin, grabbing my hand, "Let's go."

~~~~~~~~~~~~~~~~

I stepped beyond the chain at the end of the labyrinth. From this vantage, it looked like we were emerging from a darkened cave into the jungle. I wondered what my waiting companions saw— the chain didn't look special before we entered, after all.

Glenn was alert as I emerged, throwing his bow over his shoulder and racing towards us. He went from leaning casually against a tree with the weapon in his hands, to immediately helping me take the step down.

Birkita looked bored, but one hand was clamped across

LaRue's wrist to keep the wolf from fleeing.

Score hopped down shortly after I did. He nodded to the minotaur, "Looks like your debt is paid up. Thanks."

He was surprised, but happy. He whipped his enormous bull's head towards me. Glenn wrapped one arm around my waist, squeezing me as if I'd disappear otherwise.

"Truly, Matriarch?" the minotaur asked me.

I shrugged, "Yup. Have a good life."

He nodded, pulling the chain from the tree. He wrapped it in a tight coil. I watched in fascination as the links shrank down in his hands. His arm extended, offering the spring of gold chain to me. "This is yours, Siren Queen, Protectress, Lady." He bowed his head, and I flushed. It was too much attention.

I shook my head, "No, you don't—"

"This library exists only for your kind, Matriarch. It's useless to me. It serves only as a reminder of my long service. Please, *please*, take it with you."

I nodded, "Fine. Give it to Score."

The minotaur turned to my companion. "Very well." He placed the chain in Score's hand. Score sighed, unclasping a section of his guitar case and tucking it inside.

The minotaur bowed low to me. Once again, I felt uncomfortable. He raised a fist over his heart, "I owe you a debt, Matriarch."

"No," I said firmly, "we're square."

He snorted, "My lady, I will accept release, but should you ever need my aid you have my services. Ask the innkeeper at this tavern if you require me. He'll know how to contact me. I owe you a favor."

I blinked, unsure what I could ever need from a minotaur. I shook my head, baffled. "Yeah. Okay. Thanks for everything." I turned to Birkita, tossing her the enormous opal and gems. "Does this pay off LaRue's debt?"

She grinned as she examined it, turning it in her hands. She bounced it in her grip, as if trying to weigh it. Her mouth formed words silently— probably numbers.

"*Most* of it," she agreed, looking at the gem appraisingly. "He still owes on the interest, of course, but—"

"Enough you won't kill him, right?" Glenn asked, cutting her off. "So you can go your way, and we can go ours." He turned his head towards LaRue, "Well, wolf— you're at a tavern now. A hub. You even have an old friend for company."

The wolf blanched, eyeing Birkita nervously, but didn't rebuke the half-elf.

In a strange way, I'd miss the werewolf. But it was probably for the best. We'd travel more quickly and discreetly with only three in our group.

Birkita narrowed her eyes, "Yes, but—"

Score shifted his backpack on his shoulders, nodding. Wordlessly, all three of us turned, beginning to walk.

"Where we headed?" Glenn muttered.

Score stared straight ahead, "Ireland. I have some things to study, first, but we'll narrow it down later. I want to travel top-side, though, in the human world."

Glenn rolled his eyes, frowning sharply. "I *know* what you think, you arrogant—"

I let out an exasperated hiss.

Glenn changed his wording, flaring his nostrils. "Look, I understand your point of view, but I'm far more experienced than you. I'll plot our course."

Score shook his head, "You're not taking everything into account, Glenn—"

"Like what?!" he exploded, stopping in the middle of the jungle.

I rubbed my forehead wearily. The argument felt far away, distant, foggy. I felt *strange*.

"Like common sense!" Score shouted back.

The boys were standing in front of me, but it felt like I was watching a stage— like it wasn't real. The world rocked around me, and I placed a hand on my forehead. "Uh, guys?" I called out weakly.

They continued their arguments. The ground was blurring now, and I felt so… *tired*. I fell to my knees, curling up on the grass.

"Lyra?!" I heard Score call, "Lyra!"

The world went black.

Chapter Eleven

Interrogation

It felt as though I was waking up— but that couldn't have been right.

From the corner closest to me, a dull red light barely illuminated the space. Damp, cold earth was beneath my body. I was alone, surrounded only by shadows. The room was disorienting. Was it even a room?

I heaved myself upright, leaning against my knees. "Glenn?" I called. My voice sounded creaky and small, as if the shadows absorbed the sound. "Score?"

I took another fleeting look around, wondering where they were, wondering if I'd been abandoned.

I rubbed my forehead. Was this a side effect of attunement? I didn't know. Maybe.

"Awake already?" a whispering voice mused. "That's a surprise, so soon…"

I pushed forward, bringing myself up to stand. I brushed off my jeans. The dirt smeared into them, and I frowned. "Who are you? Where am I?"

"You're nowhere, and I'm no one," the voice replied. I couldn't tell if it was a man or a woman. Somehow, it sounded like both— despite my acute siren hearing.

"Show yourself!"

It could've been the grim reaper. An ominous human shape in a long black cloak stepped forward, the hood drawn over his or her face. The figure seemed to suck the thin red light from the room, making it even darker.

"Tell me, siren," the entity said, "where are you now?"

I flared my nostrils. I was terrified, but more than that, I was angry. The question was ridiculous. "How should I know? You brought me here!"

The hooded figure laughed, but it sounded more ominous than mirthful. "This isn't real. So where are you, *really*?"

I scanned the area again. It looked real enough to me. It certainly *felt* real.

"Don't bother looking for an escape," it said. "You're mine now."

My heart began to quicken. My whisper was harsh, "What are you going to do?"

"I told you," it said, stepping forward. "I want to know just where you are. Exactly. You disappeared. I want to find you."

My stomach burned. I didn't know a lot about magic, but what I did know, with absolute clarity, was that I should *not* answer this person's questions. It would be a dire, dire mistake.

"I don't know!"

The cloak swished near the figure's feet as it glided closer. I squinted, trying to make out any features from beneath the hood, but only shadows greeted me. Despite the close proximity, I couldn't detect a face within the darkness.

It crouched.

"I'll ask you again, siren. Where. Are. You?"

"I told you!" My mouth had lost all moisture. "I don't know! I don't—"

The figure reached for my ankle with a gloved hand. It passed through my jeans like a specter, moving through my flesh and grasping the bone itself.

Twist.

I heard a snap. I grimaced, falling hard on my butt before my brain caught up. My ankle! This grim reaper was breaking my ankle!

A cry escaped my lips, tears falling down my cheeks. I clutched the dirt beneath my hands, hissing in misery. The pain was sharp and hard and hot. I could feel it down through the arch of my foot into my toes, up through the curve of my calf and into my knee.

In a singsong voice, it asked again, "Where are you, little

siren?"

I cringed, both at the vocal inflections assaulting my ears and the pain in my leg. I shook my head. My eyes squeezed shut; my nose started to run. It was hard to breathe between the tears and pain.

Twist.

I screamed. In my mind's eye, I could see the break of the bone. It traveled like a crack on a frozen pond, splintering to my knee. My whole leg throbbed, but the pain was most acute where the cruel apparition gripped me.

"You will submit. Answer me."

I shook my head, feeling sick. No matter what happened, I knew in my gut I couldn't tell this person my location.

My vision began to swim. My senses were becoming obscured by pain. Maybe I would die here. Or maybe Glenn would manage to come to my rescue yet again, or maybe Score.

At the moment, I felt powerless to save myself.

Twist.

The crack expanded further, sending a wave of nausea to assault my stomach. I crashed onto my back, no longer capable of supporting myself. The pain was breathtakingly awful. I retched. Branching fractures had spread through my femur.

"Where…"

Twist.

I screamed again, my back arching in agony as the crack spread to my hip. Instead of bones, I had a web of shattered fragments. My left leg was completely useless.

"Are…"

Twist.

The small of my back burned like fire. My hands formed claws of their own accord.

"You?"

Twist.

Even if I'd wanted to answer, I couldn't. I was in such wretched torment. It felt like my back was crushed. From my neck to my toes, each bone was demolished.

I sobbed hard, but the jostling made it worse. Somehow, I managed to roll onto my side. Mercifully, the figure withdrew its hand from inside my flesh.

I felt marginally better, but my nerves still flared in

anguish. I was broken beyond repair.

It crouched next to me. I cried pitifully, shaking my head as I sobbed.

The gloved fingers stroked my face gently. "I can take it all away, little siren. Just tell me what I desire, and I will free you from this torment. I'll ask you once m…"

Everything brightened.

~~~~~~~~~~~~~~~~~

The pain disappeared in one euphoric instant. I was dripping with water. I blinked. Concerned faces were above me. Score was on my left, an emptied water skin in his hands. Glenn was on my right. Both looked terrified.

My face crumpled. I scrambled upright, clutching at them. Coarse grass in my right hand, clean cotton in my left. I leaned in, sobbing freely, burying my face in their shoulders.

Glenn pulled away, cupping my chin to turn my gaze towards him. "What did you see, Lyra?!"

His eyes were steely, trained on my own. But I didn't want to talk about that place. My whole body shook.

Score scooped me into his arms, pulling away from the half-elf. I blubbered hard into Score's chest, leaning against him.

"Lyra," Glenn pressed.

"Give her a minute!" Score snapped. "She's obviously in shock."

I drew in a long breath. Score smelled like spice and warmth and safety. At the moment, he brought me more comfort than Glenn did. Logically, I knew the half-elf understood the assault better and consequentially would be better equipped to fight it, but Score soothed me.

After a long while, I finally mumbled, "Why am I wet?"

Score stroked my hair. "I'm sorry, Lyra— it was the first thing I could think of. But it snapped you out of it."

"I'm astounded it worked," Glenn snorted.

"He was going to physically— he wanted to strike you," Score said, giving the elf a bitter look, "but I wouldn't let him."

I pulled away, wiping my eyes with the back of my hand. "Thank you. Both of you." I took a steadying breath, "I saw—" I frowned, "I don't really *know* what I saw. Mostly darkness. A hooded figure kept asking me where I was. Then…" I cringed, remembering the intense pain.

Glenn's mouth pursed thinner and thinner as he listened. He rubbed his forehead, "That…" he shook his head, "*Arashk*."

"What was it?" I asked.

He shook his head again, "I can't say for certain, only that I have suspicions." He sighed. "We should camp. I'll be off to gather firewood."

"Can we practice tonight, Glenn?" After that attack, I was even more anxious to learn how to defend myself.

His eyes were sympathetic. "It's the wrong time, Lyra. You need to rest, to recover." He tossed his knife to Score, turning towards the trees.

"You never let me have the dagger!" I sputtered.

He whipped his head back to me, giving me an incredulous look. "I don't— *what*?"

"You always leave it with Score!"

"Lyra, you've been freshly attacked. You need to rest. You're hardly—"

I shook my head, "No! You always give Score the knife. Even when his leg was ruined, you put him in charge."

His brows raised. He shook his head, "I don't even know *how* to begin to respond to that!" He muttered, "I'll be right back."

Score chewed his lip, frowning. He'd settled on the ground, the *Siren's Call* next to him. "Are you okay, Lyra?"

I shrugged, plopping down onto the dirt next to him. "I'm alive, I guess," I said bitterly.

"Honestly," Score said, turning the sheathed knife in his hands, "I don't know if it'd matter if you'd had training for whatever happened. It was weird. You were present one minute, the next you were asleep, and screaming, and—" He turned to me, his eyes forest green with rose pink at the edges, "And I don't think I've ever been so terrified."

"Me either." I leaned forward, into my fist. "But I won't just wait around until the next time I'm attacked. I need to know how to handle myself."

"You can blunder along, learning nothing with the elf," said a smooth voice across the campsite.

I jumped, turning my head.

It was Birkita. She leaned against a tree about ten yards

away, LaRue next to her. She crossed her legs casually, "Or, alternately, we can broker a deal."

"I thought our business was done?"

The banshee grinned, showing her sharp teeth. "Only if you want it to be."

I closed my eyes, feeling exhausted. I wondered if I'd be attacked again soon, or if I'd get a bit of reprieve.

"What kind of business could you possibly have with me?"

Birkita strode over, crouching next to Score and me. "If you're heading to more siren ruins, I want in. That was impressive treasure."

Score sighed next to me. "Honestly, there might not be anything you'd find worthwhile."

The banshee rolled her eyes. "The sirens were a prosperous race. There'll probably be *something*. Besides, I enjoy a good distraction."

"I doubt you have anything we need," Score countered.

"I'm good with a blade."

I leaned back into my palms, shaking my head. "I don't need another bodyguard," I clarified. "Maybe you should move on."

"That's all well and good, but I'm not offering to be your bodyguard."

"What exactly *are* you offering?" I asked, exasperated. I felt thinned out between the library and the attack this afternoon. I wished I was home, with a cup of cocoa, curled up in my bed.

"To be your teacher. I'll train you in combat."

I shook my head, "Glenn's already teaching me to use a bow." I narrowed my eyes, "You *know* that."

She grinned, her sharp teeth glinting in the low light. "Yes, I know. And it'll be great, so you can stand *way* back and be a good little girl while the big boys fight."

Score leaned forward, but didn't say anything. I bristled, "Glenn's an expert! I've even seen him use a bow in close combat—"

Birkita laughed, "Yes, and that's great for *him!* But you, siren— you're being trained to stand back and feel better about yourself. I promise you that."

I stared at the ground, gripping the lush foliage, ripping out a clump. I was sickly certain that Birkita was right.

Glenn said he'd craft me a bow if I was serious about my training, but so far he kept telling me to be patient. The progress we'd made was painfully slow. He repeatedly refused to enhance the difficulty. It all suggested he was only trying to appease me, to keep me out of harm's way long enough that he could handle any danger. I'd only *think* I was helping. It was an insulting realization.

A blush crawled from my chest to my neck. "What could you teach?"

"Self-reliance," she offered. "How to handle a blade, to move strategically, to *think* strategically. How to position your body. How to react."

I stared at the ground, "Why bother with me?"

"Because no matter how much these men pretend, you're the one with all the power. They're completely wrapped around your fingers."

From my peripherals, I could see Score blushing, but he didn't dispute it. I sighed, drawing patterns in the black dirt next to the moss.

I wondered if Glenn would ever actually let me fight, or if he'd just keep insisting I wasn't ready. If I pressed it, he'd probably give me his bow and tell me to stand back as far as possible to provide 'support'.

Yet he kept giving Score a *dagger*.

I nodded, "Yeah. Okay. You have a deal."

"Excellent," she said, grinning. "I had you pegged as sensible."

LaRue stood, brushing his hands together. "If *that's* all settled, I'll be on my way—"

Birkita grappled for his shirt with one hand, tugging him hard to the ground. "No, no, dog. You still have a debt to pay."

"But with the siren's new arrangement—"

"Exactly. A *new* arrangement. This doesn't apply to your debt. She gave you a head start, so I won't kill you. You should be grateful. As it is, I'll let you work off the rest."

He groaned, "Not—"

She nodded, smiling broadly, "*Exactly*. You're my slave until you've paid up." She turned to face me. "Would you like to begin now?"

Why not?

I nodded, "Yeah. Let's do it."

I was sore and tired, but the idea of learning something—
of *really* learning to help myself— ignited a desire within me. I
pushed myself to my feet. Score's eyebrows lifted as Birkita
passed me one of her swords, but he didn't say anything.

The blade was heavy and awkward in my hands.

"That one's a little smaller than what I usually wield," she
explained, "but you aren't as big as I am, so it might feel more
natural."

It didn't feel natural at all. I had trouble lifting it with one
hand. My grip was unsteady as I held the weapon vertically.

"Your stance is all wrong!" she barked, "Balance your
weight! You need to be able to move. Holding and swinging the
sword is the smallest part— the key is the footwork." She eyed my
frame, "Spread your legs a little further! No! Keep your knees
bent! You should be able to move at an instant's notice in any
direction. Don't lock your knees!" She rubbed her forehead. "This
might be more work than siren treasure is worth," she muttered.

I tried to follow her commands, but she spat them at me so
quickly they felt like bullets. I adjusted my stance, hoping I
reflected her instructions. I wasn't certain what she wanted from
me.

"You need... motivation," she said after a time. "Try to
attack me."

"I don't know what I'm doing. How do you want me to
move?"

"Do whatever's most natural. That way I can gauge how
we should train. Come at me."

I hauled the sword over my shoulder, swinging it clumsily
towards her. If Birkita hadn't moved, it would've sliced her torso
diagonally. Even before I'd started the downward arc, she stepped
to my left, slapping my aching ribs with the flat of her blade.

It knocked the wind out of me. I fell to the ground,
dropping the sword with a clatter.

"Hey!" Score cried. He'd been watching the spectacle
closely, and was leaning forward, "What the hell are you doing?!"

I rolled onto my knees, trying to push myself up. Birkita's
boot was on my back, pressing me down to the earth.

"She's learning," the banshee answered smoothly. I wasn't
so sure anymore. It felt like I was just being humiliated. I grabbed
the sword from where it'd fallen, rolling out from under her foot. I

picked myself up, the sword shaking in my hand.

She nodded in approval. "Better. But watch your opponent's body. That'll tell you where to strike."

"I don't like this, Lyra," Score said.

I glanced to him, shaking my head, "I don't care! I want to learn, and Birkita wants to teach me."

He frowned tightly, his forehead creasing. "Glenn won't like this, either."

Birkita just laughed, "That's unfortunate for the elf, but my arrangement is with the siren."

"My name is Lyra," I said crossly.

She smiled, arcing her arm around, slamming the hilt of her sword along my jaw and into my lip. Tears filled my eyes, my sinuses burning— more from reflex than pain. I spat crimson on the ground. My lower lip was already beginning to swell. I stared at Birkita. Maybe she was too brutal to be a good teacher. She watched appraisingly as I tentatively touched along my jaw, feeling the damage. I ran my tongue over my teeth, relieved they were all intact and in my mouth.

"You get your name when you've earned it. That's why no one calls me 'banshee'. I don't let them."

"What the hell is going on?!" Glenn yelled across the camp. His arms were loaded with twigs and fallen branches, but he dropped them, sprinting to me. He grabbed me by the shoulders and looked into my swelled and bruised face.

"I'm training the siren to fight," explained Birkita. "You should thank me. Now you won't have to come running every time someone looks at her sideways."

He glared at the banshee. Glenn moved close, getting in her face. She was tall and amazonian, but the half-elf still had a couple inches on her. He stared down at her, "You need to leave. Take your werewolf and go."

She grinned nastily at him, "Only if she wants me to." She looked over at me, "Think hard, girl. Because I promise you won't get any *real* training from him."

"She doesn't *need* real training!" Glenn yelled. Then he paused, his eyes horrified as he realized the mistake he'd made.

I blushed. He'd purposefully avoided training me. And I'd fallen for it. The archery practice had been reasonably intense, spending a few hours on the nights we could afford it, but Glenn didn't exactly expend much effort. He instructed me to change a few things and stood back. Most days I'd get frustrated, but I still had a few moments of glory. He'd orchestrated it to feel like I was making progress.

"I *do* need real training, Glenn." My voice wasn't as clear as normal, my lip too fat to speak without slurring. "I have *at least* one large group of extras trying to kill me."

"You have me," he protested, adding reluctantly, "and Score. Neither of us will let anything happen to you."

"That's all well and good, but what about the day you're not around, or the day an army attacks again? What then?"

Birkita grinned, slapping me on the back. "Good on ya, girl. Maybe you're not completely hopeless."

I took a few deep breaths. My face throbbed. With my injury, the humidity in the air felt thick and choking, like I might gag on it.

"She's brutal. She's a monster," Glenn said, staring into my eyes. "I know you're angry with me— but if you want to train harder, we *can*. We can get more serious, if that's what you want."

I stared at him doubtfully. I could see what'd happen already— he'd start with something impossible, then say we needed to scale back to basics. I'd be doing the same exercises over and over for weeks, not really improving, not given practical application. The opponents I had to face were made of flesh and blood and could move. They weren't going to stand in the middle of a field and wait for me to try again when I missed.

Score had been silent, but he finally weighed in. "Lyra… I don't want you to get hurt." He looked at Birkita, "And I don't want her to be unnecessarily hit, either. But it probably *is* a good idea for you to learn to defend yourself."

Glenn whipped his head towards Score venomously. His eyes shot a clear message: *traitorous bastard.*

Score shook his head, "What'll happen if one of us isn't there, Glenn? Could you handle it if something happened to her?" He grew quiet, "I'd rather she has a fighting chance at helping herself than risk losing her."

Glenn's frame was rigid as he considered it. His eyes moved around like he was weighing out the pros and the cons. His nostrils flared. Finally, he said, "Fine." He turned to Birkita, "But if you ever strike her face on purpose again—"

"It'll be *her* fault. She should learn to duck," Birkita finished for him. She turned to me. "Well, it seems you've learned a bit already about defending yourself. I think the lesson for tonight is over."

Glenn grabbed my face, harder than he might normally. He ran a thumb across my fat lip. I winced at the pressure.

"I probably have something to help with that," he sighed. "I swear, Lyra…" he said, exasperated. "You're going to be the death of me."

Chapter Twelve

Half-Blood

I awoke in the middle of the night.

My first instinct was panic. Since my transition, nothing good had come from stirring before daybreak. I arced my head, scanning the campsite for danger. Everything appeared normal.

Score snored lightly next to me, his sweatshirt draped across him like a blanket. LaRue was curled into a fetal position on the opposite side of the circle. From next to him, a growling snort drew my attention. Birkita. She was propped against a tree with a scowl on her face. Though she was sound asleep, one hand was wrapped defensively around her blade.

I was wide awake and in pain. My muscles were sore, but the half night's rest had improved their condition. It was the ache in my face that had roused me.

My jaw currently screamed for attention. My lower lip throbbed, sending a shooting pain into my temple. I brushed my fingertips across my swelled lip, wincing. The herbs from Glenn's bag had worn off.

The fire was a smoldering lump of red coals. Smoke wafted up in lazy curls like wisps of burning incense. The jungle was dark, but slivers of moonlight broke through the thick canopy of leaves to reach the ground. I wondered if Glenn had any more supplemental pain killers. I hoped he'd be willing to part with another dose.

My gaze swept the little circle again. A bit of panic resurfaced in my chest. I didn't know where Glenn was.

Maybe there *had* been trouble, and I just hadn't noticed.

I sat up straighter, my eyes darting about wildly, craning my neck. Finally, I caught a glimpse of his silver hair reflecting the moonlight. He was about twenty yards away, deep within the trees.

I wondered what he was doing.

I stood carefully, tiptoeing beyond the camp.

Glenn was kneeling before a small stream, rinsing his green tunic and his white undershirt carefully. He wore only his pants.

He didn't turn around when I approached, but he did greet me. "Can't sleep, little bird?"

I sat next to him on the grassy bank, dipping my toes in the cool water.

"Yeah."

I glanced at him. He wrung his undershirt out and whipped it through the air with a crack.

My gaze fell on his torso. I'd never seen him without some sort of shirt. He was thin and wiry, but surprisingly more muscular than I'd realized. His abdominals were clearly defined, rippling down to the drawstring of his pants. Black tattoos crawled along the sides of his ribcage from the arch of his hips to his armpits. The markings were sharp, but the design fluidly wove into curves, forming an intricate pattern. With my siren mind, they reminded me of treble clefs.

I reached out tentatively, touching the ink. I could feel the heat from his body before I connected. The markings were raised slightly beneath my fingertips. He tensed, turning his head to me with questioning eyes.

"I didn't know you had tattoos," I stuttered. I didn't know why I'd been so bold.

He looked uncomfortable, then went back to scrubbing his tunic. "I've had them my whole life—" he paused. "As long as I can remember, that is. I receive additional markings each year."

"Why?" I asked. "What do they mean?"

Glenn was silent, watching the moonlight glitter off the small stream. Somewhere far away, a bird cried. The chirp echoed through the jungle.

"Is this your third question?"

"No," I said, frowning. "If you don't want to answer, you don't have to."

I kicked, sending a spray up to my knees. Glenn pulled the

fabric from the water, twisting it roughly. The fluid trickled from it in a steady stream. He unfolded the grassy shirt, inspecting the cleanliness. Satisfied, he laid the tunic flat next to his undershirt.

I didn't press him, assuming the conversation was over. But Glenn surprised me by answering, "It's a warning to elves. Women, specifically. It ensures tainted blood isn't spread."

"Warn them? Of what?"

"That I'm abominable," he said softly. "Half-blood."

"You mentioned that before, Glenn, but why does it matter?"

He leaned back, gazing up through the break in trees to the waning moon. "Elves pride themselves on their innate morality. My father was human, with human fallibilities. I'm an unnatural monster."

My hands balled into fists. "Is that what you've been told?" The more I learned about elves, the angrier I became. "They're idiots."

"No," Glenn said, shaking his head, "they aren't, Lyra." He dipped his bare feet in the stream, sighing, "I'm brash. I'm violent. I was never good at my studies. I'm impatient. Honestly, I'm only skilled at fighting, yet..." he laughed bitterly, "that's a crude art."

"But you're *kind*, Glenn."

His mouth curled into a half-smile. "I'm flawed. Truth is, the markings aren't necessary. I *look* like a half-breed. My body isn't as graceful or elongated as a purebred elf. I'm thinner. My eyes are too big; my lips are too small; my hair is too short." He looked thoughtful, "Even if it *was* a different style, it's silver, which isn't natural for humans *or* elves. I'm a collection of random features, and in the end, I'm ugly."

I stared at him incredulously. The first time I laid eyes on him, I'd thought how utterly impossible he looked, how foreign, how elf-like. But more than that, I was stunned by how *attractive* he was. My nostrils flared out in pure venom for the elves. I couldn't believe how they'd treated Glenn.

I tugged on his arm until he faced me. Staring into his eyes, I said with conviction, "They're a pack of fools."

"No, Lyra, they're—"

"Are you calling me a liar?" I demanded, my face heating. I placed one hand on his bared shoulder, "Because believe me when I tell you— you're not ugly. Not at all. In fact..." I traced the lines

113

of his tattoos with my index finger. My heart sped up at the contact. "You're gorgeous," I said, leaning forward, "alluring…"

My face was inches from his, and his eyes were wide, his brows furrowed. I could feel his breath on my face when he protested, "Lyra, *you're* the kind one, you're—"

"You're beautiful," I murmured, pressing my lips against his. I slid my hand up the back of his neck, holding him close. I could feel his surprise, but he returned the kiss, balling the fabric of my shirt in his hands, pulling my body to him. He slid a palm beneath my camisole, brushing the bare skin of my back. I pressed myself closer, not satisfied until I was straddling him.

I dug my fingers into his back, but Glenn's hands caught my own. He pressed me down against the earth with a ravenous snarl, kissing me with force. I groaned, feeling my core light up with warmth.

For a moment, I wondered what I was doing. He'd asked me not to pursue him. I didn't know what I wanted from him.

Nothing, everything… It was unclear.

He nipped lightly at my lip, and I winced. It still throbbed from my earlier wound.

Glenn pulled back instantly, looking distraught. "That was a mistake."

I felt heat rise to my cheeks. "It wasn't." I gingerly ran my fingers over my swelled lip, poking at it tenderly. But maybe it *was* a mistake. Perhaps it'd been a huge blunder, and not because of my injuries.

He closed his eyes, "You should return to camp."

"Glenn…"

"Lyra." He frowned, tugging his undershirt over his head. In the jungle humidity, the fabric was probably still damp, but Glenn didn't seem to care. "I told you before. I'm not the one for you— no matter what I might wish."

I folded my arms across my chest stubbornly. "Maybe you're right, Glenn. But it'd be nice if you'd trust my judgment for once. What if you're wrong?"

He sighed, shaking his head, staring deep into the forest. "I wish I *was* wrong. But…" He turned to me, looking a bit hopeful, "Do you love me, Lyra?"

My face began to burn, spreading from my cheeks to my neck and chest. I didn't know how to answer him. I didn't know the answer myself. I was silent for a long time, unwilling to speak.

Glenn chuckled, but his eyes looked hurt. "Thought so."

"Glenn…" I said, feeling an ache in my chest. His eyes met mine. I struggled to find the right words. It felt like he was asking for all or nothing. It didn't seem right; it didn't seem fair. "Love is an overwhelming word," I finally answered. "But I care for you."

He smiled softly. "It *is* overwhelming, isn't it? Well…" He looked thoughtful, kissing my forehead, "I care for you, too, little bird. Yet I'm not willing to risk what we already have on that. I won't be kissing you again." He looked into my eyes, "Goodnight, Lyra."

It was a dismissal. He turned his gaze from me. I stood, wandering back to camp alone.

I couldn't bring myself to look back at him. An odd feeling settled in the pit of my stomach. I couldn't tell if I was more disappointed or relieved.

~~~~~~~~~~~~~~~~

I awoke with sharp stabs of regret shredding my insides. Last night's encounter had left me feeling hollow.

Glenn sat before the smoldering ashes of the fire, staring into them with a thoughtful expression. Another pang of guilt struck me.

I rolled my head towards Score. He was sitting up, reading the *Siren's Call* quickly and carefully. His gaze flickered to me when he noticed I was awake.

"Morning," he said.

"Mm," I nodded, glancing at Glenn. "What's our plan for the day?"

Score just shrugged, "We're going to Ireland. By Realm or Overworld, I have no idea, but—"

"I know. You'd prefer the Overworld," I finished.

He smiled. "I think both of us understand the dangers of the Overworld more than the dangers here. Besides, we aren't defenseless there." He meant our siren magic, our alteration.

I chewed my cheek, considering it. Glenn sighed across the camp, "I'm at a loss, to be honest." He kept his gaze locked on the ashes.

Birkita smiled, gesturing to her sword. "While the boys

discuss it, would you like to train, siren?"

"No time," Glenn grunted.

I wondered if we really didn't have time, or if he just didn't want me to get hurt.

"There could be time, if you want it," Score said. Glenn shot him a poisonous glare. Score continued, "If we take the nearest gate from here, it'll put us in the midwest United States. Near Chicago. I say from there, we take a plane straight to Ireland."

Glenn went pale. "I've told you, the Overworld is dangerous! We should travel gate by gate, taking it—"

"It takes too much time, Glenn. Besides— right now, we *can't* stay in the Realm."

The elf glared at him. "And why is that?!"

"Because," Score said, jerking a thumb back towards where we'd come from yesterday, "you can bet at least one of the creatures in that tavern will report something about us. We're not exactly traveling anonymously. At the moment, we're exceptionally conspicuous within the Realm."

Glenn glared openly at Score. The half-elf had so much venom on his face, I almost expected him to rip Score's head off. But Score didn't look like he'd back down.

Well, *I* didn't want to get in the middle of it.

I turned to Birkita, "Yeah. Let's train."

She smiled, leading me 30 yards away, where the trees were less dense. She handed me one of her swords. "What'd you learn last night?"

I watched her movements. She ran towards me, but this time I ducked out of the way. "I learned to watch my opponent's body—" She shifted out of space, flickering like static. In an instant, she was behind me with the edge of her sword against my throat.

"There are signs with magic use, too." The blade dragged, just slightly, sharp like a paper cut. If Birkita had pressed just a little harder, she'd have nicked something vital. The sword pulled away gracefully, arcing forward and back into her scabbard. "Did you see my sign?"

I shook my head, "No."

"Better hope you catch it this time; I might not be so kind." She whipped out her sword again. In a panic, I held up my own.

The blades clanged and reverberated against each other. I could feel the vibrations through my sweating palms. I kept a firm grip on the handle. Birkita pressed against me, trying to overpower me. I leapt back, and the banshee stumbled forward, almost losing her footing.

Her face twisted into a cruel smile. "Not bad."

I watched her more carefully, not trusting my instructor.

She charged forward, her sword at her side. Once again, I stepped back— this time studying her movements. There it was: her eyes. Like so many other extras', they responded to her magic. They turned electric yellow just before she shifted out of space. I adjusted my movement, jerking towards her former path.

Birkita blinked back into existence, stumbling forward. She chuckled when she saw I was no longer there. "Better," she said, "but still amateurish."

I had only one day of experience. What did she expect?

She flung a dagger from her hip sheath— a move I wasn't anticipating. I jerked awkwardly to one side, but not quickly enough. It buried into the flesh of my shoulder clear to the hilt, narrowly missing my collarbone.

"Gah!" I cried, dropping to my knees.

"A mistake like that can cost you your life," she said, striding over to me. She jerked the knife out. The blade dripped with my blood. The wound burned. My palm found the hole and pressed, staunching the blood that gushed.

I let out a dry sob. How the hell was I supposed to practice with this? I flexed the fingers on my hand rigidly. I was relieved they moved, but it was painful using the muscles. At least the nerves weren't damaged.

Birkita strode to me, slapping my aching ribs with the flat of her blade. "Get up!" she barked. I pressed into my shoulder even harder, baffled. She crinkled her nose, disgusted. "You're hopeless."

I glared, "What are you trying to teach me?!"

She crouched low, her jagged teeth extra menacing. "I'm teaching you that combat is unpredictable. You don't know 100% of the time what an opponent will do. All you can do is try to be prepared for as much as possible. Now *get up*."

I stumbled forward, pushing myself to my feet painfully. I hadn't recovered from my former injuries yet, and this new one was crippling. I released the pressure. Blood spurted from the jagged knife-wound, spraying the ground crimson. I clasped it again, "What do you want from me?" I spat.

"I want you to go see the elf. You're apparently more fragile than I thought. Then I want you to think about how you'll avoid injury next time. Siren, do yourself a favor and don't repeat mistakes. *Learn* from them."

The practice had been less than five minutes from start to finish. I fumbled, retrieving the sword from the ground. I handed the blade to Birkita. She sheathed it, waving her hand to dismiss me.

At the campsite, Score and Glenn had stopped arguing. Score looked nearly ready to leave. He was packing the *Siren's Call* into his bag and throwing his guitar over his shoulder. I staggered to the clearing. Glenn was taking inventory of his arrows, though he hadn't needed them since our last practice.

"Glenn…" I whispered. I felt ashamed asking him for help— especially since I knew my training was against his wishes.

His eyes found me, widening when he saw the blood around my palm. I awkwardly gripped the cut in my shoulder. I blinked, and suddenly Glenn was in front of me, prying my hand away from the wound.

"What'd you do?" he mumbled. He jerked his head up, yelling at Birkita, "What did you do?!"

"A lesson," the banshee said smoothly.

"A lesson?" Glenn repeated incredulously. He shook his head, digging through his bag of supplies, searching for the right remedy to help me. He gestured to the ground, and I knelt obediently. "I should stop your lessons right now." He tore my shirt in half, and I blushed. It couldn't be helped. Glenn couldn't clean the wound through my clothes.

Score stood next to me, his arms folded across his chest. He stared at the gaping, bloody hole on my shoulder. I was grateful my bra strap only needed to be shifted for Glenn to access it. At least I could keep a little modesty.

"Will she be okay?"

Glenn's brows knitted together sharply. "She'll survive. Her arm will heal eventually. I don't know if she's ever going to practice with that— that—" he took a few deep breaths, calming himself, "*banshee* again." From his satchel, Glenn removed five different dried herbs and a vial of liquid that shimmered like mother-of-pearl. He crushed the leaves together, creating a paste. He sprinkled in more herbs as he blended, ensuring it was smooth.

"Come on, boys," Birkita laughed. "You know if I was going to kill her, I'd scream."

Glenn frowned, studying his mixture, "So they say." Satisfied with the medicine, he dabbed it on the edges of my cut.

I screamed. It felt like he was rubbing salt into my wound. I tried to jerk back, but he held my arm firmly, pulling me closer.

"You're better with this than without, I promise. The fact that it hurts just means it's working." He scooped up another pinch, rubbing it into the cut in small circles. Now I knew why he'd started on the edges— they hurt so much *less* than the center did. It felt like pouring acid under my skin. I squared my jaw as he added pinch after pinch of the caustic mixture into the wound. My arm was tense, but I forced myself to remain still.

"I'm all for you learning to defend yourself," Score said, "but I've got my limits. This is ridiculous. Maybe you should go back to training with Glenn."

The half-elf's lips turned to a smile so briefly I wondered if I'd imagined it. "You should listen to him," he advised, applying more paste to the gash.

"If the siren wants to quit, then perhaps this venture is foolhardy. But I think you men underestimate her. Despite the damage you're so worried about, she's a reasonably quick study. She could do well— if she applies herself." It was the closest to a compliment Birkita had ever given me. She still wasn't using my name, though.

I took a deep breath, my teeth on edge, trying to ignore the burning of my arm.

I didn't want to discuss it. At the moment, doing anything else with Birkita sounded lunatic, but I needed to learn. There was no way Glenn would be willing to teach me what I needed to know. I watched as he so meticulously wrapped my wound. He'd never train me to face real danger; he was too intent on keeping me from it completely. So I remained silent, taking deep breaths through my nose and staring forward.

LaRue piped in, rescuing me by changing the subject, "Mademoiselle, the men have agreed to return to the Overworld, then straight on to Ireland. You'll be able to enjoy a few creature comforts then, mm? So don't look so serious."

I was surprised they'd agreed. "Really?" I asked Glenn.

"Yes. Really. Score was..." He rolled his eyes, "He was right. If we stay in the Realm, every gate within a hundred leagues of the pub will be monitored, and all of the gates that extend from them as well. So... yes. The Overworld isn't such a bad idea, this time." He grabbed a fresh leaf from his pack, placing it gingerly over my wound.

The cut throbbed dully, the ache running up and down my arm and into my neck. "You're as mended as I can make you," he said, appraising the work. "Let's get going."

Chapter Thirteen

Chicago

The gate wasn't far from our camp. We emerged in the middle of a frost covered field. I breathed out, watching a puff of white mist burst from my lips. I shivered, then winced, clasping my injured shoulder.

"Are you okay?" Score asked, noticing the attention I gave the injury.

I nodded, but truthfully it felt wretched.

He stepped in front of me. "Don't lie. I can tell when you do." He brushed my hair from my face, humming softly. My shoulder heated, the wound closing. My eyes widened. I didn't realize how far our powers stretched when we were away from the Realm. No wonder Score had wanted out so badly.

The throbbing, dull ache was gone. I rotated my arm in a huge circle, laughing.

Glenn darted forward. "What are you doing?!" he demanded. "You're going to ruin the poultice—"

Score's brows raised, "She's fine, man." He shrugged arrogantly, hitching the bags on his shoulders. He smirked, shifting his weight from foot to foot. He glanced to Birkita and LaRue, bounding through the dusting of snow to catch up to them.

Glenn frowned, wrenching my shirt down, checking beneath the leaf. "What did I say?" he muttered. "It's a total mess, not even sticking any—" His eyes widened. He smeared a dab of paste away with his thumb. "It's healed. How… this isn't possible."

I wrapped my arms around him. "Thanks for helping me, but Score took care of it."

Glenn glanced at the back of Score's head in the distance. He frowned, "I didn't realize he could do that."

"We both can. I just never remember."

"Then why didn't he heal you in camp? Why—" He shook his head, realizing. "*That's* why he wanted to get back here. You can't do that sort of magic in the Realm, can you?"

I bit my lip. It felt like a huge secret to give away. Maybe sirens really *were* naturally deceptive. I was reluctant to tell him the truth, but I pushed myself to do it anyway. "Yeah. We handle ourselves a lot better out here."

"Well…" he mumbled, looking thoughtful. After a long time, he spoke, "Better catch up to him. We may end up in the Realm again— or maybe not." He looked uncomfortable, but he strode forward deliberately.

I glanced up to Score. He was leading the group now. Birkita and LaRue followed behind. The wolf carried her swords in his arms, acting as her pack mule. The banshee sauntered next to him, filing her nails into sharp points.

In the distance, I could see a road cutting through the farmlands.

I stretched. It felt like I was home again, though I'd never been far from Washington before. There was something comforting about the human world.

~~~~~~~~~~~~~~~~~~

When we reached the road, Score halted our progress with one raised palm. The brisk wind cut into my face like icicles, stinging my eyes. I wondered why he wanted to stop.

Score dug into his bag, retrieving a mobile phone and powering it up. Apparently, he'd been preserving the battery life while in the Realm.

Was he calling someone to pick us up?

"It's about two in the afternoon," he announced. "According to this, anyway."

Oh. A clock that updated via satellite. Smart. If it was the afternoon, eventually a car should pass by.

Sure enough, a silver sedan rounded the corner of the

122

highway.

Score stepped into the middle of the road, flagging the driver down.

The vehicle skidded to a halt. A woman in a business suit stepped out, glaring at him.

"Jesus, kid!" she shouted. "You can't just jump out in front of cars like that. It's dangerous and stupid—"

As the first word left his mouth, she was compelled. "Yeah, but we need a ride into Chicago. I know it's only an hour or two from here."

"Two and a half," she agreed dreamily. Her glazed eyes moved to the rest of our party, "Okay, get in."

The car wasn't very big. I glanced at Score dubiously. "This is kind of a stretch. Where will we even put everyone?" I asked him.

He raised his brows, "You're welcome to sit on my lap, if you want."

I flushed, staring at the ground.

"Nonsense," Birkita said. She jabbed at LaRue. "I'll sit atop this one. Hopefully he makes a better chair than pack mule."

LaRue looked offended, his mouth gaping open indignantly.

I sighed, "I'm the smallest. I guess I'll sit in the middle."

Score slid into the passenger seat up front. I hopped into the back first, scooting to the middle with LaRue— then Birkita— on my left. Glenn reluctantly settled next to me. He looked a little green as the car lurched forward, and he pressed his forehead against the window.

"Are you okay?" I asked him, clicking my seatbelt.

He nodded, his eyes closed. It wasn't very convincing.

I leaned over, cracking the window for him, letting the frigid fresh air circulate.

"Is there anything *else* I can do for you?" the woman purred, brushing her hand along Score's forearm. My hackles raised, feeling instant jealousy. I gripped the fabric of my jeans, twisting them, trying to explain the emotion to myself. Score and I weren't anything but friends. Not really. I didn't have time or energy for something like that— not now. Besides, what about Glenn?

I glanced over at the elf. He still looked car-sick.

"Are you sure you're okay?" I asked.

"Yeah," he breathed. "Just… poor connection… I'll be fine."

I wasn't sure what he was talking about. I shrugged. If he needed help, he'd tell us. Well, I *hoped* he'd tell us, anyway.

Score pushed the woman away with his fingertips. "We're fine. We just need to get to Chicago. We'll get a cab from there. Something bigger."

"Oh," she said, sounding disappointed.

Satisfaction hit me, followed by shame. I shouldn't care about the woman.

I frowned, trying to think of a conversation starter. Nothing came to mind. We rode in silence.

The further we drove, the worse Glenn looked. He rolled the window completely down, sticking his head outside of the car. "What did you mean earlier," I asked him, "when you said 'poor connection'?"

He groaned, "An elf thing. I'll be okay."

I narrowed my eyes skeptically, "You don't *look* okay, Glenn."

Score craned his neck to the back seat. "Actually, you look pretty terrible."

"I'm fine," Glenn insisted.

I grabbed his hand. It was clammy and cool. I tried to decide if I should be worried or not. I didn't know enough about elf biology to determine when I needed to be concerned.

"You shouldn't worry for him," Birkita said. "He'll be good as new when we stop, I'm sure."

"What's the matter with him?" I asked her anxiously. Glenn clearly wasn't willing to discuss it.

He groaned, flapping a hand towards me. "Nothing! I'm fine."

Birkita ignored him, continuing, "It has to do with feeling connected, a part of the natural world. A car like this skims the surface, a separate mechanical entity. Breaks the connection. Usually elves and other fey avoid big human cities and other *unnatural abominations.*"

Glenn glared at her, his eyes glassy. He had a sheen of sweat on his forehead, his skin pale. He really *did* look terrible. I furrowed my brow in concern, "Glenn…"

"*Fine.*"

I frowned, staring at him. If he was this bad in a car, what would he be like on a transatlantic flight? "Can we even take a plane?"

"Yes," he snapped. "I told you. I'm fine."

"Pull over for a minute," Score commanded the driver. She obligingly turned onto the shoulder, flashing her hazard lights. Score turned back to Glenn, "Get out; take a walk. You look like crap."

The half-elf glowered at him, but yanked on the car door, stumbling out. I stared at him as he plunked down in the frosted field, pressing his palms flat on the ground. He closed his eyes, taking breaths so deep I could see his shoulders rise and fall. He did look to be perking up.

The driver pressed a button, rolling the automatic window up to keep the cold air outside.

Score sighed. "No wonder he didn't want to travel this way. Damn it." He rubbed his chin, staring at the elf. "I wonder…"

"What do you wonder?" I asked.

Score just unbuckled his seatbelt, sliding smoothly from the car. He strode down the field, crouching next to Glenn. They began to speak quickly to each other, looking surprisingly amicable. It was unusual to see after so much bickering. As they chatted, Score gestured animatedly with his hands. Glenn nodded stoically as he responded.

I wished I knew *what* they were saying.

Glenn gestured to the field surrounding him. Score nodded and began to dig through the snow. He pulled out a clod of dirt and yellowed grass. As he stared at it, I watched the stalk grow until it was green and tall. Score thrust the grass at the half-elf. Glenn looked impressed before turning his attention towards the car, towards me. I jumped, guilty. It felt like I'd been eavesdropping— though I hadn't actually heard a thing.

He turned back to Score and said a few more things, then both boys stood and returned to the car. It was… confusing.

"What's going on?" I asked anxiously.

Glenn held up the grassy clod of dirt, "Score found a remedy. Sorry I worried you."

I grabbed his forearm, "No, Glenn! I'm sorry you— you should have told us you were uncomfortable. We could've done something else, something to accommodate for you."

"Let's just get going, little bird."

Score rolled his eyes as he slid into his seat, folding his arms. I wondered what was bothering him. Maybe it had something to do with his conversation with Glenn. Score sighed, "Okay, let's go."

Glenn sat with his eyes closed and both palms against the hunk of dirt as the car moved forward. He looked focused and meditative, but he seemed healthy. It was a relief.

"When we get to Chicago," the half-elf said slowly, "I'd like to find an apothecary. If I take a plane, I'll probably need a potion. The rest... might be complicated. That's a fairly big disconnect."

Score's elbow rested against the door, his chin in his hand. He stared out the window. "I'm sure I'll think of something," he said quietly. "It won't be a problem."

~~~~~~~~~~~~~~~~~

The rest of the drive was uneventful and quiet— aside from LaRue's moans. Every few minutes, he'd make a pained noise, complain about Birkita's weight, and received the heel of her boot in his shins. Knowing first hand how brutal she could be, I was surprised she didn't dig a dagger into his thigh.

When we were almost there, I started to get anxious. I wondered how we'd keep a low-profile, especially with Glenn's dilemma.

I glanced to Score. His expression wasn't concerned, but he did look thoughtful. He stared out the window at the passing terrain. His eyes caught mine in the reflection of the side mirror, and I smiled at him. I was glad he'd found a way to help Glenn. His eyes were kind, but I didn't understand the color— bright green. I wondered what that meant he was feeling.

Maybe I needed to start writing down my own eye colors and emotions for reference. I could only decipher a few. It'd be nice if I knew what he was thinking a little more. Maybe I could sort out my own feelings better, too.

The traffic was thicker as we approached the city, slowing to a crawl as we merged from the freeway.

Glenn had been quiet, focused on the little hunk of grass in his hands. As we drove deeper into Chicago, he said, "I'll need to get out. Someplace near water... a river, a lake. That's where an apothecary will be."

Score nodded. "Okay. Yeah, that's not a problem. I'll make the arrangements for the flight." He paused, looking conflicted. "You should take Lyra with you."

Glenn raised his eyebrows. "Really?"

"Yes. She'll be able to get you around faster than anyone else. I know she'll be safe with you... so... yeah. Take her with you." Score's eyes met mine again in the reflection. He amended his words, "If she wants to go, that is."

I smiled. "Sounds like a good plan. You're right, I can get us a ride easily."

"We'll meet at the airport at seven. That'll give you guys a couple hours. I'll make sure everything is ready by then."

The woman pulled into a parking lot downtown, not far from the piers and Lake Michigan. The sheer size of it took my breath away. It was hard to believe it was fresh water. It reminded me of the ocean, going on forever.

Glenn hopped from the car, still clutching the little clod of dirt and grass— as if the tiny piece of earth protected him from the steel and glass of the sky scrapers surrounding him.

I sighed, unbuckling my seatbelt.

"Lyra," Score said as I moved from the vehicle. I gave him a quizzical look. "It's almost December." He shimmied out of his sweatshirt, offering it to me, "Here. Already warm."

I smiled a little, nodding. "Thanks, Score." I slithered into the shirt as I slid from the car.

I wondered what arrangements he'd make while Glenn and I sought the apothecary, but I didn't ask. I trusted Score. Here in the human world, he knew what he was doing. It was kind of impressive.

He'd been right about the weather, though. I zipped Score's sweatshirt clear to my chin and pulled my hands into the sleeves, chilled. The car pulled away. The wind was brisk, threatening to chap my face.

Glenn sighed, watching my teeth chatter. "I'm sure something will be nearby."

We trudged down the streets. Glenn studied the buildings surrounding us, paying special attention to the door frames we passed.

"What does an apothecary shop even look like?"

He shrugged, "Like anything else. A building. Some shops are more high-end than others. But it'll be marked with a triskele."

I had no idea what a triskele was. We walked silently for a while, Glenn preoccupied with his search.

I pulled my face into the soft cotton of the sweatshirt, sheltering myself from the wind. The fabric still smelled like Score. I smiled, breathing it in. Since returning to the Overworld, he'd made our journey as seamless as possible— even for Glenn. I'd have to remember to thank Score for everything later.

I wondered what he and I would find in Ireland. So far we'd received few answers and many new questions. It was strange to think we were ultimately looking for Atlantis. People had searched for the mythical city for years.

"Ah," Glenn said, interrupting my thoughts, "here we are."

The shop didn't look impressive. A narrow door was wedged between a pizzeria and a dry cleaner. Glenn tugged the door open, and I was immediately hit by the strong and pungent smell of spices wafting out. It was dimly lit. Tidy shelves housed neat rows of little bottled herbs and spices, racks of crystals and bags, mortars and pestles of all shapes and sizes. Another bookshelf held row after row of oils, potions and tinctures. A line of New Age spirituality books was stacked on a high counter top.

A woman sat behind the desk. She was middle-aged, but pretty, with long graying brown hair braided to her waist. She leaned back in her chair, crushing a handful of leaves carefully and methodically. Occasionally, she'd sift the herbs through a mesh screen, throwing out the excess and continuing to crush it until it was a fine powder.

"We're closed," she said, not bothering to look up as we entered.

"To all patrons?" Glenn asked.

Her eyes flicked up to meet him. She chuckled under her breath— more to herself than us. "Well, well, well. What's an elf— even a half-breed— doing this far into the city?"

Glenn smiled, "Hoping a witch would know of a potion so I could fly."

She raised a brow, "There's plenty of ways to go flying in the Realm, boy, but— you didn't mean that, did you?" She eyed him appraisingly, "Now then, you *are* unusual, aren't you?"

"Not all elves request to travel the human way, I agree."

"No," she shook her head, "that's not it."

"I don't know what you're talking about," he said guardedly.

"Nonsense. I wasn't born yesterday! Trying to fool a witch as old as I am isn't kind, boy."

Glenn's mouth formed a lop-sided smile, "And how would you know I'm a boy? I could be five times your age, uh— how should I address you, Green Mistress?"

"Matilda," she answered. She leaned forward, "And they usually retire elves from the Amaranth Guard by the time they're 600. By my book, you're still a boy— even if you're pushing retirement."

"But I'm not on the Guard," Glenn replied coolly.

She laughed, her eyes twinkling. "Trying to fool me again! What gumption! I've been around the block, young man. I know an evergrass tunic when I see one. But what's a member of the Guard—" Then she caught sight of me, her face turning pale. She shook her head violently. "No, no, no! I'll have *no* part of this nonsense!"

Glenn leaned forward on the counter, "I'm just trying to shop, Matilda."

"Ha! So casual! I don't want my head cut off! A siren! I didn't even believe it!"

My brows furrowed, "I'm sorry if I'm causing problems, ma'am, but we really *do* just want a potion."

"What's the problem?" Glenn said, "So there's a siren, here. It's an oddity but hardly reason to—"

"The *problem* is that the girl's a wanted fugitive by the council. All extras are supposed to report any sightings of a siren. And that's not all." She closed her eyes, looking conflicted. Finally, she opened them. They were narrowed but warm. "I guess there's no harm telling you. There's a bounty on you by the Hand of Fate, girl."

Big surprise. Someone else wanted me dead. I tired of the constant danger, but it'd become the norm. I shrugged, "Okay."

Glenn frowned, rapping his fingers on the table sharply, "Are you *certain* it's the Hand?"

Matilda straightened the shoulders of her baggy sweater.

"That's the rumor, but what's ever certain about the Hand?" Her voice lowered, "Look, I don't know *why* they want her, but I don't want any part of Shadowlands' business. I have enough on my plate without angering the Hand. So if you don't mind turning around, we can pretend this never happened—"

"I really *need* that potion," Glenn insisted.

She placed her hands on her hips, looking genuinely worried. Finally, she sighed, "Fine. Quickly." She appraised him, "You're a half-breed, so the dosage would need adjustment. Hmm... and how were you thinking of paying?"

Glenn looked sheepish, "I— I don't... Actually, I hadn't thought it through." I stared at him incredulously. He gave me an apologetic look, saying, "I've never *had* to do this before. Amaranthe's account usually squares things."

"Perhaps we can come to an arrangement, then." She rubbed her chin, considering. "There's one thing you could give me in payment: a very rare ingredient, something I've never had in my collection."

Glenn's features hardened. "Thanks, but no thanks. We don't have the time to traverse the Realm for—"

"You're a presumptuous one, aren't you! Who said anything about going anywhere? You have what I need right here."

Glenn narrowed his eyes skeptically, "What do you want?"

She rapped her fingers on the table, pausing for a long moment. Finally, she said, "There's a potion called the *Whisper of God*. Ever hear of it?"

I shook my head, bewildered. Glenn said, "Sorry, I'm not the most skilled herbalist. I'm unfamiliar with that potion."

Matilda smiled, walking around the counter, facing us. She was a couple inches shorter than me, wearing a long bohemian skirt. "It's not known by many, to be truthful. It's not exactly... council-legal."

Glenn raised a brow, "There are very, very few things that aren't council-legal. What exactly is this potion?"

She shrugged coyly, "The ingredients are fairly straightforward— sage, inkbatter, ashflower, candor."

"Those all create euphoria," Glenn said. "Are you looking to craft a drug experience, then?"

"Heaven's, no! There's one last ingredient that really makes or breaks the potion..." She stood right next to me, looking into my eyes with scrutiny, "Siren's tears."

I jumped, startled. "What?!"

"No, thanks," Glenn said, grabbing my hand. "We'll be leaving."

Matilda crossed her arms in front of her chest, blocking the door. "Calm down. Goddess knows I'm aware of your paranoia— I even share it, to an extent— but my shop's safe."

"What does the potion do, exactly?" I asked curiously.

"It makes a human extremely susceptible to suggestion, for a short period of time. A useful item to have in a big human city, that's all."

I considered it. It sounded relatively harmless, in the scheme of things. Still... "How *would* you use it?"

Matilda laughed, "It'd be set aside for a rainy day! I have a few potions that aren't strictly legal, for emergencies, of course."

"If they aren't legal, why would you tell us about them?" Glenn demanded.

She raised a brow, "You're both wanted. If I can't tell *you*, who can I?"

She had a point. "Deal," I said.

Glenn grabbed my shoulders, spinning me around. "Are you mental, Lyra?"

"It's not a big deal, Glenn. You need this potion. This is better than having you die on the plane."

Glenn looked unsure, but finally sighed. "I suppose you're right."

"Excellent," Matilda said, practically skipping to the cabinet behind the desk. She unfolded a small pull-out cupboard, fishing out a glass vial with a crystal cork. She tugged the lid off, handing me the bottle.

I stared at it. I wasn't in the mood to cry. I'd done enough crying the last several weeks, and I felt deflated. I screwed up my face in concentration, trying to muster some tears.

Nothing.

"Well... you work on that. I'll work on the potion."

She grabbed Glenn's arm, but he dug in his heels, hesitant to leave my side. Matilda let out an exasperated sigh, "It's hard to summon tears when there's someone staring at you. Give her a chance. Let's be productive. Both of us would benefit from haste."

Glenn nodded. Matilda plucked out a few of his hairs,

dropping them into a small mortar. She tossed several ingredients into the bowl, grinding them with a pestle.

I took a deep breath. These days, there was one thing in particular that made me cry.

I thought about Susan and Rick, my foster parents. They were in a coma because of me. Because of what I was. A siren. It was the biggest reason why I wanted answers.

The guilt bubbled up, forcing a sob to ripple from my abdomen. I gasped for air, beginning to cry. I caught the tears in the vial carefully. I wept until the tiny tube was half-filled, and I couldn't cry anymore.

It'd have to be enough.

Chapter Fourteen

The Edge of the World

Before we left her shop, Matilda leaned close to me and advised, "You look completely lost so I'll tell you this much—they think you're in the Realm, but they'll figure out soon enough that you're not. If I were you, I'd keep them guessing." She eyed me up and down, "And for heaven's sake, *avoid* being seen by extras! Keep your head down, and you should be fine."

We boarded the plane promptly at seven. Glenn clutched his potion with white knuckles as we ducked through the door.

My eyes widened as I entered the cabin. "Whoa," I said, nearly dropping my bag.

Score had not only gotten us a flight; he'd gotten us an *entire plane*. The cabin was re-tooled, the seats comfortable and wide. On one side, a mattress was dressed in full bedding—just in case we wanted to sleep. A large television was on another side of the room, a list of movies scrolling on the screen as it idled.

The back half was devoid of all seats. Instead, Score had done his best to accommodate for Glenn's issue. It was a makeshift forest: potted trees and plants were everywhere except the center aisle.

Score turned to Glenn as we took it in, "Will that be enough?"

Glenn nodded, "Yes. This is sufficient. Between the potion

and greenery, I should be fine." He even looked impressed by Score's ingenuity, running his hands gently along the leaves of the plants.

"How did you manage all this?" I asked Score.

He shrugged, sliding his backpack into the overhead compartment. He sat, giving me a smile. "It was pretty easy, once I knew what I wanted."

"He made calls to *five* different nurseries!" LaRue jumped in. "To find enough plants for the flight."

Birkita slouched into one of the seats, propping her feet up on the chair in front of her. She snorted, "Not exactly difficult for a siren."

Score shook his head, "Forget it. It's not worth discussion. We had a problem, now we have a solution. We should focus on the next step." His eyes met mine. "Which is finding this second siren ruin, so we can make it to Atlantis."

Glenn snorted in the corner. The flight crew made the rounds, asking us to buckle our safety belts as we took off. Once the plane was in the air, Glenn sighed, taking deep breaths and placing his hands on the plant closest to him. When he'd steadied himself, he said, "Atlantis is a myth."

"It's not a myth," Score replied. "The sirens are directing us there."

"You're assuming *every* ridiculous tale is true!" Glenn countered, "Atlantis is complete bollocks, you prat!"

Birkita grinned, "Now, now, boys... as far as *I* knew, Atlantis was just a story humans told for fun. But I'm willing to suspend my disbelief. If it *is* real, it's bound to be loaded with treasure."

LaRue grinned, "The violent one has a point. Atlantis— if such a place were real— it would be ripe for picking, doubtless."

"But it's *not* real," Glenn insisted. "Humans have looked for it for centuries, and no extras have come forward with information about it. No one is *that* secretive."

"Except sirens," Score countered. "They were notoriously guarded." He ran a hand through his hair, "It's where the map says we're headed."

Glenn frowned, "Are you sure?"

I sighed, leaning forward. "*I'm* sure, Glenn. I can read it now, too."

His brows raised, his eyes a mix of shocked and hurt. "When did that happen?"

"The jungle. The library, really. There was this magical chair thing, and Score—" I stopped when I saw how skeptical he looked. Maybe even for magic, this was stretching belief. I twisted my fingers together. "I can read it now, that's all. The map does mention Atlantis. It's the end goal."

"Okay," he said, rolling his eyes, "let's entertain the idea that Atlantis is real. If it is, are the sirens still alive somewhere, just lost?"

I glanced at Score. We shared a long look of doubt. Neither of us knew the answer to that, but in a weird way, I hoped they weren't. It'd be awful to think we'd just been abandoned. Who could say, though?

"I don't know," Score cut in, noting how uncomfortable I looked. "It's possible."

Glenn's eyes narrowed. Somehow, he looked even more skeptical. "Why would a council race drop off the face of the maps? It doesn't make sense."

"Maybe not," Score said, "but we don't have all the information. If Atlantis is what it's *supposed* to be— an underwater city— then I could see why sirens would live there."

I looked at him questioningly. I, for one, didn't know *what* he was talking about. I couldn't see any appeal to being disconnected from the world.

He continued, smiling a little at my confusion, "They'd have a barrier of tons of sea water to keep humanity away. It's healthy for us to sing regularly."

Was it? I hadn't tried singing— *real* singing— since the first day I turned.

"If that's true, why haven't we heard *you*?" Glenn demanded, glaring.

It was rude and hostile, but I couldn't help but wonder the same thing. Score always seemed so controlled when it came to using his voice. If it really *did* help so much, why had he reined it in?

Score stared out the window, his voice quiet, "It's personal."

"Come now!" Glenn pressed, "We're all extras here. You need it for your health, go right ahead."

Score turned back to him, his eyes filled with hostility. They were a strange salmon color I'd never seen before, and a tiny bit crimson on the edges. His nostrils flared, "Thanks, but it won't happen." He squeezed his eyes shut, leaning against the window.

I frowned at Glenn. "Why were you pressuring him?" I chided, winding my way around the plants to sit next to my guard.

He shook his head, "I just don't like it, that's all. He acts like the sodding expert all the time— and *you* haven't done any casual singing," he pointed out. He was right. I hadn't allowed myself to sing at all. Truthfully, I hadn't heard Score sing much either— only twice since I'd known him.

"Why would he lie?"

"I don't know. To get you away from me, to run off again, leaving me chasing ghosts and legends?"

I sighed. Both boys were driving me crazy. I glanced back at Score, feeling a pang of guilt. I didn't *think* he was lying to us, but I still had the feeling he was keeping something from me.

I stood, stretching my legs and wandering over to him. I sat, saying awkwardly, "Hey... Glenn's just... he's protective, that's all."

Score chuckled under his breath, "Yeah. I know."

"What you said before—"

"Is the truth. We do better if we sing."

"You haven't uttered a single note this whole trip, Score," I pointed out. "And we've been traveling for a while."

He opened his eyes, looking conflicted, miserable. Once again, I got the feeling he was keeping something from me. "Lyra, I'd love to sing for you. Every day, even, but..." He frowned, a frustrated look crossing his features, "I can't. Not right now."

"Why not?" I asked, slouching into the seat. "If it really *is* that beneficial, Score—"

"It is! But it's different with an audience."

"Even an audience of extras?"

"*Especially* that," he muttered. He stared out the window again, watching the dark clouds below us spread like a blanket over the smatterings of city lights. "Someday, you'll understand."

I shook my head, baffled, "I hope so, Score."

The flight attendants made their rounds, offering the group food and drinks. I sipped at some water thoughtfully. Whether Atlantis was real or a myth was only one of my questions.

136

I leaned into my hand, turning to Birkita, "Have you heard of the Hand of Fate?"

Her head snapped up, "Why?"

"Just something we heard at the apothecary," I responded casually.

"An assassin's group. They basically run the Shadowlands."

My heart sped up, but I tried to keep my face neutral. "Assassins?"

In my peripheral vision, Glenn shook his head soberly, issuing me a silent warning. Maybe I shouldn't continue this conversation.

"Yeah. Hire them, and you can change fate— for a price. That's what they say, anyway." She cocked her head, "Exactly what did you hear?"

"Just… something," I said, nervously playing with the hem of my shirt. "Nothing important." I looked towards Glenn anxiously. A high-powered group of assassins had been contacted to eliminate me.

Great.

~~~~~~~~~~~~~~~~

We landed in Ireland. The air was damp and cold this time of year. Score informed us that we were heading to the Western coast— the Cliffs of Moher. Apparently, it was a popular tourist attraction. We took a shuttle there.

I stared out the window as we traveled, wondering what we could possibly find at such a busy location, but Score seemed confident. The drive took longer than I'd have liked— four hours from the airport.

As we slid from the vehicle, Score thanked the driver and paid him in cash. Part of me wondered where he got the money, but I decided maybe I didn't want to know.

Glenn left his little potted plant on the seat of the car. He stretched out, breathing deeply. He looked relieved to be away from human transportation and back in nature.

A few groups of people lined up sporadically along the edge of the horizon. They gawked at the sheer drop down to the ocean. I walked to the edge, peering below. It made me dizzy. Not long ago, I'd been nervous about being 80 feet up a tree with Glenn. The cliffs had to be ten times that. Waves crashed menacingly along the edges below.

More surprising was how steeply it dropped. It was straight down, as if the hillside had been chopped in half. Yellow-green grass grew between slabs of stone in scrubby clumps. I closed my eyes, backing away from the edge.

Since my transformation as a siren, I'd had few opportunities to feel tiny. This was one of them. The scope of this place made me feel so small, so insignificant.

Score stepped next to me. "Impressive, huh?"

I nodded, "Yeah."

The wind was fierce. A pang hit me. The setting reminded me of Whitecrest, with the same chilly sharp wind and damp skies. I actually missed home more than I'd realized— especially Marin. I wondered how she was doing, if she'd forgiven me for leaving without warning.

Glenn sighed, "What now?" He stared at Score, his eyes hard. "This is your show, right?"

Score gestured to his right. "That way."

"It's marked private property," I pointed out.

"It's where we have to go."

"Let's just get on with it," Glenn muttered. "I want to find some answers so we can sort this out, and get you off these wanted lists."

We stepped away from the cliff's edge. Score led the way, ticking off his steps with his fingers. I was glad he'd taken the initiative to read the *Siren's Call* and decipher it. I felt stressed and stretched thin from the training and walking and worrying.

The tourists grew more sparse before fading completely. I worried we were going to have an angry property owner after us at any moment, shouting at us to leave. The hike wasn't difficult, though we did stumble over a few rocks poking from the ground.

"We're almost there…" Score held his hands up to form a square, as if he was framing a picture with them. He twisted his torso around, searching for something— what, I didn't know.

I sighed. Everything had been easier Score's way, despite my reluctance. If we were close to the next city, maybe he'd been right about the Overworld. Maybe it'd be better to travel like this from now on. On the other hand, I trusted Glenn's judgment.

The air shifted, the mist becoming clouds— dark and ominous.

Birkita drew her sword wordlessly with a tight frown. I could feel the crackling of energy in the air, like electricity. Magic had been invoked nearby.

"Score…?" I asked nervously.

I hoped it was part of the plan, intentional, but he bit his lip, "I need more time."

Glenn had already notched an arrow. He surveyed the area quickly. "You're almost out, mate."

No question, this was bad news. The last time I'd felt magic like this was in Whitecrest, when an army nearly killed Glenn. Anxiety pooled in the pit of my stomach, my pulse racing. My eyes flew around wildly, trying to catch sight of danger.

A misty blackness exploded like a chain of smoke bombs, detonating from left to right along the horizon. The tendrils of darkness reminded me of ink bleeding into water.

Five shapes formed from the black mist. Their darkness was so complete, it sucked the light from the atmosphere. They formed into human figures without faces. The pack approached slowly, their heads craning towards us as they glided closer.

"Shadow warriors?!" Birkita cried to Glenn.

The half-elf's jaw tensed. He loosed an arrow into one of the creatures, notching another as the monster recoiled in pain.

They'd been slow, languid even, but Glenn's arrow had provoked a reaction. Icy fear wrapped around me, taking my breath away. Birkita slashed at one, kicking and stabbing.

I realized how easy she'd been on me, despite being so much harder than Glenn. She flickered in and out of space, teleporting from one enemy to the other, slicing off limbs that grew back instantly.

The shadows seemed invulnerable. The explosions of violence dealt by my companions only slowed them.

Crowded next to Glenn, I'd remained safe so far. He kept them at a distance, delaying the monsters with a rain of arrows.

A shadowy claw slashed at LaRue. The wolf lunged forward, wrenching one of Birkita's many swords from her back. He whipped the blade forward, hopping away from the dark creature.

"Got it!" Score cried next to me.

The shadows circled, tightening like a noose around us.

Glenn whipped his head to Score, a sheen of sweat visible on his forehead, "Get her out of here!"

Score nodded, snatching my hand from my side. Glenn loosed two arrows at once, felling one of the creatures temporarily. Score took the opportunity, tugging on my hand. He broke into a sprint, dragging me behind.

"Score! We have to stay! They need help!"

He shook his head, "No, Lyra, we can't! The shadows are after *us!*"

He was probably right. Logically, it made sense, but I hated to leave anyone behind. I whipped my head back, taking a harsh breath. Score wasn't just *probably* right— he was dead on. The shadows had abandoned their pursuit of my companions, and had all turned to fixate on us, hot on our trail.

Where could we even go? Score and I were unarmed. Even siren magic could only help so much against creatures who couldn't be killed. I doubted a fortress would protect us against living shadows.

Glenn and Birkita still fought. The banshee flickered into the spaces between the creatures and slashed at them with her blades. Glenn rapidly fired at the monsters, forcing them to pause to remove the projectiles.

It wasn't enough. They still gained on us.

Score charged ahead, but there was nowhere to go but off the cliff. I dragged my feet, two awful choices before me. I stared at him questioningly, not sure what his plan was, hoping he *had* a plan.

He paused for just a moment. The edge was about twenty feet in front of us. Behind us, the shadows formed an impassable wall.

Score squeezed my hand. "Lyra, do you trust me?"

Did I?

I nodded tightly. He seemed relieved.

He scooped me into his arms, staring into my eyes with icy blue orbs, "Good."

Score sprinted hard, his chest rising and falling in exertion. He was heading towards the cliff's edge— the 800 foot drop to the sea.

I hadn't heard him hum, hadn't heard him use any of his

siren powers. What were we doing?

I became more and more nervous as we approached the edge. At the point of no return, he lunged forward, off the cliff face, into nothingness.

Chapter Fifteen

The Firmament

I squeezed my eyes shut, expecting to plunge from the sheer cliff into the rocky depths below. Then I realized we hadn't dropped. I bounced in Score's arms as steadily as if we were on solid land. I opened my eyes, confused.

He was running up the horizon through the sky, breathing hard. His face was flushed but determined.

A glance back confirmed the strange shadow creatures still followed us. They scrambled impossibly upward, trailing directly behind Score and me.

It's an invisible stair.

I let out a titter, my eyes darting below us to the churning ocean. Score counted quietly in Siren. He let out a sound of pain as one of the shadow warriors lunged, catching his heel, scratching him.

Score kicked it away and pushed forward, not losing momentum. His brow was set and determined. *"27, 28, 29—"* pivot.

Still ascending, he turned sharply to the right. Two of the creatures plunged from the edge of the stair, tumbling into the sea below.

I wanted to ask him what was going on, where we were heading, how much further this went. But Score was occupied, his face red, carrying me. I doubted he could reply if I asked.

Three shadowy creatures still pursued us. One nipped again at his heels. I wished I had a dagger, an arrow, *anything* to fend them off. I swung my backpack at one, batting it away from Score's legs as he climbed.

We'd reached a thick layer of cloud cover. The air was beginning to feel thinner but not dangerously so. I wished Score didn't have to carry me, but with the strange shadows trailing behind us, he didn't have time to stop and put me down. His arms shook with the exertion, his face and chest covered in sweat. How high had we gone now?

He turned another corner, but the creatures behind us were smarter than their companions had been and managed to stay on our heels. I glanced up at Score, worried. How much longer could he keep going like this? He was fit, but this was brutal. It seemed never ending.

We finally broke the cloud, emerging into bright sunshine. The vapor spread before us like a carpet. Oddly, sitting on the cloud top were buildings— strange, round, woven buildings.

The stairs had evidently ended, the fluff solid beneath us.

Score stumbled forward, barely capable of carrying me anymore. I tapped his shoulder urgently, trying to get him to set me down. He met my eyes with ragged breaths and desperation. I pressed my palms against his chest. He stopped. The creatures were just far enough away that we had time; they'd lost their momentum when he'd turned the last corner. I slid from his arms easily, gripping the handles of my bag with white knuckles. I didn't have anything else to use as a weapon.

The mist stirred as the creatures lunged towards us, and I braced myself to fight.

At that moment, the sky darkened. I wondered what fresh torment had arrived. The shadows stopped, bringing their gazes upward. I chanced a glance towards the sun. It was obscured by a flock of hundreds of birds— all types, shapes, and sizes.

Hummingbirds, hawks, eagles, ducks, swans, pigeons, swallows, jays— if it could fly, it was above us. The largest bird descended, raking its talons at one of the shadows. The creature was shredded, dissipating into the atmosphere. The bird was impressive: long gold, red, and yellow feathers spread wide, reminding me of flames. It circled down, landing before me with its wings out. The bird shifted, transforming into a woman wearing some sort of feathery cloak.

She was phenomenally beautiful, with sharp eyebrows and

dark skin. Her hair was long and red, but faded into gold. She tilted her head— a jerky, stilted movement— and stared at the remaining two shadow warriors. Her eyes narrowed. They were crimson, piercing.

"You aren't welcome here. This space is protected by council laws as a sanctuary. Now leave," she commanded.

The creatures hesitated for a moment, impossible to predict with their lack of features. After a few seconds, they exploded into a burst of inky black, disappearing.

I nearly collapsed with relief. We weren't going to die— at least, not yet.

Score bent over, breathing hard with his head between his knees, shaking.

"Thank you," I offered the strange woman.

As she turned to me, I realized the feathers weren't a cloak— they were wings. Looking at her head-on, she was small— probably only around five feet tall— but commanding. From the collarbone up she appeared human, with stunning and bold features. Feathers covered her torso but didn't obscure her womanly shape. She became even more avian at her legs. Her knees bent backwards, and more feathers bled down into skin and talons. She gestured, waving her right wing up. A delicate hand peeked from beneath. She greeted me, "Welcome."

The sky brightened as the birds landed on the strange structures surrounding us.

"Where are we?" I asked.

She raised a brow, "I was expecting a demand, lady siren, not a question."

She loped forward, a strange hopping movement, waving a hand for us to follow. Score panted, stumbling forward and nodding, "It's okay, Lyra. We can trust her."

"What *are* you?" I asked.

"A harpy. Their leader, in fact. My name is Avia. I've been serving the sirens for a thousand years."

Score fell to his knees, exhausted from the dead sprint he'd made up the stairs. Around us more birds descended, transforming into the same half-human form Avia had. It was a hodge-podge of appearances and sizes: crows, parrots, swallows, robins…

"Lyra!" a voice called. The clouds stirred again as Glenn burst through the mist.

He rushed forward, pulling me tightly into his arms. Avia fluffed herself up, "Step off, elf! That is a siren Matriarch!"

Glenn's eyes flashed. I pushed from him gently, "It's fine, he's one of our companions."

"Very well," Avia said. "On your authority." She bowed her head slightly, and Glenn rolled his eyes.

Birkita and LaRue appeared behind him. LaRue looked impressed by the clouds, but Birkita almost looked bored. She eyed the harpies appraisingly.

"What is this place?" I asked Avia.

The harpy's head almost snapped completely behind her as she answered. The effect was unsettling. I shrank back, but she didn't seem offended. She smiled, "It's the firmament chamber, where sirens take audience from those who wish to bargain with them." She sighed, "It had more use in the old days." Her head snapped forward, "As I'm sure you're aware, it's almost completely abandoned now."

"Then why stay?" I remembered reading that the harpies were possibly extinct, but if those birds were any indication, that wasn't close to true.

"It's our home," Avia said quietly, "and our burden." She pointed ahead. "You may find answers within."

Looming before us like a Greek temple sat the siren ruin. It was made up of pillars of marble. Several statues lined the edges— beautiful women wearing togas, holding exotic instruments.

"Let's get on with it," muttered Glenn.

"You go on ahead," Birkita said dismissively. She smiled at a hard looking male harpy standing near her, "I'd like to chat with our new friends." LaRue didn't appear enthusiastic to follow us, either. They stayed behind with the harpies.

I shrugged, grabbing Score's hand.

"You okay?" I asked.

He nodded, but his face was still flushed.

"Thank you, Score," I said sincerely. "You saved my life."

"They were after us both. Thanks for trusting me."

I had to smile at that, "Well... the cliff *did* give me pause."

We shuffled inside the wide hall. It was simple and open. Everything within the interior was marble— roof, columns, statues. Even the floor was soft white stone, etched with attractive circular patterns.

145

A single throne sat at the end of the long rectangular room. Score flopped down on it, exhausted. I had to laugh, but couldn't blame him. His muscles were probably still burning.

I walked around the empty temple. The pillars were all carved uniformly. Beautiful but bare.

"I was expecting more," I admitted. "The poem suggested this would lead to Atlantis." I sighed, running my hand over the smooth surface of the marble throne. "Do you think Avia would know where we need to go?"

"Doubt it," Score said, pushing himself up off the throne. "The poem suggested it was a secret, that we'd have to discover something hidden here. Maybe we're just missing it." he stared at the walls, the pillars, scrutinizing every section of the room. Score shook his head, "I don't see a thing that indicates... *anything.*"

I ran a hand through my hair thoughtfully. There wasn't much here. I examined the throne, sliding my hands up and down the sides and back, trying to decipher anything hidden that might hint at a clue.

Glenn didn't have any luck, either. "It's pretty barren," he agreed.

Maybe this was a waste of time. I slumped into the throne, staring at my feet. I sighed, looking at the looping design in the floor. I paused. The pattern. It wasn't siren writing— at least not in the traditional way— but...

"Score?" I called.

His shoes squeaked on the marble. He leaned against the throne's back, "Yeah? Do you see something?"

I pointed down to the markings, the spheres. "Isn't this...?" It was strange. The markings were nothing I'd ever seen, but still something I *knew*— probably from my attunement. The spheres read mathematically. It was a quick, more convenient way of writing down a musical composition. The design allowed the reader to see the whole thing at once, gaining a feel for the piece.

"It's a *song,*" he agreed. "Lyra, you're amazing!"

I shook my head, but a happy glow covered me. I flushed at the compliment, standing and folding my arms. "But what'll it do?"

He shrugged, pulling his guitar from his back. He flipped the snaps of his case open, "One way to find out, right?" He eyed the whole design, taking in every detail— even the throne was part of it— before he began to play and sing. He didn't bother with lyrics.

I closed my eyes listening to him. It was only the third time I'd ever heard him sing. Though it wasn't his own melody, it was still siren-written and perfect. But it would've been better if he'd crafted his own song. The richness of his voice soothed me. My shoulders relaxed as stress drained from my body.

It was short, but as the song wound down I realized I was smiling.

Glenn stepped forward, "Exceptional, but what did it accomplish?"

As soon as the words left his mouth, the room began to quake. I rocked into Glenn, who caught me gracefully. The throne spun along the round designs on the floor. A circular staircase appeared, winding below the temple floor.

"Excellent," Glenn said shortly, "we can sort this out and be on our way."

I nodded, following him down the stairs. It was surprisingly well-lit, with sunlight streaming in from enormous windows. The stairs ended in a wide doorway. Beyond that was a dark hall. It made me nervous, especially after the strange shadow creatures attacked us earlier.

Glenn led the way, but slammed into an invisible barrier. The edge of the passage rippled like water, distorting the air. "You've got to be kidding me!" he muttered, pounding onto the surface. The door was decorated in several ripples now, flowing from the edges of his fists to the frame. I stuck my hand out tentatively, but met no interference. I raised my brows. Glenn sighed, gesturing towards the hall, "Sirens-only. *Again.*"

I stared at the hallway anxiously, but Score slid past, stepping inside. As soon as he crossed the threshold, a bright light illuminated the whole thing, leaving it far less nefarious. I squared my shoulders and followed him inside.

~~~~~~~~~~~~~~~~~

Two rooms were across from each other in the hall. We peeked our heads inside, but they were unimpressive: simple bedrooms with small twin beds. Bathrooms adjoined, equally mundane. At the end of the corridor was a kitchen with tiny appliances and a small table. I sat on one of the chairs, resting my elbow on the table and leaning into my hand. I sighed. Everything had been such a fight to find. I wished the sirens had been less secretive and more open with us.

Score dug through my bag, retrieving the map. He re-read the verses on the back. He sank into the chair next to me, looking thoughtful.

"So we're looking for... *something*... with the Bard's words that will direct us towards Atlantis."

I laughed bitterly. "It's a good thing they were so vague. Otherwise, we wouldn't be having so much fun, right?"

Score reached over, giving my hand an empathetic squeeze. "We'll figure it out."

I shrugged, not quite believing him, "Yeah."

"Well," he said, standing up slowly and giving my hand another squeeze, "I think I saw some bookshelves in the bedrooms. I'll go check those first. Seems like the logical place. If you want, you can look around here."

I nodded. Score disappeared down the hallway. I stood, searching above the tiny fridge and inside the cupboards. Everything appeared run-of-the-mill, but it was surprisingly well maintained. It wasn't even dusty. I moved the dishes back, just in case, checking along the cracks and grooves for siren writing or anything else that might have been left for us.

"Lyra!" Score called from one of the rooms. I wandered down the hall. He was in the room to my right, holding a leather bound book in his hand. "Found it on the nightstand. The Bard's words— her journal. Or, at least, a journal she left here."

"What does it say?"

"A few things. Most of the entries are old, though. Over a century."

Well, I'd heard sirens were long-lived, though I didn't know the specifics. As the Bard, this woman must've kept her journal for ages.

"But here's the interesting part," he said, finding the correct page and turning the book to me.

The handwriting was neat and small, written precisely in Siren:

Ides of Thalia, FA:2598;

I fear we are lost. Even our magic may not save us this time. To make things worse, I was the instrument of our undoing.

How could I have made such a mistake? Even delirium is no excuse for my betrayal! Alas, my relationship to my dear one is no longer the same. It is poisoned with the burden of knowledge.

The populace is unaware of our current state of affairs for I have kept my treachery a secret. They only know we are in danger. There is still a slim hope to undo what I have instigated, but it will take us into the deep parts of the Realm to truly bring Atlantis to legend.

Only the women on the Matriarchy are aware that the danger is serious. Yet even they do not know how deep the peril runs. They have agreed: we are to fade quietly into obscurity. Truly, we were headed in this direction; our underwater city was already isolated from all else. It was only a matter of time before we sealed away the memory of our existence to live peacefully.

I fear it will not be enough. I fear that we will be ruined before our countermeasure is enacted. I fear my mistake has doomed us all.

I tell my two mothers not to worry, but they are clever siren women. I do not think I fool them. The destiny of the little ones has been reshaped. I only hope our labors are enough. All is in place for them should we fail— a chain of messages and clues to lead them.

Muses, may I be wrong! Protect us as we embark on our journey.

If the children are needed, they will likely read this entry— a strange thought. This journal was never intended to be kept as a public record; the words within are selfish and personal, a singing on paper.

No matter. The only thing they need to know is N47, W25.

I hope this is all a wretched nightmare. I wonder how deeply my people suspect.

Muses, help us.

The remaining pages were blank. I handed the book back to Score, "Well, *that* sounded ominous."

"We already knew something big happened."

"I wish she'd have just come out and *said* it," I muttered.

"Specifics probably didn't matter to her. It was her personal journal, after all. Maybe deeper within are answers…" He flipped through, shrugging, "But most of what I've read is scattered. A lot of the entries are several months apart, and even more have years or decades between them. Finding context might be difficult."

"N four seven w two five?" I asked.

"I think it's latitude and longitude," Score said.

It would make sense.

"Where would that take us?"

"I have no idea. With any luck, Atlantis."

I considered it, "Do you think there'll be sirens alive there?"

"I don't know. It's possible— especially with what the Bard was saying. It sounds like they were hoping to hide there."

"But why leave us behind?"

He shrugged, "No clue." He tapped the journal thoughtfully, "But it kind of sounds like we were never intended to have to do this. No wonder everything feels so rushed."

My brows raised, "What do you mean?"

"I mean, why didn't they just leave me a note telling me *everything*? Why should we have to follow clues from one location to the other? Unless…" He frowned, "Well, no sense worrying about it. It's probable they were just paranoid and rushed."

I tucked the journal into my already full bag. I stretched. It looked like we had a new direction.

"Is there anything here that'd be valuable for Birkita?"

Score shook his head, "Not really. I think this was just a break room for the sirens who worked here. From what I read in the *Siren's Call*, this citadel was the destination for pilgrims seeking siren favor. But bargains came with a hefty price. The siren Matriarchs took shifts here when it was functional. The rooms just made it more comfortable."

More food for thought. As we strode back through the hall, I wondered what the Bard had done that caused such a problem for her people— a big enough problem that they'd vanished.

Glenn leaned against the wall by the door. "You find anything?"

I nodded, "Coordinates. We know where we're headed, at least."

"Good. Let's get out of here." He walked a fast clip up the winding stairs.

I sighed, hitching my bag over my shoulder, bounding after him. Having a direction was one thing, but I had a thousand new questions in my head. What were those shadow creatures that attacked us? What was the sirens' full plan? Did they manage to stay safe in Atlantis? What were we going to find at 47 North, 25 West?

As soon as Score stepped from the stair behind us, the ground snapped back up, the marble floor once again intact. The room looked completely undisturbed now, as if it'd been this way for decades.

Outside, the wind was cold and brisk. I shivered and swiped at my nose uncomfortably. Birkita was animatedly talking with a male harpy who looked hawkish and strong. LaRue was braiding the hair of a pretty harpy with all white feathers.

Avia noticed our return and greeted us, "Did you find what you required?"

"I think so." I glanced at our companions, "They haven't been causing troubles for you, have they?"

She smiled, "On the contrary, the two have been giving my people some much needed social diversity. It can be lonely up here." She sighed wistfully, "But no matter! Is there anything else you need?"

My brows furrowed as I stared at the group of harpies. There were so many of them. "Avia," I said, "what exactly was your arrangement with my people?"

"You required a group of strong citizens to guard and protect this space from any who would attempt harm. It was always intended to be a safe place for travelers of all walks— regardless of status, race, age, or past. The harpies had a need for a home at the time, so a bargain was struck."

"But the other extras are under the impression you vanished."

Her mouth became small, her eyes narrowing. "Unfortunately, this space ceased to function as sirens became more and more reclusive. It's been widely unused for the past 500 years. Even before that, it was tapering off. It's been nearly 1,000 years since we've had any real interaction with this world or the Realm."

"Are you so long-lived?"

"My people are not, but I am. I'm a phoenix. My lifetimes each last a hundred years, then I'm reborn. I've led the harpies for many thousands of years."

"But don't you ever want to leave this place?"

She stared at me like I was speaking gibberish. "This place is our home. Of course we'd like to go elsewhere *at times*, but—"

"Then *go*," I said with emphasis. "The sirens aren't around anymore! And if they are, they can find new guardians."

Avia looked doubtful, "While it's true things have stagnated, do you really have authority to grant such a boon?"

I shrugged. I had no idea if I did or not, but it was the right thing to do. The sirens may have needed guards here before— and I was grateful that Avia had balked the shadows— but there was no reason for an entire species to remain isolated.

"She released the minotaur from his contract," Score said.

"What are the terms of the new arrangement?" Avia asked me.

"There *aren't* any! I just think it's wrong you're trapped here."

If they were so interested in blunt, harsh Birkita, they must have been starved for attention.

"Actually," Score broke in, "we could use a lift. We have coordinates, but no idea how to get there."

Avia nodded at this request. "That could be arranged." She snapped her head up, "Sephora! Gavin!"

The two harpies who'd been speaking with LaRue and Birkita made their way over.

As she approached, I was struck by how beautiful the white-feathered girl was. Her alabaster hair curled at the ends just slightly, though half of it was braided now. Her skin was pale and creamy, like a porcelain doll's. She had an elegant face with vibrant blue eyes. Her neck was long and graceful. Delicate and beautiful feathers adorned her, reminiscent of lace on fresh snow— intricate and glittering. She moved fluidly, contrasting with the awkward hops of her brothers and sisters.

The man whom Birkita had entertained was fearsome. His narrow, golden-brown eyes appraised me carefully as he jutted forward. He had a strong, pronounced nose and a square jawline. His brown hair was sheared closely to his head, edging into his bronze skin. He looked muscular even through the line of feathers. A scowl was on his lips as he approached with disjointed and unsettling movements.

"These are my immediates," Avia announced. "We'll be happy to take you wherever you require."

"Sephora," the girl greeted, bending at the waist to bow. She glanced at Avia, "They desire transport?"

Gavin snorted, "I'm not a taxi service, Avia. I'm a warrior."

"Then you can remain here. The siren wishes to free us from our contract."

His brows lifted, easing some of the harshness from his features, "Truly?"

"But if you'd rather stay here…" her mouth formed a sly smile.

"As usual, you are correct," he mumbled, staring into the clouds at his feet.

"Where do you need to go?"

"47° North, 25° West." Score looked relieved that we'd solved another problem. I felt the same way. Since we'd just been attacked, it'd probably be better to get to the next location as soon as possible.

"That's not very far from here. At least, not by flight. But it's in the middle of the ocean."

Atlantis seemed even more likely.

"How long will it take for us to get there?" Glenn asked.

Avia shrugged, "A few hours." She addressed me, "Matriarch, I'll personally carry you and your ma—" she paused, looking at Score, "and the male siren. Sephora and Gavin are capable of taking your companions. Are you ready to leave?"

I nodded. I wanted to go while we still had a little bit of light. I was worried about possible assassins bombarding us. If an army attacked, I wasn't 100% sure we'd survive even with the the harpies' help.

Avia transformed into her bird shape. Now that I was aware she was a phoenix, I took more time to study her appearance. She was enormous, with a hawk-like face and a gargantuan wing-span. Score and I would both easily fit on her back; there was no question of that. Her tail was her most impressive feature: long and train-like, the ends blazing with real flames that licked the air hungrily.

She jerked her head, crouching low, and nodded to Score and me. I eyed her nervously. In the span of a few hours, what if I fell?

Clearly acrophobia wasn't a siren trait, because Score was confident. He swung a leg up and over, sitting on her back like he was riding a horse. His legs dangled comfortably behind her wings. I bolstered my courage, hauling myself up until I sat behind him. I wrapped my arms around his waist, steadying myself.

Avia's body radiated heat. It was like sitting near a sun-lamp. The change from the damp, cold cloud top to her warm back was dramatic.

Sephora and Gavin transformed simultaneously.

The beautiful girl was an enormous swan— at least as large as Avia's phoenix. Glenn nimbly vaulted onto her back. The elf looked comfortable taking flight on the back of a harpy.

Gavin had transformed into an immense hawk. He let out a nerve shattering squawk, bowing low before Birkita.

The banshee grinned, hopping eagerly on his back. LaRue followed behind, folding his arms around her waist. Birkita snapped, "Oh, no. Take your hands off me, dog! You lay another finger on me, and I'll cut it off."

I had no doubt she would.

LaRue pulled away hastily, looking as terrified as I felt. He grabbed a handful of Gavin's feathers instead. The harpy screeched at him indignantly. Apparently, that wasn't polite.

Avia nodded her head with authority, crouching low with a jerky motion. She leapt, flapping her great wings, and took off. My stomach turned as we ascended, and I clamped Score's torso even tighter.

He turned his head back to me, concerned, "Are you okay, Lyra?"

I nodded but squeezed my eyes shut, pressing my face against his back. Despite the invisible stairs, despite the night in a tree, despite the Cliffs of Moher, I hadn't come to terms with heights. I kept imagining being bucked off, tumbling into the open air below, and plunging to my death.

"You're shaking."

"Just don't like heights," I mumbled.

"We're in good hands," Score said soothingly. "And there's

so much to see. Most people don't get to experience a view like this."

I pulled my face from him, but kept my arms in a death vice around his torso. I glanced around us quickly, and my hair caught in the wind, streaming behind me. I was surprised how cool the air felt compared to the heat emitted by Avia.

To our right and left, Sephora and Gavin carried our companions through the sky. Birkita was enthralled, chatting to Gavin and patting him on the back. The great hawk would jerk his head to respond. The intention of his motions were a mystery to me, but the banshee seemed to read him without trouble. LaRue, on the other hand, was green. His eyes were squeezed shut and his arms were folded tightly across his chest.

Glenn crouched low, riding easily on the enormous swan. He looked remarkably appropriate with his shock of white hair and his elvish grace, gliding through the air on such a beautiful creature. He looked focused, staring ahead with determination. I wondered what he was thinking. Had he worked out any clues as to why his Lady wanted my life, or was it just as mysterious as it always had been?

Avia shifted, tilting her body to circle around a thick cluster of clouds. I squeezed Score even tighter, knocking the wind from him. He laughed, "We'll be fine, Lyra. Avia knows what she's doing."

She screeched, as if to reassure me. I took a deep breath. Maybe I should just trust the phoenix, but it was hard to do when everything was so far below us. The sun began to dip down in the sky.

Score had been right— the view *did* take my breath away. It was a panorama of sky and sea. The sun peeked over the clouds. It stained the edges bright orange, tinting the sky pink, scattering a glittering gold reflection across the Atlantic.

"What do you think we'll find when we get there?" I asked Score.

"Atlantis," he said. "Of that, I have no doubt."

I'd been assuming the same. "But in Atlantis," I said. "What then?"

"I don't know," he admitted. "Hopefully some answers."

Chapter Sixteen

The Gate

We reached our destination: a dot of an island in the middle of the Atlantic Ocean. Avia circled downward until we settled on the ground. The landing was graceful but hard. When her feet touched the sand, I felt jostled as her muscles rippled beneath me, bumping me forward into Score's back.

Score swung his leg, sliding from the bird, and offered a hand to me. I took it, following suit. I was surprised at how stiff my muscles had become in the few hours we rode. It felt good to be off Avia's back. I leaned over and stretched, touching my toes.

Our companions weren't far behind. Glenn was the smoothest. He descended gracefully from Sephora's back as soon as she set foot on the island. LaRue scrambled off Gavin as if he was on fire and fell to his knees, kissing the earth dramatically. Birkita appeared disappointed the flight had ended. She saluted Gavin and lined up with our group. The three harpies returned to their half-human form.

It was dark out now, pitch black aside from the half-moon in the sky. The island was small and unimpressive. If this was Atlantis, it didn't look like much.

Avia approached me, "Thank you for your unexpected kindness. Despite dissolving the previous agreement…" She hesitated, "I feel I can call you a friend. If you ever need anything, the harpies will stand with you."

"Thank you," I replied. "I just hope you have the freedom to do what you'd like now."

"You're a good Matriarch. Should you need us…" She clutched at her chest, plucking out a few feathers.

"Mistress Avia!" cried Gavin, perturbed.

Avia tossed her head, narrowing her eyes at him, and they had a silent exchange. After a couple moments, Gavin's mouth tightened, and he nodded stiffly.

Avia turned to me, "Burn these, and I'll be there to aid you." I took the offered feathers. They were warm to the touch, crimson with gold tips.

She turned her head, surveying the small isle, "Will you be alright here? Have you a way to leave?"

I didn't know. The truth was that I didn't feel comfortable answering for the group. I found myself hesitating, opening and closing my mouth a few times before Avia tilted her head in that jerky manner of hers.

"Burn one if you require passage. We wish you well, Matriarch."

The three transformed again, taking off. They were much smaller this time, the size of regular birds.

Even that's magic…

"What's the next step?" Glenn asked.

"Tomorrow," I groaned. I was exhausted from the trip and the day in general. Besides, it was pitch black.

"Setting up camp?" Birkita asked, "Fine by me."

She yawned, stretching like a cat. She strode away from the beach and onto the island proper. It was hard to see in the darkness, but from what I could tell, the island was less than a square quarter mile in size.

We stood on a wreath of beach that surrounded the whole island. The bulk of the land mounded into a slight hill, flattening out at the top. A few bare trees towered in the darkness like sentinels. Scrubby grass grew in scattered clumps along the dune.

I pushed my aching limbs to the top of the hill and sat, the grass tickling my arms as I leaned back. I was tired. Tired of running, tired of thinking, tired of searching for answers.

Glenn plopped down next to me, whispering, "I'm not trying to push you."

I sighed, "I know."

"We just… things are getting more urgent. If we can find some tangible answers, we can go to the council and present them

157

with evidence. Then things won't be so dangerous for you."

I smiled, appreciating the thought. It'd be nice to return to our lives, to not have to worry about assassins or the council or following clues. There's only so long you can go on a scavenger hunt before you long for home. I missed Marin, painfully so. We'd become so close in the months I was living with her. It was strange to not see her every day.

I pulled my boots off, peeling my socks from my feet, and dug my toes into the sand. It was coarse and dry with a few yellowing stalks of grass in it, but it felt good. It reminded me of home.

"What were those things that attacked us?" I asked. It was a question I'd been wanting to ask for a while, but we hadn't had a moment until now.

"Shadow warriors," he said grimly. "They're conjured to terrorize or kill a specific target. Shadowlands business."

"Because assassins are out to get me?" I asked, exhausted.

"Yes. The Hand has used them in the past, but they typically only send one. Dark magic. Rare magic. Shade magic."

"A ghost?"

"No, a *shade*. A creature imbued with shadow who can manipulate the darkness. Dangerous, uncommon, and dreadful."

"So if they usually only send one, why did I warrant five?"

"I guess someone really wants you dead. They're hard to kill. Maybe impossible."

That much was clear when we fought them. They were only slightly fazed by the blows struck against them— blows that would've been fatal to another opponent.

"Does loverboy know where you're supposed to go from here?" Glenn asked.

I frowned. "I don't think Score knows. And I've told you before—"

He laughed, "I know, I know. Sorry I said anything." He picked up a twig from the ground, flexing it between his hands. "It was awful, though. Being locked from that siren place."

I rolled my eyes, laying back. "Trust me, you didn't miss much. Just a couple bedrooms and a kitchen. Nothing exciting."

He kept his gaze on the twig, snapping it in two, "It wasn't that I was expecting anything exceptional. I just hate it when we're separated. I worry something will happen, and I'll be powerless to help you."

"Well," I said wanly, "it's not as though things are always safe when I'm with you."

"But at least then I'd go out fighting. Not knowing— not knowing is more terrifying."

I grabbed his hand, squeezing it, trying to reassure him. "If I can help it, you'll be with me. Does that make you feel better?"

"Actually… Yeah, it does."

Score approached us with an armful of branches. "I've gathered supplies for a fire," he said with a gentle smile, "and I checked the island to see if I could find any clues."

"Anything?" I asked, leaning forward.

He set the wood in front of Glenn, settling next to me. "A couple things. There's ruins here. Just a crumbling, foot high wall and sinking foundation, but *something*. Looks like this was actually busy, once upon a time."

I glanced at the stalks of grass and bent trees. I couldn't imagine anyone had set foot on this island in a long, long time.

"More interesting is a boulder on one section of the beach. It has a marking carved on one side— one word, in Siren: 'sunrise'."

Glenn picked through the branches, tossing a few aside. He knelt down, stacking them into a neat start for a campfire before coaxing the dry grass into a spark, then a blaze.

Birkita was already snoring, propped against one of the trees. LaRue sat glumly next to her. He was probably even more tired of traipsing about the countryside than I was. At least I had incentive.

"We should try to sleep," Score said, "I think we'll want to be near that stone at sunrise."

Sleep did sound good. I curled up next to him. He propped my head on his lap and stroked my hair soothingly. Friend or love, Score was good to me. I tried to picture doing any of this without him. Impossible. I needed him. He identified with me and saw the world with a siren's perspective.

I cared deeply for Glenn, but he'd never really understand what being a siren felt like anymore than I'd understand how he'd forgive the elves for the awful things they'd done to him. Even now he defended them, and they'd done nothing but tell him how unnatural he was.

If I was in Whitecrest, I could confide in Marin. In a lot of ways, she understood me better than anyone. I'd have never believed it six months ago, but now I wished she was here with us. She'd have been incredibly helpful in navigating this nonsense. Even so, she'd never understand being a siren, just as I'd never understand being a mermaid.

Score shifted his weight so he was propped against a tree, falling asleep quickly. The rhythm of his breaths lulled me until I, too, had fallen into slumber.

~~~~~~~~~~~~~~~~~

"Lyra, you need to get up."

Glenn?

I was groggy. I rubbed my eyes. I didn't know how much sleep I'd gotten, but it didn't feel like enough. Score shifted beneath my head. I pushed myself upright, scooting forward. I felt dirty and wished I could change my clothes. But there wasn't a place I could change discreetly, so instead I just tugged on a fresh pair of socks and slipped into my boots.

We stretched, shuffling to our feet. It was too early to be functional.

Score looked at me, rubbing his eyes. He scanned the horizon. Noticing the glow in the east, he let out a soft grunt, "This way."

He stumbled tiredly, leading us to the south side of the beach. He paused before a huge, lumpy boulder. Score gestured to the base of the stone where the siren symbol was cut deep enough to withstand the lapping tide.

The spray of the salt water hit my face. I wrapped my arms around myself, cold. The fire had given more warmth than I'd realized. Without it, the air was frigid.

The sun crested the horizon. As the beams fell across the boulder, I could feel it— a crackling charge in the air. Magic.

I steeled myself, nervous. In my experience, magic was followed by trouble.

The ocean rippled, the tide stilling. A sphere of water rose from the glassy sea. The globe stretched, forming the shape of a woman. She was pretty, with an hour glass figure and long flowing hair. She had a face like a Greek statue. Her lips were

160

heart-shaped, her mouth pouting. The water creating her form still flowed, dripping down her body to return to the ocean. She reminded me of an ice sculpture— transparent and fluid, but somehow still firm, still solid.

"What *are* you?" I asked the spirit curiously.

She glided closer, her feet skimming the top of the water, leaving a rippling trail beneath her toes. "A Nereid. I guard Atlantis; I have for centuries." Her voice was strange. It surrounded the entire space, the sound as tangible as fingers caressing my spine.

"She's not real," Glenn said. "Nereids are artificial. Magical constructs."

The creature's lips turned up. "True. But real or not, I'm capable of my position."

She swept a hand out over the water. An enormous wave formed behind her, high and menacing. It was eerie— the water had been relatively still, the tide low.

"I am in the presence of siren." she bowed her head reverently, and the water fell down around her. "The doors are open to you and your sir alone, Matriarch, though the journey is far yet."

Glenn sighed in frustration, growling, "I'm so tired of this! The sirens had a real trust problem."

I stared at the Nereid, "How long will it take to get there?"

"An hour? A day? Perhaps ten. Perhaps a hundred. I don't know the distance, nor when you'll return."

"But it's close, right?" Score asked.

"Perhaps. This is the way forward, certainly."

Birkita leaned back on her heels, folding her arms across her chest. LaRue stood next to her, looking depressed.

"Chances are, it'll have the best siren treasures. The sooner they leave, the sooner they can return with the goods," Birkita announced. LaRue just sighed next to her.

She had a one-track mind, that was for sure. I considered it. We'd come so far forward— too far to not keep going. But this leg of the journey was only for Score and me. We were never intended to have additional companions.

"We should get going," I said reluctantly.

"No," Glenn stated decisively, leaning against the tree. He wasn't arguing, nor was he opening discussion. To the elf, it was fact. The subject was closed, and we weren't going.

"What?!" Score exploded. "We've been doing everything to get to this point, and now that we're *this close* to finding some answers, you're trying to tell us we can't go?!"

Glenn glared at him, standing up straighter so his full height towered over Score. He didn't look impressed.

Glenn snorted, "There's not enough details. How long will you be gone? How far is it? Is it safe? Can the Nereid answer *any* of these questions?!"

"I don't know the answers," the Nereid admitted, "but I can promise that it'll be safe for sirens, but no others."

Score's brows raised, "See? It's safe for Lyra and me. That's good enough."

"The two of you..." Glenn shook his head, "It's too dangerous! If the journey takes days, or weeks, or even months— both of you are hopeless. You *need* me!"

"We *don't* need you! And that's the real problem, isn't it?" Score growled. "The sirens aren't setting up to hurt Lyra. The only thing the Nereid seems to know is that it's safe for us! And I won't allow your attachment to stand in her way."

"Lyra," Glenn said, turning his head towards me. "This is completely mental. Tell your mad boyfriend to let it go." He hitched his quiver up, shifting it on his shoulders.

"Score isn't my boyfriend, first of all. And second," I looked to the Nereid. She was impassive, almost bored. She didn't care about the spectacle in front of her. She was only created for one purpose— to tell us what to do, where to go, to keep out those who weren't sirens. "Second, we've come too far to not see it through. We can handle ourselves."

"You're being ridiculous!" Glenn said, shaking his head firmly. "Maybe we don't need answers. We'll run instead. Hide within the Realm. I'll keep you safe."

"No!"

Glenn sighed, exasperated. He grabbed me by the waist and hauled me over his shoulder, walking away from the Nereid. I smacked his back, but he wasn't fazed and continued moving up the sand.

"Put me down!"

"I'll put you down when we're back in the Realm, when we're safe and sound and—" we stopped abruptly. "Get out of the way, Score."

"Look. With all due respect, I know you're trying to save her life, that you want to keep her safe. I appreciate that more than you think. But honestly? *Fuck off.* It's not your call to make."

Glenn's grip on me loosed, and I shimmied, slithering down to the ground. I glared at him. I'd never felt more disrespected by the elf than I did right now.

"How *dare* you!" I seethed, slapping him hard across the face. He looked hurt, shocked. "I will make my own choices. And you need to deal with that." I turned to Score, gripping his hand tightly in mine. "We'll be fine. We're going to go, to find out what the hell is going on, get some answers, and we'll be back!"

Glenn's eyes met mine, looking pained, "When… when will you be back?"

"I don't know. I can't answer that! I don't even know how long it'll take to get there."

Score scratched his shoulder, staring at his feet, "Give us a month. If the journey takes longer than that, we'll turn around and head back. But we need *some* time to figure things out. It's not Lyra's fault there's a sirens-only clause."

It was the right thing to say. I saw the tension diffuse from Glenn's features as he finally nodded. "Okay. Yeah. A month." His eyes met Score's, "Anything happens to her, I'm holding you responsible."

Score just nodded in response, then turned to me. "No pressure, but whenever you're ready, we can leave."

I took a few breaths, collecting myself. If we were potentially going to be gone for a month, I should say my goodbyes.

I glanced at the half-elf. Glenn looked so worried. The edge of my anger fizzled away. He'd been wrong before, but it was for noble reasons. He just didn't want anything to happen to me.

I stood on my tiptoes, arcing my clasped hands over the half-elf's shoulders. He really did care for me. I pressed myself against him, leaning into his chest. He returned the embrace with a squeeze.

"I'll be back before you know it. Promise."

He grunted. I dug into my pocket and retrieved the feathers Avia had given me. "Take these. Summon the harpies if you need to go."

"I'm not leaving until you're with me."

I had to smile at that. I grabbed his wrist, bringing his hand closer. I dropped the feathers into his palm and curled his fingers over them. "Just in case," I said. "Besides, if we're gone more than a couple weeks, you'll need a way to get LaRue out of here before he turns."

The wolf looked a bit green at the prospect of riding the harpies again, but he sighed loudly and nodded. "Mademoiselle is correct."

I hesitated for a moment. "Will you be alright?"

Glenn gave me a lopsided half-smile and nodded, "I'll be fine. There's life everywhere around me. The banshee and wolf, however…"

Birkita grinned nastily, "I'm more stalwart than that. A month on an island? Please. Simple. As for the dog… well, he's tougher than you'd think. Just make it worth my wait."

Glenn's hand cupped my face, and he ran a thumb along my jaw. From my peripheral vision I could see Score tense at the interaction. I didn't care.

"Be careful," Glenn told me.

I nodded. He pressed his forehead into mine. We stood silently for a moment, eyes closed.

I pulled away, turning to the Nereid. "Ready."

She gestured, and the water parted to reveal a stairway.

"Below this, you'll need to be able to survive underwater. Once you reach Atlantis, it won't be a problem. If you're truly siren-born, you'll have no difficulties making the journey."

I already had a way to survive the water— the potion Marin gave me before we left. I dug through my bag and retrieved it. I unstoppered the bottle, watching the viscous liquid fall from the cork.

"Marin gave this to me," I said, glancing at the group. "She said it lets anyone breathe underwater."

Score nodded, "That should work."

I swallowed a few mouthfuls. It smelled sweet, but the taste was sickly and reminded me of an infection. I gagged on it, but managed to choke it down. With glassy eyes, I passed the bottle to Score, coughing. I felt a little different. The liquid spread out into my chest, making it hot. My skin felt a little thicker, too, better insulated. I doubted the cold of the water would be a problem.

Score downed his dose, taking it like a shot of alcohol. He closed his eyes, shivering. It was nasty stuff. He took a few deep breaths, steadying his stomach, then nodded. "Let's go."

I grabbed his hand nervously, and we descended the stairs. It was unnerving with the water on either side of us. A churning roar echoed at our backs as we took each step. I whipped my head to the sound. As we walked, the water crashed down behind us, sealing the passage. I had a moment of panic, claustrophobia hitting me. I hoped Marin had given me the right potion.

The path ahead was lit dimly by a dark green glow. A cluster of underwater anemones gave off the light. Everything else was blackness. We'd be truly below water soon. The stairs were leveling off, sinking down into the waves.

"Score?" I asked nervously.

"Hmm?"

"How could we have done this without the potion?"

"Our magic."

He said it so matter-of-factly. I was always reluctant to use my voice. I'd almost forgotten we were capable of such magic.

"We won't be able to speak again until we're outside of the water," I said, feeling anxious.

He squeezed my hand, reassuring me, "We're close, Lyra. And we're in this *together*. If you need help, just look at me. Look at my eyes. You'll know what I'm thinking." The colors would help, but it was still a gamble. I steeled myself. We took another step forward. The ocean water invaded my leather boots.

Another three steps, and it was at my waist. Another three, and my head was the only thing above the water. I sucked in a deep breath of real air, and sank down, keeping my eyes open. The path was straight and narrow, the way illuminated only by the strange anemones. A small school of silver fish darted past, flashing in the green light. The glow gave Score's face a strange cast.

I tucked my shirt into my pants to keep it from floating up around me. Hopefully my bag was sturdy enough to reasonably shelter its contents from the water. I was certain that my dulcimer was protected, at least. Score had assured me that our instrument cases were waterproof at the beginning of our journey through the Realm. I hoped that the music box was also constructed to withstand the water.

165

My lungs were burning, but I didn't have the courage to exhale yet. The idea of taking a breath of water terrified me. I didn't have gills like Marin did. It was hard to have the backbone and faith to take that first deep breath. I looked towards Score, who was in similar discomfort. His face was red, ruddy in the greenish light.

He stared into my eyes. His were black, revealing how terrified he was.

I squeezed his hand. As hard as this first breath would be for me, I trusted Marin. Score barely knew her. I released the air from my lungs, watching the bubbles stream from my mouth and rise upwards. Score closed his eyes and did the same.

Pure panic gripped my heart, but I took another breath.

Cold water streamed through my nose. I waited for the seizing, the coughing, the response my body normally gave me, but it didn't come. The liquid was heavy, but it filled my lungs comfortably. I didn't feel lightheaded. The water was truly breathable.

I exhaled. While it took more effort, the fluid pushed out of my lungs so I could drag in another 'breath'.

Score looked as relieved as I felt. Strangely, breathing the ocean water wasn't as terrible as it could've been, though it was cold sloshing around my windpipe.

I pressed forward. We didn't know how long we'd be down here. If we had to surface for food, or for fresh water— best to move forward as quickly as possible.

The path was long, stretching ahead of us as far as I could see. Our steps were laboriously slow, hindered by the water. The buoyancy caused more complications than it solved. I wished there was a practical way to swim through, but the path was too narrow, too obstructed, and too dim. It sloped downward steadily, sinking us deeper and deeper into the ocean as we progressed.

It felt like hours before we'd reached a change in terrain.

Eventually, coral began to sprout up on either side of us. The further we wandered, the more it grew, until the tangle encapsulated us completely. Below our feet, the sand gave way to a slick paved road, completely covered in algae. Hanging tangles of lights flickered to life as we moved forward. The path forked into a T— right and left, identical.

Which way?

We paused. I glanced at the paths, trying to decide. Score looked frustrated, beginning to pace back and forth.

I felt a warmth tingling in my limbs. It dawned on me that I *knew* the right way. I could feel it in my bones as easily as I could craft a melody.

I grabbed his wrists, jerking them so he'd stop moving. Score was overthinking it. He looked into my eyes, and I smiled, nodding my head to the left path. His brows lifted, confused, then his eyes widened as he realized I was right.

The paths were easy to navigate now. We followed our instincts right, left, left, right. It was as though Atlantis called to us.

Hours passed. The silence was absolute, giving the atmosphere an eerie quality. Sound had become more important to me as a siren. Given a choice, I'd actually give up almost any sense before my hearing.

Score's hand was reassuring as we made our way through the winding paths. It was still so dim, so quiet, so... *wrong.* Though my instincts assured me we were moving in the right direction, the tangled reef itself felt unnatural and dangerous. It had the same strange, inherent danger that the Broken did. The path we walked was safe, but if we strayed... I shuddered. There was no curiosity, nothing compelling within the dark depths worth the risk. Score didn't waver from our intended course, either. I knew he felt it, too.

After a long while, I began to tire, my legs cramping. How long had we been hiking through the ocean? I pulled on Score's hand. He looked wearily into my eyes. He was exhausted, too.

I gestured to the floor. The hallway was narrow, but not so narrow that we couldn't sit. We lowered ourselves to the slick ground. I rolled my ankles around, enjoying the reprieve. I was so tired, so sleepy. The idea of laying on the slimy ground disgusted me, though.

As if reading my mind, Score pulled me against him, letting me lay back on his chest as he sat upright. He stroked my hair comfortingly.

I closed my eyes. I hoped we'd arrive soon. This winding labyrinth was more terrifying and bleak than the minotaur's, and certainly a lot longer.

Despite my busy mind, I fell asleep against Score.

When I awoke, I wasn't sure how much time had passed. The light was unchanging, the surroundings identical.

When Score saw I was awake, he nodded at me. I pushed myself upright, helping him to his feet. We needed to keep going.

More hours. More monotony.

Then finally, without warning, we'd arrived.

A wide set of double doors appeared before us. They looked like they were made of pale blue glass. No algae or barnacles clung to them despite being under the water. Above the doors, etched perfectly in siren lettering was one word:

Atlantis

We both reached out, touching the smooth surface of the doors simultaneously. A ripple in the water thundered from our contact. The glass crawled out, sinking into the reef, allowing us passage. Within the chamber was a brightness, a soft blue glow. The light was more natural than the strange baubles that illuminated the coral maze.

We stepped through the doors, hand in hand.

Part Two
Atlantis

"The end of a melody is not its goal;
but nonetheless, had the melody not reached its end,
it would not have reached its goal, either."

- Frederick Nietzsche, *Human, All Too Human*

Chapter Seventeen

Message

We crossed the threshold reverently. The doors shuddered closed as we passed. We'd finally made it inside.

Atlantis.

I brushed my fingertips along the smooth glassy surface of the wall. As we walked through the water in the long hallway, it began to glow a crisp, clean turquoise. The lighting started dim, but grew steadily brighter, accommodating our tired eyes. After a short time, the passage was well-lit.

Above us, I could see the break in the water. A stairway was directly ahead. I gripped Score's hand nervously as we took the first steps up. What would we find here?

To my intense relief, we broke the surface. I exhaled the last of the ocean water from my lungs. It poured from my nose in two streams. I coughed despite the magic, grateful for the lightness of real air again.

After a few more steps, I could feel the true weight of my clothes and bag. The buoyancy of the water had given way to the heaviness of gravity. My clothes were soaked, as was my hair, but the air was warm and humid. It wasn't uncomfortable, aside from the additional weight.

"We're finally here," Score breathed. He laughed loudly, as if he was bursting with tension. "It's so nice to *talk* again."

"It's so nice to *breathe* again."

I turned back fleetingly. The watery hallway that led from the ocean looked like a long reflection pool from here.

This room was beautiful. The ceiling was rounded and made of the same transparent turquoise material as the hall. The soft glow cast enough light to reveal the ocean outside. Fish swam in schools; crabs scuttled near the sand. I wondered how deep we were. Probably not as far as it seemed.

Great pillars stood on either side of us, twisting up to the ceiling in spirals of the same glassy material. Ahead of us was another hallway that branched into a crossroad a few yards from where it began.

"Can you feel it?" Score asked.

I nodded, because I *could* feel it. A profound relief shuddered through me. For the first time in my life, I was home.

I smiled and leaned over, giving Score a kiss on the cheek. Who knew what we'd find here? Maybe even *who* we'd find?

A bubble of excitement started at my chest, igniting my nerves like a spark of electricity. We stepped forward, hand in hand. I was relieved that Score was here with me, that I didn't have to do this alone. As we took our first steps into Atlantis, a soft humming emanated from the walls. The very place sang to us— a quiet, ethereal melody. It was soothing, but haunting.

The hall branched out into three directions: right, left, and forward. The two sides curved, as if the hallway eventually made a huge loop. Directly ahead, the glass was cut into an enormous arch that opened into a great room.

My eyes were drawn to a round table in the center, ringed by five chairs. At the head of the room was a large opal throne. I'd seen something like it before— at the first council meeting I'd attended. It looked like it'd been carved from one enormous opal, the colors flashing beautifully in the calm light.

We stepped inside. The high backs of the chairs were decorated in opal patterns, each distinct.

Two of the designs were remarkably similar. Their shared prominent feature was a bird with open wings, as if in flight. But the animals faced opposite directions, and the backgrounds were different. Behind one was a sun shape; behind the other was a crescent moon. I ran my fingertips over them. My dulcimer and music box were decorated with similar designs.

The other three patterns were more varied: a sword, a gemstone, a quill.

The room was open and perfectly circular. White silk

tapestries covered the wall. The ceiling was domed, revealing the fish, sharks, and even turtles swimming above.

I paced the circumference, feeling the edge of one hanging curtain. I stood, listening to the soothing melody of Atlantis. I sighed in contentment.

"Lyra?" Score called, standing at the table.

I turned to face him, "Yeah?"

He picked up an object from the table and turned it to face me. An envelope.

I raised a brow.

"See for yourself."

I moved next to him, taking the parcel from his hands. It was heavier than I'd expected, but softer than any paper I'd ever felt before. I flipped it over and nearly dropped it.

In siren lettering was my name, along with Score's.

I sank into one of the chairs, staring at him.

"You can open it, if you want."

I bit my lip and stared at the cream colored paper in my hands. I took two deep, steadying breaths and tore the envelope open.

I pulled out a thick parchment, and read:

Lyra & Score~

This letter feels like a surrender. If you have survived to read it, you are the last with siren blood flowing in your veins. It is an unusual message to write, as I assume that from your perspective I have been dead for many cycles.

It proves the resilience of our kind if you are indeed holding this parchment in your hands. Our clever plan has come to fruition, though it was always intended as a failsafe.

The universe is a fickle mistress; the Muses may smile or frown on you. This time, it would seem, they have frowned on us. Yet all is not lost! For within the two of you lies the hope of our kind.

As each other's ideal match, you will be constant companions from now forward.

Atlantis lies before you! This great hall has been home to the sirens since before its submersion. The location is a well-guarded secret. You will be safe here. To the right is our

171

industry, to the left our residency. Everything is marked clearly. Do not concern yourself with food— you shall be provided for in our kitchen.

As you are our great hope for survival, I am proud you have made your way home. While it pains me to hinder your freedom, you have been sealed within these walls to ensure the survival of our species. The doors will unlock after a century, when you have had ample time to recover from your journey and provide children.

> *May your voices swell,*
> *Bard Shiri*

A wave of dizziness struck me. I set the letter down on the table, resting my head in my hands.

"Lyra?" Score asked shakily.

...you have been sealed within these walls to ensure the survival of our species. The doors will unlock after a century...

I took a couple deep breaths. "We have to get out of here, Score."

I bolted from the chair, running in my wet boots back the way we came. The potion was still active— we had enough time to pass through the maze and return to the real ocean. I heard Score behind me in the hall, our wet shoes squeaking on the glass as we ran.

I dove into the icy and unforgiving water, splashing madly forward. I reached the glass doors that'd slid shut when we'd entered. The water invaded my lungs again, slithering down my throat, cold and heavy.

I pounded at the doors, screaming uselessly through the water. I kicked them, trying to slide my fingernails into the crack between to force the doors open. The water made my movements slow and erratic. The fluid was too thick to get any weight behind my swings.

Score came from behind me, grappling my wrists. He shook his head, his hair floating like a halo. My hands were bleeding— I had split the knuckles open. He pushed me aside, kicking earnestly at the gate. A few minutes passed, but the doors did not yield. All that Score had accomplished was wearing himself out. He shook his head glumly.

172

I let out a silent wail in the water, crouching down miserably. I clutched my hair, falling onto my knees.

He let me despair for a few moments, but after a time, his strong arms wrapped around me. He picked me up, stepping away from the doors. We emerged from the pool. In my grief, I sputtered out the water I'd been inhaling, coughing it onto Score's shoulder. I sobbed, bundled in his arms, crying hard. The melody of the walls was broken by my own wretched wailing and the sound of our hair and clothes dripping.

He paused in the hallway, kissing me fervently on the top of my head. I choked as I inhaled, trying to control my feelings long enough to get my bearings.

I had only one thought: we were trapped. We were trapped, and I'd left Glenn behind. I'd promised him I'd return.

Score ran his hand through my tangled wet hair, trying desperately to soothe me.

I buried my face in his shoulder, sobbing hard again. He sighed, "Let it go; let it out."

I shook my head, ashamed of my tears, "I can't. I have to be strong. I have to find a way."

He pulled away, so I was looking into his eyes. They were a murky purple. "You don't have to be *anything* right now. Not strong, not a fighter, not Sarah, not even a siren! Nothing… except Lyra. Just be Lyra for a moment, with no expectations."

At that moment I loved him. It seemed like since this journey had begun, everyone, including myself, wanted something from me. But not Score. He was asking for the opposite— to tear that down, to be myself, to fall apart if necessary.

I clutched his dripping t-shirt in my hands and leaned in. I could smell the cold, fishy salt water on him, but beneath was the same spice and warmth that always comforted me.

"If I put you down, will you be able to stand?" he asked gently.

I nodded.

"I promise," he said, wiping a tear off my cheek with his thumb, "we'll figure this out. But for now, I think you need some dry clothes." He smiled lopsidedly, "You look like a drowned rat."

I laughed thickly. He looked less than polished himself in his soaked jeans, frayed shirt, and squeaking tennis shoes. Nodding, I said, "Yeah. Okay."

Chapter Eighteen

Cope

Walking through the left side of the hall, we found the residential half to be large, comfortable, and clear-cut. Small silver plaques were posted at the forks in the road, directing us right or left. If we were trapped here, at least it'd be easy to navigate.

We followed the signs to the bedrooms under the assumption we'd find some sort of dry clothing. What we found was more surprising— we already had rooms of our own.

Thick velvet curtains covered doors that lined the hallway. Each residence was marked with another silver plate bearing the owner's name. I didn't recognize any until I stumbled across my own.

Shock went down my spine, but I wasn't entirely sure why. Logically, why *wouldn't* I have my own room? While it was a little eerie, it made sense.

I swung the purple curtain back.

The room was bigger than I'd anticipated. I assumed space would've been more of a premium, but it was at least the same size as my room at Marin's house— maybe even a little bigger. A huge bed sat in the center, draped with plush blankets in exotic indigo, white, and purple fabrics. A bookshelf lined one wall, but it was empty. On top of the shelf were several thick wire hooks— made to display my dulcimer. Next to the shelf was a cream colored chaise lounge, loaded with pillows in the same hues as the bedding.

A midnight blue curtain separated the living space from an

opulent bath. I peered inside, gawking at an enormous tub, sink, and a huge wardrobe with curved silver handles. A large shower was in one corner, and off to the side was a toilet.

"I suppose if we're stuck here, at least they made sure we're comfortable," Score said wryly. "I hope my room is even half so nice."

"Why wouldn't it be?"

His brow raised, "You're the woman. I'm less important than you are."

I put my hands on my hips, "If we really are stuck here for a hundred years, we can find you a decent room, even if they gave you a shoe box. It's just us, right?"

I gripped at the silver handles, tugging the wardrobe open. Dress after dress after dress. Not exactly my style. I pulled one from a hanger, sighing. Of course it was my size. It'd be a perfect fit. I turned to Score. "I'll meet you in that throne room in an hour. I just need a little while to decompress, to get dressed."

"All right. I'll go see what I can find. It'd be nice to be dry again," he added, disappearing from sight.

I closed my eyes, gripping the silk fabric of the dress I'd pulled out. It was a lovely thing— slinky and ice blue, with feathery sleeves that would barely cover my shoulders. The back was low-cut with ties by my neck. I set it down on the vanity, staring at the bathtub.

Rinsing the saltwater from my body sounded amazing, but I wasn't sure how the tub functioned. There wasn't a handle or plug, but it was obviously intended for bathing.

I sat on the edge of the basin, peeling off my leather boot. I wiggled my toes, wondering if I'd developed a blister. Sure enough, a red welt had formed between my first and second toes, the start of an angry one. I tugged off my clothes. Everything was wet, sticky, and colder than I'd noticed before.

I crawled into the bath tub, wondering if there was a trick to it. Maybe I'd have to sing?

Surprisingly, as I settled into the tub, it automatically filled with silky, scented water. I inhaled, recognizing the fragrance: lavender. A scent to calm my frayed nerves. I leaned back. The water was my ideal temperature— hotter than most people preferred, but not burning. I closed my eyes and tried to focus.

I still had at least a dozen questions for the sirens, despite arriving at the pinnacle of their society.

First and foremost, what happened? Were they killed off? Or did they vanish? What calamity could cause an entire society to collapse?

Why? Why did it happen? Why did Amaranthe want us dead? Did any of the other extras feel similarly? What provoked such hostility?

What did that letter mean, Score and I were each other's ideal match? The fact was I did care for Score, but how would the sirens know that? Just the thought made my stomach turn. It implied that our entire friendship, our entire companionship, was predetermined.

I scrubbed at my skin with the soapy water. There it was again. Another pang, one that I'd buried before.

Glenn.

What I felt for him was different than what I felt for Score. How long would Glenn wait for us to emerge before he left his post? How long until he decided I'd abandoned him completely?

I pulled myself from the tub, drying with a huge towel that hung on a bar to my side. I slid the blue dress over my body and gazed into the mirror before me. Beautiful. Like always. I strode barefoot through the halls, the glass eerily warm underfoot.

Score was already in the throne room, spinning the letter in his hands again and again. His hair was dry. He wore a soft white dress shirt and black pants. His eyes were murky gray— confused. When he realized I'd arrived, his gaze moved up from the paper and fell onto me. He stood.

"You look incredible."

I frowned. I didn't want to be complimented right now. I just wanted to be able to find answers and leave. I wondered if that would happen, or if this really was just one giant trap the sirens had planned for us.

"Thanks," I returned, sighing and stepping towards him.

"The library will be down the industrial half," he said. "I read a couple signs, but didn't explore very far. We might find answers there. It'd be where I'd start, anyway." He tilted his head sympathetically, "There's no reason to push it today, though. We have time."

I slumped against him, resting my head in the crook of his shoulder, weary. The thought of doing anything at the moment was overwhelming.

Score always smelled so good. Fresh and clean, with just a hint of warmth and spice. He stroked my back, running his fingers through my hair. I gripped his shirt, balling the fabric in my fists, clasping onto him tightly.

If nothing else, I wasn't here alone. Even if I felt used and betrayed, I had to admit I was happy Score was here with me.

In a fluid, gentle motion, he lifted me into his arms, supporting me. I leaned against him with my eyes closed, breathing deeply. Score carried me back through the hall to my room and sat me on the bed.

"Tonight, I told you— you don't have to be anything but honest to yourself."

He kissed me on the forehead, then turned to go.

I caught him by the wrist.

"Stay with me," I murmured. I didn't know if I could bear to be alone. He nodded but remained silent, sitting next to me on the bed. I leaned into him, my heart picking up speed, surprising me.

I lay on the bed, pulling him down with me and wrapping his arm around my waist. I buried myself into his chest. He sighed, rubbing my back. Maybe we could sleep like this. I felt... safe.

"Score?" I breathed.

"Hmm?" He looped his other arm around me. I slumped against him, closing my eyes.

"What do you think the letter meant?"

"That we're locked in? Some sort of spell," he said with a sigh. "But from what I read in the minotaur's library, and from what Glenn's told me, all spells have counters. Now, whether or not we can—"

I shook my head, "No. Not that." I peered at him through my lashes, taking in his handsome face, his beautiful eyes, his jawline, his slightly mussed hair. "That we're... each other's ideal match?"

His face flushed slightly. From beneath my head, I could hear his heart begin to race. His brows furrowed. He pulled back from me, his fingertips brushing through my hair. "I don't— I don't really know what that means," he said slowly. "But..."

My heartbeat pounded in my ears, my breaths coming quicker now.

"But?" I whispered, looking up to him.

"You're all I've ever wanted…" He took a breath, lacing his fingers through mine. "My heart sings for you."

It was overwhelming to hear. He loved me, that's what it meant. The phrasing was crystal clear to me. Yet it made me wonder how I felt for him. I buried my face deeper into his chest, breathing him in. I closed my eyes. If I *did* love Score, I was afraid to admit it.

"Stay with me tonight?" I mumbled into him. "Stay with me?"

He let out a long breath. He kept his arms wrapped around me, not moving. "As long as you want me," he offered.

It was a relief. I was exhausted. I let myself drift off, enjoying Score's touch. He softly ran his fingertips along my bared back. It felt good. It felt…

Like home.

~~~~~~~~~~~~~~~

It was the best night of sleep I'd ever had in my life. I was awoken by the slight brightening of the lights. Score's arm was slung across my torso. I cracked my eyes open. He was looking at me with sleepy rose pink eyes.

"Lyra," he mumbled, "you're awake."

I smiled, rubbing my eyes. "Hey," I said, yawning. "Thanks for staying."

He gave me a lopsided grin, "*Anytime.*"

I pushed myself away from him, sitting up and stretching. "How did you sleep?"

"Amazingly well," he said. "You?"

"The same." I glanced around, "Is it just this place, because it's built for sirens?"

"Maybe," he admitted, staring at his feet. His eyes had shifted, a slight yellow murkiness bled into the rose. "You want to return, though," he said thoughtfully, leaning against his knees.

I nodded. "Yes. I promised—" I hesitated for a moment, though I wasn't sure why. "Glenn. I promised Glenn."

Score swung his legs off the edge of the bed, bringing himself up to stand. "If it's what you want, I'll find a way out."

"Don't you want to leave?"

178

He smiled, putting his hands in his pockets. He walked the perimeter of the room, looking at the furniture and other objects. "I… I'd like the *freedom* to leave."

My brows furrowed. Wasn't that the same thing?

He turned to me, "And I've confused you…" He laughed, shaking his head. He cast his gaze to his feet, "I mean, I wouldn't mind exploring a little more. I do hate that we're locked in, though."

Oh. That made sense.

I pulled my knees to my chest, leaning forward and hugging them. "How do we even go about finding any answers?"

"The library, first," he said. "That's my guess. If that doesn't produce anything, I don't know. We'll just have to rethink it."

My stomach grumbled. Between the ocean trek and the nerves of yesterday, I hadn't eaten anything in over a day. "Do you think we can get breakfast somewhere?"

Score yawned, "The letter said the kitchen was stocked. I hope there's coffee."

He gripped my hand, and we stumbled down the hall. My dress was rumpled, and so was his shirt, but we were still clean. Overall, I felt more put together than I had since we began camping.

Beneath my feet, the glass was warm. It felt like it hummed. The melody continued to tone from the walls, but it relaxed me. I was surprised, given how irritated I was by most music. I supposed if there was one thing sirens knew, it was the art of composing songs.

We followed the silver plaques to the kitchen. It wasn't what I'd been expecting— there were tables lined up like a school cafeteria. One end of the room had a few counters, but there wasn't a sink, oven, or microwave. There *was* an object that looked similar to a black fridge. Score tugged it open.

"It's not cold in here," he said, frowning, "and it's empty, anyway." He shut it, sighing.

There was nothing else of note in the room.

I rubbed my forehead, "Did they forget the food?"

Score leaned against the glass wall. "All I really want is a cup of coffee," he moaned.

A tone sounded, drawing our attention. A small red light

blinked in the corner of the black appliance. I raised a brow. Score tugged the handle again.

Sitting on the center shelf was a ceramic cup with steam rising from it. Even from here, I could smell the coffee in the air. My eyes widened. Score pulled the mug from the device and took an experimental sip.

He slumped down in relief, "That... is damn good."

"So if I said I wanted a mango smoothie?" I asked hopefully.

The tone sounded again, the light blinking red. I tugged at the handle. Sure enough, a smoothie sat where Score's coffee had been moments ago. It even had a straw. I pulled it out, taking a tentative sip.

It was good. In fact, it was the best smoothie I'd ever had.

I glanced at Score. His eyes were closed, savoring the coffee. I settled into one of the chairs. "Does that work for anything we want?" I wondered aloud.

He shrugged, still nursing his java. He took the chair next to me. "I don't know. We could find out. Just start requesting things."

I grinned, considering it. For now, I figured I'd probably be fine with my current breakfast. But...

"You can't honestly expect to run on only a cup of coffee, Score," I chided.

He laughed, "It's actually my usual breakfast. I just haven't had much opportunity for it lately."

I pursed my lips. "Usual or not, I think you need something with calories. Waffles?"

The black box chimed, and I laughed, standing and pulling open the door. Sure enough, a plate of the fluffy pastry, complete with a small carafe of syrup. I set it down before him, "There. Much better."

His mouth twitched, "And what if I said I don't care for them?"

"Too bad," I said shortly, giggling.

He shrugged, his mouth a cheerful grin. He took a bite. "Oh my god! Lyra, you have to try these."

I laughed again, "No, thank you, I have my smoothie—"

He shook his head, "No, really. Just..." He cut off a small bite and lanced it with the fork, offering it to me, "Indulge me, will you?"

I shrugged, opening my mouth. He popped the slice of waffle on my tongue. It *was* good. Better than good. My eyes widened, "Holy cow..."

He pushed my shoulder, "*Holy cow*? You're the type of girl who says *holy cow*?"

"Only when something is genuinely amazing!"

"Okay, fair enough." He laughed again, "They are pretty amazing. Maybe not *holy cow* amazing, but amazing." He glanced around the room, fixing his gaze on the ceiling. A few fish darted past. "This whole *place* is amazing."

It was. But it was still a prison.

I frowned, "I hope we can find a way out."

Concern clouded his features, turning his eyes a deep forest green with rosy pink edges. He leaned forward, squeezing my hand, "I'll figure something out. I promise."

We finished breakfast, sharing the rich waffles between us. When we couldn't eat another bite, Score gathered the dishes together, leaning back and sighing. He eyed the plate disdainfully.

"What's wrong?" I asked him.

He sighed, shaking his head, "Nothing. Just... if we *are* supposedly stuck here for a hundred years, it's going to get pretty full of dishes."

I laughed, "We can wash them."

"They come from thin air, Lyra. Even if they're clean, we don't need a new set of dishes for every meal."

Leaning against my fist, I swept my gaze around the room, wondering if we could store them somewhere nearby— at least at first. I stood, pacing the room. There weren't any cupboards or shelves. I was about to give up when I noticed a small hole cut through the counter top. A small plaque marked it: *Recycling*.

"Score?" I called, "What about this?"

He stood, appraising the hole. "That doesn't *go* anywhere."

"Well, it doesn't hurt to try," I said, pulling the plate from his hands. I dumped it down the chute. With a soft hum, the plate shuddered, breaking apart into a powder that faded into nothingness.

Score's eyes widened, "That... was seriously cool."

"I don't know about that," I said, laughing, "but it solves a problem." I sighed, leaning against the counter, "They thought of everything."

Score gazed into my eyes, his brow furrowing, "Come on, Lyra. Let's get to the library. The sooner we start looking, the sooner we'll discover the way out."

He grabbed my hand in his, leading me from the kitchen. We meandered slowly towards the library.

As we walked, I noticed just how huge Atlantis really was. "This place is enormous," I said, shaking my head. "How'd they manage to keep it hidden?"

Score shrugged, "I have no idea. It'd be fascinating to research, though."

I doubted that. Still, I had to admire Score's curiosity. It'd seemed nearly impossible, but the industrial half of Atlantis looked even bigger than the residential side. The curtains were all white, but every doorway was labeled with the little plaques.

"The library's this way," Score said, tugging on my arm.

At the end of the hall were double curtains, both white. I dragged a fingertip over the siren lettering on the nearby plaque.

Library.

We moved simultaneously, each pulling aside a heavy curtain, stepping inside.

Chapter Nineteen

Research

It was gargantuan. I'd assumed the library guarded by the minotaur would've been the larger of the two, but standing at the entrance I couldn't even make out the back wall. In the center was a spiral staircase, leading to a balcony stuffed with more books. Above that, the ceiling was domed glass. It glowed pale blue. Even from here, I could make out the graceful forms of fish gliding outside.

Books crowded the space. Rows of shelves formed aisles in a sunburst pattern. But the room wasn't limited to books. There were filing cabinets, cryptic devices, and a row of human computers that were probably pretty impressive thirteen years ago. The area in the center was open, broken only by the staircase and a few comfortable chairs.

The scope of the room overwhelmed me.

"Score, how will we even know where to start?" I asked, taking in every shelf. We could be here the entire century and still not open half these books.

His brow raised, considering it. He glanced at me with dark brown eyes ringed with rose pink, "We'll find a way." Score grabbed my hand, lacing my fingers through his, "Come on."

His eyes flew from shelf to shelf, studying the room. He shook his head. "We probably want to be upstairs, on the balcony. It looks like everything down here is music, plays, fiction— nothing that will help us. We need references. Hopefully, they'll be up there."

I was glad he could make sense of everything so quickly. I took a breath and nodded, following him up the spiraling stairway. These bookshelves were just as dense, but there were fewer aisles.

"Well," he said, appraising the area, "I guess getting some information about Atlantis itself would be the best place to start."

Despite being tall— over six feet— Score stood on his tiptoes as he ran a finger along the top shelf, mouthing the titles of the books as he passed them. Occasionally, he'd pull one down, holding it in the crook of his arm before continuing.

I found myself smiling as I watched him. He looked at home here in the library.

When he had six books, he shrugged, turning to me, "This is a start, at least."

I nodded. We made our way to a long table in the center of the stacks. I pulled one of the books over, raising a brow at the title.

Limitations of Magical Constructs
& Abstract Arcana Within Atlantis
Penned by Rhythm Octave Lark-fire, HRT, ATA, Physicist

Just reading the cover gave me a headache. "This is…"

He grinned, watching my expression, "I'll take that one." He handed me a slimmer book, "Here, this one might suit you better."

The Factions and Functions of Atlantis
By Sonore Alaudidae

I was relieved, flipping it open. It was on basic day-to-day life and the organization of Atlantis. I read quickly, happy to be doing something productive.

Score tapped his index finger on the book in front of him. "No… but… the *reference* it's using is probably here, somewhere," he mumbled to himself. I almost laughed at how absorbed he was. He pulled away from the table, abandoning the book and darting back into the shelves.

I leaned against my hand, trying to focus. A symbol on one of the pages caught my eye. It was the same marking that was on my dulcimer— a bird with open wings, a crescent moon behind it.

184

I read:

The Nightingale Faction of Atlantis

Devoted to serving the siren community with moral judgment, Nightingales maintain indispensable balance within the rest of society. Symbolically, they have chosen the Nightingale as their mascot because it brightens the darkness with song. The faction colors are shades of violet and blue.

Patron Muses: *Polyhymnia & Urania*
Current Matriarch: *Harmony Cadence of clan Nightsong*

Jobs often undertaken by Nightingales include clerics of the Muses, gardeners, councilors…

"Score?" I called.

He peeked out from the stacks. "Yeah, Lyra? You find something?"

"Maybe. I think… I'm a Nightingale?"

Score pulled the book from me, flipping through it. He read the text so quickly, I wondered if he could possibly have retained any information. He grinned. "I think you're right, and…" he turned another couple pages, "I'm a Lark. Hmm." His eyes met mine, rose pink and beautiful, "Nice work."

My stomach flipped at the compliment. My face flushed a little. "I don't— I don't know if it's *helpful*," I faltered. "But it's interesting, at least, and—"

He leaned closer to me, grabbing my hand with a smile. "Every bit of information is helpful, I promise. It's all a piece of the puzzle. This piece tells us what kind of people lived here. So, yeah, nice job." He hesitated for a long moment, looking into my eyes. Finally, he leaned in, barely brushing his lips against mine.

My heart pounded in my ears. I pressed forward, kissing him back.

What am I doing?

I broke away abruptly, my face prickling, burning.

"I—" I stammered, staring at the book in front of myself. "Sorry— just— sorry."

I looked up into his eyes. Score was as scarlet as I felt, his eyes wide, pink and orange orbs staring at me. "I don't— we don't— I mean—" he stuttered. He turned away, "I'm going to find some more books."

He kissed *me*… So why did I feel so strange about it?

My hands were shaking. I flipped the pages of the book. My eyes skimmed over the words, but I didn't register any of them.

Okay, maybe that was a mistake, then? Maybe he just wanted to say thank you, to show a little affection?

I stood. I needed to clarify things. I needed to let him know I wasn't pressing for anything, *especially* if we were stuck in Atlantis. How awkward would *that* be? Getting involved would be the last thing we needed to do. I couldn't imagine having a nasty break up and being trapped with baggage between us for a hundred years. I'd seen enough of that kind of drama at Whitecrest High.

I nodded, steeling myself, and walked into the stacks. He stood leaning against one of the shelves. His eyes were closed, and he sighed.

"I…" I began, twisting my fingers together, "Score, I—"

His eyes snapped open, revealing light blue and pink irises. Within a second, he had me pinned against the other shelf in the row, kissing me hard.

His tongue traced against my teeth in a wave of cinnamon sweetness, making me moan.

Drama be damned, I wanted him. I'd wanted him since the moment I saw him so many months ago. I met the force of his affection with my own, gripping feverishly at his shirt. He kissed down my neck. One of his hands grazed along my waist, sliding down my hips, until it cupped my butt. A soft hum escaped my throat. My body was filled with an aching need, a frantic desire only he could fulfill.

His other hand tangled in my hair. I pulled away, kissing along his jaw line, down his neck. Passion engulfed me, urging me onward— I wanted to cross this line.

His hand slid beneath my dress, so his palm was against my bare thigh. A tingling charge ignited the nerves beneath his fingertips, filling me with even more yearning.

"Score…" I breathed. I tugged on his shirt, trying to remove it.

He broke from me, groaning, leaning against the stacks

again.

"Lyra…" he sounded so reluctant. "I— do you *really* want this?"

My heart beat like a bass drum in my ears. My body heated with a flush that began somewhere in my core and seemed to spread to the edges of reality.

Did I want him? Oh, god *yes.*

But was this a good idea? I didn't know.

"Do you love me, Score?" I blurted.

His eyes were on me, following the lines of my face. He moved forward, cupping my jawline in his palms softly. "Yes, Lyra. I've loved you for a long time."

With him looking at me now, it was obvious. The rose pink in his eyes, the color I'd seen him wear for so long— it was the color of love, the color of passion.

I was shaking. Score brushed aside a few hairs that had meandered wantonly across my forehead. I was nervous, but there was no hesitation on his part— only deliberate movement. He kissed my forehead, then each cheek, then the tip of my nose. His thumb ran along my lower lip; I shivered at the sensation, my lips parting of their own accord.

One of his hands slid down my neck. He leaned in, colliding his lips against my own once more.

My body responded automatically, returning the kiss eagerly. I wanted him. I wanted every part of him with absolute clarity. I clawed at his back, pulling him closer to me. One of my hands crawled up, seeking his hair— the same hair he ran his hands through when he was nervous. I broke from him, kissing down his jaw line, his neck, along his collarbone.

He moaned, "Lyra…"

Everything was so easy, so automatic, so… *right.*

My hands had found their way beneath his shirt. I dragged my fingertips across each cut of his muscle. The bare skin of his back radiated with a heat that reminded me of a sunbeam. He was warmth, and light, and summertime.

It stirred a frenzy inside of me. I had to see him, to touch him. I tugged the tee up, over his head, tossing it behind us carelessly onto the floor. He was beautiful: defined muscles on a lean frame. I brushed my lips tentatively along his pecs.

Score grunted, grabbing me by the waist and pulling me

187

towards himself. The motion took me by surprise and I giggled, glancing into his eyes. They smoldered in pink. He brought his lips to my own, flicking his tongue playfully against mine. I pressed my hips against his, dragging my hands across his chest. I could feel his heart racing beneath my fingertips, the rise and fall of his breaths.

Did I love him? I didn't know. But in this moment, I needed him.

I trailed kisses down his torso. Score pushed me hard into the stacks of books, inflamed. He drew his lips and tongue along my neck, near my collarbone, along the tops of my breasts.

Then his hands were at the ties of my dress, tugging— and I wanted it; I wanted him.

But a thought…

Glenn. I'd kissed Glenn. I'd kissed Glenn, and I didn't know what it meant. I didn't know how I felt.

My body went rigid. I caught Score's hands behind my neck, pushing them away reluctantly.

He pulled his face from mine. "What's wrong?" he asked. His eyes shifted a little, the rose pink now invaded by dark violet and forest green.

I gently set his hands back at his sides, shaking. Though I'd reined in our passion, I still wanted him more than I'd ever wanted anything in my life. He was beautiful— his rippling muscles, his gorgeous eyes, his strong jawline, cheeks flushed with the exertion from our activities, straight nose, full lips. His hair was a little mussed, but still perfect and shiny. He watched me with beautiful, patient eyes, waiting for an answer.

I sighed, leaning my head into his chest.

"Nothing's wrong, Score. I…"

I couldn't finish the thought. How could I possibly explain my conflicting emotions?

He sighed, folding his arms around me, leaning his head onto mine. "Okay. If it's what you want… okay."

I felt guilty. This wasn't fair to him.

I pulled back, twisting my fingers together awkwardly. "It's not that I don't want to," I tried to clarify, "but—"

"You don't need to explain, Lyra," he said, smiling lightly. "Besides, we have work to do, right?"

I wasn't having much luck with studying. I wasn't sure if it was due to a lack of information, or just scattered thoughts. I kept glancing at Score, biting my lip. He was always deep within his book— I worried he just didn't want to look at me.

He said we were okay, but maybe I'd ruined everything.

I chewed on my cheek, staring blankly at the book before me. I really hoped Score wasn't angry with me.

He didn't move his eyes up. "You haven't turned a page in that book for the past half hour at least," he said, finally looking at me. "So either it's extremely interesting, or you're not really into this." He offered me a soft smile.

My shoulders slumped. His eyes were a rosy pink, and he *sounded* good natured. The coloring should've made me feel worse, more guilty. Instead, I was comforted by the hue.

I returned his smile. "Yeah… I've never been a great student," I admitted. I was suddenly curious, "What about you?"

He grinned, threatening to melt my heart again. His eyes crinkled. "I actually love studying."

"Really?!" I blurted, surprised. The only people I knew who loved to study wore thick glasses and snorted at their own jokes. I stared at him incredulously. He began to laugh.

His cheeks turned slightly pink, and so did the tips of his ears. He kept his gaze on the book, but he was still smiling. "You once asked me what I was like before I turned. Well, *this*. This is what I was like. Buried in a book, always learning something new." He leaned onto his hand, resting his elbow on the table. "I was the stereotypical geek. Early college courses, straight-A student, always tutoring everyone else. That sort of thing."

My jaw dropped. Score turned away, embarrassed. I grabbed his hand, tugging him back to me.

"I know," he said, his gaze sheepishly falling back to the table, "it's really—"

"No!" I returned. He'd misunderstood me. "It's *impressive*, Score."

His eyes met mine, "Really?"

"Yeah! I could never do something like that. It's amazing!"

"I'm sure you're underestimating yourself, Lyra. You're— you're the most incredible person I've ever met," he said shyly.

I shook my head. He was nuts if he thought there was any way I could riddle out half the information in this library.

"No... I'm pretty much useless right now. I'm terrible at this sort of thing," I lamented, groaning into my arms.

He brushed one hand against my forearm. I brought my head up. He offered me a small smile, "Hey, if you— if you *want*, I can keep it up here, and you can maybe, um, go relax?"

I shook my head, "It's not fair to you! I can't make you do all the work, and—"

He cut me off, "The thing is, Lyra..." He flushed, "The thing is, you're really, *really*, distracting to me."

Oh... my eyes widened. *Oh.*

"I don't— I mean, I'm not trying to—"

He laughed, leaning back in his chair, "Trust me, it's not your fault, and it isn't... It wasn't... It's not because of what happened." He tilted his head, looking into my eyes, "From the moment we got here, I haven't been able to focus. So maybe it'd be better if you go do something else." He shrugged, "I've got this."

"Are you sure?" I asked, my forehead creasing. "It just doesn't seem fair—"

"It's fair! Trust me, it's *more* than fair. Besides," he added, "you still haven't unpacked your bag. As optimistic as I am, I doubt we're leaving in the next few days. Getting settled wouldn't be a bad thing."

It felt like charity, an excuse to let me leave. But I wanted to take the out.

I nodded, folding my hands, "Okay. Yeah."

I stood, pushing in my chair. I moved slowly down the spiral stairs. When I'd descended a few steps, I took a fleeting glance over my shoulder. Score watched me, smiling softly. He offered a wave.

"I'll see you this evening. We can meet in your room."

I nodded again, continuing down the steps.

Chapter Twenty

Forte

I took the opportunity to do as Score suggested. I began to sort through the soaking wet objects from my backpack.

I started with my clothes. They were wadded into bundles that smelled like sea water, coated in lines of sand at the creases.

I rinsed them in the bathtub, which mercifully filled as I did so. I shook out the dirt, draping them over the shower stall. My boots were beneath the bathroom vanity where I'd left them last night, so I retrieved them and gave the leather a quick rinse. The boots would never be the same after our ocean walk, but the stitching had held up. The shoes I'd found in Atlantis weren't practical, and I wanted to hold on to what I could from the outside.

My toothbrush was destroyed from the journey, the bristles mangled. After some searching, I discovered several new ones still in the boxes. Next to them were multiple containers of floss, toothpaste, and many other toiletries.

I crinkled my nose, wondering if it was perishable. Thirteen-year-old toothpaste sounded gross, but it had to be better than the sour taste still coating my mouth from yesterday's trek. I decided to chance it, swiping a line across a fresh brush. Surprisingly, the ancient toothpaste was palatable.

I took a brief break to grab some dinner, hoping Score would remember to do the same, before I returned to my task.

Finally, I moved on to my inheritance. I pulled out my dulcimer first, unclasping it from the case. I'd place it on the display hooks for now.

I smiled at its appearance. I'd almost forgotten how beautiful it was. I had a sudden urge to play the instrument, but I quashed it down.

Though Score insisted that playing and singing was healthy, I'd never been comfortable with it. Even playing my dulcimer felt like it'd be a slippery slope to disaster. Instead, I stared at the instrument, tracing my fingertips over the Siren lettering bearing my name.

It'd seemed like such a mystery when I'd first received the dulcimer, but now that I could understand the language, the designs were laughably obvious.

I turned it over, following the lines that made up the Nightingale symbol. It gave me the strange feeling that it connected me to a completely different era— something I hadn't even known about myself. I wondered if I used to live here.

Nothing about Atlantis was familiar, except for the water.

I gingerly set the dulcimer onto the display, pulling out the music box. I opened the lid, snapping the rings into place. I waited as the familiar mechanical whirs and clicks sounded, the map popping up on its tray.

I retrieved it, keeping it folded. I placed it next to my dulcimer on the bookshelf with a sigh.

Snapping the trap door shut, I opened the lid again, prying the rings from their slots. I placed them neatly next to the map, running my fingertips over the edge of siren writing along the music box. Since being attuned, I'd never taken the time to read it. The symbols below the birds said:

Joined, the Songbird

I'd been expecting the writing to hint at the map, so this was a surprise. I shrugged it off— maybe if we'd grown up in siren society, it would've made more sense.

There was only one thing left: the letter my parents had left for me with the attorney and the rest of my inheritance, the letter written in English that'd proved laughably inadequate at preparing me for what was to come. Glancing at it was almost an afterthought.

Despite getting it less than three months ago, holding it now filled me with nostalgia. Receiving the letter was one of the last experiences I'd had before my transition. I unfolded the page, smiling, skimming the words quickly.

Then I froze.

Beneath the familiar English letters was a line of scrolling Siren writing. I'd completely forgotten it existed. My hands trembled, reading the words over and over again.

In a corner of the Atlantis Library, you will find answers through the Songbird.

I wondered, for an instant, if I should return to the library. I could find Score and take my discovery to him. I chewed my lower lip, considering it, then glanced at the small silver clock on the wall.

It was late. We'd awoken mid-day, and it was almost seven in the evening already. Chances were, Score would be here soon to tell me if he'd made any headway.

I was pleased that I'd found something worthwhile to share with him. Though I wasn't certain of the connection, it felt like the music box and the library were linked. Both the letter and box mentioned the 'Songbird'. While there were two birds listed as siren factions— the Nightingales, which I was apparently part of, and the Larks, which Score belonged to— I'd seen no mention of a 'Songbird'.

Score would most likely decipher it. I was still impressed that he was so intelligent. Clearly, I hadn't given him enough credit before. I couldn't believe he was self-conscious about it. I wished I was that talented.

I set the box on the side table near the chaise lounge. I lay back on the bed, taking a few deep breaths.

The curtain swung open. Score sighed as he entered, rubbing his forehead tiredly.

"I'm sorry, Lyra, I didn't really find much today."

"It's okay!" I chirped, patting the bed next to me.

"No," he said, frustrated. He sank into the mattress at my side, "It's not. I told you I'd find a way out, and I will." He sounded so determined.

I grabbed his hand, grinning, "Score!"

"Turquoise," he breathed. "You're excited. What's up?"

"My parents didn't leave me as high and dry as I thought!"

I pushed the music box to him, gesturing to the words.

He sighed, "Yeah, I know, Lyra. I saw it before. I figured it was alluding to our rings. It actually came together for me today, when you figured out we were members of those factions. Our two faction rings, joined, to—"

I shook my head, "No, I mean, that makes sense, but—that's not everything. Look at this." I unfolded the letter from my parents.

Score read the English. He scowled, "This is really all they left you? All the warning you had?!"

His eyes were a brilliant red with that rose pink on the outer edges. The letter had made him *angry*. But he was missing the point.

"No, Score," I said, gesturing to the Siren at the bottom.

His eyes grazed over it. "This is—!" He turned to me, beaming. His own eyes were turquoise now. "This is something, Lyra!"

I laughed, "So it's helpful?"

"Definitely!"

I leaned in, kissing him on the cheek. He wrapped his arms around my waist, giving me a tight squeeze.

Score fell back on the bed. "Finally," he whispered, "some guidance."

I let myself tumble next to him, giggling. "It's a start, at least. A place to begin."

He turned to me on his side, propping himself up with one hand. "You little genius."

I flushed at the compliment, shaking my head. It was luck that I found it. I looked into his eyes. "I just happened to stumble on the right thing."

"Do you want to check it out now?" Score looked tired even as he asked, though.

I shook my head, my waves brushing against my back. "It can wait until tomorrow. I think you've worked hard enough today, and honestly, I'm tired. Besides," I added, "I have a good feeling about this."

"Well, then…" he said, sitting up, "I guess this is good night." He swung his legs off the bed, but I caught his hand.

He tilted his head, looking down at me. I blushed. I wasn't sure why I'd grabbed for him, but in that single instant when he said he was leaving, panic struck me. I didn't want him to go.

Score looked at me expectantly.

"I..." I started. My eyes fell to the comforter, but I didn't release my grip. "Stay with me again? I mean... Just stay with me?" I brought my gaze back to his face. He smiled softly, nodding.

"Anytime, Lyra," he said, settling back down on the bed, folding his arms around me. "As long as you want me. Always."

~~~~~~~~~~~~~~~~

I awoke as refreshed as I had the previous morning. Score's leg was wrapped loosely around mine. My arms were tucked around him, gripping his shoulders. I took a few moments before I opened my eyes, breathing him in, enjoying the warmth, the spice.

"Mm..." I murmured.

Whatever I felt for Glenn, it wasn't this. This was something entirely different.

I opened my eyes. He was still asleep, his breathing soft and rhythmic. He looked incredibly serene. I sighed. I probably should get up, take a shower, and find a clean dress to wear. I began to pull away, but his arms circled my torso, trapping me.

I had to smile. It was nice.

"Lyra..." he breathed. His eyes opened, hazy. He broke into a huge grin, his gaze falling onto my face. "For a while, I thought I was dreaming."

A warmth settled into my stomach. I pulled from him. "I want to shower this morning and get some fresh clothes." I stretched, swinging my legs off the bed. "Did you sleep well?"

"Fantastic, once again."

"Me, too." I yawned. "When we're more awake, we can check out the library and maybe get some answers."

"I'm anxious to see what we'll find." Score moved from the bed, turning to me regretfully. "I guess I should probably go shower, too. I'll meet you at the library, though? Around ten?"

I nodded, pushing the curtain of the bathroom open. "See you soon."

The clothes I'd washed haphazardly last night weren't quite dry yet. I tugged them from the stall, draping them across the vanity sink instead.

I stepped inside the shower. It operated the same as the bath, the water streaming down instantly at the perfect temperature. It was soothing. The flow was scented lightly with a citrus fragrance— lemon, orange. I rolled my shoulders, feeling good. If we could find some real answers, if we could make it out of Atlantis, then I'd have zero complaints at all.

I scrubbed my hair and shivered, reliving the feeling of waking up in Score's arms. I'd never felt so comfortable with someone before. I was surprised I was thinking it. When we'd been on the road, on the way here, it felt like half the time I wanted to rip his head off. But tensions had been higher then, and he and Glenn had never gotten along.

Standing here now, thinking about Score, I felt a few butterflies in my stomach. If I could properly sort out what I felt for him and what I felt for Glenn, then maybe I could decide what to do with myself.

I slipped out of the shower, drying with a towel. I yanked open the wardrobe. I grabbed a midnight blue dress— long and form fitting with an empire waist. The back laced up complexly. After some fumbling, I was pleased to find I could loosen the crisscrosses, slip inside, and tug to tighten it. I tied it at the base of my neck, taking a quick glance in the mirror.

I looked pretty, of course— I hadn't had a day where I didn't feel like I looked nice since I'd turned into a siren— but today it made me especially happy. I squeezed the water from my dripping hair, braiding it to one side, and stretched again. I left my feet bare to walk along the warm glass.

After grabbing another smoothie, I made my way to the library to meet with Score. I carried the music box in my arms, anxious to discover its secret.

Score was waiting for me in the hall. He looked casual but handsome in a pair of black jeans and a loose shirt. He grinned when he saw me, taking my hand in his. "You look lovely today, Lyra."

I smiled, shifting the music box in my arm, "Thanks."

We flipped the curtain open, walking the perimeter of the library until we finally found a mark on the wall, tucked away in a far corner. The symbol was a blend of the Nightingale and Lark symbols: a bird with open wings, a sun with a crescent moon inside of it. The space was quiet, surrounded by a couple wooden chairs and a table. Near the wall was a little octagonal pedestal.

I brushed my fingers on the symbol, "What does it mean?"

"This must be the Songbird." He gestured to the pedestal, "It looks like your music box would fit there."

It *was* the same size as the heirloom. Holding the box close to the pedestal gave me a strange sensation in my stomach, like a current was passing through my hands and down my spine. I set the box in place, and it sank down with a click.

This time, the music box began to play a short, sweet melody. As the notes trickled out, the box flipped at the seams, the edges unfolding further and further. I was grateful that I'd already removed the map from the hidden compartment. Nothing would be retrievable from the box now. It was completely flattened.

I'm not sure what I thought would happen, but what came next was a surprise.

The two birds on what had been the lid lit up, melding together to create the same symbol that was on the wall. That triggered the pillar to sink into the floor with a groan. My heart sped up. There was a flickering of illumination from the former music box and pillar. The light's spindly beams swirled and stretched, forming a shape— a man. He looked defined but transparent. If I'd known less about ghosts, I'd have been convinced I was standing before a specter. As it was, I knew he was something else completely.

He had olive skin that flickered, a handsome face with a rugged square jaw and a line of dark stubble. His hair was dark, practically black. A shock of it fell near one of his eyes. He looked as young as Score and me. Of course, that didn't mean much to an extra. He could be ancient or as fresh as the moment— there was no way to know.

His eyes snapped open. They were disconcertingly all white without iris or pupil to distinguish them. I gasped a little bit, and next to me Score went rigid, his eyes widening.

The man held a hand up, then laughed. It was an infectious, familiar sound. A wave of déjà vu struck me, the laugh echoing in the back of my mind.

"Hmm…" he mused. He turned his hand back and forth, examining it. He glanced at us, his gaze falling on Score. He grinned, "If we weren't certainly dead, I'd say your father owed me some of his time in the singing chambers."

"You— I know you!" Score said, his eyes narrowing.

The man nodded, pacing the little corner. "Yes! Always my astute pupil, Score! I will get to your questions, I promise!" he exclaimed with a quirky smile. "But tell me, Lyra…" He paused, still smiling, looking directly at me, "Do you remember me? Do *you* know me?"

I didn't know this man from Adam. I shook my head, baffled, "No."

His face fell. He nodded, sighing, "As I'd suspected." He laughed, "No matter!"

It'd seemed important to him. I twisted my fingers together, "But, sir, I— I feel like your laugh is really familiar."

He grinned, "Is it?! If I had real emotions, I'd say that makes me happy, indeed. When I was alive, I was your father, Lyra."

My knees went weak. I almost collapsed on the ground, but Score caught me by the shoulders. His eyes were still fixed on the strange hologram, this ghost of my father.

"Forte?" he whispered.

"Well done, Score!" the hologram responded, laughing again. His white eyes crinkled at the corners, his hands on his hips.

"Why do I remember you?" Score asked, his brow furrowing.

"Probably because I taught you for about three months," Forte said. "Right after you were attuned. It's why Beat created this construct, this imprint of me. It was a way I could teach you, as intended, now that you're home."

"You were—" Score trembled beneath my fingertips, blinking. I wrapped my arms around him, trying to make it so we were somehow supporting each other simultaneously. "You were very kind to me."

The hologram laughed again, "Hmm… I guess that's what people used to say about me. It's good to see you both made it here, though. That plan…" he shook his head, "You didn't have trouble with it, did you?"

"It was confusing," I admitted, feeling dazed. "Figuring out how to get the map, I mean, and—"

"Well," Forte explained apologetically, "we didn't have much time to sort the details out. But we needed you two to get here, and we needed everything to be secure for both of you, and we needed you to meet first, and—"

I swallowed thickly, "But why all the detours? Why not send us directly here?"

"Now, Lyra," he said, his hands on his hips. He switched over to Siren, "*How would you get attuned without being led to the library?* Hmm?" My face heated. He laughed again, "Teasing, baby-girl. Teasing.

"There were several reasons, most of them obvious. Atlantis has always been a closely guarded secret— considered only a legend. That makes it more secure, but it complicates things, too. We weren't certain you wouldn't be followed, despite our hopes. Escaping to one of the other citadels would ensure your privacy until you could be safe. And, of course, we were concerned you didn't have enough time together to develop properly as matches, and—"

"Matches?" I asked him, confused.

"Well, yes," he said, his brow raising. "At any rate, we wanted to give you enough time that it was evident, and—" He cut himself off, staring at me. After several long seconds, he turned to Score, "She has *no* idea, does she?"

I whipped my head to him, my heart pounding loudly in my ears, drumming out a rhythm I couldn't escape. "What— what is he talking about?"

Score sighed, pulling from me. Shame washed over his features, coloring his eyes a soft lilac. "I… she couldn't read my letter when I met her," he mumbled, staring at his feet, "and I didn't— she didn't ask to read it when she could."

"What do you mean?!" I demanded, turning to the hologram of my father. "What are you talking about?!"

He seemed to take a breath. "Lyra… Score is your *match.*"

"I don't— I don't understand what that means," I said, my eyes darting between the projection and Score. "Are we— *were* we an arranged marriage?"

Forte smiled, shaking his head. "No, no, no… nothing like that. That's thinking too basic, too simplistically. Matches are more than that, they're—"

"They're what?!" I cried, feeling a heat creep onto my cheeks again. I didn't like where this was headed.

The projection stared at me with his unnervingly white eyes. "It's a *process,* Lyra. Sirens are born deliberately with predetermined destinies. We map out the type of *people* we want to create, the children we'd like to have— their personalities, what would work best within our population, what is needed for our society to thrive. We manipulate it with magic.

"Sirens are always born in pairs, matches. Each match corresponds to the other. Matches balance each other, have a connection to each other, could love each other. They—"

I wasn't even registering the other words. Bile rose in my throat, and all I wanted was to escape. It was stuck in my head: I was only a plan, manipulated and crafted to suit the purposes of the sirens. And Score...

I couldn't stomach another moment of explanation. I spun around, slamming hard against Score's shoulder as I stumbled out. Everything about me had been premeditated. Even my *feelings* were all mapped out from the start— enough that the sirens could predict my every move, right down to stumbling into Atlantis, right down to being attracted to Score.

My cheeks blazed and my eyes stung, filling with tears.

I was half-way back to my room when I heard the steps behind me.

"Lyra!" Score called. He was jogging now, trying to catch up.

I broke into a run, needing to escape. I just wanted to go back to the bedroom, to bury my face in the comforter and cry for hours. White-hot tears streamed down my face. It still burned with shame.

Yesterday, in the library...

Score caught my wrist, tugging sharply enough to whip my body around so I faced him.

"Why didn't you tell me?!" I demanded, "Why did you keep it a secret?!"

He ran his hands through his hair, looking lost. He kicked the floor with his sneaker. "Lyra," he said, sounding tormented, "the letter didn't go into that much detail! It just said—" He groaned, slumping into the wall, "It just said that when the compass led me to someone, she'd be my destiny. My soul mate."

"You lied to me!" I cried. I felt so betrayed— first by the sirens, for locking me away here, and now by Score.

"I didn't!" he said, his cheeks warm. But his eyes remained pale purple. He *knew* he wasn't completely guiltless. He knew he couldn't escape the responsibility of withholding this from me.

My lower lip trembled, but I tensed my jaw.

He groaned, agonized, and slid down the wall until he sat with his head in his hands.

"I mean," he sighed, tilting his head to me, "I didn't *lie*— not exactly. Things just didn't go according to plan." His eyes had shifted to a piercing, true blue. He was speaking with conviction. He truly believed it. "I figured that when we first met, you'd already be able to speak and read and write siren as fluently as I could. I'd planned on just letting you read my letter, the one I got when I was sixteen. And you'd laugh about it, but maybe… maybe you'd give it a chance— give *us* a chance. But then—" he groaned again, dropping his head between his knees. "Then you *couldn't* read it, and… and what do you say to someone who you've just met, who's already suspicious? 'Hey, I know this is sudden, but guess what! We're soul mates!'? How creepy would that have been?!"

My stomach clenched, though I could understand his hesitation. "But why hold off for so long, Score?" I asked, my voice cracking under the weight of my emotion.

"I don't know, Lyra! I don't know! By the time you could read it, it just— it seemed like it was too late to show you, and…" he hesitated, "Glenn."

My cheeks grew even hotter. I squashed the feeling down, my nostrils flaring, "Glenn has nothing to do with this!"

Score frowned, pounding a fist into the glass floor. "Really? Can you tell me with a clear conscience that he didn't affect our relationship at all?"

"He's my friend!" I protested, feeling my jaw harden.

Score gave me an incredulous look. I knew somewhere in the back of my mind it wasn't as simple as friendship. I didn't care; it wasn't Score's business *what* I felt for Glenn.

Score pushed himself up, shaking his head. He stared at the floor, as if he was afraid to look at me. "There are a hundred questions I have for Forte," he said quietly. "I *know* I'm not who you want to be with right now, but maybe you should hear some of it, too." He turned on his heel, his head still down, looking almost heartbroken.

For a single moment, it made my own chest ache for him. Then I felt a wave of disgust pull up from my stomach. Right on cue, my feelings were manipulated. I *had* to like Score.

Maybe even love him.

My hands formed tight fists, but I stalked after him, scowling. He'd been right on some accounts. If nothing else, I deserved some answers.

We reentered the library. The projection of my father still stood in the corner, the Songbird symbol behind him.

His brows furrowed. He looked concerned. "Is everything okay, Lyra?"

I shook my head, "No."

"You need to understand, baby-girl, you need to know that—" but then he stopped, frowning. "Let's just move on. I'm sure you have more questions."

"Is anyone besides Amaranthe after us?" Score asked evenly. His eyes didn't stray from the projection. They were a serious dark brown, tinged with light purple.

Forte's brow raised, "The Lady of Flowers? Really? Are you certain?"

I stared at my feet, balling my hands into fists. I wished he'd just answer the question. The room felt constricting and uncomfortable.

"Yes, we're sure," Score said next to me. "Is there anyone else?"

"I'm afraid I don't know the answer to that. I didn't even know the Lady Amaranthe held any animosity towards our race." His lips pursed, "She must have known."

"Must have known *what?*" I muttered impatiently.

He spread his hands wide, tilting his head back, "We couldn't always use alteration. Our Bard wanted us to shine like opals, to raise us up as the greatest magical race of all." He sighed, "She was greedy. She was wrong. But it's an easy dream to chase. The truth is, she found a way— at a price. Shortly after she altered the flow of magic to benefit us, something peculiar began to happen to the Borderlands of the Realm."

My heart felt like it stopped. I whispered, "The Broken."

Forte nodded, "Exactly that. Exactly that."

My stomach turned. The Broken was the sirens' faults, a product of greed and lies. I felt dizzy, sick, remembering the tentacle of the grog on my ankle. I'd been so panicked, so confused, so hurt by that creature. But if it weren't for the sirens, there'd never have been such a monster in the first place. There were thousands of extras who'd been displaced from their homes, thousands who'd turned into terrors, thousands who were forced to run for their lives.

I leaned into my hand, blinking back tears. I whispered harshly, "How can we fix it?"

"Oh, Lyra." Forte said empathetically, "Now isn't the time to worry about that."

I shook my head. What a selfish thing for him to say. How could the sirens prioritize suffering?

"No!" I barked, tearing up. "We need to—"

Forte interrupted me, "No, you don't, even if you thought you could do something about it." His brows turned sympathetically, "This place is sealed, honey. For a century, it's sealed."

Score looked thoughtful beside me, rubbing his chin. "But maybe we could find a counterspell? A way to exit before the hundred years?"

Forte laughed, "Good luck with that! Beat crafted that spell. Took him *weeks* to construct it, double-checking to make sure there weren't any loopholes."

Score's gaze flickered to me. I saw an ounce of hope in it. I frowned, still furious with him. He squared his jaw, "I *will* find a way."

"Well," Forte mused, "if anyone could, it'd be you, Score. You're very intelligent."

My face prickled again at the reminder that Forte knew us completely because he'd helped plan our personalities. I suddenly thought I'd throw up, disgusted. I wanted to get out of the claustrophobic library.

"I think I've heard enough," I muttered, walking away. To my great relief, Score didn't follow this time.

Chapter Twenty-One

Matched

I wandered the halls in a daze, the pit of my stomach burning. My thoughts churned with Forte's revelations. The sirens were worse than I'd thought, but I didn't know what I'd expected.

I found myself crying, my thoughts cyclical. I kept thinking about the Broken— a problem created by the sirens' thirst for power. How stupid, how *selfish* could an entire race be that they'd displace everyone else for their own gain?

Almost 700 years they'd allowed the corruption to spread. Almost 800 by the time I could leave this prison. I groaned, squeezing my eyes shut. I leaned against the glassy wall. The worst part was they hadn't even tried to fix it. Instead they focused on creating an elaborate plan to trap Score and me together. The races that were after the sirens had every right to be angry, every right to attack, every right to kill all of us.

I swiped at my face miserably, wishing for the thousandth time I wasn't a siren at all, that I was just a simple human girl, Sarah Mills. Maybe one of these days, I'd wake up and find it was just a nightmare.

I blinked, sweeping my gaze over the hall. I wasn't sure where I'd wandered or how far I was from the library. I'd been moving in the basic direction of my bedroom, but I wasn't near the purple velvet curtains surrounding it.

I blinked, checking the little silver plaque near the door closest to me.

The curtain was white. I drew it aside, expecting to find a gymnasium with weights and equipment.

It was bigger than I'd imagined anything down here *could've* been. Even the library was minuscule in comparison. The traditional weights, jump ropes, and medicine balls were in a nearby corner, but the majority of the space was trees and grass— an outdoor park.

My eyes caught the glint of a glassy reflection in the distance. Walls.

No, not outdoors.

But the illusion was grand. A track loop, probably about a half mile, circled a cluster of trees. A lake-like pool filled with crystal clear water took up a quarter of the space. Against one wall was a rocky formation with ropes and pulleys, made for climbing. Further up there were even hiking trails cut into a broad hillside. I couldn't see how far it went— the foliage was too dense.

Squinting, I made out a few dummies and targets near a rack containing several weapons. Next to them sat mannequins wearing armor. It seemed there was opportunity to become proficient at whatever you chose.

I was surprised. Training meant work— and the sirens as a whole were clearly lazy and selfish. But perhaps they just enjoyed having the options available.

I stumbled my way across the arena to the weapons. Beneath my bare feet, the grass was soft and springy. I wondered how it could be such a perfect length despite being abandoned for so many years. It felt like I was really outside. There was a brightness to the light above, though I couldn't tell where it came from. It felt like sunshine on my skin. A soft breeze blew, carrying the scent of the grass and trees with it.

The smell made me miss Glenn, and I let out a sob as I moved towards the equipment.

What could he possibly be thinking by now? Score and I'd already been away from him for days. I'd promised to return. As it was, I might be stuck here, miserable, for a century of loneliness.

As I made it to the combat training section of the arena, I placed my hands on my hips, appraising the weapons. Axes, bows, shields, long swords, short swords, broadswords, daggers, maces, hammers...

It was an impressive selection. They were beautiful—much flashier than the weapons that Glenn and Birkita used. Jewels adorned some of them, glints of gold and silver caught the light. Everything sirens did had to be needlessly opulent.

I grasped a more modest sword. It had a purple handle and a blade flecked with indigo. Along the hilt was a Nightingale symbol embedded in opal. I tossed it between my hands. It was a good weight, well balanced for me. It felt like the kind of sword I could wield for hours but wouldn't tire me out.

I brought it through the air in a quick arc, causing it to whistle. The sound was satisfying. I smiled, thrusting it forward, trying to remember my form. My dress bound my lunge; it was too constricting to properly practice.

I sighed. Today, at least, I couldn't train with a sword.

I replaced the blade on the wall, chewing my lip.

I selected a golden bow instead, slinging a quiver of silver arrows over my shoulder. I stared at the weapon. The shiny, pretentious metal was nothing like Glenn's bow. He'd personally crafted that weapon, decorating it with carvings of nature. The grip had been well worn from his use. This new bow was pretty with an opal Lark symbol breaking the gold just above a flawless grip. Even the string glinted with the precious metal. I rolled my eyes. At least it was light and felt balanced.

About 30 feet ahead of me was a target dummy. A bullseye was painted across its straw chest. I notched one of the arrows, trying to remember everything Glenn had taught me, and drew the string back. I released. Though the arrow flew, it only grazed the dummy's shoulder and clattered against the glass wall.

The bow felt strange in my hands. I wondered if it was the way it was set— the weight of the draw— or if it was the smooth surface of the grip throwing me off. It felt nothing like Glenn's bow. I bit my lip as a pang of longing to see my bodyguard ripped through me.

I pulled a second arrow from the quiver. I drew it back, taking my time to adjust my aim. The exertion made my brow bead with sweat. The draw was indeed tighter on this bow. My shoulders began to burn dully, fatiguing.

Glenn was always too soft on me, I supposed.

I released the arrow. This time it embedded itself in the

dummy's shoulder.

"Dammit," I hissed through gritted teeth. I'd been aiming for the head.

A third arrow. I took a deep breath, staring at the silver fletching.

"And... Glenn..."

"Glenn has nothing to do with this!"

"Really? Can you tell me with a clear conscience that he didn't affect our relationship at all?"

"He's my friend!"

My thoughts replayed the conversation. I didn't know how I felt about Glenn— not really. I'd told him before that love was an overwhelming word. I still felt that was true. I didn't think I loved him— at least, not like that.

I drew the string back, ignoring the ache in my shoulders. I took a few moments to steady my breath, keeping my core tight, before I let the arrow fly.

It arced towards the target, embedding into the other shoulder this time. I'd compensated too much.

If I had the chance, if I was more normal, if things hadn't been so completely screwed up from the beginning, then maybe Glenn and I could've become something.

I grabbed another arrow, sliding the notch along the golden string. I pulled back, releasing it without bothering to aim.

Surprisingly, better. It embedded into the neck this time.

How did I feel for Score, after all this?

I frowned, returning the bow to the wall and slinging the quiver onto the hook next to it. Pulling the purple sword down again, I swung it hard through the air. I ran forward, letting out a snarling cry. I embedded the sword deep within the chest of the dummy.

Straw poked out around the blade. The dummy wasn't created for sword-play, but I didn't care. I swung the blade forward and around, lopping the head clean off. The straw stuffing flew, falling through the air like confetti.

How *did* I feel about Score?

Angry. Manipulated. Used.

I whirled, dragging the blade across the chest. The attack struck the two arrows embedded within the shoulders, snapping them apart.

I heard silk rip. My dress had split at the seams on my thighs. I didn't care. I had nothing but time— it was all Atlantis had to offer me.

My jaw tensed. The *worst* part was that I still kind of loved him. Even after everything I knew, I still wanted him, still desired him, still—

I let out a barking growl, stabbing the sword forward again.

My arms shook with exertion now, my face flushed. This wasn't helping me to learn anything; this wasn't helping with my skills. But damn, it felt good.

How dare the sirens do this to me?!

To us?!

Score acted like he was fine with this, but he was a victim, too. The victim of a horrible trap. We weren't people to them. We were a product— a useful product to keep the species alive— nothing more.

How could he pretend it didn't matter? How could he possibly take this in stride? How could he ignore how unfair this was?

I fell to my knees, leaning against the broken dummy, sobbing into my arm.

None of this was fair.

~~~~~~~~~~~~~~~

I was relieved Score avoided my bedroom that night. I didn't want to see him. I didn't want to feel the tug of longing for him I'd certainly have in the pit of my stomach. I didn't want to be reminded yet again of the sirens' despicable trap. Somewhere, I was sure, he'd have his own room. If not, then he could certainly find some vacant space to crash. He must have unpacked his things somewhere.

I closed my eyes, trying to relax, trying to coax myself to sleep. But my body betrayed me. Without Score's presence, I didn't slip into the easy slumber I had the past couple days. It was even more proof of how much our connection was crafted by magic. He was a drug to me, and I needed to go cold-turkey.

My eyes popped open again, and I groaned. This was impossible.

What would I even *do* for a century? If Score and I were

trapped here, it'd be an uncomfortable hundred years indeed. I glanced at the little silver clock on my wall. 2:43 a.m.

Maybe there was something interesting to read in the library.

I swung my legs over, pushing myself from the bed. I wandered slowly and steadily back to the industrial half of Atlantis. At this time of night, I was grateful that I'd almost certainly be left alone. Score was probably sleeping somewhere.

I didn't know what he'd done after I'd left. I forced myself not to care.

After a brief walk, I reached the white curtains of the library. I pushed my way inside. What could I read? Along each shelf was a small silver plaque, similar to the ones marking the door ways. Each labeled the genre of books housed within.

So far, there were only volumes of music— fascinating, but a painful reminder of what I was. I didn't want to feel like a siren tonight.

I moved deeper into the stacks. Music history, performances, theory… I sighed. I probably wouldn't find what I wanted here.

"Can't sleep?"

I whipped my head towards the sound. There, still pacing the corner of the room marked with the Songbird, was Forte.

I flushed, moving my gaze to my bare feet. "I wanted something to read."

He chuckled. I wondered why the projection bothered to show that kind of emotion. "When you were about two, you liked the fables." He nodded towards one of the shelves to his right, "Over there. They're some of my favorites."

I wove through the stacks until I found the row marked with 'Tales and Fables'. The titles were all unfamiliar to me, but they did sound interesting. I tilted my head, reading each one.

The Lyre and the Bard, The Singing Fern, The Whisper in the Dark, The Lark and the Nightingale, The Muse and the Jackal…

I tugged one out at random, flipping through it. One of the thicker volumes. It was brightly illustrated, the text precisely written in the scrolling script of the sirens. In a few sections, songs were labeled. The music was easy to read and added depth to the stories.

209

"Thank you," I said to the projection. He laughed again. I had to ask, "If you're just a mechanical— or magical— construct why do you have so much... personality?"

"Hmm..." he mused, smiling. Despite the white eyes, Forte looked kind and gentle. I tugged one of the chairs over to the corner, sinking into it. I looked up at him expectantly.

"I think this is better than some robotic voice barking out information, don't you?" He shrugged, "To be honest, this was probably easier for Beat, too. It relied on the same technology as attunement. He just expanded on it."

"Beat?"

"Score's father," Forte clarified. I went rigid at the name of my match, but the hologram just laughed. "You were always stubborn. But then again, you had to be."

I frowned, my hands forming tight fists. "It's *creepy* how much you know about me. My room is stuffed full of clothing that fits perfectly; you didn't seem the least bit surprised at how I looked or how I acted..."

The projection tilted his head a little, his mouth forming a lopsided grin, "It only *seems* strange to you. You were raised human," he sighed. "We had no intention of things playing out the way they did. You have to understand that."

I glared openly at him, "You're telling me you didn't think for a *second* that lusting after power would cause problems?!"

His hands were on his hips now. "I'm not getting into a pointless argument with you. Yell at me all you'd like, Lyra. It's not going to make much difference. I'm dead."

My nostrils flared at that statement. I gripped the book hard in my hands, squaring my shoulders. "I should go."

"You're right. You *should*. You should stop being so stubborn. You should go to Score and apologize for—"

I stood, slamming the book down on the floor. "What?!" I demanded incredulously. "He kept *everything* from me! He knew we had this strange connection, and—"

"And you *didn't?*" Forte asked skeptically.

My face flushed, instantly heating. Forte had called my bluff. It was impossible to miss our bond. I'd noticed it the moment I'd met Score. I'd felt it in the days before I was even aware he was a siren— way back in Whitecrest when I was still calling him Will.

"He loves you, Lyra," Forte said, "and you're being cruel."

"He *has* to love me!" I spat back, "Because of you, and—"

"No," the projection said shortly. "He doesn't."

I just stared at him, my lip trembling, shaking with rage.

Forte shook his head, "You grew up with so few advantages, Lyra. It was unfortunate, but necessary to keep you alive." He looked thoughtful, "Maybe you've never heard of the five basic principles of the arcane arts, but one of them— one of the unbreakable ones— is that love *can't* be created from magic."

My heart hammered hard in my chest. I had the impulse to run, but I had to consider his words. "But you said—"

"I *said*," Forte agreed, "matches are created to be the kind of people who *could* fall in love with each other. But we can't create that emotion, Lyra! We can't create that kind of connection. Score loves you because he allowed himself to fall. He was in here past midnight, searching for a way out— among other things— for *you*."

I bent down, collecting the book from the ground where I'd thrown it. I shook the pages out, making sure none were bent. I wanted nothing more than to run out the door, convinced Forte was telling more siren lies.

I hugged the book to my chest. I stared at this man, this ghost of my father, nodding curtly. "Thank you for the book recommendation. Good night." I spun on my heel, walking a steady clip away from him.

He sighed behind me, "Lyra…" I turned my head back, just for a moment. The projection smiled lightly, "If you keep that chip on your shoulder, it'll be a very long century indeed."

I scowled, stalking back to my room.

Chapter Twenty-Two

Clash

I awoke from a pitiful sleep the next morning, feeling tired and cranky. My stomach growled loudly. I swung my legs off the edge of the bed, trudging into the bathroom. I snatched my jeans from the stall where they hung. They were stiff, smelled like lavender, and crunched between my fingers, but they were dry. "Hallelujah," I muttered. At least I wasn't stuck with a dress today.

I shimmied into the rough denim, glancing at the mirror. My eyes were crimson, ringed by dark violet.

My stomach complained again. I sighed, heading towards the kitchen. I'd have breakfast, then— then what would I do with myself?

I didn't know.

I didn't care.

I was too angry to care about anything.

As I pulled back the white curtain to the kitchen, a jolt thundered down my spine. Score was here, eating breakfast. My stomach burned; my back tensed. I'd lost my appetite.

His eyes moved up from his cereal at the sound of the curtain, "Lyra?"

My face was on fire. I was still furious with him. I couldn't believe he'd known we were soul mates— at least, whatever twisted idea the sirens had about them— and kept it from me. My nostrils flared.

"I'm... would you care to join me?" he asked hopefully.

I glared at him. Scowling, I whipped my body away from

the kitchen.

Score sprang to his feet behind me, making the chair clatter. Within seconds, he'd caught my wrist, tugging me back. "Lyra, I'm *sorry* I didn't tell you," he said carefully. "I'm sorry."

I just stared at him.

He looked… *in love*, I realized. In love, and hopeful. It filled me with so much rage, so completely, that everything boiled over inside of me.

I arced my hand up, slapping him hard across the face. Score was stunned. His eyes shifted to a wounded blue gray. I stomped off, feeling a few tears slither down my cheeks. I swiped at them impatiently. I didn't want to feel broken anymore. My heart raced, pounding in my ears.

I took a hard right, marching down the hall. From behind me, I heard, "Lyra!"

Apparently, Score wasn't finished. He still wanted to speak with me.

But I didn't want to speak with him. I broke into a run, taking several twisting turns. I could hear him chasing behind me.

I couldn't handle Score today. I darted into a bedroom, done up in shades of red. A large side table displayed two siren instruments, drawing my eye. I folded my arms across my chest, standing before them. A drum and a lyre, beautiful and perfect instruments. They were inscribed with names— *Melody, Treble*. I was so soured with sirens at the moment, I wanted to break them. If I'd thought I could do so silently, I would have.

I took several deep breaths. From outside the room, I could hear the squeaking of his shoes. He moved past, then turned, returning to the door. My stomach ached. I wanted to be left alone.

I didn't get my wish— Score burst through the crimson curtain. For a single moment, I wondered how he'd known which room I'd chosen. Then I saw the compass he clutched in his fist.

I closed my eyes, shaking with rage. I wasn't allowed privacy. I wasn't allowed anything.

I kicked at the glassy floor. It squealed loudly underfoot.

"Lyra!" His expression was pleading, his eyes rose pink and forest green. "What can I do? How can I fix this?"

I remained silent. He couldn't fix it. I had no desire for his comfort or love or concern. More than anything else, I wanted to escape him.

Here he was, in the flesh, the greatest representation of siren manipulation of all.

"I—" he started, "I don't want you to be angry with me."

What a stupid thing to say. How could I be anything but angry?

"You *knew,* Score!" I cried, pressing my hands against his chest, pushing him away. "You knew all along!"

He paced, "The thing is, Lyra— the thing is, I'm not sure how it makes a difference."

Was he kidding?

"It's siren tricks, Score!" I hissed, "It's being used at its finest! I don't even know if *I* really like you. Would I have liked you if I wasn't a siren?! Would you even care about me?!" I leaned forward, my head in my hands, feeling sick.

"Does it matter?!" he cried, a pained expression on his face. "We *are* sirens!"

"Exactly! That's why—"

"You know what your problem is?!" Score snapped, interrupting. "You're so consumed with self-loathing just for being what you are. You don't even see the good! I may have made mistakes in the past, I may have deep regrets, but when *I* look in the mirror, I can stomach what I see!

"You hate every single thing about your heritage— you have since the very first day when you sang for your foster parents. So, honestly? It's not a surprise I'd fall into that category, too!"

I wanted to say something then, I wanted to protest, but so far he was uncomfortably on the mark. Score was created to know me, created to understand me. I trembled, trying to hold back tears that burned my eyes.

He ran a hand through his hair, laughing bitterly. "And the *really* terrible thing? The really messed up part?! I *love you!*" he cried. "I love you so much that even now, when I'm practically *shaking* in frustration and anger, my eyes are probably giving it away. How could they not be?! Every instinct I have is to abandon this argument and pull you into my arms!" His jaw tensed, and he slammed his hand against the tabletop. He stared into my eyes, "Well? Are they?!"

I swallowed thickly, nodding. His irises were a deep red that bled into pink at the edges. My lip began to quiver.

He laughed again, shaking his head, "It doesn't matter,

does it? *Your* eyes certainly don't reflect love for me. And they never will. You'd never let yourself— even if it's destiny! *Especially* if it's destiny!"

He leaned against the wall, his shoulders shuddering, "So I'm screwed. You've already spun me into your web, already got me so tangled up in you that I'm trapped. So just tell me what you want from me, and I'll do it. You want me to find a way out of Atlantis? I'll find you a way. You want me to figure out how to start collecting stars in bottles? I'll *cheerfully* do it. Cure a disease? Why not? I have nothing but time! Cut out my own heart? It's already yours, already bleeding, crushed in your hand.

"But *none* of it will matter. None of it will make any difference! You'd rather dig in your heels and pretend to be human! But feign all you'd like, Lyra. It won't make it true." He took two steps forward, digging into his pocket, producing a small vial. He slammed it on the table.

I jumped, timidly inspecting it.

"Score?" I asked in a meek voice.

His jaw tightened. "That, my *darling* Nightingale," he scoffed, "is the cure for a siren's song, *Lethe*. Consider it my gift to you. I've been hunting for it since you told me about your foster parents."

My face prickled, my eyes filling with tears. The inside of the vial held a clear liquid with silver specks that caught the light, flashing like diamonds.

"Score…" I mumbled, feeling guilty. What could I say? I took a sharp inhale, but the breath caught in my lungs.

He turned from me with his hands in his pockets, staring at the exit. "Don't worry, Lyra. I'll figure out how to let you escape from here. I'll figure out how to get you out, as far from me as possible. I know I disgust you." His head was angled towards the floor. "I'm sorry I'm not enough," he muttered. He pushed through the curtain, leaving me alone.

My breath left my body in a shuddering sob.

~~~~~~~~~~~~~~~~~

I sat in the red room for what felt like hours, not moving. At first, I was too stunned, too numbed to do anything but cry. After a time, I found myself turning the little vial of the cure— the

Lethe— over and over in my hands, watching the sparkling silver flashes catch the light.

This tiny bottle— more than anything else in Score's loaded monologue— affected me profoundly. I'd been looking for this since my first and only siren song. Now that it was in my hands, a strange mix of relief and dread settled in the pit of my stomach.

I finally had the way to fix my biggest, deepest regret. Yet I was trapped, unable to utilize it. There was little point in waiting for the century to pass. Human lives just weren't that long. The vial would be useless to Susan and Rick by the time I escaped. I could only stare at it with emotions that swung back and forth from hope to sorrow like a pendulum.

Score had understood this was important to me. He knew I didn't like talking about Susan and Rick— he hadn't even brought it up since we'd first discussed it. But he'd remembered. He'd filed it away until he could do something about it. He didn't give up, even though I almost had.

Score did this for me— for no reason but love.

I leaned against the table, cradling my head in my arms. A wave of guilt washed over me again.

Forte had been right. I was being cruel.

I owed him an apology.

It was easy for me to blame him. Score was the only person available to act as my punching bag. But in the end, it wasn't his fault— none of it was. Sure, he'd withheld that we were connected, meant to be, but in the scheme of things that wasn't so bad. The truth was, Score had been just as manipulated as me.

I rubbed my forehead wearily. It'd be painful, but I needed to let him know I was sorry. I needed to find and speak with him.

I didn't know if I loved him. Maybe I did— but how much was genuine affection and how much was magic? I couldn't say. But it'd be better to act as friends than strangers.

I pushed myself from the room, walking reluctantly down the hallway towards the library. It's where he'd spent the last couple days. I had to hope I'd find him there now. I knotted my fingers, pushing aside the curtain.

The library appeared empty— except for Forte's projection. He raised an eyebrow at me, noticing my arrival.

"Now this is a surprise. What brings you here?"

I stared into my hands. After a few moments I asked, "Have you seen Score?"

Forte smiled just a little bit. "Not since yesterday. Are you finally coming to your senses?"

I frowned, "I'm just realizing that none of this is his fault. The true demons are you and the other sirens who set us up!"

Forte's mouth twitched, "I'm not sure which demons you've met, baby-girl, but they've certainly changed in the past thirteen cycles. Gotten more handsome, at the very least."

My nostrils flared, but I deliberately ignored the comment, "At any rate, there's no reason Score and I can't be friends."

The projection just laughed. "Well, it's a start."

I glared at him, "Do you know where he is or not?"

"If it were me, I'd start by searching the Lark faction rooms— the curtains are gold there. Score's name will be next to his. After that," he looked thoughtful, "I'd try the singing chambers, maybe, or the kitchen, or the fitness arena. Atlantis is big, but it's not *that* big. You'll run into each other soon enough."

"Thank you," I said stiffly.

Forte smiled. "I'm here to help you. I'll answer questions if you have them. I hope you remember that."

I sighed, turning away from him. I walked back out of the library.

I followed Forte's advice, first seeking the Lark faction rooms, separated by their golden curtains. After a short search, I found the little silver plaque bearing Score's name and swung the curtain aside.

He'd been right. His room was quite a bit smaller than my own— perhaps a third of the size. The bedding was made up in Lark colors— rich gold, cream, yellow, with a few small pops of red and orange. Score was nowhere in sight. The bed was neat and tidy, the pillows arranged decoratively. I wondered if he even stayed in this room. It was pristine.

Then I noticed his guitar in the corner, propped up proudly on display. I tugged the handles of the wardrobe, peeking inside. All of his clothing was neatly hung, arranged by color and type.

I smiled, looking at it. He was so orderly and organized. I rapped on the wall near the bathroom, calling, "Score?" just in case.

No answer.

Curious, I pulled the curtain back a crack, peering in. The bathroom was also significantly smaller than my own. It was still nice, but it was probably half the size of mine. There was only a shower, sink vanity, and toilet.

I dropped the curtain, continuing my search. He wasn't in the kitchen, either. I didn't know *what* Forte had meant by singing chambers. At least I could check the arena.

I wove my way through the hall, my nerves threatening to swallow me whole. I wasn't looking forward to this conversation, but it was necessary. I took a breath and swung back the curtain to the arena.

Score had changed into shorts and a tank top. He was running the loop of the track, pushing himself hard. His face was red with exertion. He was still angry— his eyes matched the color of his cheeks.

I smiled in spite of myself, watching him. He could move faster than I'd realized. I didn't even know he was a runner.

I caught his gaze. He began to slow, jogging to meet me on the grass. He narrowed his eyes, "You here to yell at me?"

I flushed, chewing on my lip, "No… I actually came to apologize."

He raised a brow, gesturing. I walked next to him as he cooled down from the work out. He didn't say a thing, keeping his eyes forward.

"I'm sorry, Score. For slapping you, and— and for being so—"

Stumbling through the words, I could feel prickles of embarrassment surface on my face. I plowed forward, "I've decided that even though I don't like that you kept it from me, you're right— it didn't really matter. Not in the long run. You didn't know the details." I sighed, tucking a piece of hair behind my ears.

I folded my arms around myself as we walked the track.

"I *am* sorry I didn't tell you earlier," he offered. "And I'm sorry I didn't anticipate this would be a trap, that I didn't realize we'd be stuck here. And I'm sorry—" He took a breath in, looking at me with light purple and rose pink eyes, "I'm just sorry."

We'd stopped moving. I sank down onto the grass, sitting with my legs sprawled in front of me, leaning on my palms.

Score followed my lead so we faced each other. We didn't

speak for a long time. I closed my eyes, pretending I was outside, on the surface. The silence was comfortable— the same ease we always slipped into around each other. I wondered briefly if it was because we were matched, because we were created for each other.

Probably so.

Even if I hated that it was magic, I had to admit it was nice to feel so relaxed with another person.

I opened my eyes and smiled. Score was doing the same thing I had been. His eyes were closed, his mouth upturned into a slight smile, head tilted back.

"Score?" I murmured. His eyes opened— beautiful, rose-colored. I felt a fresh pang of guilt hit me in the heart. "Can we start over? Be friends?"

"I'd like that, Lyra." He looked past me, at the trees. "I can still search for a way out."

"I—" I hesitated, because I didn't want him to think that I only wanted a way out to escape from him. That wasn't true. "I'd appreciate that," I admitted. "For a couple reasons." I leaned forward, into my knees, offering him a smile. "I mean, you found the cure for my foster parents, right?"

"Yes. It should work. I'm sorry for how I delivered that, I'm—"

I shook my head. His words fizzled out. In the end, he'd had every right to say what he did. It'd felt cruel, but it was honest and necessary.

"Don't be," I said with a sigh. "The thing is," I gripped at the grass, ripping out a handful. "How I feel about things…" His brow rose, and his eyes shifted to deep brown fading to rose pink. "I don't think I can stomach being a siren, right now."

"But you're beautiful," he said. "Inside, outside, in every way. More so because of what you are."

I shook my head again, scattering the torn grass through my fingertips. "Right now I'm so ashamed of the sirens. The Broken…" I closed my eyes, "Because of our kind, there are *thousands* of extras who are homeless. Who knows how many have been turned, twisted into creatures like the grog." I opened my eyes, "Knowing that, even if it isn't my fault personally," I folded my arms around my knees, making myself smaller, "I don't feel pride in being a siren." A light breeze picked up, blowing the leaves around. It made me ache for the outside, the *real* outside. "I want to fix it."

A long pause stretched between us. Score was thoughtful, absorbing what I'd said.

Finally, he nodded, "Okay."

My gaze snapped to him, " 'Okay'?"

"Yeah," he said with a shrug, "okay. Let's do it. Let's fix the Broken."

He said it like it was a simple request— like I'd asked him to scratch my back or get me a glass of water.

"I don't even know if we can!"

"Hey," he said lightly, smiling, "I'm already looking for something impossible. This won't add much to the work load." He moved to his feet, "I'll find a way, Lyra. I *promise* you, I'll find a way— a way out and a way to make things right." He offered me his hand. I took the help up, standing next to him.

"What can I do?" I asked. I wasn't as smart as he was, but maybe I could still help in some way.

He laughed, scratching at the back of his neck awkwardly. "Honestly, Lyra? Don't take this the wrong way, but the best thing you could do would be to let me work. I'm— you distract me. So just let me do it. Let me take care of this for you— for us."

"Are you sure?"

"Yeah. I'm sure. I'll find a way. I promise."

He sounded so confident, so completely certain, that I believed he'd succeed. A bubble of warmth burst in my chest. I jumped over, wrapping my arms around his torso and squeezing hard, "Thank you, Score! Thank you..."

He seemed startled, but he returned the hug, leaning his head against mine. "No problem."

"We should spend the evenings together," I chirped, surprising myself.

Score looked taken aback, pulling away from me, "Really? But—"

I could feel a flush working its way up my neck. I wasn't sure where I'd found the enthusiasm, but I didn't want to withdraw the offer. "You can't work *all* the time, Score," I said, staring at my feet. "And... we're friends, right?"

"Yeah. Okay."

"So then," I said, nodding once to punctuate the point, "I'll see you tonight for dinner, I guess. Around five."

He smiled softly, making his way out of the arena. "See you tonight."

Chapter Twenty-Three

Exploration

We met in the kitchen that evening. I felt nervous. There wasn't any reason— Score and I were just friends, after all. This was just two people, spending time together, hopefully having fun.

I rapped my fingers impatiently on the table as I waited for him. I'd arrived at five on the dot. It was after six. So I ordered some nachos and waited. I recycled the plate when the cheese started to congeal. Score had yet to make an appearance.

Maybe he didn't want to be around me anymore. Maybe that's why he was so determined to find a way out. Maybe I'd soured him completely after my outburst this morning.

I groaned, leaning into my hands. Just as I was about to call it an evening, he burst through the curtain.

"Sorry, Lyra," he mumbled, requesting a sandwich from the machine. He pulled it out, sitting next to me. "I was just reading about the nature of magic— how it works, I mean. And I got to thinking that it reminded me of photons, in a way, like it's a *particle*, and then I realized it—" He cut himself off, blushing. "I got caught up. Sorry," he said again.

I chuckled weakly, relieved he'd arrived. "It's okay, Score." I leaned into my fist, watching him devour his sandwich, "Did you have any luck?"

"It'll be a process, unfortunately. I've been focused on Atlantis, and I haven't even started to think about the other problem. Ideally, once we're free, we'll come and go as we please. If I can pull it off, you can help your foster parents, and maybe we can get some outside assistance before we tackle the Broken."

I nodded. If we could leave and return, preferably with Glenn and Marin, it'd make things much easier to research. I slumped in the chair, happy he'd worked out a basic plan.

Score finished his last bite, taking a swig of water. I asked, "What did you want to do tonight?"

"If you're up for it, I'd like to explore."

I nodded. Exploring was a good idea. We needed to get our bearings. Atlantis was vast, after all, and we'd barely scratched the surface. I stood, stretching. He followed me out of the kitchen.

We wandered the halls. The nearest rooms were surrounded by red, like the one I'd run into earlier today.

I chewed on my cheek. "So these are residential, obviously..."

Score nodded, "Yes. The Songsmith faction. Their color was red."

"What was the point of separating everyone into groups?"

"Mostly it's by job. But also..." He hesitated a moment, "By personality-type, I guess? It took specific kinds of people to make Atlantis function. The Songsmiths, for instance, crafted instruments."

"So," I listed, "there's the Songsmiths," I gestured back to the red curtains as we passed, "the Nightingales—"

Score grinned, "The moral core of Atlantis."

"The Larks?"

"Scientists, researchers, historians..."

"The Songbirds?" I asked, curious. There was that symbol in the library. It *looked* like a faction emblem. It seemed important.

He stopped, looking stumped. "I don't think that was a faction, Lyra. I'm not sure why it was used as the marking... unless it was to point out how we're both *in* factions named for songbirds..." We were at a huge, double red curtain. He pointed to the plaque, "The Songsmith common room. When the Matriarch addressed her faction, it was in here." He leaned against the wall. "I only know what I've read about," he admitted.

"How many factions were there?"

"Five."

"What were the other two?"

"The Minstrels— they dealt with trade, mostly. And the Chanters— writers and performers exclusively."

Across the hall, opposite of the red curtains was a row of white drapes. Each was marked with a symbol representing a number—

7, 8, 9

Curious, I swung one open, stepping inside.

The room was glassy and the walls were plain. Above me, in the domed ceiling I could make out a school of fish gliding through the water outside. There were a few small, comfortable looking stools, and a tiny stage.

"This isn't big enough for a real performance," I said, folding my arms across my chest. My voice bounced around the room, amplified. The acoustics in here were amazing.

Score was still in the hall, inspecting the velvet of the curtain. He stepped past it, "Sorry, I missed that. It was really hard to hear you out—" he blinked. "The sound quality is brilliant in here, but outside it was almost impossible to make out anything you said."

It dawned on me. I ran my hands across the stage, "Forte mentioned something about singing chambers…"

"Oh," Score said, his eyes softening, "that'd make sense."

I tilted my head to one side, looking at him. "Is it *really* healthier for us to sing regularly?"

He grinned, running a hand through his hair. "As far as I can tell, yeah. In California, I had a room built for myself. It had great sound quality, even better sound proofing, and an *exceptionally* sturdy lock on the door." He laughed, "I used that thing everyday. It's like…" he paused, looking thoughtful. "It's like something between a stretch or yawn, mixed with therapy. The sensation is *amazing*, and you feel so much better after— mentally, emotionally, physically…"

I twisted my fingers together. "I only sang once," I said softly, glancing at the high ceiling. Even whispers echoed, amplified.

"I know…" He sighed sympathetically, his eyes a murky purple tinged with rose at the edges. "It was a terrible shame it happened the way it did." He gestured to the room, "But you should take the time to try it while you're here, at least. It's not like anyone can stumble in, and there's tons of water to separate you from human ears."

I nodded, though I doubted I would. Singing, as with all siren activities, was a sour notion to me. A new question sprang to my lips, "But, Score, if they didn't worry about humans, why doesn't the sound travel beyond the chamber?"

Score stared at his feet, looking uncomfortable. "Because, Lyra… Singing is… It's *personal*. Really personal."

"What do you mean?" My own experience was so limited, I mainly remembered the horror that followed my song. But what I *did* remember of the actual singing was spot-on with what he'd described. It felt like I'd been draining the hurts of my day, replacing them with contentment.

He leaned his head back, "When you first heard me in Whitecrest, before that ridiculous double date…" His eyes met mine, "Do you remember how panicked I was?"

"Yeah," I said, "but I figured you were worried I was one of your parents, maybe, or—"

Score shook his head, "No, no. I knew it was you, Lyra. I did a quick sealing spell— I *always* do when I sing. You were the only person who could've entered the house, and even that— it seemed weird to lock you out. I'd *never* have risked my parents or anyone else."

"Then why were you worried?" I asked. "Unless you thought it might harm me, too?"

"No. Nothing like that." Score took a deep breath, leaning against the stage next to me. "I was a little concerned because of how profoundly intimate it made things. It was *embarrassing*. I was pouring my heart out, every emotion, how I was feeling—" he paused, staring into my eyes. "*Especially* how I was feeling for you. The relief, the hope, the gratitude that there was someone else like me out there— all of it was there, and— and even more. And I was letting it go, but you walked into it, right at the apex. So… it freaked me out a little. But then I guess I realized you couldn't understand the language anyway, and maybe it'd be okay."

I shrugged, leaning back into the stage next to him, crossing my ankles. "I honestly had no idea *what* you were singing about."

"It's good to know these are here," Score said thoughtfully.

I glanced around the room dubiously. Even in a hundred years, I couldn't imagine wanting to repeat my singing experience. Chances were, these rooms would mostly collect dust.

I grabbed his hand, needing to escape from the little room. All of Atlantis was built for sirens, but this, more than anything else, reminded me of what I was. I tugged on him, "Come on! We've hardly seen anything!"

He laughed, tumbling with me from the chamber into the hallway.

We continued to explore, following the meandering pathways. Score gestured to the right and left, pointing out the different rooms. Each faction had their own ideas of recreation— the Nightingales had tiny spaces crafted for meditation, the Larks small study chambers. There were also opulent temples in every faction space. Score told me they were dedicated to the devotion of the Nine Muses.

We wandered the residential half until we reached a far off corner with a double curtain. It was silver and shimmery. There was no marker next to it. I gestured, "What's in there?"

Score shrugged, "I have no idea."

"But you have all the answers!" I protested.

He just chuckled, staring down at his feet. "I don't. Like I said: I know what I've read, what I've seen, and what I've researched." He glanced at the curtain, "But there's one way to find out, right?"

He swept the fabric aside. My heart leapt into my throat.

The room was tiny— minuscule, even. It formed a small offshoot of Atlantis's main dome, a bay. The curved exterior wall filled the room with light and placed the ocean in full view. I watched fish glide near the glass. A shark loomed further back.

Beneath my feet was the same thick springy grass that covered the arena. The lawn expanded about two yards before meeting a huge stone slab, set like a stage. Flowers bloomed everywhere, crawling on trellises along the wall. Some of the blooms glowed. The room had a fragrance, thick and heady. It wasn't floral, but it was sweet. I bit my lip, trying to place it.

At the very back of the room, just beyond the slab of stone, was a large silver plaque inscribed with siren lettering.

I padded over, curious.

The Joining

I join my life to her
I join my life to him
From the ocean's depths,
To the sun's flames,
We'll sing together.
In a single moment,
Or a millennium,
We'll sing together.
For my heart sings for her
For my heart sings for him
We are one, soul and body
Joined.

I flushed. The room's purpose was suddenly obvious. I swallowed thickly, petrified.

Score cleared his throat, sounding uncomfortable, "It's a place to get married."

I nodded, keeping my head down, making a beeline for the curtain. I needed to leave the stuffy room. The perfumed air felt dangerous now.

I rounded the corner, leaning against the wall and taking a few deep, soothing breaths. Score wasn't far behind me, but he gave me a few moments before he said anything.

It could've been a loaded moment. After all, this was obviously what our parents had in mind for us. Arrive in Atlantis, marry— or join, or whatever— and have children immediately, saving the species.

Mercifully, Score instead said, "So... I wonder what's in the rest of the industrial half?"

I smiled gratefully at him. "I don't know. I've only seen the library. You haven't been anywhere else?"

"No, same as you."

"Well, let's find out," I said, thankful for the reprieve. I pushed away from the wall, moving from the shimmery silver curtains.

The industrial side was quite a distance from the residential, especially from the tucked away corner of the joining room. Our silence was awkward— abnormal for Score and me.

I blamed it on expectations, personally. But the longer we walked, the more I felt like one of us should be speaking to the other. Finally, after what felt like an eternity, Score sputtered, "Did you know a day on Mercury is longer than its year?"

I blinked, looking at him. It was the most random thing I'd ever heard. I started to laugh, bringing my hand up to cover my mouth.

He blushed, his eyes turning a peachy color. He stared at the ground, groaning, "I'm— forget I said that, will you?"

I giggled, pushing lightly against his shoulder, "Dork."

Score squeezed his eyes shut, his face turning even brighter red. He looked so anxious and uncomfortable, I wondered if that sandwich was going to make a reappearance. I shook my head. What would I do with him?

I grabbed his wrist, tugging him back to me. He cracked his eyes open— they were still that mortified salmon color. "I didn't mean to upset you. It was an interesting fact, just a little random." I changed the subject, "So, earlier, you were running. I didn't know you were into that. Or are you? I don't know, I guess, I just— do you run?"

His eyes relaxed back into rose pink, though he walked with his head down. "Yeah. I started running a long time ago. When I was around eight."

My brows lifted, "So young?"

He reached a hand out, sliding his index finger along the glass wall as we moved. Score nodded, "Had to. I'm lucky I enjoyed it."

"You *had* to?"

He took a breath. "I was picked on a lot in school when I was a kid. I was always the smallest guy in class— at least until I turned. And... and I guess I'm *weird*. I like studying. I like books. I like learning new things..." He groaned, "I like random facts."

I laughed, then the realization hit me hard in the chest. Score had been called names before— and worse, probably. No wonder he'd seemed so embarrassed. I chewed my cheek, "Score, I— when I called you a dork..." He turned his gaze to me, his eyes questioning. He looked like he was going to be sick. I sighed, wrapping my arms around him. I gave him a quick, tight squeeze. "I meant it in the nicest way," I finished. "So I'm sorry if it hurt you."

"You don't have to apologize, Lyra. I'm fine. I'm—"

I grinned, cutting him off, "Hey, we made it!"

I gestured to a white curtain, the first one on this half of Atlantis.

My fingertips ran over the little plaque of siren lettering, labeled *Workshop*. I pushed aside the white curtain, stepping inside.

The scent of sawdust greeted me. My breath caught.

Instruments. Hundreds of instruments, all in different stages of completion. None were finished. There were twelve large workbenches with supplies, and a gargantuan wall of wood and crafting materials.

I stepped forward, picking up a half-finished mandolin. The strings hadn't been placed on it yet, and it wasn't stained, but the instrument was beginning to be carved into an attractive and balanced form. There wasn't a faction symbol or name on it yet.

It didn't belong to anyone.

Score was next to me, "This is impressive. Songsmith work."

I nodded, replacing the mandolin on the bench. "I wonder if we could finish any of these," I said wistfully. It seemed like such a waste.

Next to me was a nearly finished violin. The spaces were carved with flowers and vines, but there were a couple large empty sections as well. One bare space on the side, and another larger section on the back. It hadn't been stained yet, but the strings were already placed— probably for testing purposes.

A bow rested next to it. Curious, I held it carefully in one hand, running my thumbnail sideways across the hair. A soft puff of rosin was barely visible for a single moment. Smiling, I picked up the instrument, propping it beneath my chin. I drew the bow across the strings.

The sound quality was so beautiful that it made my knees weak.

Score tilted his head to me, looking surprised.

I replaced the instrument on the bench, "What?"

"It's just… that was very *siren* of you, to test it out."

I blushed, "I was just— it was—"

"No, I understand," he said, pulling the violin to his own

chin, playing a quick melody. It was only seven notes, but it made my heart catch in my throat.

I missed music more than I'd let myself know.

He gingerly set the instrument and bow down on the workbench. "I doubt I'd know where to start to complete any of these. I suppose if I really had a hundred years of study, *maybe* I could figure it out. But I have no intention of trying now."

I rapped my fingers on the table, "It's too bad. They're beautiful. And that sound…" I closed my eyes, remembering it.

"You can have that sound again, Lyra," Score stated. "Not everything about being a siren is awful. Some things are pretty great."

Did he mean us? Or something else? With my eyes closed, I couldn't guess what he was feeling at this moment. I cracked them open slowly, my heartbeat beginning to quicken.

He was turned away from me, looking thoughtfully at the violin with one hand against his chin.

I felt the familiar tug of longing in my core as I stared at him. I needed to leave. I couldn't trust myself here, now— not with him.

"Thank you for the evening, Score. I'm tired, I think I'll head to bed."

"Oh… okay." He looked at me, "Can we really spend the evening together tomorrow, too?"

I should've said no. It was the safer response. But at that moment, he looked so hopeful that I just sighed, "Yeah… of course we can. I'll see you tomorrow night."

Chapter Twenty-Four

Strength

Sometime in the night after we parted ways, I made a decision.

If Score was going to be productive, if he was going to research and find a way out of Atlantis, I'd do my best to keep busy too. I'd train until I became strong, fast, and self-reliant. It seemed like a much better use of my time than sitting around or exploring Atlantis.

I hoped we wouldn't be stuck here for the full century. If we could make it out, building my strength was in my best interest.

The next morning, I pulled on some cotton yoga pants and a tank top, then made my way to the kitchen for a light breakfast. When I was finished, I headed to the fitness arena.

The scope and size of it was still dizzying, but I walked to the far corner where the weapons were laid out. I chose the purple Nightingale sword, entering a basic stance. I tried to remember all the points about form Birkita had barked at me— keep my core tight, make sure I was balanced on the balls of my feet, hold the sword with authority— but none of it would matter without a sparring partner.

I sighed, replacing the beautiful purple blade on the wall. I turned to the armor, considering it.

There were five sets for women— the rest were obviously for men. Each one was made of a different material. I was too petite for most of them, but there was an indigo leather set that looked like it'd suit me. I heaved the breast plate from the mannequin, lacing it across my body. Snug, but not constricting. I systematically removed the boots, greaves, gloves, and so on from the dummy, until I'd successfully stripped it. I slipped the armor over my own appendages. It was more comfortable than I'd been expecting— I could move fairly easily, despite the additional weight.

Near the now naked dummy, glinting, was a small plaque on the wall.

Song and intention summon opponents
The greatest challenge is yourself
Muses bless those who must fight

I raised my brows.

Song and intention sounded like our alteration magic. It hadn't occurred to me to sing in this space.

I pulled the sword from the wall again, swinging it absently in one hand, listening to it whistle.

I *didn't* sing, but humming was usually enough to activate magic. I doubted anything here would truly harm me. I hummed three notes.

She stepped from my body like a ghost. It was *me*— identical in every way except one: her eyes were completely black with no iris or whites. She even wore the same indigo armor I did, carried the same sword. I leaned forward, squinting at this near-perfect copy of myself.

She didn't give me time to study her. A snarl escaped her lips, and my double lunged forward, swinging her sword down hard into my shoulder.

I cringed as the metal bit into my flesh. It burned as she drug it through my muscle tissue.

I glanced at my wounded shoulder, expecting torn leather and oozing blood. Instead, the armor was completely intact. The ache was beginning to diffuse, though I still felt prickles of pain throbbing down my arm. Apparently, my doppelgänger's blows hurt but did no actual damage.

She jabbed her sword forward. This time I darted to the side, rolling out of the way. My heart quickened as she lunged again.

Search for a weakness, I reminded myself.

232

My eyes scoured her form. I ducked to the left, avoiding an arcing swing of her blade. I tried to watch her balance and movement as I avoided the attacks. What was her weakness?

She grunted, swinging for me.

She was too aggressive— too offensive. She left herself undefended in almost every possible way.

I let my legs drop from beneath me as the sword whistled horizontally through the air— where my head had been a second before. I pushed forward, catching her in the gut with the hilt of my blade.

She fell on her butt, her legs splaying out for a moment. That moment was all I needed. I slashed her abdomen. She let out a cry, enraged, and sprang to her feet. She brought the blade up high above her head with both hands.

I thrust, burying the sword into her chest clear to the hilt. She stopped moving, frozen.

I'd won the battle.

As I jerked the sword from the double, she vanished in an explosion of dust. The blade was clean; she hadn't bled. A trickle of sweat dripped down my neck.

"That was good," I said aloud, humming to summon a new opponent. "But this time, show some defense. Again."

The new doppelgänger didn't hesitate. With a snarl, she jumped forward, slashing at my belly.

I hopped back, narrowly avoiding the blade. The double eyed me warily. We circled each other.

I lunged forward, swinging my sword towards her gut. She batted it away almost carelessly, following it with a riposte. The blade caught my left cheek, making my eye water and sinuses burn. I hissed through my teeth, jerking hard to the right.

She moved much more confidently than the previous doppelgänger had. We continued to circle each other. I took a breath. While I'd wanted her to be more defensive, I didn't want the challenge to be impossible.

I glanced down. Maybe her footwork would give me a clue as to how to continue.

The moment I moved my eyes from her face, she grunted, charging me. I panicked, lurching blindly away from her.

Crack! Pain exploded behind my eyes in a red-hot wave. Blood trickled down my brow bone and across the bridge of my nose. I grunted, pushing away from whatever I'd crashed into. Prying my eyes open, I saw what had thwarted my escape: one of the armored dummies.

I sucked in a hard, snorting breath. A thick layer of blood drizzled down my throat. I placed a hand to my forehead, trying to get my bearings.

Pausing was a mistake.

Slash! I barely saw the flash of purple blade as it dug through my arm into the shoulder joint. A wave of nausea pulled from my stomach— I couldn't feel my arm anymore.

I took a stumbling, disjointed step backward, glancing to my ruined arm. Relief shuddered through me. Like the previous blows struck by my double, the blade had not left any physical damage. Nevertheless, the limb was useless to me now, swinging numbly at my side.

The double screeched.

What did I get myself into?

Panicking, I grappled for one of the other weapons on the wall— a chakrum. I threw it in desperation, running in the opposite direction and clutching my ruined arm.

An agonized sound wrenched my gaze to the double. Miraculously, the disc-like blade I'd thrown had struck her in the neck. She fell to her knees, taking gurgling breaths.

I swallowed bile and blood, swiping at my forehead. A wave of pins and needles hit my numbed arm as fresh sensation hit the nerves. I took a deep, relieved breath. I slumped against the wall, spitting bloody saliva onto the grass.

"Okay," I breathed. I moved to the frozen double and grasped the chakrum, tugging it from her neck. Like her predecessor, she exploded into dust. I turned back, replacing the blade on the wall. "That was… interesting. Let's try again, but maybe a little less intense." I swiped my sweaty palm across my thigh as I hummed, "Again."

~~~~~~~~~~~~~~~~~

My training had gone well, and I was happy I'd decided to treat this as my job. When I nearly couldn't stand, I shuffled back to my room, exhausted. I settled into the bathtub to soothe my aching muscles. I wondered if I could find an icepack somewhere— my back was killing me.

I hauled myself from the soft water, glancing in the mirror. My eye had begun to swell from my dive into the mannequin, and a dark and shiny bruise was beginning to surface.

But compared to Birkita's training, it'd been a walk in the park.

I slipped one of the pretty dresses over my head, glancing at the clock on the wall. I was supposed to meet with Score in less than five minutes.

I wound my way through the halls as quickly as my aching legs would carry me, entering the kitchen.

Score was already there. He looked tired, his head propped up in his hands. His gaze met mine when I entered. Concern immediately clouded his features, turning his pink eyes to forest green. "Lyra, what happened to you?" he asked, bringing one hand to cup my face.

I pushed him away. "It's nothing."

His brows furrowed, "You never remember to heal yourself." He reached up again, "Here, I can—"

I caught his hand, shaking my head. "I earned this Score. And I don't want to take the easy way out."

He eyed me suspiciously, "*How* did you earn it?"

"Just doing some training. Some swordplay," I said innocently. "It's not like anyone ever died of a black eye."

"I don't want you hurting yourself."

"Calm down, Score." I rolled my eyes, "It's not dangerous. I'm in *Atlantis*. What could possibly harm me here?"

His mouth puckered a little more. He looked conflicted, but after a few moments he sighed, nodding, "Yeah… I guess so. But maybe you should take up a new hobby tomorrow."

"You have your job; I have mine."

"But you don't *have* to do this."

"Maybe not. But I *want* to. I want to be strong and self-reliant. When we get out of here, I want to take care of myself."

Score stared into his hands, taking several breaths. "Okay. Will you at least promise to stop if it gets out of hand?"

"Yeah." I shifted my weight awkwardly, "What did you want to do tonight?"

He shrugged. "I did a little bit of exploring today at lunch. I found the Bard's old chambers. It was really interesting. Want to check it out?"

I sighed, feeling indifferent. I turned to the little machine, requesting a bowl of potato soup. I didn't care about the stuffy siren queen. On the other hand, I didn't have any better ideas.

"Like, her bedroom?" I asked.

"Yeah. Bedroom, bathroom, living room. It's a good sized space, considering only two people lived there."

"I don't know, Score, that sounds—"

"It's interesting, I promise! I mean—" he turned slightly pink. "I think it's interesting, anyway." He sighed, "It's probably stupid. Forget it."

His eyes were a disappointed violet. I rubbed my forehead tiredly, shoving a spoonful of the thick soup into my mouth. An explosion of flavor hit my tongue, making me moan. If there was anything I'd actually miss about Atlantis when we finally escaped, it would be the food.

Score was just trying to make our time fun. That was obvious. I took another swallow of soup. "So... her *bedroom*?" I asked in a teasing tone, "You aren't trying to seduce me, are you?"

His mouth twitched, "Perish the thought."

I continued to eat, studying his eyes. Rose pink had made its way into the orbs now, but the centers were a piercing honest blue.

"Alright, I'm up for it." I scraped the sides of the bowl. When every drop of the delicious soup was gone, I stood and dumped the dish into the recycling receptacle.

Score smiled, brushing his fingers against mine. I flinched from his touch, jerking my hand away. After yesterday's exploration, I needed to be extra vigilant in my resistance to our magical connection. He pulled from me hastily. His eyes revealed his disappointment though his face remained neutral.

I cleared my throat, following him through the door, "So... make any headway?"

He shrugged, keeping his gaze forward. "I'm still narrowing it down. But I'm going to do my best. If it exists, I'll find it." He scratched the back of his neck. "The problem is I'm still a novice. And my father's spell was advanced."

I sighed. It felt like he was making excuses. But I had little to complain about— it wasn't like I was helping Score in his pursuit. "So you're just out-classed?"

"At the moment, yeah." He grinned, glancing into my eyes, "But don't worry, Lyra. I'm a quick study. I'll figure it out."

He said it with such conviction, I couldn't help but believe him. I smiled shyly, glancing at my feet. "I really appreciate it, Score."

"Well," he said, "it's not like the lock-down doesn't affect me, too." He gestured in front of himself, "We're here."

Double curtains in blood red broke up the glass wall. There wasn't another door for quite a distance in either direction. I eyed the little plaque.

Bard Shiri & her Consort Jaren

Score hefted the curtain aside, waving me in. "After you."

I stepped through. Though it was opulent, it didn't seem special. My room was just as nice, but smaller. Shiri's quarters were larger than the other bedrooms, but not as enormous as the library.

Closest to the door was a seating area with several crimson couches and chairs. They were all decorated with thick plush pillows. Behind the largest couch loomed an ivory bookshelf.

To the right, a small round table set with a golden cloth provided an intimate area to take meals or have a discussion. Two well-worn high backed chairs faced each other as if they were old friends. It was probably the most charming part of the space.

A further corner housed a large wooden desk. Though kept tidily, it was cluttered with neat stacks of paper, rolls of parchment, small knickknacks, and a few quills.

A gauzy black curtain separated the remaining space, obscuring about a third of the room from view.

I laced my fingers together. While the room was pretty, it wasn't interesting. "So… this is it?" I asked.

Score grinned, grabbing my hand, "Don't look so dour. As they say, the devil is in the details." He gestured to one wall, broken by a silver doorway framed in gold. "For example: A door."

I rolled my eyes, "So?"

"So? *So?*" He raised a brow, "Lyra, how many doors have you *seen* in Atlantis?"

It hadn't seemed unnatural to me before, but now that he mentioned it, he was right. The hinges and frame were all shiny gold, but the door itself was silver. It looked out of place on the glass wall. I wracked my brain. I couldn't recall a single instance of another door in all of Atlantis. Every entryway was covered by a curtain.

I gripped the knob, feeling almost nervous. "What's inside?"

"Open it."

I twisted the handle, jerking the door open. My heart sank. "The bathroom?"

"Weird, right?"

"She probably just valued privacy," I pouted.

Score laughed, "It's *weird* because every other bathroom is only covered by a curtain. Shiri may have valued privacy, but only her own." He leaned against the wall, "There are stories everywhere in this room."

"What kind of stories?"

"Well," he said thoughtfully, leading me to the bookshelf behind the couches, "For example, this." He pointed to the top shelf. It was completely crammed full of books bound in dark green. He tugged out one of the tomes, dropping it into my arms.

It felt like a brick. I stared at the cover. The writing was cryptic and unknown to me. I looked into Score's eyes, "So Shiri spoke multiple languages?"

"That's not just any language, Lyra. That's Ancient Siren."

My brows furrowed as I studied the shapes. The writing was square and blocky, cumbersome. It did not remind me of the delicate, scrolling script I'd been attuned to read. I puckered my lips, flipping the pages. The lettering was consistently foreign, bold, and ugly. I wrinkled my nose, "How did our language evolve from *that*?"

"It didn't." He took the enormous book from my arms, sliding it back onto the shelf, "In fact, when I asked Forte about it he said that Ancient Siren stopped being used entirely 4,000 years ago, though it had been declining for longer. Shiri outlawed its use 2,000 years ago. Our current Siren doesn't have etymological roots in the old tongue— they have entirely different evolutionary trees."

I stared at him.

He blushed, "I mean— um, Ancient Siren and current Siren

don't have the same origins. They're completely different languages. That's all."

I smiled, squatting before the shelf. The entirety of the top row was full of the stuffy old writing, but the bottom was more friendly. Two bookends shaped like stars propped up a line of small tomes bound in a rainbow of colors. I tugged one out. *Musings* splashed across the cover in current Siren.

I grinned as I flipped it. "It's poetry," I whispered. Most siren books were crowded with music, but this was simply words. I traced the lettering. Though there was no melody, the rhythm was pleasant.

"Those weren't Shiri's," Score informed me.

"Then whose were they?"

He pointed to the inner cover. A handwritten note adorned it:

To my darling Jaren: may you never lose the poetry of your soul ~ Shiri

I'd almost forgotten that the room didn't belong exclusively to the Bard.

"Shiri tended to favor the practical. The other books are all technical." He helped me to my feet. "She was a little peculiar."

I shook my head, "That seems awfully judgmental, Score. I mean, just because she preferred to read things that were more—"

"That's not all," he said, interrupting me. He tugged the black shroud away from the remainder of the room. My brows raised. Score grinned, taking in my expression, "See? Peculiar."

It was her bedroom, essentially. But it wasn't exactly conventional. I glanced into his eyes, "Three beds?"

He nodded, "Yeah. I have no idea why she would need so many."

I stepped into the chamber. Not only were there three, but each bed was distinct. I pressed my hand against them. The largest bed was an over-sized four poster in a wine shade that was hard as a rock. The smallest looked more like a day bed, but the mattress was softer than the first, and the blankets were white. The third was queen size, adorned in black, and so soft my palm sank deep within the blankets when I leaned against it.

Did Shiri have a Goldilocks complex or something?

Another curtain broke up the wall in this section of the room, drawing my eye. It looked like spun gold. "What's through there?" I asked.

"What Birkita was hoping we'd find." He grinned, tugging the curtain open. "The wealth of a nation."

The flimsy cloth was all that separated us from a stockpile of jewels, antiques, and gold coins of all sizes. The room was on the smaller size for Atlantis, but it was piled high. The stacks were well above my head, glittering in the soft light.

I picked up an emerald the size of a basketball, holding it in front of myself. It distorted Score, multiplying him through the facets.

I replaced the jewel, looking into his eyes. Score's were a tiny bit turquoise, but mostly rose pink. He was excited to show me this room. I sighed, "Even if we could leave, there's no way we could take this with us. It probably weighs tons."

Score leaned against the wall, rolling his eyes, "I doubt very much that two lessons that left you *injured* are worth even the smallest bit of this wealth, let alone the whole thing. She'd have to be satisfied with a necklace or something."

"There's a fortune here," I said, squatting in front of the treasure pile. A glittering tiara caught my eye. I pulled it into the light, studying it. "I can't believe it's so open. It should be in a safe or something."

Score shrugged, "It's not like the sirens were going to steal from their own Bard. Besides, what was valuable to Shiri wasn't in this room."

"If not here, then where?"

He grinned, tugging on my hands and sprinting. I laughed in spite of myself. Score's enthusiasm was infectious. He led me to the bathroom door, tugging it open and gesturing to a vanity.

I glanced at him, deflating. Going into a bathroom wasn't exactly thrilling. "Score, this is—"

"This is where Shiri kept what she valued." He tugged open the drawer of the vanity, holding up a little white compact.

I raised a brow, "What's that supposed to be?"

"This is a mix of talc and pigmentation. It's makeup."

"So?"

He laughed, "So she was vain enough to wear makeup,

even though she had siren genetics. She applied it privately, probably so that no one knew she wore it."

He pointed to the top of the vanity. A cracked hand mirror sat next to an opal comb and an intricate key made of the same precious gem. The key drew my eye.

I picked it up, turning it in my hand. The teeth curved gently like notes on a staff. A treble and bass clef formed a heart shaped handle. The tiniest current hummed beneath my fingertips as I held it, recalling the echo of a song in my mind. I shivered, "Are these all magic?"

"Maybe," Score said. "Or maybe just sentimental." He gestured to the looking glass, "What type of woman hangs onto a broken mirror?"

I set the key back on the table top, staring into his eyes. "What kind of woman traps two people?"

He shrugged, returning my gaze. His eyes shifted to a sympathetic murky purple, "A desperate one."

It sounded almost like Score forgave her. Or maybe he was just more levelheaded than me.

I was sick of dwelling on the dead.

"I'm tired. I have to train tomorrow."

He sighed, nodding. "Okay. Goodnight, Lyra."

"Goodnight, Score."

~~~~~~~~~~~~~

A few weeks into training, I could already see physical results from my efforts. Along my arms, my biceps were slightly more defined. They popped out just a little when I swung my sword.

I'd been training hard. Today I trained harder.

Sweat trickled into my eyes. I grunted, stabbing at the double in front of me, plunging a blade into her belly.

Desperately, she arced her own sword up.

Clang!

My second sword blocked her first.

I grinned, parrying the blow. The additional blade was a good choice, though I'd been nervous when I'd first pulled the red short sword from the wall. I'd been using it the past week, and found my instincts to be more in line with the second weapon than a shield.

I was in a foul mood. I wanted this to be painful, though I doubted my double felt anything.

I thrust my foot out, lashing across her chest. The doppelgänger fell to the ground with her arms splayed.

I stood over her, pinning her wrists beneath my feet. I squeezed my eyes shut, panting. With a shriek, I jammed both blades down in a cross, severing her head from shoulders.

I waited until I felt her dissolve into dust under my feet before I opened my eyes.

I may have wanted to cause her pain, I may have wanted to lash out, I may have been in a foul mood— but I didn't want to see a decapitation.

"That was brutal," a voice called to me.

I turned, swiping at the hair plastered to my heated face.

Score stood with his arms folded in front of his chest, about twenty feet from me.

"What are you doing here?" I asked.

He gestured to himself. He was wearing a tank top and shorts. "I was going to go for a run."

"I thought you were researching?" I said with a frown.

"I was," he agreed. He ran a hand through his hair, "But I was going around in circles. I needed to clear my head. Runs usually help."

I sighed, snapping my long Nightingale blade into my scabbard. I wasn't sure why, but I balked at letting him watch me train. I slid my second weapon into its sheath, striding to the rack.

"Don't stop on my account."

I shook my head, glaring as I jammed the swords into their proper rack.

"Is it me? Did I say something?" he asked.

I rolled my eyes, tugging impatiently at the laces on my leather armor.

"Lyra, I can see in your eyes that—"

"It isn't you!" I snapped.

His brows furrowed, "Then what's wrong?"

I shook my head, bending to unlace my greaves. When I'd removed them, I balanced carefully, rolling my ankles to coax blood flow back into my legs. I took two deep breaths, letting them out slowly.

242

"I'm not angry with you," I said again.

"But you *are* angry?" he pried gently.

I strode towards him. "I'm angry at myself." I shook my head. Anger wasn't quite the right word. I sighed, folding my arms across my chest. I stared at the grass beneath my feet. "I just hate that I'm a liar."

"But you're not—"

"It's after the New Year. We've been in Atlantis for 32 days."

He let out a soft sound. "I— I hadn't realized it's been that long."

I shrugged, trying to let the emotion roll off my back. "The days bleed together here." I glanced into his eyes. Forest green had obscured most of the usual pink. "It's hard to mark the time without weekends." I tipped my head back, feeling miserable.

The days may have been a blur in Atlantis, but I knew that for Glenn the time passed slowly. I wondered how disappointed he was with me. I wondered if he would remain patient.

Grief settled into my bones, and I sobbed harshly. I raised a fist to my face, keeping my head down. I didn't want to cry in front of Score, least of all over this.

"Lyra…"

"Just leave me alone!"

But he didn't. Instead, within ten seconds, he pulled me against his chest. "I'm sorry," he murmured.

I shook my head, crying against him. "I hate it here."

"I'll skip my run," he offered. "I can work late tonight— I— I'll find the way, Lyra. I'll find it. I promise you: I'll find it."

I took a breath, collecting myself. I pulled away from him, "No. You should run. I need to go shower."

He gripped my shoulders, staring into my eyes. "I'm going to grab lunch— something quick— and take it back to the library with me. And you're not going to worry. I'll find the answer, Lyra. I *will*. And you'll be back home before you know it. And you'll see Glenn again. I promise."

I nodded, feeling numb and grateful. He turned from me, striding towards the exit of the arena.

"Score?" I called.

He paused, turning his head to me.

"I—" I took a breath. "I'll see you tonight, right? For

dinner?"

He smiled, just a bit. "If you still want to."

"I do."

He nodded, "Alright. See you then."

Chapter Twenty-Five

Play

Despite Score's best intentions, we still hadn't discovered a way out by May.

During that time, I'd grown substantially in my sword play. I was getting faster, more nimble, more adept with the swords with each passing day. Working with my double on my own had been exactly what I needed— not so brutal as Birkita's training, but more challenging than Glenn's.

Over the past months I'd experimented with adding additional opponents. I hummed twice during my practice, requesting a second double to work in tandem with the first, or sometimes a third. It was harder— exponentially so— but I was learning to divide my attention between them effectively.

I'd still taken a fair share of beatings. I seemed to emerge from my training each day with new bruises or scrapes. Most of my pain was the good, deep ache of tired muscles working to build themselves. Though I'd shattered my promise to Glenn, I had yet to break the one I'd made to Score: none of my injuries were serious.

The work felt productive— even if it might have been pointless.

I was in good spirits today. I tugged a clean tee over my head, shimmying into a pair of jeans.

I'd flawlessly defeated my opponents in seven battles today— even when I requested to increase the difficulty. I was on form. I felt good about what I was achieving. Maybe soon, I'd move on to a fourth sparring partner.

I took a few deep breaths, checking the clock. 5:17 p.m.— I was running late to meet Score for dinner. I smiled, tying my hair back with a silver cord as I jogged down the hall. Things had been going well with him. I enjoyed our time together, entering into an easy friendship.

Too easy...

I quashed the thought down. I was aware of my connection to him, and I had it under complete control. I'd go insane if I tried to isolate myself from him. Atlantis would be far too lonely.

For his part, Score surprised me. When we were in Whitecrest, he was always confident to the point of brash. He slipped into social scenarios so easily, commanding every situation. Since we'd been here, I'd seen a different side of him.

He was filled with more determination than I'd ever seen, all to find the answers we needed to escape this place. Not only that, but he was quieter than he'd been on the surface. Occasionally, he'd come from the library bursting with excitement, so thrilled he'd discovered something new and interesting. His breakthroughs were almost always over my head. Half the time, I'd just grin and say, "And that's cool?" Score would always laugh, nod, and respond with something like, "*Way* cool."

Sometimes, when we were wandering around, he'd surprise me by pointing out things around us and mention a new fact. Score told me that the light glowing from the glass around Atlantis was a special frequency that was antibiotic. The light also kept the glass free of algae and prevented anything from growing on its surface.

Once I'd wondered aloud how it was so warm here. Score just got really excited and told me Atlantis wasn't just powered by magic. The warmth I felt every day beneath my bare feet was caused by the electricity the city generated through harnessing the tidal power.

Almost any question that left my lips— even if I just pondered it on a whim— could be answered by him. I wasn't sure where he kept all the information. His mind seemed to store it infinitely. Most of the time, I felt like whenever *I* learned a new fact, an older piece of knowledge slipped out of my skull to make room. Not him, though. He was easily the smartest person I'd met in my entire life.

I rounded the corner of the kitchen, nodding at Score,

"Sorry I'm late."

He smiled, continuing to eat his steak. He closed the open book before him.

"You're not still working, are you?" I asked, quickly requesting a plate of pasta and some water. The machine toned. I pulled out the meal. It was hot, fresh, and certainly delicious.

"No," Score said, shaking his head. "This is just for fun, that's all." He pushed the volume aside. I stared at it curiously, taking a bite of my dinner.

My fingers found the edges of the book, flipping it open. It was page after page of siren music, all written in the strange round way we'd seen at the Firmament Chamber. I closed the cover, disinterested. I took a sip of water, pushing the book away from me.

"So," I asked cheerfully, "what did you want to do this evening? We could hike, or maybe swim, or—"

"Actually," he interrupted, "I was hoping today we could maybe… play a little?"

"What do you mean?"

"Just…" He chewed his lower lip, "Have fun. Let loose?"

"Score…" I sighed, finishing my plate.

"Will you just *humor* me, Lyra?"

I leaned against my fist, frowning.

Score put a look on his face. It was the same expression he'd used when he'd asked me to attend his house party in Whitecrest. Huge, dramatic puppy dog eyes, his mouth twitching just a little to let me know it wasn't serious.

I laughed, shaking my head, "Okay, okay!" My stomach turned a little, "We're not singing, are we?"

He shook his head, grabbing my hand, "No, Lyra. I told you, that's really personal. I'd never, *ever*, push you into that."

My stomach relaxed. I nodded, "Then, okay. We can play… Whatever that means."

Score grinned, pulling me to my feet. We walked side-by-side through the hall, towards the industrial half.

I tilted my head, giving him a curious look.

He just laughed. "Patience! It'll be fun."

I shrugged, clasping my hands together. We walked steadily onward. I wondered where he was leading me, but in the grand scheme of things I didn't know much about this half of

Atlantis. In general, I'd avoided coming over here if possible—mostly because of Forte.

Finally, after several twists and turns, Score paused at a white curtain. He rushed to the side, propping himself against the silver plaque next to it. "So, here we are." I tilted my head, grabbing his shoulders to push him aside and reveal the label. Score dug his heels in stubbornly, leaning back, laughing. "Go inside!"

I shrugged, pulling back the curtain.

Set before me was a large stage, hundreds of instruments on it, all beautiful and polished. There wasn't much space for an audience— maybe about ten chairs— but it looked comfortable.

"Are you putting on a show?" I asked, my mouth twitching in amusement.

Score grinned, "No, Lyra. I told you, I just want us to let loose. That's all."

"I don't understand."

"Come on," he laughed, grabbing my hand and tugging me down the short decline, then up the stairs to the stage. As we stood, I shifted my weight awkwardly, surveying my surroundings.

Every conceivable instrument I could imagine, all pristine, laid about me. They weren't as decorated as my dulcimer, but a glance told me each was as perfectly crafted. Songsmith work.

"So...?" I began, "What *are* we doing?"

"Playing," he said again. He began to tap his foot, creating a short, quick staccato rhythm.

I folded my arms across my chest.

He spun around, standing before a drum. He added a new beat, complicating it, then looked at me expectantly. I twisted my fingers together, unsure. Score laughed, urging, "Come on!"

"What do you want me to do?" I asked. A smile crept onto my features in spite of myself.

"Add something! *Anything!* Make it better."

I chewed my lip, my heart racing. I nodded, grabbing the first instrument I saw— a harp. I added a quick, fun melody to the rhythm.

Score was up like a flash, still tapping his feet to keep the beat. He sat before a piano. His fingers danced across the keys, weaving a new harmony to our session.

I laughed, whirling. I brushed my hands across a set of

chimes, punctuating the melody at just the right moment.

The song was living, breathing, created from thin air. We used probably half the instruments, giving each a few moments to shine before we grappled for a new one.

I twirled and whirled and laughed. I let my body move more on instinct than on conscious thought. It was enthralling— a dance between us. I was surprised I was having so much fun with music. It was *freeing*.

Score was right; we were playing. This was a game— one part skill, one part luck, and a hundred parts anticipating each other's choices and movements. Perhaps, if it'd been anyone else but Score— even another siren— it would've been more difficult to create something so lovely from nothing. But we were made to know each other down to the bone. I had to admit this wasn't something I'd expected.

I spun around again, laughing, bumping directly into Score. I stood with my hands against his chest, panting lightly. He watched me with rose colored eyes and a soft smile across his lips.

"I wish…" he began. The words faded out. He sighed, turning from me.

"I'm surprised how much I enjoyed that," I admitted.

"Why?" he asked, folding his arms around his chest. He looked thoughtful, staring out at an empty audience.

I shrugged, sitting at the edge of the stage. I leaned back into my palms, swinging my legs. "It's just— I didn't realize music could feel like that."

He sighed again, settling next to me. His eyes were tinged with a bit of sad blue gray. It was strange he'd look so forlorn after that. He should feel happy, invigorated, *alive*.

"What is it Score? What do you wish?"

He turned his gaze to me. "It's just… You hardly ever give yourself permission to be happy. You're always punishing yourself. I wish you were more open to siren experiences. They aren't *all* bad. But you had the unfortunate luck of having a terrible transition." He turned back to face the empty chairs, "I feel bad for you, Lyra."

I frowned, looking down at my feet. "You shouldn't. Unless you feel bad about us being trapped here. If that's the case, you should feel just as bad for yourself."

"What we did just now, that's—" he sighed, "that's really

nothing, in the scheme of things." He slid off the stage, landing lightly on his feet. He turned from me, "Thanks for indulging me. I'm calling it a night."

Score was never the first to say goodnight. I felt a little bad about it. I shook my head, trying to clear it. "Goodnight, Score."

He nodded in response, not even looking back at me. His steps echoed as he walked from the theater.

Atlantis was isolated and huge and imposing, but this was the first time I'd felt lonely here.

~~~~~~~~~~~~~~~

In bed that night, I kept mulling over what Score had said to me in the theater. I rolled onto my side, chewing my lip.

"I wish you were more open to siren experiences. They aren't all bad."

I sighed. My eyes wandered to my dulcimer on display. How long had it been since I'd last played it? The idea of mistreating or losing it physically repelled me. But I'd done nothing with the instrument since playing for Aldan in Whitecrest. Months ago.

It'd been longer since I'd sang.

I pressed myself upright. My heart settled in my throat. If there was ever a time to experiment with song, it was now, within the safety of Atlantis. I swung my legs over the edge of the bed. I carefully pried the instrument from the display, tucking it in my arms. I peeked out of the curtain.

It was still and quiet, but I felt a tiny amount of panic bubble up. What if Score caught me? What if he saw?

I didn't want to be judged, and I didn't want to worry about impressing him or elating him. I had low expectations. But I was curious, and playing with Score had been fun. More fun than I thought it could be.

I padded through the hall until I reached the first singing chamber. I scanned right, then left, before sharply tugging the curtain aside and darting through. My heart pounded in my ears, but the room was otherwise quiet inside. Even the soft melody of Atlantis was dulled within the confines of the chamber.

I waited a solid 30 seconds, listening for any sign of Score's presence. I relaxed a little at the silence. My hands shook as I sat, perched in my cotton shorts and camisole on one of the plush stools. I eased my grip on the instrument. I had to take several deep breaths before I'd settled enough to think straight.

It's just a song. I'm just singing a song, all alone, in private, with no one around to harm, no one to judge. It's just a song.

I let my fingers glide across the strings of the dulcimer, closing my eyes, letting myself go. After a few moments, I added a melody with my voice. I sang in siren-tongue, unraveling every trouble and heartache I'd experienced since I'd transitioned.

My song liberated my emotions in a tumble of notes, allowing them to bleed into the open air and dissipate. But there was more than sorrow and heartache. There were good feelings, too, and more neutral ones. Confusion— there was so much confusion.

I bent the song down, unexpectedly finding myself singing about Score. My deepest, most genuine feelings surfaced, impossible to contain. I wished I could let myself love him, I lamented. The song had turned into a heartbreaking anthem.

Tears rolled down my cheeks, but they didn't hamper my ability. I continued to sort through my feelings, stacking them up neatly, replacing the aches and pains with a sense of completion, of contentment.

The song was far longer than I'd intended. I didn't know how pent up I'd been until I was nearly finished and realized I felt so much better.

The song wound down, and I sobbed harder. But my tears weren't from any negative emotion— just sheer, complete relief.

This *was* healthy for me. This was good. This was something I needed to do, something I had to release. I felt physically better than I ever had. For almost eight months, since turning sixteen…

I'd been starving myself, essentially.

I sat on the stool, my fingers caressing the edges of my dulcimer, staring at my feet and taking a few deep breaths. There was a lightness to my body now, something I'd never experienced before. The thoughts that'd been rattling so persistently in my head had been quieted. My concerns were still present, but they no longer haunted me so much.

I stood, hugging my dulcimer to my chest. I slipped beyond

the curtain, back to my bedroom. For the first time in months, I felt like I could breathe.

Chapter Twenty-Six

Eavesdropping

I sank my blade into my doppelgänger, pleased when she exploded into dust. I ducked, hearing the whistle of a blade as it barely missed lopping off my head.

I'd never experienced *that* type of defeat while training. I was grateful now that I'd lucked out again. I couldn't imagine how it would've felt to 'die' by decapitation in training. Probably not pleasant.

I whirled, lunging my blade forward, skewering the last double. She fell apart into ash as I pulled away. That made five. Five opponents taken on, all at once.

I'd never beaten so many before.

I let out a happy little squeal, dropping my swords carelessly on the ground and jumping around in excitement.

I was shaking, exhilarated. I'd been stagnant for three weeks, trying to overcome that illusive number five. Until today, I'd always been defeated— feeling a flaying pain course through my body before the doppelgängers faded and the whole thing reset.

I swiped at my forehead with the back of my hand, taking a few deep, panting breaths. I couldn't stop smiling. This was a huge milestone for me.

I retrieved the swords, replacing them on the weapon racks along the wall. I cheerfully unlaced my breastplate, dropping it on the wooden dummy.

Yes, I thought, *I'm finally getting somewhere.*

I rolled my shoulders, enjoying the reprive from the

weight of the armor. I nearly skipped back to my room. It was still early in the day, but this was a breakthrough for me. I didn't want to ruin it by practicing again. I might find out it was all dumb luck.

I hopped into the shower, rinsing the sweat from my hair and body. I grinned, a thought popping into my head.

I should tell Score about this.

Then I frowned. Score was busy. He was working in the library for at least three more hours. I could tell him about it over dinner, at five.

But I didn't *want* to wait. I wanted to share it with him right this minute.

I shook my head, pulling on some loose cotton pants and a tank top. I flopped down on the bed, sighing. I grabbed my book from the nightstand. I was reading fables about the muse Calliope— the same fat book I'd retrieved so long ago from the library. I'd already finished it a few times, but I still read a chapter or two before crashing for the evening.

I stared at the open page.

Calliope had a son. His name was Orpheus, and he was the Father of Songs.

I read the line seven times, not getting further in the story.

I grunted. My thoughts nagged me. I was happy, but— it felt like I'd somehow be happier with my achievement if I could talk to Score about it.

I still wasn't sure what I felt for him. If the additional stigma, the additional complexities of our relationship weren't there, I'd have said with certainty I was falling in love with him. When we were together, it felt like I could finally relax. But that was magic, predetermined, something manipulated by the sirens to guarantee that we'd procreate and save the species. It wasn't *real*.

Or was it?

I found myself reading, then re-reading that same sentence over and over again, the words never sinking in.

You were falling in love with him in Whitecrest...

I flushed. It'd been so long since I'd thought about those early days that it felt strange now. Of course, it practically didn't count back then. Neither of us knew what we did now.

So stop worrying about the sirens and their grand designs

and decide if you like him personally, a stubborn voice prodded me.

I *did* like him personally— truly, I did. But would I have, if we hadn't been sirens? If we'd have been left to develop on our own?

I rapped my fingertips on the book's cover, closing it again. I set it back on the table.

At this rate, I'd have been better off failing in combat. The thoughts I had were far more painful and tormenting than the blades of my doubles.

So just go tell him. Then he'll stop cycling around in your head.

It was worth a shot.

I picked myself up off the bed, making my way out of the room. I strode quickly through the winding halls, reaching the library within five minutes. I scanned past the shelves, spotting him. Score was absorbed and didn't notice my arrival.

He was leaning over a table near Forte. There were at least twelve books open in front of him. He tapped a pencil on one of the pages. Score glanced up at the hologram, "Okay, what if I adjust the limitations a bit? Tweak the spell so—"

Forte smiled, "A brilliant train of thought. Your father would be proud of that conclusion. *But* it's impossible. To do that, you'd have to be able to access the seal. Beat put that *outside* of Atlantis, but inside the sirens' gates." Score groaned, leaning into his hand. The hologram just chuckled, "You should stop worrying about it."

"I have to find a way. For Lyra."

My heart felt like it'd stopped. I was eavesdropping, but I didn't care. I froze in place, backing against one of the shelves, watching them.

"I'm glad she's decided to be amicable."

"Yeah… but I don't know if it's because she really wants to be, or if it would just be too lonely otherwise." Score frowned, leaning into one of the books. "And I can't blame her. None of this is what she wanted."

"And what about for you?"

Score sighed, "I guess— for me— I just want her to be happy." His eyes skimmed over the text of the book in front of him. He frowned, shuffling it to his left and tugging over a new tome. He flipped the pages, "So I guess in that way, I'm not happy, either."

"It wasn't supposed to be like this," Forte assured him. "You two… you were *always* good together, did you know that? Best friends, even as toddlers. A better match hadn't been seen in a millenia."

Score just shrugged, "People change. *I* changed. But she's…" He leaned into the book, taking a deep breath. "She drives me crazy. It's like everything I was after I turned has been completely torn down. I'm just—" He shook his head, looking bewildered and a tiny bit bitter. "I'm just that same ridiculous kid I used to be, feeling insecure and wanting so much for someone to like me but failing miserably. And all the confidence, all the bravado, all my pride— it's just come crashing down."

Forte was sympathetic, "Score, the thing you don't seem to understand is that your looks and abilities aren't what make you who you are." The projection looked sad, "It was a deep, deep shame that you grew up in the human world. It should never have felt like there was a big personality shift when you transitioned. It should only have felt like you were taking the next step forward. I regret what happened. I regret how much was robbed from you— and Lyra." He sighed, "*Especially* Lyra. She was born with such a big destiny. My only consolation is knowing she has you. You can be there for her like I can't. If any man deserves her, it's you, Score. You love her."

He shook his head again, tapping on the page, "Except I'm not the only man who loves her."

Forte's eyes narrowed, "What do you mean?"

Score sighed, "Never mind. It's not important." He scratched some notations in the margins of the page.

"You know," the projection reflected, "you could probably relax. My daughter is stubborn, but give it time. A hundred years is nothing in a lifetime, but it's too much time to spend pouting. Give her a year or two, max. She'll come around."

"Sir, with all due respect, I don't want her to love me because she has no one else. I want her to have *choices*. If that means clawing my way out of here…" He shrugged, "I guess I have to try. Besides, I've pretty much given up on winning her over at this point." He laughed joylessly, making my chest ache. "I just— I just want her to be *happy*. I don't think that'll happen unless she's able to leave. So whatever it takes, I'll find a way to let her out of Atlantis. And I *will* find it within the next year."

"A cycle isn't much in the scheme of things. You've already been here for… um, eight moons? Is that right in human time?"

Score laughed, nodding. "Yeah. Eight months."

The projection looked relieved that he'd been correct. My heart pounded in my ears. Had it really been that long already?

"Honestly, Score, your father—" Forte began again.

"Always used to underestimate me," Score finished. "I'm older and wiser now. I'll work it out."

"Do you remember him?"

"The longer I'm here, the more I seem to remember. Mostly, I recall that I thought you were kinder than he was. I remember him treating me like I was a moron for asking questions. That's all." His eyes hovered over the page, "But I've read his journal. He was arrogant. That's where I'll succeed. There'll be a chink in the armor, somewhere in here…" Score flipped the pages, "He was brilliant. I just have to be more brilliant."

"He always wanted you to surpass him. Both of your parents did. Maybe you *can* figure it out. If it's possible." He sounded doubtful. Forte's head tilted up, his white eyes boring into mine. I knew the hologram had caught sight of me. He smiled lopsidedly, "So if you could get my stubborn daughter to actually listen to you, what would you tell her?"

Score sighed, setting the pencil down. He leaned forward, running his hands through his hair. "I guess— I guess I'd tell her sorry. Sorry things aren't the way she hoped. Sorry I'm not what she's looking for."

Was that what he thought? A knot formed in my throat, my eyes tearing. I hadn't intended on making Score think there was something wrong with *him*. It was the situation that was so terrible, nothing more.

He laughed hollowly, "And I guess I'd tell her that, whether the affection's returned or not, I'll love her until the day I die. That she's the most bewitching girl I've ever met, that I hated the idea of soul mates, too, once upon a time— but it didn't *matter*, because it was *her*, because she's just so…" He paused, looking up at the projection, "She's my everything."

"Well… I hope she gets the message soon," Forte said

knowingly.

Heat rushed to my face, and my pulse pounded in my ears. I squeezed my eyes shut, taking a deep breath. I slipped away from the shelf. This had been a mistake.

I walked as quietly as I could, darting to the door. The desire to talk about my tiny achievement today felt so ridiculous now. I slid beyond the white curtains and propped myself against the wall.

The fact that Score thought he wasn't *good enough* for me. I took a few deep breaths, gulping the air down, feeling overwhelmed and suffocated. The truth was, Score had become my best friend. The fact that I'd felt such a strong impulse to tell him about my victory today was testament to that.

I rested my palm on my forehead, closing my eyes.

If things were different...

I pushed away from the wall, wandering back to my room.

If things were different— if Score and I weren't sirens. If I'd been Sarah Mills, if he'd been William Sanders, if we were just human and normal... If we'd met then, I wondered: would we have fallen in love?

The complication, of course, was that we weren't human. Nothing about our lives was normal. Everything had been predetermined from the start.

I glanced fleetingly over my shoulder, back towards the library. My brows furrowed.

The truth was, even now, even knowing how much of it was all lies and tricks, I thought I *did* love him. But I couldn't trust my feelings. Even if I was willing to think about pursuing it, there was another complication: Glenn.

A pang hit my chest thinking about him. Score and I had already far surpassed our month long limitation. I wondered if he had even bothered to wait any longer, or if he'd given up.

It didn't matter what Glenn was doing now— I'd kissed him. He may have admitted how he felt, but I was the one who pushed it. I was the one who'd instigated the results. Glenn had always been forthright in his wishes to remain friends and nothing more, despite his feelings.

It made me feel guilty now. I *did* have feelings for Glenn, but it wasn't the same way I felt for Score— wasn't what I wished I could *let* myself feel for Score. In a way, maybe I did love the half-elf. Maybe it was more honest, because I didn't have strange siren magic interfering with it.

Or maybe I was just fooling myself.

I'd never told Score about my kisses with Glenn. I wondered how he'd feel if I did mention it.

Somehow, I made it to my room. I sank into my bed, lying down.

I glanced at the clock. It was already 4:48p.m. I'd been wandering longer than I'd thought. Score would be done soon, and then he'd meet me in the kitchen for dinner to spend some time together.

Tonight, I dreaded it.

Chapter Twenty-Seven

Destiny

I couldn't sleep that night. My evening with Score had been amicable enough, but I was quiet and withdrawn, and I could tell he was suspicious. I'd feigned a headache. Mercifully, he'd let me go without additional pressure.

I rolled over again and again, staring at the silver clock. It was almost eleven.

I thumbed through the book of fables I'd been reading, the one about Calliope. I sighed, replacing it on the nightstand.

I'd read the stories several times, and reading them again didn't appeal to me. At this rate, tomorrow I wouldn't start training until the afternoon.

Maybe I'd take the day off.

I swung my legs over the bed, grabbing the book from my nightstand. I'd exchange it for a new volume. Maybe after I read for a while, sleep would overtake me.

I made my way through the twisting halls. The pathway to the library was fairly routine, now. I stepped through the curtain, making a beeline for the proper shelf.

"I didn't think I'd see you here," I heard Forte muse behind me.

I sighed, running my fingertip over the spines of the books, tugging one out.

"Of all the stories you could have chosen…" the projection said with a chuckle.

I turned to him, frowning. "I know you saw me earlier."

He nodded, leaning casually against the wall. "I did."

I sank into the chair Score had occupied earlier. His books were still scattered about, each marked where he'd left off to continue his research tomorrow.

I slumped against the table, resting my head in my hand. I couldn't look at the projection. "If you wanted to make me feel bad, you succeeded."

Forte made a soft sound, something between a sigh and a whimper. "No, Lyra, that isn't what I wanted at all. I just thought you needed to hear it."

I looked at him, feeling so tired of my life. "It's terrible that he thinks there's something wrong with him. None of it is his fault. I've told him that before." I shook my head, "I don't know how to fix it."

"I think Score's wishes are pretty clear."

I laughed hollowly. "Give in to my 'siren needs'?" I rolled my eyes, sitting back, "That's not an option."

Forte burst into a furious laughter, like I'd just told him the greatest joke in the universe.

It made me feel self-conscious. I sat up, rigid, "What? *What?!*"

He shook his head, still chuckling, "It's just funny, that *you* of all people are so against the sirens."

I frowned. I didn't understand the humor. My mouth tugged down into a thin line, "Why is that funny?"

He gave me a quirky grin. "Because of your destiny. Because of your path. Because of the reason you were born."

I glared at him, "It's funny because I'm supposed to be saving the sirens from extinction, funny because you trapped me here, because—"

Forte just held a hand up, shaking his head, "No, Lyra. You're misunderstanding."

My nostrils flared, my hands balling into tight fists.

"Do you honestly think we had children just so you could be— what, our breeders? Why would the sirens all *choose* to die out?" The projection leaned forward, against the table. "No, Lyra, you had a much different path set before you. But things changed when the attacks started."

I took a few steadying breaths, closing my eyes.

"Most sirens didn't even know we were the cause of the

Broken. Did you know that? Most didn't know why anyone would even want to go after us," Forte told me. "Some speculated jealousy— we had *power*, that much was true, and a seat on the council— though we were few in numbers."

"If it was a secret, why did *you* know?"

Forte shrugged, casually sitting in another chair next to the table. "Because I was married to your mother, mostly. Because Harmony was my match, and because we liked to talk about her business. And..." he took a breath, "because of you."

I raised a brow. Until I'd turned sixteen, I always felt like my life was so inconsequential— and I preferred it that way. I liked being invisible; I liked being left alone; I liked fading into the background.

"What did Harmony do?"

He smiled, "Harmony was on the Matriarchy. She worked with the Bard and the other women to govern us."

I rolled my eyes, "So she's one of the morons who caused this whole mess? Great."

Forte frowned sharply, his eyes narrowing. "You should be more respectful of your mother, Lyra. And you should hold your tongue if you're planning to insult my match in front of me." He shook his head, "If she was alive now..."

"Sorry," I said sarcastically. "I'm just not that impressed with someone who—"

He slammed his palm onto the table. I was surprised it rang out with sound as clearly as if I'd struck it myself. Was he physical? But the table itself remained still and didn't vibrate at all. It was a trick of the hologram, but it had made me jump.

"Lyra, I can tolerate an awful lot, but do yourself a favor and listen," Forte snapped.

I glared but settled into the chair. I folded my arms in front of my chest, raising a brow. Forte understood the gesture: I was listening.

"Your mother was privy to that kind of information. Everyone on the Matriarchy was— and probably their matches, too. One day, Shiri approached the group with a plan to obtain more power. Those were harder times. Most of Atlantis is automatically maintained now, but back then— let's just say, a lot of us were excited at the advantages more magic could bring us.

"Shiri promised she had the answers, and that it wouldn't

harm any of the other extras— Harmony wouldn't have tolerated it otherwise. *None* of us knew there'd be such terrible consequences. Most of us were unaware of the ones that did occur.

"252 sirens are probably dead, and they didn't even know why they were being attacked," Forte said sadly.

"*Probably* dead?"

"I'm just an imprint, Lyra. I'm a great representation of your father, exactly as he was before he left for the singing. But I can't say for sure what happened at the end of his days— or even if his days *did* end. But look at this place," he held his hands out. "It's a ghost town. I can't imagine I'd have left you two alone here if there was still breath in my lungs."

I chewed on my cheek, "What was the singing?"

"We'd known danger was growing. The Bard kept returning from council meetings shaken up and worried. So two plans were created— though the majority of sirens only knew about one," Forte explained. "The first part was the singing. Most sirens assumed once the singing was complete, so was our plan. But really, we just needed to buy ourselves a little time, to work up to fixing our mistake. That was our second plan, the big secret. Because— believe it or not— those who knew about it *wanted* to fix it. The singing was complex magic. We planned to seal ourselves away here, in Atlantis. Not forever— that would've been foolish, and I'm sure the general population would've gotten antsy. But if we could've made the world *forget* about us, Atlantis would have remained secure. And we'd have bought time for the next part of our plan to be enacted."

"Hiding? That seems cowardly."

Forte shrugged, "Maybe it does. But you have to remember, most sirens were completely innocent. They were being attacked, abused…" His brow lifted, and he looked forlorn for a moment, "The moment I knew we'd fail was the moment we lost two of our people." He shook his head, "They were good men, scouting locations in the Realm to work our magic."

"But our magic doesn't work in the Realm," I protested.

"I told you the singing was complicated. Our alteration pulls from the Realm to draw magic into the Overworld, that's true. Normally it's useless in that plane. But our plan was to alter things in three stages— draw a great amount of magic in the Overworld near a gate, pull it through the gate to seal ourselves in

263

the Realm, then push it back to the Overworld to tie things together.

"Bass and Treble were looking for a location that'd be private enough that we could perform the singing without fear. Even with all our knowledge and power, they were attacked. Most smaller gates wouldn't work— we had too many people— and the larger ones were too heavily trafficked."

From my own experiences, I understood what he meant. I tried to imagine drawing almost a hundred people through a single gate. It'd have to be sizable indeed, especially if it needed to be nearly simultaneous. Depending on how long they'd been scouting, it suddenly made sense how well documented the gates were on the map I'd been left.

"So what happened?" I asked, leaning forward.

Forte shrugged, "I don't know, Lyra. My knowledge is completely limited to what I knew before I left. I can't imagine my projection being necessary if there was a possible way to have—" He sighed heavily, "My best guess is we were ambushed, then slaughtered. The Bard worried that would happen. That's why your mother and I, along with Alondra and Beat— Score's parents— had to scramble to craft a plan to keep you both safe."

"Sounds like my destiny was pretty much set in stone, then. A siren baby-factory," I snorted.

Forte frowned, "Hardly the truth. You should know, for me personally—" he sounded choked for a second, "for me, at least, I wouldn't have been able to bear it if you'd died. You were loved. More than you could possibly know."

My breath caught a little at that statement. I'd spent my entire life trying to just slip by quietly. I didn't remember mourning my parents' death, and I'd never allowed myself to feel pitied for being an orphan. I often speculated on what my life might have been like, but it was more a curiosity than an emotional journey. At this moment, I felt a burning loss in my stomach. A tear trickled down my face. I didn't bother wiping it away.

I stared at the open book in front of me. The words were all big and complex. I wouldn't have been able to make sense of it if I tried. A fresh wave of guilt hit me in my chest at what Score was doing for me.

"So no, Lyra, we had no intentions of you having to do any of this. It isn't fair, it isn't right, and it's not what we had in mind for your destiny." He sighed regretfully. I looked up at him, wiping my tears away with my fingertips.

"Then what was it? Why was I so special?!"

Forte smiled, "You were going to start a new faction, first of all." He leaned forward, "Merge the Nightingales with the Larks to form the Songbirds. Reason and passion, together."

My brows furrowed, "Like the symbol on the wall?"

The projection laughed, "Yes, Lyra. Most siren matches aren't outside of their factions. You and Score… you're an oddity."

My stomach tumbled a little at the thought. I whispered, "And?"

He smiled, "Most people didn't know the rest. It was a secret between only the Bard, the Matriarchy, Beat, and me. When you had your bearings, you were going to become our new Bard."

My eyes widened. I blanched. Even though it'd never happen, it sounded terrible. "Why?!"

Forte laughed at the reaction, "Because you're what we *needed*. Someone who'd stubbornly do the right thing, who wouldn't take no for an answer. Someone who'd be generally well-liked, with enough bravery to take a stand. And you are those things, Lyra."

The words made me dizzy. I leaned into my hand, squeezing my eyes shut. Even in this hypothetical scenario, I wasn't allowed to be normal. Not even relatively.

My father's projection grinned broadly, "And that's why I was laughing, Lyra. I was laughing because you were supposed to *care* for the sirens fiercely, but you grew up so estranged from us you've painted us as the villains of the piece! Even though you're the closest to a princess we'd ever had."

I groaned, leaning into my arms. "But I hate that kind of attention!"

Forte just chuckled, "I know. Of course you do, baby-girl. We needed someone who'd be humble, not someone who'd let power go to their head." He looked thoughtful, "Score would've helped to balance that out. With him next to you, it would've made things easier."

"He was really good at that in Whitecrest," I admitted, smiling weakly. Score had been the one to take me under his wing and teach me how to keep my voice in check. He was always so commanding and perfect at taking the pressure off of me. I leaned into my hand, considering it. He'd pushed me, but only enough that I managed to grow a little— never so much that it caused anyone harm. I turned my gaze to Forte, "Does Score know all this?"

"Score knows better than you do all your best qualities. But I've never spoken about your former role with him. It seemed sad to bring it up."

"Maybe it is," I said, running my fingertips along the open book. "Does he at least know about the singing, and—"

"Of course. He was quite interested in that. Especially within the context of figuring out how to fix the Broken." He sighed, shaking his head, "I wish you wouldn't have him chasing such nonsense now. There will be time for that later, Lyra. After you've had a family, after things have settled—"

"Even if Score and I *were* something, I'd still want to fix this mess before bringing new sirens into this world!" I snapped.

Forte just sighed, staring at his feet wearily. He rubbed his forehead, "This overly noble quality of yours— right here— is why I asked Beat to create the sealing spell in the first place."

I glared, standing. "You asked for it?!" I demanded. "It was your idea?!"

"Yes. I wanted you to be safe. Lyra, you're so young, and I already knew that you'd be so *good*, and so moral, that you'd also be incredibly reckless—"

"You—" I was flustered, so I took a moment to take a deep, even breath and collect myself. When I'd calmed, I growled, "You said my good quality *is* my morality. How can you be so set on not accomplishing the right thing?"

"Maybe because I want you to survive. Maybe because I love you."

I leaned into my hands, tearing up. "If you loved me," I said quietly, "you'd be trying to help me leave." I blinked, "Are you *really* helping Score in his search?"

"I'm doing what I'm supposed to do," Forte said simply. "I'm teaching. Score's asking me questions, and I am answering to the best of my ability. I've been honest with him. He knows my role in crafting the spell. But I'd be surprised if he succeeds. And he knows I think it's a waste of his time and talents. But he loves you so, so much, that…" he sighed.

"This isn't fair for Score," I murmured.

"No," Forte agreed, "it isn't. But the truth is, I doubt you could call him off even if you wanted." He tilted his head to one side, looking at me. "You should probably stop pretending you don't love him," my father advised. "It'd be better for you both."

The muscles in my core tightened, pushing my breath from my body in a whoosh. I jerked my gaze up to the projection, "I don't—"

Forte was smiling broadly, his brows lifted, *"Don't* you?"

I groaned, leaning into my hands, "I should go…" I pulled the chair out, standing to leave.

The projection laughed, "Goodnight, Lyra. Enjoy reading your fable about the Nightingale and the Lark!"

I flushed, stalking off to my room.

~~~~~~~~~~~~~~~~

I still couldn't sleep. At some point, near three in the morning, I thought I'd work out some of the fresh disharmony. I tried to sing, but the melody was jagged, the words forced. What came easy was not what I wanted. In desperation, I decided to train again.

I wasn't focused. At one point, I made a huge mistake. I arced my sword through the air at one my doubles while dodging, accidentally catching my leg with my second sword.

I hissed in pain, humming a quick dismissal. I teared up, my swords clattering to the ground. It hurt, and badly— much worse than the fake injuries my doppelgängers inflicted. I clutched my leg and took several deep breaths before I felt I could even stand.

My victory against five might have been a fluke.

I pushed myself to my feet. The cut gushed blood.

I groaned. This would set my training back, without a doubt. I'd also ruined one of my only pairs of pants beneath the greaves. I couldn't replace anything in Atlantis.

I hobbled out of the arena, shuffling to my room. I slumped onto my bed, unlacing my armor slowly.

The leather was slashed through. I pulled it off, throwing it to the floor in frustration. I peeled off my ruined jeans and staggered to the bathroom to rinse the cut.

It was long, running diagonally along my thigh from my knee to my hip bone, and deep. At least it was clean— that was a mercy. Keeping it closed might be challenging.

I pressed the sides of the wound together, biting my lip, glancing around the room. I needed to hold it tight and allow it to mend.

I rifled through the closet, grabbing one of the silky purple dresses. I tore it into strips, binding my leg gingerly with the fabric. It'd have to do. I'd never seen anything resembling a real bandage in this place.

Then again, the cut looked like it needed stitches.

I blanched. I doubted I could sew evenly on fabric, let alone flesh. The thought wasn't comforting. I hobbled to bed and elevated the leg, wrapping a towel beneath it. My blood was already seeping through my make-shift wrappings.

I frowned, blaming Forte for this mess. I grabbed the book I'd taken from the library, reading it. Halfway through the story, I flushed.

No wonder he'd been so amused. The book was about a Nightingale girl who falls in love with a Lark boy, only to deal with great adversity— mostly having to do with their lifestyles and families. Part of me wondered if this fable was written specifically for Score and me.

I closed my eyes, replacing the book on the nightstand. It really wouldn't surprise me, knowing what I did now.

I couldn't believe I was supposed to become the Bard.

How ridiculous.

I smirked, thinking about it— me, trying to lead people, trying to speak in front of them, trying to deal with council meetings and pomp and ceremony. I began to laugh. The whole thing was too nonsensical to fathom. Then I couldn't *stop* laughing.

Tears rolled down my cheeks as I considered it. It was difficult to picture. I couldn't even make proper friends, not unless I was forced. But somehow, I was supposed to mingle with dozens of people each day— attempting to socialize and— oh, it was just priceless! More than that, the fact that I was supposed to be in charge of anyone was completely laughable. I didn't know what *I* wanted half the time, often *more* than half the time. How could I have been expected to lead an entire race?

268

I giggled madly, swiping at my tears and gripping my stomach, trying hard not to laugh myself off the pillows propping up my wounded leg.

The sirens were so flawed that they thought *I* was leadership material.

I let out another loud chuckle, dimming the lights. I laughed myself to sleep.

Chapter Twenty-Eight

The Garden

My bandages were drenched in blood when I awoke. I groaned as I hobbled to the bathtub to rinse the wound. I had no idea what I'd do about it. I certainly wasn't going to train today.

I awkwardly pressed my leg together, trying to keep the edges of the cut sealed. I sighed, limping to the wardrobe.

I pulled out a silver halter dress that was shorter in the front and longer in the back, tugging it over my head quickly and tying it before gripping my leg again. On the vanity was the remainder of the dress I'd cut up yesterday.

I'd have to use the rest of the fabric. I hoped it was enough.

I sat perched on the edge of the bathtub, ripping the cloth into strips. I wished I had a second pair of hands to make this easier.

As if my thoughts summoned him, I heard a soft knocking on the wall outside the bathroom.

"Lyra?!" Score sounded distressed, but he still respected the border the curtain made between us.

"Crap," I whispered. My stomach flipped. I didn't want him to see the cut I'd made.

I wondered if he'd try to limit my training from now on— but it couldn't be helped. If I tried to wrap it on my own again, it'd only keep bleeding through.

"I'm— I'm decent, Score," I responded.

The curtain fluttered open. He stepped through, his brows turning up when he saw me. His breath left him raggedly. In an instant he was kneeling, "What happened?!"

I shook my head, my face burning, "My own clumsiness, that's all. An accident while training. It's fine, but if you can help me wrap it—"

"You're an idiot," he muttered, pulling my hands away from the cut, inspecting it.

I bristled, "I'm not an idiot for training—"

"Unnecessarily? Yeah, that, too…" he said, shaking his head. His eyes met mine. They were rose pink, "More importantly, you're missing the obvious."

He hummed. I felt a warmth blush around my leg, the cut mending before my eyes. My face grew even hotter. I ran a hand through my hair. He was right. I *was* an idiot.

"Thank you," I mumbled, staring at the floor. But it was unusual for Score to come around in the morning. I wondered if Forte had told him anything about last night. "Why are you here?"

Score stood, leaning against the vanity. "To check on you…" He shook his head, "Actually, to check on us— as friends, I mean. You were really standoffish last night. Saying you had a headache." He stared at the wall, scratching the back of his neck. His cheeks colored, "Maybe I'm being paranoid."

"I'm— you're not entirely wrong," I admitted, feeling my own face grow warm again. I stood tentatively, checking to see if my ruined leg really was good to go. It was fine— better than fine, actually. It felt healthier than the rest of my tired and aching body.

Another jolt of guilt rose up, knotting my throat. Score was pushing himself too hard on my behalf. I knew he thought I didn't want to be with him because there was something *wrong* with him. He didn't blame the situation at all, like I did.

"I think both of us need a day off," I said, deciding in the moment.

"But, Lyra, I have a lot of research mapped out today, and—"

"It can wait," I said, cutting him off.

Score looked at me for a long moment, his eyes that guilt-inducing rose pink. I offered him a soft smile.

"I owe you some time together for last night, anyway."

"Okay, Lyra… If it's what you really want."

We wandered Atlantis, and I chewed on my lip. I needed to convince Score that the amount of pressure he'd put on himself on my behalf was unnecessary. But I wasn't sure how to say it. So I just walked silently beside him through the halls. We took each winding turn slowly, meandering along.

A deep green curtain contrasted in the sea of purple Nightingale drapes. No plaque marked it.

"What's through here?" I wondered aloud.

Score smiled, staring at the floor. "You should look. You might like it."

I hooked a finger on the edge of the curtain, tugging it back. The view took my breath away.

It was a garden. It was dimly lit despite the daylight hours, when most of Atlantis was bright. The flowers bloomed strongly, defying the darkness. It looked like everything was healthy, if a little wild. A large, twisting tree with a white trunk bloomed with dark purple flowers. The branches bent down, weeping with the fat blossoms.

A few star-shaped midnight blue flowers grew at the base in a thick jumble. The whole room smelled intoxicating. I was grateful I didn't have any allergies to flora, or this place would've been a nightmare. A glass bench lined the round edges of the room. I sat on it, taking a few deep breaths. The scenery was beautiful.

Beneath the bench a swath of tiny ice blue flowers grew, adding dots of color like stars in a pitch black sky. A couple of brilliant, turquoise butterflies hovered around the room. A smattering of fireflies added pinpoints of light to the garden's perpetual twilight. A tiny waterfall churned in one corner.

It was peaceful here— the best place I'd seen in all of Atlantis. Below my feet was a thick layer of grass. It was so springy and soft, it may as well have been a carpet. I ran my fingers through the blades, closing my eyes and trying to pretend I was outside, on the surface.

I leaned back so I was lying on the bench, pulling my feet up. I stared at the rounded ceiling. It was surreal to see the dark forms of dolphins and sharks languidly passing by overhead, above branches and flowers.

Score sat next to me, slipping his shoes off. He tugged the socks from his feet. He closed his eyes, digging his toes into the grass.

"If I do this, I can almost pretend I'm outside, on the surface, back home in California, dusk settling in…" He sighed, "Almost." It nearly made me smile; we were so similar. But I still felt guilty. Instead, I leaned forward against my knees.

"I heard you yesterday, talking to Forte about me."

"Did you?"

"You've been different since we've been here, in Atlantis. Is this how you were before you changed— before you were a siren?" I asked, staring into his eyes.

They were orange. He was nervous. I wanted to reassure him, but I couldn't. I needed to hear his answer.

After a moment, he took a breath. "Yes. It is. Aside from looks," he added, holding his head his hands.

"I… I like this version of you better," I confessed, peeking over my knees at him.

He chuckled, "After everything, *this* is what you prefer?"

I reached a hand down, weaving my fingers through the grass below. It was cool. Under the shadow of the bench, a light layer of dew had settled on the blades.

"Actually, when we first met, you were kind of intimidating," I admitted.

"I wasn't trying to be. I was just trying to act confident. And I wanted to win you over so badly."

"But I never liked attention— and some gorgeous, confident, popular guy approaching me…" I sighed. I'd been flattered, but my first impulse had been to run.

"I can't imagine this is better, though," Score said, leaning into his knees. "I'm— I'm *awkward*, Lyra. I wasn't lying to Forte— you stripped me down, took away all the confidence I'd gained since transitioning, made me feel foolish…"

"You aren't awkward, Score," I said, shaking my head. "Compared to me? Not even close…" I leaned back again on the bench, my stomach aching a little.

"You always seem composed, Lyra."

"Appearances are deceiving, I guess."

I squinted. If I looked carefully, maybe I'd see some hint of light way up, beyond all the water. But all I could make out were the fireflies hovering lazily overhead.

"I'm not any closer to figuring out an answer," he

murmured, breaking my thoughts. I glanced at him. He was staring forward at the twisting white trunk of the tree. "Not about the Broken, not about the lock down, none of it." He turned his eyes to me. It made my heart hurt. Rose pink, regretful light purple, a touch of dark purple at the edges.

"Maybe you won't," I whispered. The longer we were here, the more it seemed plausible we'd be trapped the full term.

"I can't fail you," he said, raking his hands through his hair. "After everything else, after all the other parts of me that are a let down— I can't disappoint you again."

My heart pounded hard in my ears. "Score, you don't need to put that pressure on yourself, you don't—"

He shook his head, gripping the back of his neck. "You've *never* let me down, Lyra. Never. But it's all I can seem to do."

Every instinct I had rebelled against hurting him more, but I knew what I needed to say.

"Score… I'm not perfect," I mumbled. I sat up, bundling myself against my knees, trying to make myself smaller.

He laughed bitterly, "You are, Lyra! You don't see it, but you are! And when I'm around you, I feel like I'm just trying to keep up with you, to—"

"I kissed Glenn!" I blurted.

His eyes remained forward, on the tree. I'd expected him to be angry, or look hurt, or shocked, but he just looked tired. His eyes hadn't even shifted to anything new. They were still the maddening pink and purple combination.

"Did you?" he whispered. He rolled his bare feet over the grass a few times, back and forth.

"Twice," I sputtered.

He nodded to himself, keeping his gaze on the trunk. "I— I see."

A long silence filled the room. I suddenly realized that in this muffled little corner of Atlantis, I couldn't hear the soft singing that normally permeated the walls. It was eerie. I'd gotten so used to hearing it in the background. The only sound was the churning of the waterfall in the corner.

My face prickled. The silence felt like a third person between us. I wanted him to be angry with me— to yell, to realize how incredibly imperfect I was, to be frustrated, *something.* Instead Score still stared forward at the tree, silent.

"Is that it?!" I snapped, "Is that all you have to say?!"

His shoulders rose and fell in a single shrug. "What else *is* there to say? Do you love him?"

It was the million dollar question, but I didn't know the answer.

"I—" the second half of the sentence stuck in my throat, as jagged and unforgiving as swallowing a pine cone. I balled my hands into fists. "Would it even matter if I did?"

Why is he being so patient? Why doesn't he react? Doesn't it bother him?

Score just sighed again, "Of *course* it'd matter, Lyra."

"You don't even care!" I accused. I finally evoked a response. He whipped his head towards me, his eyes flashing in shades of red.

"How can you say that?" he demanded, standing. "What do I have to do to prove myself to you? If I could, if I wasn't trapped here, I'd love the chance to tear him apart! But I can't. Even if I could, even if I did, I doubt it'd make you happy." He began to pace the grounds, his hands balled into fists. His eyes snapped up, looking directly into mine. "I *hate* him!" he said finally, with venom. "I hate him for loving you, I hate him for trying to sabotage us, but mostly? Mostly I hate him because I *owe* him so much! Because without him, you'd be dead somewhere." He tilted his head back, looking tortured, "And I'm trying to understand. I'm trying so hard to be patient with you, because god knows I don't deserve to judge. I don't deserve to be picky or unforgiving— but you're pushing me. So yes, it matters! Yes, I care! Do. You. Love. Him?"

I felt dizzy all of a sudden, blinking back tears, not sure what to say. "I—"

"Do you?!"

"Just give me a second, to—"

"Answer me!"

"No!" I finally screamed. For a single moment, time stood still. Score's form went rigid, his eyes a swirling mixture of every color of the rainbow. "No," I said again more quietly. "Not like that, anyway." The confession was oddly liberating. It cauterized the wound, allowing me to move on.

Score sank down on the bench again, staring at the ground. He gripped the glass at the edge so tightly his knuckles were white.

"It'd be a relief to hear, but I know you don't love me either," he said with a hollow laugh.

Yes I do. I have to.

My chest felt tight, aching, looking at him. He was miserable. In that moment I could see it— I held his heart in my hand, squeezing it, causing him pain.

"Can't you understand, Score?" I asked, turning my gaze to the glass bench. I couldn't stomach the agony on his features. "Everything, *everything* is a manipulation of the sirens."

"So that's it, then?" he said. "That's how you see us…" He relaxed his grip, sliding his hands up to his sides.

"How can you see it any differently?" I asked. "We were used, viciously. They trapped us here, and— it's all fabricated. A lie." My voice broke as I added softly, "I hate that everything you do makes me love you more."

Score turned to me, his eyes gentle, rose mixed with an anguished blue gray. "I guess that's just another one of the ways we're so different, you and I…" he picked up my hand and ran his fingertips along my palm, tracing it. "You see us as being inorganic, tainted, and terrible. A product of manipulation. But I…" he laced his fingers through mine, and my stomach fluttered a little in spite of everything.

Our hands locked together like two pieces of a puzzle, connecting us. Score's eyes met mine again, "I think it's less complicated than that. I guess I just see us as being *made* for each other. In every sense of the word."

All my resolve came crashing down at that moment. The image of my life, of how things were, had shattered into a million pieces.

In the end, Score was right: it didn't matter *how* it came about; all that mattered was what we were. A perfect match. And I loved him. I'd loved him for a long time. Longer than I cared to admit. Longer than I was willing to try to pinpoint.

Even in Whitecrest, I'd fallen for him, right from the start. There were a million reasons: the physical— the line of his jaw, the shape of his lips, the size of his nose; the superficial— the way he sounded when he laughed, his bravado, even his cocky swagger; that he was like me— his changing eyes, the way he could pick up an instrument and know if it was in tune just by looking at it, how much he hated human music.

276

But being in Atlantis had given me a new depth of perspective on him. It allowed me to see the man he was beneath all that. He was beautiful, smart, and humble. He tried so hard, gave so much, and he loved me so strongly.

Tears filled my eyes. My breath caught for a moment before I whispered, "I'm such a fool…"

"Lyra?" Score said, his brows turning up, "Your eyes are—"

I sprang forward, holding his face in my hands, pressing my lips into his. I fell into him. I don't know why it'd taken me so long to see what was right in front of my face. Why had I been so stubborn? Why did I try to dig in my heels and refuse this?

Score wasn't the enemy at all.

He was a gift.

He returned the kiss, running his hands through my hair. He pulled away sharply, "Does this— do you— do you really love me?!"

I took his hand in mine, kissing each fingertip. I closed my eyes, leaning into him. "Everything about you, Score. Everything. I love you."

He pushed me down into the glass bench, kissing along my neck. His hands grasped for mine. I pressed back into him, bringing myself up. I left a trail of kisses along his jawline, running my palms down his back, along his hips. I wanted to touch and feel every part of him.

He picked me up, holding me in his arms. I twined my legs around his waist, kissing his lips, loving that they tasted like the same spice I could smell on him. I ran my hands through his beautiful hair, down his neck, along his broad shoulders.

My fingers found the edges of his shirt. I tugged it, my heart racing in my ears, but Score caught my hand in his own. He gently pushed me away. His eyes were still beautiful, still rose, but they searched mine. "Lyra, don't tease me," he breathed. "I couldn't bear that again."

I pressed my forehead against his, kissing him on the tip of his nose. I shook my head, biting my lip as I pulled away. I slipped my hand from his grasp, sliding it back beneath the hem of his tee. "I'm not teasing you. Not anymore."

His lips were on mine in an instant, a dizzying whirlwind of kisses and passion. I pulled off his shirt, finally, running my palms

277

over his warm skin. I allowed myself to touch him with abandon.

Score's hands were at the ties of my dress. He tugged, freeing the knot. The silk slithered down, bunching uselessly at my waist, leaving me exposed. He pulled back for a moment, admiring my naked torso before burying his face along my throat. He kissed my collarbone, moving down, drawing his tongue over my skin.

I pressed my hands into his back, lost in the sensation. I closed my eyes, moaning. The sound returned his lips to mine. He nipped at my lower lip softly with his teeth. My hands traveled downward, finding the clasp of his belt, tugging feverishly at it.

What I needed, right at this moment— more than anything— was to lose myself, to lose him, to only become *us*. I loved him, I wanted him, and I would have him.

He lifted me by the waist. I shimmied the silk from my hips, and Score gathered me back into his arms. I'd finally freed the buckle on his belt. With a swift motion, I tugged it from his jeans, clawing at the button, unclasping it.

I grappled for the waistband, my hands shaking. I stared at the sharp line at the arch of his hips. Score placed his hands over mine. I glanced into his eyes. They were questioning— we could stop if I wanted. My nerves dissolved, and with a laugh I pushed the fabric down.

He kicked the pair away, gently setting me on the soft grass. His fingertips caressed the sides of my hair, my cheeks.

We were both completely exposed. Our clothes lay abandoned on the grass around us, but somehow I didn't feel embarrassed or self-conscious. Whenever I'd pictured this moment, I'd worried about feeling awkward or terrified. All I felt now was a strong desire for Score, an unrelenting need to be with him, and enough affection for him that I wanted to close the gap between us as far as we could.

I loved him.

Chapter Twenty-Nine

Entwined

Everything had changed.

We lay on the grass for a long moment. Score's eyes had settled into a sea green color I'd seen but had never pinpointed before. The serenity on his face made the hue easy to decipher—contentment. He stroked my arm with his fingertips, smiling. Every few seconds he'd look over at me, as if he was checking to make sure I was real. It was like he couldn't believe I was still with him.

"Holy cow…" he whispered.

I giggled, huddling closer to him. I breathed a happy sigh as I cuddled against his chest.

I thought about what we'd just done, and a titter escaped my lips. Then the moisture left my mouth completely, and my heart began to beat fast in my ears.

I sat up, groaning.

Score's eyes shifted immediately, deep forest green, rose pink, and a tiny bit of black. "What's wrong?" he asked, panicked.

"We didn't— we—" I stuttered. I leaned forward, cupping my face in my hands.

"That was a mistake?" he asked, sounding sad.

I glanced over at him, shaking my head, "Yes, but, no, I mean—" I took a ragged breath, finally whispering, "Score… what if I get pregnant?"

His eyes shifted back to the light green color. He laughed, pulling me down to the grass with him, running his fingers through my hair. "You won't. Don't worry." Score kissed my forehead, shaking his head just a little bit.

"But you can't be sure," I said, still feeling anxious.

"Lyra..." he sighed. His mouth twitched as he fought off laughter. "Sirens— we don't reproduce the human way. It takes more than that to make a baby."

I rolled over to face him, pressing my body against his. "Are you *sure*?"

"I've read some siren biology books in the library. And I've discussed it with Forte a little bit, too." He smiled, caressing my cheek with his thumb, "Sirens have to sing while they make love if they want a child."

My heart began to calm. I settled into him again, "Promise?"

He laughed, "Yes. I *promise*. But we can still enjoy ourselves, right?"

I closed my eyes, relaxing, "Right."

~~~~~~~~~~~~~~~~

Atlantis was different now. I found I couldn't bear to part with Score unless absolutely necessary. Even during brief separations, it felt like I was missing an essential part of myself. When we were together, life fell into an easy rhythm.

He was the harmony of my soul.

He told me his deepest wishes, desires, dreams. I told him my hopes, my insecurities, even what Forte had revealed about my previous destiny.

Score refused to stop seeking the way out. He was determined to succeed. He told me nothing had changed, that our union made him want to free us even more.

We'd combined our rooms. He moved into my large chamber, bringing his guitar, his wardrobe, and the desk from his Lark room. With him beside me, I slept deeper and more comforted, slipping into slumber with ease.

In the daytime, I parted from him reluctantly, letting him puzzle out the spell that trapped us inside Atlantis while I continued my training. I'd occasionally return alone to the singing chambers, letting my emotional turmoils and triumphs bleed from my voice to free my mind.

I was getting better, stronger, faster with my blades. I was more capable of defending myself, more capable of striking out. I could take on up to eight doppelgängers at once, deflecting and defeating them quickly. I'd learned to dodge, duck, twist, and roll to evade their attacks. I used the walls for leverage, jumping and tumbling through the air.

The evenings were when I felt most alive, though. We continued to explore, but our hikes and wanderings were now punctuated by kisses, caresses, and more. The whole of Atlantis became our playground in the night. Tangled up in each other, it'd blossomed into a paradise.

It was the happiest I'd been in my whole life.

One afternoon, five weeks from our interlude in the garden, Score burst into our bedroom. I'd been lying on the bed, lazily reading a book. I grinned at his arrival. He wordlessly pulled me into a long kiss, making my legs melt. His lips followed the line of my neck, down my shoulder. I moaned.

"Score…" I breathed, "What did you want to do tonight?"

He chuckled into my shoulder, "*This*. Always, this…"

I laughed, drawing my hands over his shoulders. "Mm… you're in a good mood today."

"Every day I'm with you, I'm in a good mood," he said. He tugged my tee over my head.

"I feel like this is a trap," I muttered, my lips turning into a smile. "You usually don't sneak attack me like this."

He laughed, pressing his lips against my torso. "You have more muscle now, Lyra." For a second, my heart beat a little faster. I wondered if it was unattractive to him— maybe deviating from my predetermined body type left me inadequate. His eyes met mine, beautiful, rose pink. He smiled, "It's sexy."

I pulled him up until his lips met mine. He groaned. My hands wandered, dragging across his chest. Score pulled back, sighing happily. I stared into his eyes. They were almost completely pink— but there, on the edges, was a tinge of violet.

I sighed, moving away from him. "What's going on, Score?"

He closed his eyes, laughing. "Dammit. I'd hoped to put it off at least a few more minutes…" He shrugged, opening them again, "Forte's— he wants to speak to you."

I flushed, leaning back into the bed, groaning. My hand

fumbled across the covers, finding my shirt. I tugged it over my head. "Well, *I* don't want to talk to *him!*"

Score settled next to me, propping himself up on one side with his fist. His eyes were still mostly rose, but the edges were a dark, serious brown. His inflections bordered on stern, "What are you so afraid of?"

My face prickled. I squeezed my eyes shut, sputtering, "I just— he's going to be so self-satisfied, Score!"

My match chuckled, taking one of my hands and giving it a squeeze. "Maybe not as much as you'd think."

I'd gone out of my way to avoid the library at all costs. I'd even asked Score to trade my books for me. "What did he say when you first told him?" I asked.

His mouth formed a lopsided grin. He cast his gaze down to the comforter below us, "Well…"

"Score!" I pressed.

"Actually, I didn't have to tell him. He took one look at me the next day and said, '*finally*'. Then he dropped it."

I groaned. It didn't exactly make me anxious to speak with the projection. My eyes cracked open, looking at Score. "So why did you approach me like *this*—"

He chuckled again, "Just in case you were mad later. If Forte said something that upset you, I wanted to at least have a *little* bit of—" I thumped him in the face with my pillow.

"Selfish jerk," I complained. But I wasn't really mad at him.

He leaned forward, pressing against me. "Isn't that what all the girls like? The jerks?"

"That's what they say," I responded, "but I've always liked the nice guys."

"So how can I make it up to you?" he whispered, kissing my fingertips. He worked his way up, trailing kisses along my arm.

My heartbeat quickened. My toes curled into the bedding with desire.

I pulled his face to me, nipping at his lower lip. Forte could wait.

I smiled, "I'm sure you'll find some way…"

I still wasn't anxious to visit Forte that evening. I dressed reluctantly, sighing, "Well, at least I can pick out my *own* library book."

"You didn't like the last one?" Score asked, grinning.

I rolled my eyes. He thought it was hilarious to give me educational materials. I wanted fluff. I shook my head. "No, Score. I wasn't especially interested in the emotional sufferings the Minstrel clan endured when they first brokered a deal 27 centuries ago over *clay.*"

He kissed me, "My mistake, heart-song."

I leaned into him, closing my eyes. "Do we *have* to?" I smiled slyly, sliding my hand on his belt buckle. "We could blow him off, Score. We could—"

He pushed my hand away, tapping me on the nose with his index finger. "Nope, we can't. But…" he slid one hand beneath my shirt, cupping my breast. I groaned. "After," he breathed, immediately pulling away.

"Tease," I grumbled.

Score just laughed, lacing his fingers through mine. "Come on, let's get it over with."

"What does he even want?"

"I don't know, Lyra. He wouldn't tell me. But he's been bugging me for over a month, almost since—" He stopped talking, but I knew what he was going to say: since I'd come to my senses, since we'd been together properly.

That didn't bode well for the impending conversation. I could only assume the projection would gloat. I tipped my head back as we walked down the hall, sighing.

My heart sped up as we stood before the heavy curtains of the library.

"Ready?" Score whispered.

I nodded, trying to fill myself with resolve. It's not like the projection could do anything to me, after all. At least not physically. And if I needed to, I could always walk away. Forte had a limited range.

We pulled the curtains back, stepping through.

He greeted us immediately, "You came. Good."

I folded my arms across my chest, leaning into Score as we walked to the corner where Forte paced. Score slung his arm over my shoulders, sensing my nerves. It was reassuring.

"What do you *want*, Forte?" I asked.

The projection sighed, "Honestly, I've *missed* you, Lyra. You look good, by the way. Much better. Healthier…" He tilted his head to one side, "You've been singing."

I flushed. Score's brows raised. He turned to me, "Have you, Lyra? I didn't know that."

I squeezed myself a little tighter, looking at my match, "I— Yes, I have. A little bit. It's been—"

"It's *good*, baby-girl," said Forte. "It's not bad; it's not evil. It's what you *should* do."

I groaned, leaning against Score, squeezing my eyes shut. "Yes, okay! I was wrong on some accounts! I'm not perfect!"

Both men laughed. Score brought his arms around me, holding me tightly, his head leaning against mine.

"You *are* perfect, Lyra," he murmured. "Perfectly imperfect."

I frowned, pulling from him. "So you missed me, and wanted to berate me, and—"

Forte grinned, "Oh, Lyra, calm down. Water under the bridge."

I stared at him dubiously. "That easy?"

The projection just shrugged, "It's my nature, baby-girl. I just decided that if you're putting aside some of your nonsense, maybe I can talk to you like an adult now."

I slid into the chair. Score pulled up a second one, sitting next to me. I took a deep breath, "So, what, then?"

"I thought if you were more comfortable with your destiny, I'd walk you through why you were born in the first place."

"I already know," I snapped. "I was supposed to be the new Bard, which is *still* completely ridiculous."

"It's less ridiculous than you think. But why did we need a new Bard, Lyra? Score, I'm sure you've already pieced it together."

I looked up to my match, curious.

"There's really only two possible conclusions," he explained slowly. "The first, of course, is that the sirens wanted a new Bard because they were dissatisfied with the leadership. That's instantly discredited, though. Shiri was aware that Lyra was going to take over. Which means…" he sighed. "It had something to do with the Broken, the sirens' big problem."

My back went rigid. I stared at my father with wide eyes. "What did I have to do with the Broken?"

The projection sat on the chair across from us. "It came down to how the Bard managed to get our additional power in the first place. She breached the Source of Magic."

"But that's impossible!" Score cried.

Forte just shook his head, "No. It was clever. It involved a lot of sneaking and thieving on our parts, I'm ashamed to say."

"How did you even?!—" Score sputtered. "I thought the Source was sealed with a key from each council race— even the angels and the demons, and they haven't been involved in extraordinary business for 4,000 years!"

"You're correct. But we managed it," Forte said calmly. "Every key was taken discreetly. The Bard collected most herself. Then—" he paused a beat, "then she traveled to the Sea of Phantoms with a small choir of sirens and used the keys."

"What does that even *do*?" I asked.

"The Source of Magic is where *anything* is possible," Forte replied. "But there are rules with magic, even there. The Bard wanted to affect every siren, and to do that—"

"It's tied to responsibility," Score broke in. "That's why she went personally. She was Bard of the sirens, so only she held the fate of the species in her hand." He shook his head, baffled, "But the Source also dictates *flow*, at least according to my father's journals. He said that all documented cases of the Source's activation were one-time, major events. Nothing that would've *permanently* altered flow. Fluctuations had been noted, of course, but—"

"Yes," Forte agreed. "But nothing like what we attempted had ever been done. The natural rhythm was interrupted. As the stream of magic flowed to our species, it drained the Realm. Magic's not an infinite resource, no matter how much it may seem like it."

Score frowned, staring forward with narrowed eyes, "Why didn't my father note that?"

"Beat was actually the one who put it all together, Score. But that information was highly classified. He wouldn't have been allowed to write it freely in his journal. Other Larks could potentially find it."

Score ran a hand through his hair, "Okay, then why didn't

Bard Shiri just return with the keys and undo it?"

"Ah! Therein lies the problem," Forte replied, leaning back in the chair. "The keys mark the individual who uses them as a failsafe to avoid continual breach. The Bard could never return to that sacred space once she'd altered the flow in the first place." He sighed, "Hence, we needed a *new* Bard. One who was better, more moral. One who we could trust." His disconcerting white eyes stared directly into my own.

Goosebumps rose on my skin. My destiny had *always* been to fix things. "So that's how I can do it," I said, my heart pounding. "I can get the keys, go to the Source of Magic, then—"

"Yes, Lyra. And *someday* you'll do that. But not until the century is finished, not until you've had time to learn the best ways to do it." Forte tilted his head, "The throne in the Matriarchy— the big room where you found the Bard's letter? That's connected to the council grounds. It's how the Bard did most of her business in our last days. I'd suggest taking your council seat, getting comfortable, and forging relationships. Then you can appeal to the councilors individually to gain their keys and right this. But *take your time.*"

"But I'm not the councilor, I'm just—"

"You're the Bard, Lyra. You have been since you transitioned."

My face prickled, but it wasn't hot. I wasn't blushing; I was just supremely uncomfortable. A wave of panic struck me between my brows, making my vision swim.

"I *can't* be the new Bard!"

"Well," Forte said with a chuckle, "Score certainly can't do it. No boys allowed."

Score pulled me closer to him, kissing the side of my head. "Why are you telling us this now?"

"So Lyra can use the next century to prepare for what she needs to do."

Score narrowed his eyes, "Unless we find a way out before then."

Forte shook his head, "Give that up. Get joined, have a family, study the best approach to fix the Broken, and—"

"I'm not having children with this— this stigma attached!" I cried, shaking my head. I stood, "I don't want to bring new sirens into the world when they're just going to pull more magic out of

286

place! I'm not that selfish, Forte!"

The projection sighed, "In the long run, it won't matter, Lyra."

"Maybe not!" I said with quaking shoulders, "But it'd matter to *me*. I want my son, or my daughter— I want them *free* of this mistake. Absolutely not!" I crossed my arms in front of myself.

Sorrow clouded Forte's features. "That's too bad," he whispered. "I'd have liked to know my grandchildren."

The comment toppled my rage over the edge. I slammed my palms into the table, "Well, *I'd* have liked to know my father! I'd have liked to know my mother! But the sirens didn't think things through, did they? So now I'm stuck cleaning up your damn messes!"

I whirled around, furious. Behind me, I could hear Score sliding his chair out and standing.

"I'm sorry, Lyra," the projection said.

I didn't want to hear it. I marched from the library, not looking back. Score was at my heels, his footsteps padding behind mine.

When we were in the hall, Score bounded forward, catching up to me so we were side-by-side. He laced his fingers through mine, "I'm sorry that upset you."

I shook my head, frowning. "Well, one question answered, anyway," I said bitterly. "So now you don't have to search for a remedy for the Broken. We have it!"

Score grabbed my arm, spinning me back to him. He had a slight smile on his face. "Suddenly, Lyra, I'm grateful I conducted my diabolical plan this afternoon."

In spite of my mood, my mouth began to twitch. "Oh? That did you well enough for *today*," I said, turning from him. I glanced coyly into his eyes over my shoulder. "But what about *tomorrow*? We already know I can hold a grudge."

"Is that so?" he said, laughing. "Then I'll just have to try my best to lift your spirits." He scooped me into his arms, racing through the hallway, carrying me.

I laughed, feeling my tension dissolve away. I stroked his cheek fondly as we bounced down the hallway, "I love you, Score."

"Not nearly as much as I love you," he said with certainty.

His eyes shifted to a true blue as he spoke. "I was saving this for a special time. Now seems appropriate."

We wove though the halls to the residential half. As he blazed through the corridors, I noticed he was leading us away from the Nightingale section where our room was housed. Instead, he carried me into the midst of the golden curtains— the Lark area.

"Score?"

He shifted my weight, so I was balanced in one of his arms. He grinned, pushing open a green curtain. "You enjoyed the Nightingale garden, right? Well, let me show you *my* faction's garden."

It was late— probably around eight or nine— but when he pulled the curtain back, I felt like I was being bathed in sunshine.

"Oh!" I cried, enjoying the warmth on my skin. A light breeze blew. As my eyes adjusted to the brightness, I had to smile. Along the edges were trees, and thick tangles of roses in yellow, red, and cream colors. A few snapdragons, pansies, and marigolds grew in islands to break up a carpet of grass. A perfectly round pond crowded one side. Next to it was a bench beneath a few trees.

I turned to Score, smiling, taking a few deep breaths. It felt like we were outside on a summer's day. Above us, a few fluffy clouds appeared to drift through a bright blue sky.

"It's all illusion, of course," he said regretfully. "If you go beyond the trees, you'll see the glass and the fish, but…"

"It's beautiful here, Score," I said, slipping from his arms, enjoying the feeling of the grass beneath my feet. "All sunshine," I kissed him, "like you."

"Has your mood improved?" he asked with twinkling eyes.

"What if I say no?"

Score laughed, slipping his hands beneath my skirt. He pulled me closer to him. "Then I guess," he said with a mock-sigh, "I'll just have to keep *trying* to make you happy."

As he leaned in, my stomach quivered in longing. His lips met mine, and I clutched his shirt, feeling my knees go weak.

It just wasn't possible to be unhappy when I was with him.

Chapter Thirty

Duet

Days faded into weeks. I stopped asking Score about his progress. I had confidence that if there was an answer, he would find it. The sharp edges of my guilt had dulled in my contentment with him, and escape felt less pressing.

One early morning I awoke before the lights had brightened to signal dawn. I rolled over, inhaling the cinnamon spice in the bedsheets, smiling.

I reached a hand out, searching for him. He was gone.

My heart leapt to my throat.

"Score?" I called, sitting up, glancing at the vacant space on the bed.

"Mm… Heart-song? You're awake?"

He sat at the desk, open books before him. He was shirtless, facing away from me. I bit my lip, looking at the muscles along his broad back.

I drew my legs up under the blankets, circling them with my arms. I leaned forward, "What are you doing?"

"Studying. Trying to figure this out…" he sighed. "Not having any luck, though." He turned to me, a tired smile on his face. A pair of spectacles framed his eyes.

I hopped up, bounding to him. "I didn't know you wore glasses!"

He flushed, snatching them away from his face immediately. "I don't! I mean, *normally* I don't, but this text is *very* precise, and these were my father's for working, and—" he groaned, tipping his head back. "I'll put them away."

I straddled him, pulling the frames from his fingers. I grinned, sliding them back onto his face. "I like them. You look distinguished."

He chuckled, shaking his head. "Is that so?"

I nodded stoically, "Yes. They frame your beautiful eyes."

Score leaned in, kissing me slowly, deeply.

I pressed myself closer to him, resting my palms against his chest. "Mm…" I pulled back, giggling, "You're prickly today."

He smiled, staring into my eyes, "I haven't shaved yet. I've been so focused on deep intrinsic arcana that—" His mouth twitched, taking in my lost expression. "I'm distracted. *Clearly* neglecting my duties to you, heart-song," he said in a mocking tone.

I yawned, "You should come back to bed. You have all day to study."

I stood, lacing his hand through mine.

"I don't," he countered, shaking his head. He closed the book, removing the glasses and setting them on the desk. "Today, I have other obligations."

I tugged impatiently on his hand, "No, you don't!" I argued. "You work too hard to—"

His lips were on mine again, cutting me off. He stood, pulling back but keeping his arms around me, "What kind of man would I be if I ignored my match's birthday?"

I glanced into his eyes, feeling confused. "But— it's only—"

"It's September 21st. That's the day, right?"

Had we really been in Atlantis for almost a year? I swallowed thickly. "I— oh."

He sighed, pulling me down to the bed. "I know. I promised you." He ran his fingers through my hair, "Yet here we are." He pulled his gaze from me, staring at the thick blankets instead.

"I'm trying, heart-song. I'm trying. It's just—" He laughed, shaking his head. "My father was brilliant. Deciphering his notes alone took me three months. He wrote everything in this shorthand that no one else seemed to use, but it saved himself time. And this spell is *complicated*. He used about fifteen layers to make sure it couldn't be broken, so any loopholes were closed before the magic was in place." He sighed again. He looked so tired, with shadows under his eyes. "But I *think* I might have found something worth looking into."

"What is it?"

He shook his head, "Oh, no. No, no, no. I'm not about to tell you and jinx myself." He grinned, staring into my eyes, "But it'll probably take a bit more research for me to get there. So today, my love, we're going to do anything you'd like. Anything at all."

I smiled, curling against him. I kissed the hollow of his throat, and Score made a deep sound like a purr.

"Can we spend the day in bed?"

"Definitely," he breathed.

I tucked my head against his chest, "Will you shave?"

He laughed at that, running his hand along my shoulder, "Of course." He started to move, but I twined his leg with my own.

"No. Stay here."

"Anything else?"

I nodded, "Kiss me?"

"You're very demanding on your birthday," he teased.

"*Now.*"

He brought his lips to mine, brushing his thumb across my cheek. I shuddered closer to him, feeling my body relax. He caressed my arm, and I began to drift.

A thought struck me when I was on the edge of sleep.

"Score? Does this mean you had a birthday, too?"

He laughed, "That's usually the way it works."

I smacked his shoulder, "No, I mean— when was it?"

His mouth twitched into a smile, "July 19th."

My brows furrowed, "But— you never said—" I pouted, "I didn't even do anything!"

He traced the back of my hand with his index finger. "Three days before I turned eighteen…" he smiled, "was the first time we were in the garden together."

"Why didn't you tell me?!"

"Because I already had everything I wanted. It was the best birthday of my life. And I thought sixteen would be hard to top, but you blew it out of the water."

I shifted. "I hated my sixteenth."

"I know… hopefully this one will be better."

"It already is." I curled closer to him, wondering how many

more birthdays I'd spend in Atlantis. I sighed.

"But you're sad? I'm not doing my job, am I?"

I shook my head, "It's not you, Score. I just wish…" I wasn't sure what I wished. The truth was, I felt guilty about how *little* it bothered me that we were trapped here.

"What conflicting emotions," he said, staring into my eyes. "Guilty and happy and sad, all at once. I can't have that," he chided. "Not on your birthday."

I smiled at him weakly, "I'm fine, Score, and—"

"Nope. Not allowed." He rolled away from me, padding from the bed until he'd reached the wardrobe. He stood on his tiptoes, reaching for something in the way back. He retrieved a little box, packaged in a shiny white paper flecked with iridescence like opal.

He sat with one leg beneath himself casually, holding the box to me. "Happy birthday, Lyra."

"You got me a present?" I asked. I wondered how it was even possible— Atlantis already had everything we could possibly want within its glass walls.

"Yes… no. Not exactly. But it's for you."

I shook my head, tugging off the paper. I slipped the lid from the box, revealing something shiny and metallic, glinting in gold.

As I brushed my fingertips across it, the gift sprang to life. It soared up, escaping the box. I jumped back, startled, bumping into Score.

He laughed. "Heart-song," he said, pointing to it, "look."

Hovering in front of my face was a golden bird. It darted around the room, landing on my shoulder.

"What is it?" I whispered. It looked impossible.

"It's a clockwork Nightingale. My father made it for my mother over 500 years ago." He cupped his hands, and the bird hopped into his palms. He glanced into my eyes, his own shining with turquoise, "Listen." He stroked the bird along its breast with his index finger.

It opened its mouth. First there was laughter: feminine giggles and more masculine chuckles.

"Are you sure this works, Beat?"

A lump formed in my throat. It was Forte's voice, though he spoke Siren.

"I'm certain. Alondra, my love, are you absolutely positive you want to—" Another man.

"Yes! I want to memorialize this moment! My best friend's frozen heart has melted," a feminine voice responded in a teasing tone.

"Ally, bring Score closer. He's meeting his match for the first time." I could almost hear the smile in my mother's voice. A few tears fell from my eyes. There was the sound of cooing. *"In just sixteen cycles, my darling, I will let you listen to this. And on your transition you will know the joy your birth brought us."*

"You rarely wax so sentimental, Harmony," Forte said.

"Hormones," she dismissed.

"Shh... look at the children." The other man— Beat. *"Look how he observes her. He can't decipher her."*

"Yet he still reaches for her!" Forte laughed.

"And she for him," Alondra agreed. *"So, a message— though this is already lengthy."*

"May you have a fruitful life, little Lyra," said Beat, *"and a happy transition."*

"I don't know what I'll tell you in sixteen cycles," Forte said, sounding choked, *"but I never thought I'd be so happy to be a father."*

"I'm looking forward to knowing you, little one. Happy transition." Alondra, Score's mother, again.

"I— I'm bad at this. But, Lyra... I love you very, very much. And I'm certain I'm proud of you now. Happy transition." My mother's voice was quiet, almost a mumble.

The recording clicked, turning off. The bird settled onto the end of the bed.

"Sorry it's a year late," Score said, lacing his fingers through mine.

"I don't— I—" It was a lot to process. I leaned against him, closing my eyes. "How did you know about it?"

"It wasn't a secret. The bird was in my parent's room. But Forte mentioned that it had a message to you when I asked what day your birthday was."

"You asked Forte?"

"I didn't know the exact date. I knew that we met right after you turned sixteen, but I didn't know the specifics. Asking Forte made the most sense."

I pulled him closer to me, "Thank you."

"Do you want to go back to sleep?"

I shook my head.

"Do you want me to go shave?"

I giggled, shaking my head again. "No."

"Well, I'm at your disposal today. For the whole day."

A few butterflies hit my stomach. I'd had the desire to ask this for the past two weeks, but I hadn't gotten up the nerve. Today was probably the day.

"Score, I was hoping..." I trailed off, my courage failing.

"You're so nervous." He grinned, "Are you going to scandalize me?"

I flushed, smacking his shoulder again, "No!"

"Then what is it?"

"I was hoping that maybe— maybe we could sing together?"

His breath caught. His irises shifted to an unfamiliar warm brown with flecks of gold in it. The edges remained pink. "I've never even heard you sing properly."

"What are you feeling?" I asked, curious. These days I was comfortable asking when I didn't know, though it was rarer and rarer.

"Amazed. In love. Grateful, mostly."

I rolled from the bed and pulled my dulcimer from the display hooks. I was less anxious with singing in general, but this was still a big step. Score grabbed his guitar from the corner, and we walked hand in hand to the first singing chamber we could find.

"Are you *sure*, Lyra?" Score asked gently. He knew as well as I did— maybe even better— how intimate this would be, how potentially painful. But if he was willing to pour his heart out to me, I could do the same for him.

I nodded, feeling a flurry of nerves for just a moment. I plunked down on one of the stools, and Score settled next to me.

I closed my eyes. I let my fingers go to work, beginning the melody. I started with something easy— how much I loved him, how happy I was with him, how grateful I was to have him in my life. He began shortly after I did, adding an accompanying harmony. His own voice blended seamlessly into mine, creating something more beautiful.

And oh, how he loved me! In the heady magic surrounding

us, it was undeniable and beautiful. The weight of his emotion surrounded me like a warm and comforting blanket. My chest ached with the magnitude of it.

It was like the song was alive— something growing between us, twining us together. For a moment, it felt like our souls were dancing somewhere in the ether, our bodies left behind long ago.

I allowed myself to open up my eyes. I had to smile as I sang. Score's eyes were a haunting white, the iris lined with a sharp gold ring. They sparked in colors like our opals.

Most of our song was happy, but there were other emotions lurking beneath the surface. We sang of our love, mostly, but also of regrets, of promises, of fears. The singing didn't allow for dishonesty— it was a clean, vibrant look into each other's minds. It was our souls— raw, honest, and bare.

After a long while, our duet wound down. We finished the song simultaneously. We stared into each other's eyes as they faded from the sparkling colors to the deep rose of love. Our hearts and bodies felt lighter than they had before. There was a silence for a few moments, our final notes bouncing off the rounded walls of the chamber as we collected our thoughts and ourselves.

It was a new connection that we'd forged. If sex had been intimate, this was a million times more so. Never were we more vulnerable than when we were bleeding our notes out into the air, and both of us were keenly aware of it.

If it'd been anyone but Score who'd heard me, I'd have been profoundly, deeply mortified. But it was him, so I only felt relieved, connected to him, and most of all, loved.

His song was flawless, and so was mine, but together we made something better than either of us could alone. The feeling of the melody stuck with me. More than anything else, sirens were creatures of emotion. Maybe we felt things more keenly than other races. Maybe it was just part of our nature to have higher highs, deeper lows, and a million colors in between. It was why we needed to sing. It was why our eyes revealed how we felt. It was why our libraries contained so much music and performance pieces. We needed an escape, a conduit for our passion.

I reached over to him, finding his hand, interlinking it with mine.

He tugged me to him, propping his guitar against the stage.

He wrapped his arms around me. I leaned forward, breathing him in, feeling blissful. I was closer to him than I'd ever been.

"I love you," he whispered.

I pushed up on my tiptoes and kissed him, feeling the warmth of him bleed from my lips down my core. It blushed out to my limbs, spreading like a wildfire. He pressed his hands into my back, returning the kiss in perfect rhythm.

I wished we could stay this way forever, interlinked. I wished our troubles would spontaneously dissolve away, and that it could be just the two of us, together. Without the Broken, without my foster parents, without any of life's cruel pain. Instead, it could be this— happiness, and fun, and joy— so much joy.

There's a cruel truth about life, though:

Nothing lasts.

Chapter Thirty-One

The Way

I was finishing my training session three months later when Score stumbled into the fitness arena. I barely had time to register him as I dodged the attacks from my last couple of doubles. But Score *never* interrupted my training, so I knew it was important.

I hummed, dismissing my opponents. I sank breathlessly to the mat.

Score looked more wretched than I'd ever seen him. His face was etched with despair, his lips pulled into a tight frown, his eyes glassy. The look could only have one meaning.

I stood, feeling numb. "You found *proof*. Definitive proof we're trapped here."

He shook his head and gasped out, "No!"

I sprinted to him, ignoring my aching limbs. "What's wrong?"

His eyes searched mine desperately. They were a deep blue gray, the color of sadness, of anguish. He kissed me, a hungry, needy kiss that made my lips tingle. He gathered me into his arms, ignoring the sweat and heat my body radiated from my practice.

I pulled away from him. "Score," I said, running my hand along his face. I wished I could probe into his mind. His eyes revealed that he was emotionally hurting, but they offered no clue as to *why*. What could possibly be wrong?

He closed his eyes miserably, tipping his head back. His hands balled into fists. "I found the way. The way to leave."

My brows knitted in confusion, "But that's great news."

He shook his head, a hollow laugh rumbling in his throat. "I can only get one of us out. One of us has to stay."

The room seemed to sway beneath me as I absorbed his words. I shook my head, "No. We have to stay together."

"We *can't*. My father made the spell airtight, but a Realm gate can be opened as long as one of us is here. One of us needs to act as a conduit for it to work."

"There has to be another way."

"If it was possible, I'd have found it," he said, resigned. "You're going to have to go."

My heart sped up. "Me? Why not you?" I shook my head, "No! This is crazy!"

"Don't you see? It *has* to be you. You're the Bard. You can reverse the Broken. You're the one who's been training. You're the one who's contacted the council."

"I can't leave you behind," I choked out. It was too cruel to be forced to separate. I tried to even picture him staying here alone. It was heartbreaking. The loneliness would be soul shattering. The only reason Atlantis was bearable now was because we were together.

I wrapped my arms around him, burying my face in his chest. We could be patient. We could delay and fix the problem later.

"It can wait, Score."

"You *have* to leave me," he repeated.

"No."

"You deserve more, Lyra."

"You're enough. You're everything."

"You have to help your foster parents."

My breath caught. Susan and Rick. I'd almost forgotten them. Guilt blossomed at the base of my spine, catching in my chest. I wanted to tell him they didn't matter, but I couldn't do it. The weight of it crashed down, sitting on me like a ton of steel.

My eyes met his, "I have to leave."

He nodded, gasping, "Yes! You do."

I stumbled numbly forward. I felt vulnerable and disconnected within the enormous arena. I needed to get away from this stark place, back to the security of the room I shared with Score. I dashed forward, unlacing the breastplate on my armor.

Hot tears ran down my face. Score walked behind me

silently. I tore away our curtain, casting it and my armor to the floor. I peeled out of the gloves and boots, kicking the suit aside.

I sat on the bed, burying my face in my hands. I could hear Score beside me, and the bed dipped down with his weight. I leaned against him. He felt solid, steady, reassuring.

"I can help Susan and Rick, then come back," I said. "I could be gone for less than a day." I looked to him, catching his eyes. They were that same sad color.

Score shook his head, "You *can't*. You need to finish it, to fix what the sirens have done."

"I don't think I can."

He pushed me away gently, holding my shoulders so I was looking into his eyes. He smiled, "You're so strong. You'll manage to fix it." He closed his eyes, "I wish I could do it. I wish I could keep you here, just so I knew you'd be safe, alive. I wish I could give up my life to fix everything."

"Don't say that," I told him, "I need you."

"You don't need me."

"I do," I insisted, pushing into him, kissing him. I needed to touch him, to make sure he was still real, still with me. "I love you."

He turned from me, swallowing thickly. "This is ripping me apart, Lyra. But it's what's *right*. You can't come back until it's finished, because…" He took a breath, "Because Atlantis will remain sealed when you've left. There's no way to get inside except changing the flow of magic. Then my father's seal will break. It won't have enough magic to function the same way— actually, a lot of Atlantis will change."

I felt a sickness blossom in my stomach at that thought. "How much of Atlantis?"

He shook his head, "I don't know, Lyra. Some of the systems in place are mundane— the heating, the ventilation, the water filtration. The lighting's magical, but there are emergency lights. It might not be viable to live here without the additional magic."

I leaned against him, tears rolling down my cheeks. "But… it's *home*, Score."

He ran his hand through my hair, comforting me, "I know, Lyra. I know. I'll see what I can do. Maybe I can find a work-around. But it's possible we won't be able to return when we leave." He took a deep breath, "Even more so because our own powers will be severely limited."

"What do you mean?"

"Everything Bard Shiri added when she visited the Source will be taken away. So no more alteration. We'll be able to compel, to play, to sing, but— we won't be able to do much more."

"How long do we have?"

"The longer we delay, the harder it'll be. We can hold off another week. Just enough time to prepare. Enough time for you to contact the council. Maybe they'll agree to give you the keys."

"What if they won't?"

He cupped my face, wiping away one of my tears with his thumb. "Then you'll *fight*. You'll make them. And when you've succeeded in changing things, in making it right…" his eyes shifted to a murky yellow color, and he turned his gaze from me. "Then I can leave here, and we can be together again."

I fell backwards onto the bed. The stakes had always been high, of course. Now they were personal. A selfish part of me wanted to ignore the Broken, ignore Susan and Rick, and stay with him. In a hundred years' time, we could try to fix the problem together.

But I couldn't do it. I couldn't abandon my foster family.

Score's lips found mine, tender and comforting. A sob rippled from my core, breaking the kiss.

"I love you, and I have complete faith in you. You'll find me again," he affirmed.

I was dirty and tired and emotionally exhausted, but I still found myself gripping his clothes. I needed to be with him deeply. Reading me easily, he slid off my loose pants, pressing himself against me. He wrapped his hands around my torso.

I tugged off my tank top, throwing it in the corner. I ran my hands through his hair, closing my eyes and wishing that this was it, that this was my whole life. He kissed down my neck, my breast bone, along my stomach, across my hip bones. His hands skirted up my sides, leaving a tingly charge in their wake. A moan escaped my lips, and he sank into me.

~~~~~~~~~~~~~~~~

In the quiet that followed, we lay with our arms and legs tangled together, staring at the glass ceiling. Schools of fish languidly passed overhead. For a moment, I could almost forget the task ahead. But not for long.

"Do you really think I can do it?" I whispered.

"I do."

I hoped he was right. I twisted my fingers in his.

"It isn't like you're going to be alone," he pointed out. "You know Glenn will be there, if nothing else."

I considered that. We'd been in Atlantis for so long, I didn't have much faith that my guard had sat around patiently.

"There's no way he's been waiting this whole time."

"I wouldn't be surprised if he has."

Score said it as if he didn't have a single doubt. The certainty surprised me. He looked into my eyes, explaining, "We've been gone for over a year now, but I doubt he'd willingly leave. When you were on lock down in Whitecrest, I'd have waited for you for a *lifetime*. Glenn's a lot of things— a lot of things I'm not necessarily crazy about— but flaky isn't one of them. He'll be there." He swallowed. "He loves you, Lyra."

With the clarity of time behind me, I knew my match was right. I wondered what Glenn would say when I told him how I felt for Score. I supposed it was what the half-elf expected— what he claimed he wanted, even. On the other hand, it would hurt.

"What if he isn't there?"

"He'll be there, Lyra."

I chewed my lip, staring at the fishes swimming outside. "But what if he's not? What if—"

"If he isn't, there's zero probability that he'd just disappear. He'd leave behind a message, or something else to let you know where he is. I know it."

"How do you know?"

Score shrugged, running his fingertip over the back of my hand. "It's what I'd do. If I were him, and something dragged me away from my vigil, I'd make sure that the first thing you saw was from me. So that you knew where to find me."

He was probably right. I sat up, looking down at Score. He looked so casual, lying there. "Do you trust me with him?"

He took a deep breath. "I do," he answered. His eyes said otherwise— they were a bright, piercing green, not the brilliant blue I associated with honesty.

I grabbed a pillow and smacked him on the head, "*Truth.*"

He closed his eyes, chuckling. "How I *feel* has nothing to do with what I believe. I *do* trust you."

"Then why the green eyes?" I demanded.

"Honestly?" he pulled me down to him again, kissing me softly on the forehead. "I'm jealous. I'll be trapped here, and he'll be out there with you."

My heart ached for a moment. Every time I thought about leaving Score, panic settled into my bones. I shook it off.

"At least I can attend a council meeting," I said with a sigh. "Test the waters?"

That was a slight relief, anyway.

"Should be able to…" He embraced me, "And my work is done, at least for now. When you're getting ready, I can spend as much time with you as possible."

I could feel tears filling my eyes again. "Don't leave me at all until— until it's time, okay?"

"I belong to you. I promise."

Chapter Thirty-Two

Plea

The council met once a week to discuss events and policies, laws and treaties. The timing was always sunrise, often lasting until late in the day. Communication magic made time zones irrelevant. Even when Glenn and I'd spoken with them in the afternoon, the council members had been meeting at dawn. It was strange, but Score assured me it was just how it all worked with magical communications— coordinating time was too much of a hassle when crossing lines between the Realm and Overworld. Workarounds increased efficiency. The meeting was always on Monday— unless there was an emergency.

Recognizing me as the Bard, the throne in the Matriarchy would connect me psychically to the meeting space. I simply had to envision the council circle. I couldn't physically go to the site like I had before, but I'd be more present than when I'd interacted through the scrying pool. This time, I would attend the meeting as a councilor. I hoped I'd be well received.

"You're nervous?" Score asked as we awoke that Monday morning. It was early; the lights in the halls were still dim.

I nodded, "I am. What if they don't want to help?"

He stroked my arm comfortingly. "They might not. But it'd be stupid of them to withhold aid. You're going to set things right."

He had a point. What I was trying to do would only benefit the other extras. I couldn't see a logical reason they'd resist. Still, I didn't have enough experience to feel confident.

I slipped into one of the dresses, determined to look professional for the meeting. I twisted my hair into a tight bun, securing it with a silver cord. None of my shoes were appropriate, so I left my feet bare.

We made our way down the dark halls. I went over potential scenarios in my mind again and again. Unfortunately, I didn't know what to expect. The council had seemed rigid before. I had a feeling their meetings were usually outlined in advance. Who knew if they'd even hear me out?

"Don't be nervous," Score said, giving me a quick kiss. "You'll be fine."

I nodded, squaring my shoulders. I forced myself to descend onto the opal throne, gripping the arms. I took several deep breaths to calm myself.

Imagine the meeting grounds.

I pictured the space clearly. A ring of thrones surrounded by a scrubby beige patch of the Broken.

My vision blurred, Atlantis fading away. Directly ahead of me was Amaranthe's woven throne. I glanced around the circle. It felt like I was actually there, physically present, but I could hear the soft singing of Atlantis humming in the back of my head. It was reassuring.

The council members weren't there. I scanned the circle right to left. Maybe the meeting time had changed.

"Well, *this* is a surprise," a velvety voice mused next to me. I whipped my head sharply to the right. Sitting in his plush Victorian chair with red cushions was the vampire representative. His slice of the meeting space was covered in a cloak of night, protecting him from the light. I wondered if this glare— this sick fluorescent of the Broken— even counted as sunlight.

"Councilor," I responded stiffly.

He laughed jovially, sipping on a chalice of blood. I'd only seen the vampire a handful of times, but he'd always gone out of his way to make me uncomfortable. "I'd assumed we'd never see you again. After all, you disappeared on us." He clucked his tongue, "Naughty, naughty. So what are you asking for now? A new bodyguard? Did you wear through the old one so soon? Or are you just going to complain about your lot in life?"

I narrowed my eyes. "I'm a councilor just as much as you are, sir. I'll remind you I need respect."

"Do you think so?" he asked, grinning. "Girl, I'm 563 years old. You know *nothing*."

The circle began to fill out. Most of the councilors looked at me with mild surprise followed by boredom. I wondered if any of them wanted to be here. None of them looked like they enjoyed these meetings. I had the impression most councilors just slogged through them.

Amaranthe faded into view before me, taking a seat on the wicker throne. My heart beat faster. It was strange to see her now that I knew she'd wanted me dead.

Her hair draped over one shoulder in a complicated braid interwoven with morning glories. A cluster of lilac blossoms fell across her décolleté, complementing a soft violet dress. Her eyes reflected the color of the flowers: pale purple.

She regarded me in surprise but remained silent, sitting rigidly on her throne. She was again flanked by two members of her Guard. I recognized the bulky elf from when I'd first met Glenn, but the fiery redhead was new to me. He was thicker than Glenn, but still smaller than the other guardian.

I swallowed thickly, my eyes flickering over the other council members. I recognized all but one— at least passingly. The new centaur representative had ebony skin that bled into cream fur with cocoa spots. Her red-brown tail flicked a few times in irritation as I looked at her. Unlike Aristos, I'd call her beautiful. She had a small, heart-shaped face and huge eyes with long lashes and a pouting mouth.

King Dorian was the last to arrive. I smiled at him, happy to see another familiar face. I wished Marin attended council meetings regularly; it would've been nice to have her support. At least her father was here.

He stared at me, confused, his eyes the same blue as the water surrounding him. "Why are you here, siren?"

I took a deep breath, "I have an important matter to discuss with the council."

"We have protocols," Amaranthe seethed. "We have business set for each meeting. How presumptuous you are, how *arrogant* to assume we would drop everything to listen to your nonsense. You have taken advantage of the council's generosity, made us look like fools, and have absconded with one of my own guardians." She cocked her head, "Tell me, where is Glenn now? I would like to speak with him."

"Glenn is… indisposed," I answered carefully.

"Is he?" she said with a cruel smile. "Typical."

Dorian gazed at me, frowning. He sounded regretful, "Why did you vanish from my home like a thief in the night, Sarah? We painstakingly arranged your safe foster with the naga."

My nostrils flared, and I sat up straighter. I couldn't back down; I needed to assert myself. I took a deep breath, keeping my voice steady, "My name is Lyra, and I am of clan Nightingale. I'm the last siren Matriarch, the last of the siren Bards. You *will* respect me as my position dictates." There was a bristling at that. Around the circle, a few of the council members murmured amongst themselves. I kept my face impassive, "I've arrived here not only to take my place as representative of my people—"

"Your people!" snorted the dwarf. "You don't have any people!"

I ignored him, "But also to bring attention to a dire problem my species created. While I was unwitting in the conception of this issue, it's my duty as the last siren councilor to rectify it."

The elf queen's mouth twitched in amusement. She nodded, "Fine, little siren. We shall hear you out. What grave trouble *have* you discovered?"

I cast my eyes on the ground, to the scrubby beige grass and reedy light. "The Broken is a problem that's persisted for hundreds of years. It's— it's due to a tampering of my people. While they've died for their crimes, the consequences of their actions still prevail. The Broken continues to spread in the Realm."

"That's ridiculous," said a man with a thick accent. He wore a nice suit and tie, standing in a fire to the left of Amaranthe's throne. A djinni. His body was slightly transparent, and it wavered and moved like he was made of the smoke from the hearth. Maybe he was. "The Broken is a natural phenomenon."

"It is *not*," I responded firmly. "It was created when the sirens attempted to steal power by altering the flow of magic. Our kind used to be limited to the manipulation of mortals, but we changed things so we're capable of altering the world around us. This allows us to use our voices in almost limitless ways."

One of the dragon twins, the girl, spoke softly in Japanese. Her brother translated for the rest of us, "Then to adjust it, you will need to relinquish that power. Why would anyone agree to lose something so valuable?"

"Because," I answered, "the Broken will consume the Realm if it's left unchecked. I don't *need* the extra power. I just want to make things right."

"Even if we believed you," Amaranthe said with a slight edge to her voice, "what plan would you have to 'make things right'? What is it you require of us in your solution?"

I pursed my lips together, feeling nervous. I wasn't just asserting myself or explaining something now— I was asking for help. "It would require undoing it the same way that it was done— traveling to the Isle of Arcane at the center of the Realm. I'd need to use your Source Keys. My ancestors stole them from you the first time. Today I'm asking you to give them to me willingly so I can fix it."

Another round of harsh whispers surrounded me. The vampire spoke first, "That is not a light request."

"I understand. But—"

"Absolutely not!" cried Amaranthe. She openly glared at me. My heart pounded in my ears.

Why would she reject it? I was trying to *help*. Changing the flow of magic back to its natural current would benefit the council far more than it would benefit me.

She tilted her head to one side. "I see you're confused, so I'll explain why you won't be getting the key from the elves. The Source of Magic is a volatile place. It's nestled within a poisonous sea, riddled with enough dangers that I could hardly imagine you surviving the journey. Should you arrive within that sacred space, there's very little you couldn't do.

"If you have all twelve keys— which would be almost impossible to acquire this day and age— you'd have the building blocks of all creation at your disposal. You could do anything, become anything, manipulate the world into *anything*. There are almost no limitations. It's why the keys were created in the first place— they're a failsafe, to prevent any single race from getting to that sacred space.

"*If* what you say is truthful, I'll admit it'd answer many questions. The Broken is indeed a problem that we've been combating for many centuries. However," she leaned forward, "if the whole of your story is true, the problem should resolve itself when you *die*, my dear."

I fought to keep my composure. After all this, she was implying that she still wanted to kill me. My voice was harsh, "Why?"

She leaned back, "You are the last siren, hmm?" I kept my face neutral. She didn't know about Score. It was a relief— he'd be safe, at least. She brushed her hands along her skirt, smoothing it. "You cannot create more sirens without a mate, and you will die eventually. When that happens, the stream of magic will have no place to go but back to its natural path, the flow no longer impeded. It might be painful and slow, but it *will* correct itself. Faster, should the council decide to help..." she looked into her lap, lacing her fingers together. Sounding reluctant, she finished, "*Speed* the process along."

"Who are we to say she has to die?"

I jumped. Someone was actually defending me!

The tiny Japanese girl. I'd never heard her speak English. Her accent was subtle, and her voice was clear and bright.

She continued, "We dragons have a saying— if you set fire to the world, you have two choices: to let it burn to ash or to collect water. It sounds to me like this siren, this Lyra, is trying to put out the fire her people created. She has our support."

Her brother went rigid next to her. He began speaking quickly in Japanese. The girl just smiled and spoke soothingly in their native tongue, caressing his cheek. He seemed quelled and nodded. "She has our support," he said grudgingly.

I turned to King Dorian. He looked thoughtful, his brow pulled tight. He glanced at me, then shook his head, "I'm sorry, Lyra. Our people have long been allies, but I cannot abide this. It's too risky and far too foolish to give you our key. While I *hope* your intentions are noble, I can only say with certainty that you disappeared from my home without a trace over a year ago. Unfortunately, you've abused the council system and caused embarrassment. We had to explain to the naga family that we lost you, to thank them for their generosity, to compensate them for their wasted time. I must think about what's best for the people."

I couldn't believe it. I wasn't expecting Amaranthe to give me her key, and most of the councilors' allegiances were total mysteries, but I'd at least hoped the mer king would honor our alliance. When we'd met, Marin told me our peoples' friendships ran old and deep. I thought we'd always depend on each other. It was the reason she'd helped me in the first place.

I struggled to keep my face neutral. I was starting to feel despair seep into my bones. "Is that all then?" I asked.

Amaranthe sneered, "Naturally not! We're not animals. The council will take a vote." She looked up to the head of the circle. The twins were the first in the loop.

"The dragons wish to give the siren a chance," said the man. "Yes."

Dorian sighed, "It's too risky. I apologize, siren. No."

"Absolutely not," said Amaranthe.

The djinni in the fire sighed, "No. At least— not without compensation."

"Eh…" said the dwarf, stroking his beard. "Give her a chance. Yes."

The pixie was the next to speak. She flew to me with stiff yet graceful movement, reminding me of a hummingbird. Darting so she was in front of my face, she spoke in a voice so quiet it was hard for me to hear her despite the close proximity. "The faeries abstain from this vote. We'll agree if the siren can retrieve the keys from the angels and demons. Otherwise, this vote is pointless." She flew back to her perch.

The vampire swirled his bloody wineglass before he took a sip, "I think not."

I felt dizzy. That was four firm nos, two yeses, and one maybe. Unless everyone else at this circle agreed, there wasn't a chance.

I blinked, realizing the group was looking at me. "Obviously I support it," I said. That made it three yeses. I'd forgotten about my own vote.

The centaur stared at me, her face scrunched up, looking indecisive. After a long while, she said, "I feel the centaurs owe you a debt, personally. For what it's worth, you have our support."

Four yeses. The vote was tied now. I kept my gaze locked forward. There was only the ghost left. I wished I could see her more firmly, but she was a creature of the peripherals. I knew that I'd see less if I trained my gaze directly to her. Her voice made me shiver.

"There are none who should have business within the Sea of Phantoms," she said slowly. "While her intentions *appear* honorable, I must decline. I'm sorry."

309

I stared at my bare feet, my face flushing. I'd lost the vote. I wasn't going to get any help here.

"Well," said Amaranthe smugly, "with that delay concluded, we can start our *actual* business." Her eyes flickered over to me, "You may go or stay, if you wish." She paused, "If you see Glenn, tell him he's needed."

I couldn't stand another minute. How could the council members take me seriously when most wanted me to die? I had no place here. I stood from the throne, severing the connection. The ground rocked around me as my eyes readjusted to Atlantis.

Score sat in one of the Matriarchy chairs at the end of the table. His hands were folded in front of him. "How'd it go?"

I shook my head, "They won't help us."

He stood, walking around the table to meet me. He wrapped his arms around my waist, "What happened?"

I shrugged. I felt exhausted from the meeting and the early morning. "They took a vote. The council decided it was too risky to give me the keys." I pulled from him, slapping my palm against the tabletop. "The thing that's really irritating is that I was so *close* to having that vote." I closed my eyes. If King Dorian had stood with me like I'd expected, I'd have won.

"The elves disapproved?" Score asked, sitting on the table to face me.

"Yeah, but I was expecting that. I'd hoped the Lady of Flowers would've seen reason, but I knew it wouldn't be easy to convince her if she's spent so much time trying to kill me." I folded my arms, "No, what surprised me was that the mermaids didn't have my back."

His brows furrowed, "I thought that Stacie— Marin— was their princess. Isn't she one of your best friends?"

I closed my eyes, shaking my head, "It was her father's decision. He didn't think it was wise."

Score grabbed my hand, squeezing it comfortingly. "We'll find a way."

Will we?

"They've opted to wait for me to die, unless Amaranthe can convince them to take a more proactive approach. That'll supposedly fix the Broken."

"If you were the *last* siren, maybe it would," he mused. Then his brow raised, "So... they don't know about me?"

I shook my head, "No. They don't. They think I'm it, and when I'm dead the problem will solve itself." I wrung my hands together. They were wrong, of course. If the sirens' plan had worked, if Score hadn't found a workaround to leaving Atlantis, we'd probably have had a family together. Another group of sirens to pull the flow of magic out of its natural place.

"It's too bad you can't talk to Marin," Score reflected. "You could probably convince her to talk some sense into her father. Maybe if she let him know what's really at stake, that we're sincere, that I'm a factor— it might make things more dire. Maybe they'd be more likely to respond if they realize we won't just snuff out."

It was a shame Marin wasn't with King Dorian at the council meeting. I wondered if she'd have tolerated the decision. Of course, she had such a strange relationship with her father, she may have just accepted his choice without argument.

"Maybe if she'd been—" I paused, suddenly remembering the vial containing her tear. I'd completely forgotten about it abandoned in my bag. "I— I actually *can* talk to Marin! She gave me a way before we left! She has a really strained relationship with her dad, so it might be useless. But it's worth a shot, right?"

"Absolutely. If she's the princess, she has to have some say in things."

I wasn't certain that was true, but Score had never seen Marin around her father. In fact, Score hadn't really seen much of Marin at all. What he *had* seen was almost exclusively her alter-ego, Stacie, who wasn't the same. He only knew her from what I'd told him, which was admittedly not much.

But we had to try.

Chapter Thirty-Three

Mermaid Tears

I took a long nap, curling under the blankets with Score wrapped around me. It was too early to contact Marin. Knowing her, she wouldn't wake up until right before she had to be at school. I'd have better luck trying to speak with her in the afternoon.

Truthfully, I was grateful for it. I was exhausted from the meeting, and I felt deflated. As much as I'd worried, I hadn't expected the council to reject me. I was naive— too new to this world to understand how things worked.

I awoke late in the day.

Score was staring at me, a soft smile on his lips.

"You were watching me sleep?"

He chuckled, "Maybe."

I smacked him with a pillow, laughing, "Well, stop. It's creepy."

"Oh, come on," he said, smirking, "Glenn used to do it all the time."

"Glenn doesn't sleep, though," I said. "You do."

"I wasn't sleeping just now."

"There are so many more productive things you could be doing," I said with a giggle.

"Such as?"

"Such as this," I said. I kissed him hard, running my fingertips over his back.

He pulled away, "And ruin your beauty sleep? How cruel

do you think I am?"

"I'd hardly call that 'ruining'."

He brought his arms around me, clasping his hands at the small of my back. I leaned against his chest, sighing happily. Somewhere in the back of my mind, a little voice nagged me: five more days. Five days until I'd leave him.

"You're sad."

Sometimes I forgot how much my eyes gave away. I didn't want to spoil Score's mood. His eyes were a brilliant gold— or at least they were before I'd made him worry. Now they were forest green.

I tried to play it off, "I'm just going to miss you, that's all."

"It'll be fast." He didn't sound convinced.

Guilt welled up in my core. Now his eyes were heartsick blue gray. I'd ruined his mood.

I kissed him, "It will be. I'm going to hurry to fix things so it'll be fast." I sat up, looking at the silver clock on the wall— 4:17 p.m. I suspected Marin would be available now.

After fishing out my abandoned bag from the back of the wardrobe, I dug through the dregs remaining inside. Sure enough, deep within was the bottle with the tear, still bundled in Marin's handkerchief.

"I need a shallow dish or bowl," I told Score.

"Already grabbed one while you were asleep," he said, sitting up and stretching.

I pulled a dress over my head, lacing the back up as quickly as I could manage and haphazardly tying it.

Score leaned over, grappling for a shirt, but I laughed. "Nope! Not allowed. Only pants. And only if it's *completely* necessary."

He raised a brow, his mouth twitching in amusement. "Well, I'm at my Bard's disposal." He bowed cheekily at me.

I loved him so much.

I combed my fingers through my hair hastily, sitting on the chaise. I dragged the side table closer. Score had set up the scrying saucer on top of it. I was impressed to see it was extremely similar to the one Marin and I had used to speak with King Dorian so long ago. The only real difference I could see was the size; this dish was much smaller, allowing for only one person to peer inside.

I unraveled the bandanna from the bottle, examining it. It

didn't *look* like much, but sometimes magic was like that. I trusted Marin. I tipped it into the saucer and waited. After about a minute, the water rippled and I could see her.

She was as clear as if I was standing in the room with her. I felt a strange desire to reach my hand through the water, pull her out, and hug her. It didn't work like that, though. It was just for communication. I'd missed her more than I'd realized.

She was sitting on the edge of her bed in her room. I swallowed the homesickness that burbled up as I watched her. Her hand was on her forehead, and she was squinting.

"Marin?" I asked. Her eyes widened. She could see me. "Thank god," I said, relieved. It was nice to talk to another friendly face. I hoped she wasn't mad at me for leaving so suddenly, for taking off without a proper goodbye.

She smiled widely, "Lyra?!" Her face fell, "Are you okay? You just disappeared."

Score interjected, "Ask her if she can talk reason into her father."

I waved at him, shooing him away. I knew what I needed to do. "I'll ask her!" I turned back to Marin, "There's a lot I want to tell you, and—"

My friend jumped, her skin taking on a lighter pallor.

"I don't have long, Lyra," she whispered hastily. She craned her neck, calling, "Just— give me some time, Dylan! Please!"

She looked nervous. Something about the name was familiar— then I remembered why.

"Dylan? As in—"

Marin sighed, rubbing her forehead wearily, "My betrothed. I can't really get into it right now."

"Is there a better time to talk to you, or—?"

She shook her head, "Unfortunately, no. There's not. Just— what's up?"

I sighed, trying to prioritize my thoughts. Marin obviously didn't have a lot of time to chat. "A lot's happened, but here's the main part: Glenn and I ran— you knew that," I smiled softly. "But Score came, too. You remember, Will."

She looked a little confused, "I knew he'd stopped attending school. His parents moved away."

I whipped my head back towards Score. I hadn't realized

he'd completely cut ties from them when we'd left. I felt a strange combination of flattered and appalled.

I blinked, trying to focus. I didn't know how long Marin would be able to talk to me, and I needed to take advantage of the time I had. "Well, the map I'd told you about— we followed the clues and found the siren ruins. Everything happened the way our parents planned, but…"

"What happened?" she leaned forward, interested.

I bit my lip, "It turned out to be a trap."

"A trap?" she raised a brow. "Why would they set up their own kind?"

I rubbed my forehead wearily, "The good of the species, it seems."

"What?!"

"Let me back up," I leaned into the chair, crossing my ankles. "The map led us— Score and I, and no one else— to Atlantis."

"Atlantis?" She sounded skeptical, "As in, 'underwater lost city of Atlantis'? Pretty sure that doesn't actually exist."

"It definitely exists. It was the sirens' main city, their home. They were supposed to disappear forever within it, but instead they were all killed… somehow."

"How'd they die?"

"That part's still fuzzy, unfortunately."

She stared at me expectantly. Marin looked different than before we'd left Whitecrest. It could've been worry for me, but it didn't seem like that'd be enough to make her look so subdued. I blinked, remembering I didn't have time to get sidetracked. "When we got here, it became clear. They'd left us a note— Score and me." I sighed, "They locked us inside."

"What?! Why the hell would they imprison their own—" Realization dawned on her, and she flushed. "Oh my. I mean, Score's a good looking cat and all, but—" She furrowed her brows, "Do you guys even really *like* each other like that?! I mean, enough to be— *forever*— I mean—" She was stumbling over her words. Something was definitely up with her. Marin was never like this; she was confident to the point of cocky most days. I didn't have time to ask her what was wrong, and I felt selfish for it.

"Score and I are actually…" I paused, glancing over to him. "He's the best thing about being here," I finished affectionately.

"I'd ask for details, but there's no time."

"There *isn't*," I agreed regretfully. It would've been nice to just be a girl for a moment. "The thing is, we also learned that the whole reason the sirens were being attacked is because they caused the Broken."

"But no one knows what caused it."

"Greed caused it. Score and I want to set it right, so maybe the Realm won't become completely devoid of magic in a few hundred years. I found a way to attend the council meeting—"

"Then we can meet there later tonight, and I'll just pull you out to Whitecrest that way!"

I shook my head, "Not so simple, unfortunately. There's a link between a throne here and the one there, but it doesn't actually transport me. It just lets my consciousness travel. It's how the last siren Bard attended the meetings but still ran Atlantis."

"I'm honestly surprised there *is* such a thing. It's a running joke down here. Every seduced human a mermaid drags underwater automatically assumes he's going to Atlantis."

"Well, if we can sort everything out, maybe you can visit sometime." Marin could visit Atlantis easily, as long as we could remove the defenses. It'd be nice to show Glenn, too, though it was probably too artificial for him. "The truth is, I need your help. At the meeting, I asked for all the Source Keys from the councilors."

"Whoa. That's a tall order, Lyra," she said, twisting a lock of hair around her index finger. "Why do you need them?"

"To fix what the sirens did with them the first time around. They stole the keys and altered the flow of magic. That's why the Broken happened. The magic's being funneled from the Realm to—" I swallowed, "Well, to me. To Score. To Atlantis."

"That explains why your race was rumored to be so powerful, at least," Marin muttered. "So the council told you no, right?" She didn't sound surprised.

I nodded, "Yeah. But it was actually a close vote. Your father could've changed things. I'd have won the vote if he'd stood with me."

"He didn't?!" She sounded outraged, genuinely shocked. "But we have an alliance!"

"I know. I was surprised, too. I just— I really need to get those keys, to undo everything. That'll unlock Atlantis."

"Even if you *had* their keys, how can you use them if

316

you're stuck there?"

"I…" This was the part that hurt the most. I sucked in a deep breath, "Score found a loophole. He's going to create a Realm gate."

"Really? I thought you had to be a skilled sorcerer for something like that."

I glanced at Score, smiling in admiration. I looked at Marin. "Score's just… brilliant, that's all. I don't know the details. But when I leave here, I'd like to have a head start. I can meet you at your house in about a week. I mean, I figure your father is a good place to begin. So will you talk to him for us?"

"Yeah," she muttered. She looked distracted and angrier than I'd have expected, "Something like that."

"Thanks, Marin!" I said, relieved, "I'm counting on you. See you on the other side."

She nodded, moving away from the bed and into her closet.

I uncorked the vial and slid a funnel into it, tipping the dish back to return the tears to the bottle. I quickly covered it with the bandanna.

I turned to Score, "Did you really abandon your parents?"

He shrugged, settling next to me, clasping his hands together. "I— they think I'm in college. If they don't hear from me for five years, they'll forget to even worry. They'll think I died, but— but it won't be painful for them. I made sure, I was really careful with the compulsion."

It was cruel— not to his parents, Score had made certain of that— but I knew how much he loved them. "I can't believe that you'd—"

"Lyra," he murmured, wrapping his arm around me. He hauled me over to him, speaking into my shoulder with his head buried near the crook of my neck, "I love them, and I appreciate them. But I had to give them their lives back, and…" He sighed, nuzzling my neck, "If it's the choice between you or them, you're going to win. Every time."

My stomach tumbled around, "But Score—"

His eyes met mine, "You're better than me, Lyra. In every possible way. And you make me want to be better, too."

I felt a heat rising to my cheeks, "I'm not, though, Score, I'm—"

"You have no idea how special you actually are." He

turned me to him, "It's going to be a really, *really*, long wait for me. It could be a minute, and it'd be too long without you. But if I tried to— if I convinced you to stay— you'd be worse off, in the long run. So you're teaching me to be more selfless," he said quietly. "And that's a lesson I needed."

It was silly for him to think he was selfish. He spent so much time, so much effort, trying to help me and make me happy.

"But you give me so much of yourself, so much—" I started.

He just chuckled, "And I get to see you happier, Lyra, and that fills my brain up with all sorts of lovely chemicals: dopamine, serotonin…" I furrowed my brows. He was beyond me again. He smiled, "You make me happy, Lyra. That's all I'm saying."

"But that *is* selfless," I protested.

"Not the same way," he said, shaking his head. "You give because it's the right thing to do. If not…" He looked into my eyes, "Do you really want to leave Atlantis?"

No.

I hated the idea at this point, which was almost insane considering how desperately I'd wanted to leave when we'd arrived. But now, if we could just manage to open it to visitors, I'd feel like Atlantis was perfect. I was happy here.

"I have to…"

"Exactly, heart-song, exactly."

I leaned into his chest, closing my eyes, taking a few deep breaths. I tried to imagine spending a hundred years away from him, and I began to tremble. Score's hand ran lightly down my back. I turned my gaze to him, "I'll miss you, Score."

"Mm…" he murmured. "Look at those blue eyes. So sad… it'll be okay, Lyra," he soothed, pulling me tighter to him. "It'll be okay."

Chapter Thirty-Four

A Goodbye

Four nights later, I was having trouble sleeping, my heart racing. My thoughts kept returning to how much I'd miss Score, how I'd possibly do what was needed without him. For his part, my match was peaceful, his arm slung over me, breathing rhythmically.

I didn't often see him like this, the still hours when his mind wasn't so busy. He was beautiful. His hair mussed, his long dark eyelashes resting on the top of his cheekbones, mouth parted just slightly, breathing out a soft hum.

I sighed. I'd been putting this off, but it was time.

I shifted Score's arm, careful not to wake him, and slipped out of the bed. Pulling a dress from the wardrobe, I tugged it over my head. I ducked beyond the curtain to the hall.

The warm glass underfoot reassured me as I padded through the dim hallway. My heart leapt in my throat, urging me to return to the comfort and safety of my bed. Instead, I pressed onward until I reached the library.

Forte's projection appeared seated, leaning forward into his hand. He stared at the shelves ahead. Score's books had been left open on the table. The hologram looked like a statue collecting dust. Abandoned as he was, the scene felt melancholy.

"Hello… dad?" I said awkwardly, making my way to his corner.

His mouth tugged into a smile, his gaze forlorn. "You actually used to call me papa, Lyra."

"Then hello... papa."

"Hello, baby-girl."

I slid into the chair across from him, taking a deep breath. "I'm leaving day after tomorrow," I announced. His eyes met mine, his brows lifted. He looked unhappy— but I'd been expecting that. "It's the right thing to do."

Forte shook his head, sighing, "And what about Score?"

I felt a pang hit me in the heart, hard and cruel. Of course I'd miss him. "I'll see him again."

The projection laughed sadly. "My darling girl, so brave and stubborn. Are you really willing to risk his life like this?"

My heart seemed to stop. I leaned forward, "What... what do you mean?"

Forte's mouth curled into a smile, but he still looked sad. "Clever boy," he muttered. "*Too* clever..."

"Risk whose life?" I whispered harshly, "Score's?"

Forte nodded, "This plan he's put together is dangerous, Lyra. It's experimental. Bold, yes. Safe... no."

I felt like I was going to be sick. I leaned into my hand, groaning. Score had told me nothing about danger— only that he would be trapped. My gaze moved up to Forte wretchedly.

"So he could *die*?"

"He could die, Lyra," Forte agreed.

It wasn't anything I could bear. I closed my eyes, fat tears rolling down my cheeks.

"You could wait it out," Forte said. "I could walk you through every detail to fixing the Broken. Every step. You'd be so, so prepared."

If it weren't for the reason Score had given me before that forced my hand, god help me I would've. But as it was...

"Papa," I whispered, "I can't wait that long."

"Why are you so stubborn?!" He demanded, pained. "The Borderlands surrounding the Broken were evacuated in my own time! The decay shouldn't be spreading very quickly with only two sirens alive. You have to see, Lyra! Waiting is the right thing to do! It's the *only* thing to—"

I shook my head. "I can't wait, papa. It has nothing to do with the Broken."

His mouth closed. He stared at me, and I wished suddenly that he was real and whole— not just the memory of my father, but the real person standing before me. I wished I knew what emotion he was feeling right now. I wished I could know what was on his mind with a glance. Instead, I was looking at a blank slate, trying to keep my voice even.

"I grew up human," I explained, "and I've made mistakes."

"*Everyone* makes mistakes, Lyra," he told me. "That's no reason—"

I held my hand up, stopping him. My eyes were on the table. "I wasn't like Score was. No human family adopted me. I was pinched and ugly and skinny and introverted. Maybe I'm just not very lovable," I said, considering it. I leaned into my hand.

"That isn't true at all," Forte protested.

I just smiled. He was my father. He almost had to love me.

"But for the last three years, I was with a young couple," I continued, brushing my fingertips along an open book, "On the day I transitioned, I sang for them."

His brows turned up, "Oh, baby-girl..."

I blinked a few times. I'd already shed my tears for Susan and Rick. I was going to make amends, one way or another. I rapped my fingers on the tabletop. "So you see," I finished, "I need to deliver *Lethe* to them."

"Where are they now?"

"Sleeping. A human hospital." They'd been comatose for far longer than they should've been. A day was too long, and it'd been over a year.

Forte just sighed, his face tormented. Finally, he surrendered, "There's no way I'll possibly talk you out of it." He leaned into his own hand, eyes cast down at his feet.

"I wish you were real," I sobbed.

Forte's eyes snapped up to me. "You have no idea how much I wish that was the case, baby-girl," he said. "If I'd survived, things would've been so different."

"I wish I could at least touch you!" I gasped, reaching a hand for him. It passed right through the projection's body. "Will you even be here when I come home?"

"Atlantis is *home* now?"

"Of course it is," I said weakly.

Forte laughed, "If you truly do fix the Broken—" He shook his head, "No. Without alteration, my projection won't function."

"I'll miss you," I admitted. In the strangest way, I'd

developed an odd attachment to Forte, despite being at odds with him so frequently.

Regret washed over me. I'd made a lot of mistakes since arriving in Atlantis, but none worse than ignoring my father. I'd squandered my opportunity to know so much, all because I was angry with him.

Suddenly I was crying, "What was she like?!"

He understood the question without clarification. "Most people thought that she was cold and difficult, but she loved, deeper than anyone I've ever met," he said thoughtfully, smiling just a little. "She loved you, especially. She was wise, too. It was her suggestion that we have you, that we'd finally have a Bard who'd fix our mistake. She was chiding, but I could tell she was fond of you and Score. She didn't allow for much fun, or horseplay, but she'd often sneak one or both of you sweets.

"And she was more than that," he declared. "She was my match, my wife, the mother of my child. She was brilliant and beautiful and kind, as hard and unyielding as she had to be, a great Matriarch. She was just, and always knew the answers when there was a problem within the Nightingales. She and Score's mother were best friends— to the point that they wanted to merge factions.

"Oh, and Muses, was she beautiful. She had golden hair that draped down to her waist. The ends curled no matter what style she wanted to favor that day. Her mouth was a little wide, and she was so serious, so often, that when you were lucky enough to get a smile from her, both Realm and Overworld lit up. She was my world, for a long time. Then she was only half my world because you'd stolen the other piece of my heart, Lyra."

I cried thinking about it. I wanted it. I wanted this picture that Forte was painting. I knew almost nothing about how my childhood could've gone, but I wanted my family— the family that'd been ripped from me before I even remembered it. I felt a hollow sense of loss in the pit of my stomach. I wondered if soon I'd lose Score, too. I didn't know if I could bear it.

Forte could read the hesitation on my features, or maybe he just knew me well enough. "Are two human lives worth Score's?" he asked gently.

I took a ragged breath, feeling wretched. In the back of my mind, in my heart, I didn't think so. But that was selfish.

"I want to tell you no, they aren't, but I know, I *know,*

that's wrong." I chewed on my cheek. "Maybe I can do it," I said. "Maybe I can be the gamble, and Score can go—"

Forte shook his head, "Do you honestly think he'd agree to that, Lyra?"

"Agree to what?" Score asked, his hands on his hips standing behind me. I jumped, feeling guilty. He slid into the chair next to mine, pressing his lips to my neck. "You weren't in bed, heart-song…"

I turned to him, my heart heavy, "Is it true this is dangerous, Score?"

He sighed, opening and closing the golden compass he'd used to find me. "How long have you been talking to Forte?"

"Long enough," the projection responded. "Long enough to know there are risks, though I didn't spell them all out for her."

Score bit his lip, turning to me, "I've done the calculations, Lyra. There's a margin for error, of course, but I should be fine."

"That 'margin for error' is bigger than he'd like you to believe," Forte rebuked.

Score narrowed his eyes at the projection, "But I'll be *fine*."

"Maybe we can find another way?" I asked hopefully. "I can speak with Marin, and maybe she can… make some *Lethe*?"

Forte sighed, "Unfortunately, that won't work."

"Why not?"

"Because to craft *Lethe*, you need siren blood, and the only two sirens are locked away. Unless you have some blood frozen somewhere on the surface?"

Score offered, "I donated blood once when I was fifteen. They barely let me do it because of my bodyweight. I doubt it's still around."

"It wouldn't work anyway, because it's from before your transition," Forte told him. His eyes turned to me, "Lyra?"

I slumped into the chair, feeling defeated. A burning pain seared my stomach. "I certainly lost enough blood since transitioning, but none of it's been saved."

"This *has* to be done," Score said, squeezing my hand tightly. "Don't let ghosts scare you, Lyra. I'll be fine."

Forte glared at him, "You're brilliant, Score. In fact, Beat and Alondra pushed that when they had you— pushed your intelligence right up to the edge before it'd spiral back into madness. Maybe they went too far, though."

Score's nostrils flared, looking at the projection. "It'll be fine," he asserted. His head snapped back to me, "It's what needs to happen."

I shook my head, staring at my hands. "Isn't there— isn't there another way?" I asked desperately, "The spell can't be completely airtight, can it? Forte? Papa?"

The projection let out a long sigh. "There was never a precedent for it *needing* to be breached. In fact, we didn't *want* it to be breached. That was the point. If for some reason, Muses forbid, you both grew up hating each other, we wanted there to be enough time for you to reconcile. We needed you both to be together and safe."

"But it's so *long!*" I protested, my voice cracking.

Forte shook his head, "It's incredibly short, in the scheme of things."

"Then let me do it!" I cried, looking into Score's eyes.

Horror crossed his features at the suggestion. It proved to me how dangerous Score's plan was. He cupped my face in his hands, "Absolutely not!"

"You can go, cure my foster parents, and then—"

"And then what, Lyra?" he asked, shaking his head. "Wait a century for you? Spend the time tortured, alone, on the surface?"

I sobbed, feeling miserable. "Then we can push it back, push it further away. It doesn't have to be so soon—"

"You'll regret it if we do," Score said with certainty. "And if we start now, we'll only keep doing that. It needs to be—" his eyes moved up, along the wall, to the large clock near the stairs. It was after midnight. "Tomorrow. As planned, as intended."

I growled against Score, squeezing my eyes shut, frustrated. I was so angry with the situation. A deep rumbling echoed from his chest. I cracked my eyes open— he was laughing.

"You think it's funny?!"

He wrapped his arms around me, leaning his head against mine. "I was just thinking that a year ago, everything would've been so different. You'd have said good riddance, and—"

"That's not true!" I protested, my face on fire.

"But mostly," he said, pressing two fingers beneath my chin so I looked into his beautiful rose eyes, "I was thinking how nice it is to be so loved."

"I don't want to leave," I whispered.

"Then don't!" Forte erupted, breaking the intimacy of the moment.

"She needs to," Score responded, his brows furrowing. His eyes were a beautiful, bright blue laced with lilac— it broke my heart. "I don't want Lyra to ever experience the kind of regret I have." He stood, offering me his hand. "So if you don't mind, I'd rather we get some sleep so we can enjoy our last full day together."

"In that case," the projection said with a sigh, "I wish you both the best. *Hopefully,* I'll be seeing more of you, Score." The uncertainty in his voice made my heart ache. Forte turned to me, "And Lyra— my beautiful, darling Lyra. Your parents loved you. Don't forget that. I love you. More than you could possibly know."

"Goodbye," I said softly, "I— I love you, papa."

The projection just laughed, "Go, then! Off with you! And the very, *very* best of luck with everything."

I laced my fingers through Score's. We turned, walking out of the library. I felt a crushing weight settle on my shoulders. Everything felt so final.

Score's fingers ran soothingly through my hair. "Don't worry, Lyra. Everything will be okay."

I could only hope.

Chapter Thirty-Five

Conduit

I awoke the next day, glancing at the clock. It was already after ten. I was sad it was so late, sad I spent so much time asleep. Score's arm was draped around me. He leaned on his other hand, studying my features, a soft smile on his face.

"Why didn't you wake me up?"

"You need your sleep," he responded. "I'm content when you're with me."

It was a true enough statement, something I might have said if the situation was reversed. I twisted my leg around his, burying my face into his chest. "I don't want this to be our last day together."

"It won't be," he soothed, looking thoughtful. He ran his fingertips lightly along my bare shoulders. "You know, I never realized before that even our names complement each other," he said, kissing me, tucking a stray piece of hair behind my ear. "But they do. Music, Lyrics…" He ran a hand down my side, near my back. I shivered. "We'll find each other again."

Even if the creation of the gate didn't kill him, there was still no guarantee that I'd survive my mission or that I'd even be successful. A hundred years of being alone couldn't be good for Score. My stomach tumbled at the thought.

Score pulled away from me, kissing me before standing to retrieve something from the top of the shelf.

He returned. Balanced in his palm were the two opal rings our parents had left us.

"There are over 10,000 opals in Atlantis," he murmured, holding one of the rings to the light.

I sighed wistfully, "I've always thought they were pretty."

"Me, too. But they're more than beautiful. You know the siren word for them…"

"*Asosae,*" I whispered.

"Siren eyes."

I nodded. I'd understood the meaning in my core since my attunement.

"Have you read the Exposition?"

I smiled. Normally I was out of the loop compared to Score, but the Exposition was a tale I knew. "The Nine Muses were leaving the Earth and Realm forever. But before they departed, they left a gift to the world. They carved a man and woman from a glittering stone, breathed life into the pair through song, and placed opals within them to serve as their eyes. Then they ascended to the heavens to watch over their children made of song and artistry and emotion."

"The sirens believed that was true," he reflected. "The first of us. Matched by the Muses themselves."

First. Last. I wondered if I would ever see Score again. Maybe we really would be the last of our kind. Maybe the line would end here.

"Do *you* believe it's true, Score?"

"Hmm… Well, my father thought it was nonsense, but if you ask Forte, he doesn't have a doubt it happened. But me? As a Lark, I'm inclined to believe in science and facts. On the other hand…" he smiled, staring into my eyes with devotion. "I'm matched to a Nightingale. So I believe in miracles. I think it's possible. Maybe it's exactly the way it happened. Maybe the Muses are watching over us now." He held up the feminine ring, "I never told you this before. But this was always yours. I knew it from the start."

It seemed so obvious to me now, but the first time I'd spied it, the ring appeared to be a family heirloom.

I plucked the simpler man's ring from his palm and gazed into his eyes, "Then this must be yours."

"So when you're gone," he said with a grin, taking the larger band from my hand, "I'll wear my ring. You wear yours. And we can both know we're connected." He slid the silver over my finger. My heart raced in my ears.

Was this a proposal?

I stared into his eyes, but he just laughed cheerfully. His irises turned a liquid gold with that familiar rose pink on the edges. "Someday," he added, "I'd like to ask you to marry me. But now isn't the time."

My stomach leapt to my throat. I wrapped my arms around him, kissing along his neck, "It could be, Score..."

He grinned, pulling me into his strong arms, tumbling me onto the mattress so I bounced. He ran his lips across my torso, leaving a trail of kisses from my navel to my breast bone. "No, my Nightingale, my heart-song, this separation will be a test of patience for us both..." his lips moved up, along my breasts, and I groaned a little at both the statement and the sensation. "And when I *do* ask you..." he whispered, running his tongue lightly over my neck, "I won't want you half-way."

I couldn't take it anymore. Desire engulfed me like a flame. I whipped us around, pressing him into the bed until I straddled him, kissing his lips. My hands ran over his chest and down, down, down his body.

"Lyra?" he asked, surprised at my boldness.

I pinned his hands in mine and kissed him deeply, quenching the fire.

~~~~~~~~~~~~~~~

I stood over the objects strewn out on our bed, trying to decide what to take with me. I pursed my lips. Packing to return to the surface was harder than I'd have thought.

It was the big day— the day I was leaving Score. I stared at the potions, clothes, papers and other miscellaneous items that had invaded my life. There was a definite 'take' pile formed in one corner of the enormous bed. The rest of the stuff was all 'maybe'.

In the 'take' pile was the vial of *Lethe*, the Realm map, my dulcimer, and the opal key of the sirens— retrieved from Bard Shiri's chambers.

Everything else was undecided.

"You should take the water breathing potion," Score insisted, pushing it towards the 'take' corner.

I shook my head, "I want you to keep that."

"You may need it."

I sighed. I wouldn't take no for an answer. "Yeah, and if I'm successful, Atlantis is going to change. I know you said you'll still have air, but…" I slid the bottle towards him, "I'd rather you have an option. Just in case." I could probably get another dose of the potion from Marin if I needed it, anyway.

The definite 'no' section was even smaller than the 'take' pile. I only knew I would leave the vial with Marin's eye scale, and now the water-breathing potion. I'd already made Score promise me he'd at least take the tears so he'd have *someone* to talk to besides Forte, even though he didn't know Marin very well yet. It'd also allow us to communicate— through an intermediary, but it was still a relief.

"You could take this," Score said, fishing the minotaur's chain from his guitar case.

I sighed, "You'd get better use from that library than I would. You'd also benefit from a change of scenery and some real sunshine."

"A skylight isn't much better than the Lark garden."

"I still think you should keep it."

I leaned back against the smooth wall of the room, rubbing my forehead with the flat of my palm. What else would I need? I didn't know. The scope of this mission, this quest, was too much. I wasn't familiar enough with the Realm to know what problems could potentially arise.

"Take some clothes," Score suggested.

"I don't really *need* clothes. I still have a closet full at Marin's house, and until I get there, I'll be in the Overworld. Human items aren't exactly difficult to procure."

"Take your armor."

My brows raised. It was a good idea. "The armor's too bulky for my bag, but I'll wear it when I leave." I ran my finger over the swords, the bow. I'd brought them from the arena, but I didn't know if I'd actually need them. I hoped not.

"Those should be going," Score said softly.

"Should they?" I asked, my voice almost cracking. I traced the hilts. He was right. I'd strap them to my back when I left.

"I hope you don't have to use them, but take them with you. Just…"

"Hmm?" I stared into his eyes. They were mournful blue.

They had been all day. I was sure mine matched the color perfectly.

"Just try— if you *have* to fight, please fight smart, not hard."

"Yeah. Sure."

"I mean it, Lyra. You're so good, so moral, but you don't always think through actions. Remember what's practical before jumping headfirst into danger. Remember that you have the power of your voice when you're outside of the Realm— at least until you change things. If you remember, your limitations are so infinitesimal—"

I smiled softly at the rant, brushing my fingertips over his hand. He'd seen me forget, time and again, to use my voice. It was always obvious to him, but I only thought of it as a last resort. I needed to remember I had the option, especially when I was in a pinch.

Even with the weapons added to my back, my bag was still almost empty. "Why is this so hard?" I groaned.

Score wrapped his arms around me, encircling me completely, pinning my arms to my sides. He kissed my temple. "What do you *want* to take with you?"

You.

It was on the tip of my tongue, but I couldn't say it. It was too heartbreaking.

I shrugged under the weight of his chin, "I don't know, Score. I don't know. Morale, I guess?"

"Morale?"

You.

I took a moment to collect myself. If I started to cry now, I wouldn't *stop* crying. "Yeah. Something to remember why I'm fighting."

"Oh," Score said thoughtfully.

I bolstered my courage, steeling myself, promising I wouldn't shed a tear if I said it.

"I don't even have a picture of you."

He dropped his arms from me and began digging through our shared wardrobe. He reached deep in the back of the top shelf, retrieving his phone.

Score held it up. "You want one?" he asked, turning it on. The device made a pitiful beeping noise. I hovered over him, staring at the screen. The wallpaper was a picture of me sleeping soundly.

"Creepy," I said, smiling.

He chuckled at the remark. It hadn't been charged in over a year. I was impressed it still had ten percent battery life. In Atlantis, of course, there was no signal available. "There's not much time left on the battery, anyway, and I'm nervous to keep extending it with magic." He shrugged, "It's not a big loss to me. Click a picture."

He handed the phone to me. I held it up, snapping the photo quickly. Score looked sad, but I wasn't going to ask for a second one. I turned it off, setting it with my bag. "Thank you."

He smiled, pointing to the clockwork Nightingale, "Are you going to take your friend?"

Grief hit my chest, making it difficult to breathe. "I think I'd rather keep it here." I smiled, but I was certain I didn't fool Score. "I'll see it again when I return."

"If—" he paused, looking conflicted. I tilted my head, waiting for him to complete the thought. "If you're leaving it, would you—" He took a breath, smiling, "Would you mind saying something into it? For my own morale?" He paused, his eyes wide and almost frantic, "It won't delete the original message, I— I just…" he stared at his feet, "I just know I'll miss your voice."

I moved closer to him, standing on my tiptoes. I brushed my thumb across his cheek, kissing him. I grabbed the bird, squeezing the body until I heard a rough click. "I love you, Score. Forever. And I'm going to see you again."

I released the clockwork animal, taking in a rasping breath.

He reached for my hands, caressing them in his own. "It's not like you won't be hearing from me," he said, gesturing towards the bottle with the mermaid tears.

I nodded. We'd had this discussion twice now. And I was grateful for it, truly— but I wasn't Marin, and he wouldn't be talking to *me*. I was still anxious, though. "You'll speak to her first thing after I leave, right?"

"*Yes*, Lyra."

I gripped his hands, pulling him closer. I stared into his eyes, "I just want to know, for sure, as soon as I speak with her that you're fine— that there weren't any complications with the gate."

He pressed his forehead to mine, "I know. First thing.

Promise."

I clutched his back, leaning against his chest. I closed my eyes, breathing him in. How could I possibly succeed without him? After all this time, it felt more and more like he was my strength.

"Is there anything else you should take?"

"There's only one thing I'd like to bring with me, but I can't."

Score gently lifted my chin up towards him with two fingers and kissed me. It was a sweet kiss— soft and comforting. When he pulled back, he said, "Sirens live *at least* 3,500 years— usually more, Lyra. Did you know that?"

I shook my head. I knew we were long-lived, but none of Aldan's books had pinpointed exact ages. There were too many conflicting reports. Long-lived could mean anywhere between 200 years and 10,000. None were completely immortal. Forte had implied we lived a long time, too.

"Well, we do," he continued. He ran his hands up and down my arms, "So in the span of 1,000 years, or 2,000, or 5,000, what's a year? What's a decade? What's a century?" He brushed my hair back, draping it all over one shoulder, leaning close to my ear, "A drop in the bucket. That's all."

That didn't mean that it wouldn't be a painful year, or decade, or century. Small bites of time could have big impact. I turned to him, my eyes wide and sad, "Score, we've only known each other for a little over a year. We've been together, like this, for less than half of that." I placed my hand on his cheek, feeling the roughness of his stubble. He hadn't shaved today. "Sometimes," I said carefully, "the smallest drops in the bucket make the biggest ripples."

"Lyra," he groaned. He grabbed my waist, swooping me to his lap, sitting on the edge of the bed. "We're not going to be sad today."

"You say that as if only *my* eyes are blue, Score."

He smiled, "Inner turmoils aside— we aren't shedding tears. We're not going to frown, and we're not going to wallow in self pity. We should *celebrate*."

"And why is that?"

"Because after today, you'll finish your mission. You'll fix this mess our species made and return to me. And then..." he smiled, his eyes actually turning gold. "Then it'll be our time to be together. And we'll never part again. I promise."

"You can't know for sure, Score," I pointed out to him. "In the span of a thousand years or more, a million things could happen that could—"

His lips silenced me, hungrily fixing on my own. I melted into him, wishing for the billionth time today that the Broken was all a nightmare, that Susan and Rick would spontaneously get well on their own, that the only *real* things were he and I and our life together.

When he broke the kiss, he smiled. "Everything after this mission— I don't care what it is. I won't part from you. So fate had better only bring the kind of nonsense that takes *two*."

I laughed, swiping at my face. "Okay. Let's be happy, then."

He glanced at the clock, his eyes anxious, "It's probably about time. If we wait too long you're going to have trouble getting anywhere."

Score was right, as usual. I had no idea where I'd emerge, but the first order of business would be to find Glenn. After that, we'd need to get our bearings and return to Marin. Depending on how far we were from Whitecrest, I might have a long journey ahead.

I tucked the few possessions I needed in my bag, making sure to wrap and re-wrap any glass in fabric. I couldn't afford for a single item to break. I zipped the phone into the side pocket. It was the most precious thing I was taking. I looped a silver chain with the sirens' opal Source Key around my neck, tucking it beneath my shirt.

I laced my armor methodically. It felt good to do something so *normal* for Atlantis. I could almost pretend I was just getting ready for an average day of training. Score would spend the day in his research, and we'd meet in the evening.

I slung both swords across my back, angling them carefully so they were easily accessible. I packed a bow below them, hanging a small quiver of arrows from my hips. I wasn't as skilled with the bow as I was with my swords, but it was a good idea to carry a ranged weapon.

I gripped my bag nervously. It felt deflated, especially since I wasn't taking nearly as much as I had the first time. Even with my dulcimer shoved inside, it was still smaller than the bag

I'd carried while I trekked across the Realm.

True to his word, Score pocketed the vial with Marin's eye scale before we left. He wouldn't even pause to rest after the gate was opened. He'd inform Marin first thing of our plan.

I laced my fingers through Score's as we headed to the arena. He chose it because the space was wide open and would allow magic to channel freely. As we walked, I said, "Tell me how it works. Exactly."

"Okay." He'd explained it all before, but I hoped hearing it again would reassure me. "Every magical race has their own methods of creating gates. Some work better than others for each species. Sirens very rarely created gates, but we've passed through one before— the minotaur's chain. That's why it felt so natural for us, like we were just opening a door.

"Though each race guards how they create their own gates carefully, the basics are simple. Two points, linked magically from object to object to create a portal.

"Normally, to effectively create a sirens' gate, many years of meditation are required to charge the two objects. However, this isn't always the case. One way gates are also possible, which is what we'll be attempting. Most species use gates to link the Realm to a point on the Overworld, but there are other functions. There are gates linking two sites in the Realm, gates linking two sites in the Overworld, and even gates that link to other places.

"The problem is that it'd require vast amounts of singing on our parts to imbue anything with enough magic to create such a portal. A conduit has to be capable of channeling a *tremendous* amount of magic, which normally requires a minimum of 70 years to refine. We don't have that kind of time.

"But sirens are organically capable of handling vast amounts of arcane energy. By utilizing *myself* rather than an object, we bypass the timing issue. A second object *might* be problematic, but as a siren I'm already linked to an object outside— the opal we gave Birkita. This will negate the need to meditate on a second point, and will place you outside of Atlantis. If you're near Birkita, you can probably hire her to help you get to Glenn. At the very least, I doubt Birkita let anything happen to the opal, though you might rip her bag when you arrive next to it."

We'd been over that part of the plan a hundred times.

"And the risks," I said softly. We stood on the grass of the arena. The breeze blew my hair across my eyes.

He sighed, "There's a risk transferring that much magic through me, yes. Best case scenario, I walk out of this with a headache. Worst case… I don't survive."

I hated hearing it, but needed to accept it.

"Are you ready?"

No.

I nodded.

"When it's time, you'll know," He said. "You can approach then."

"Okay."

I felt numbed. This was it. The last couple seconds I had with him.

"Score!" I called. He turned to me, surprised. I kissed him anxiously. "Goodb— I'll see you soon."

He smiled, backing up. "See you soon, Lyra."

He began to chant softly in siren tongue, with the slightest hum below it:

Power Travel Magic Power Travel Magic…

The chant shifted, changing to a melody with a chord backing it. Score's body began to glow, dim at first, but then it was bright— so bright it hurt my eyes.

Now was the time. I stepped towards him. He wrapped his arms around me. I leaned my head against his chest, looking up at his face. It was screwed up in concentration. I could feel it now, a wave of magic, the static charge in the air like a lightning storm. He squeezed me tightly, his mouth forming a grimace. My stomach quivered involuntarily. The air seemed to hum, the chanting still echoing though Score wasn't making the sound now. It felt like there was a cloud of locusts around me, stinging, buzzing, biting.

His legs buckled, his arms going slack, and he fell forward.

"Score!" I shouted.

He passed through me, as steadily as if I was a ghost. The light swelled, blinding me.

I blinked, clearing my vision.

He was gone. Atlantis was gone. I was standing at the edge of dunes, not far from the shore of the island where we'd left Glenn.

I felt an aching pain in my heart. Score! He fell. Was he alive? Did he survive?

I wrenched my gaze upward, stumbling forward. "Glenn?" I called, my voice dried up and creaky. I was parched, my mouth ashy from the influx of magic. A wave of dizziness struck me, and I placed a hand against my head, trying to steady myself.

My eyes were fixed on the ground. Near my feet lay the huge opal, toppled out of Birkita's satchel. Two of Avia's phoenix feathers were scattered beneath the leather, half-buried in sand but protected by the pouch.

That's strange...

I'd assumed I'd be right next to the banshee, but I didn't see anyone nearby. I shook my head, running my hands through my hair. I hadn't expected to be here. Maybe Glenn insisted that Birkita leave the opal with him?

I squeezed my eyes shut, trying to get my bearings. When I felt steady, I opened them.

A make-shift shelter of sticks and dry grass was ahead of me, no more than a ramshackle hut. It looked like it was one gust away from falling over.

I stumbled forward, calling, "Glenn?!" again. Even if he had abandoned the island, there would probably be a note— or something to direct me to my bodyguard. I stepped through the opening.

Signs of a struggle greeted my eyes: snapped bushes, scrapes in the branches of the shack, burnt cinders, ash and soot smearing the grass.

A rust colored stain blushed from the center of the sand, tracked by deep ruts that faded into obscurity at the doorway, weathered away by time. It looked like a body had been dragged out.

Discarded near the bloodstain was a twisted, leafy necklace. It was Glenn's.

I swallowed thickly, falling to my knees. Dread slithered down my spine like a snake.

He was gone.

Read Ahead for an Excerpt From...

Caprice

Book Three of the Rhapsody Quartet

by A. M. Hodgson

"Sarah… Wake up, Sarah. You're going to be late."

I rubbed my eyes, cracking them open. "Wha— what?"

Susan loomed over me, a broad smile on her lips. Her hair fell near her face like a curtain. "School starts in half an hour."

I shook my head, trying to clear it. I craned my neck. I was in my room— my *old* room. The room I'd had at my foster parents' house.

"Score?" I called, blinking. No, that wasn't right— I'd just arrived in Whitecrest…

"Where's Marin?"

"Who? What are you talking about?" Susan shook her head and glanced at the book on the nightstand— *Andersen Fairy Tales*. She smiled, "Fairy stories before bedtime again? You know they give you nightmares."

I groped near the foot of the bed where I kept my swords, but my fingers met only carpet fiber.

The room was dimmer than I remembered.

"Magic," I muttered, my stomach clenching.

Susan laughed, "Oh, Sarah, there's no such thing as—"

I leapt to my feet. Pushing her away, I moved to the window. It was covered in drab gray curtains. I tugged on them, expecting to see— what? A dream landscape? Darkness? An illusion?

All that met my eyes was the same view I'd always had from this bedroom. A vantage overlooking dreary skies, trees, and other houses in the suburbs. Too far to see the ocean. Too far to even hear it.

"This is impossible," I whispered.

"Are you okay, honey?" Susan asked, her brows knitting in worry. She wove her way to me, placing a hand against my forehead, "You don't feel feverish."

I glanced down at my body. My pajamas hung on my frame, the way they always did before my transition. Stringy hair fell across my shoulders.

I shook.

"This isn't—" I swallowed, looking into her eyes. Only concern met my gaze. "You were in a coma."

She laughed, "So it *was* a nightmare. Well, it's over now."

I plopped down on the foot of my bed, staring out the window.

Everything had felt so real, though.

My stomach clenched as I recalled Score's touch, his kisses, his song.

Of course he'd be a dream. Nothing is that perfect.

I swallowed, "What's— what day is it? I don't remember."

"Tuesday," Susan supplied. "We just got your graduation announcements. We need to mail them soon."

"Graduation?" I whispered, blinking.

I didn't remember a single thing about my senior year, but I was supposedly half-way through it.

"Yeah," Susan said. "Just a few months left." She handed me an announcement. Whitecrest High's blue and green crest greeted me, complete with our shark mascot. I ran my fingertip across the embossed surface, flipping it open. A picture of my own face met my eyes. I smiled brightly in the image, though a single snaggle tooth marred the radiance. I was skinny, and my skin was sallow, sickly— less olive than it'd been since the transition I remembered so clearly. My hair had been pulled half up, but despite the extra effort it remained lackluster. I wore a white cardigan and floral print dress that buttoned up the front. The outfit hung on my frame like a tent, highlighting my lack of curves.

I had no memory of the picture.

"Susan when did we—"

"Autumn. Right after your birthday this year."

I nodded, rubbing my forehead.

"Remember? We went out for cake and ice cream at the European Bakery?" she prodded.

I nodded again, though I had no idea what she was talking about. My only memory of my seventeenth birthday was a cherished one— singing with Score for the first time.

"You know what might make you feel better?" Susan asked, moving to the closet, "A present. I'd planned on giving this to you closer to graduation, but you seem so out of sorts today that I think you should have it now. Then straight to school."

I swallowed, glancing outside again.

A few seagulls flew past the window.

"Ah!" Susan said behind me, "Here we are."

I glanced over my shoulder at her. She held out a little velvet box, opening it.

A necklace woven with silver filigree, black onyxes, and white diamonds rested in the box.

"It's pretty," I mumbled.

"The gems are fake," she said with a sigh. "But I thought it'd look nice on you."

I stared out the window again. A horn honked in the distance.

It'd seemed so real...

"Here. I'll help you clasp it." She moved behind me, holding up the necklace.

A sick feeling settled in my stomach.

The silver in Susan's hand caught the dim light, glinting in the window pane.

I glanced at the reflection. My heart stopped.

I was exactly the way I'd been since transitioning. Curvy, with changing eyes and bright skin, a siren. Wearing a camisole and yoga pants.

That wasn't the important part. Within the reflection, I could see Susan— and it wasn't Susan.

It was a monster.

Sagging skin and sharp bones formed the carcass of a hideous old woman. A few stray wisps of white hair grew from her spotty skull and sprouted off of long pointed ears. Gray skin hung from her limbs like a coat. Red eyes burned in her hollow sockets, fixed on my neck. A jagged smile spread maniacally across her black lips as though it'd been carved into her flesh.

And in her hands she held not a necklace, but a knife. A knife that inched closer and closer to my throat.

I ducked, batting the weapon from her hand and stumbling forward.

A shrill sound met my ears, loud enough that I clapped my hands over them, squeezing my eyes shut.

My swords— I need my swords!

The glass of the window shattered in an explosion, raining into my hair. I peered through the hole, seeing sky and tide. A glow in the west marked dawn's arrival, but it was still dusky.

The illusion had been severed.

I jerked my head up towards the creature who'd assaulted me.

She still wore the rigid smile across her black lips. "Oh, Lyra," she murmured. I'd expected something grating, but instead the sound was like silk floating through the air. "Don't you know it's rude to look into the reflection of a dark elf?"

I rolled away, snatching my swords from the ground and

jerking them free of their scabbards.

A shadow glided across the broken window. I snapped my head towards it, seeing a flash of green but not much else.

"I was so close," she pouted. "The Hand would've been pleased."

I turned to her, holding my blades before myself. "Tell the Hand of Fate I'm not going to die today."

"Oh? Maybe you won't." She chuckled, her grotesque form melting away. Her hair grew and shone in white curls, her gray skin firmed, her body softened into defined curves. A snappy suit faded onto her body, red and ornate like a general's dress regalia. Her crimson eyes sparkled through long dark lashes. She grinned, looking the picture of youthful health, though unnatural. "I'd have been disappointed if it'd been that easy." She drew a long rapier from her side. I wondered if it was real, or more illusion. "But killing you would've been a bonus. I was sent to give you a message." She jutted forward with the sword.

I jerked to the right, dodging the blade. Broken glass dug into my bare feet.

I swung my sword, hearing it whistle. "And what message is that?"

She stepped aside gracefully, smiling more broadly.

The light filtering through the broken window dimmed again.

I glanced towards it. An enormous green dragon blotted the thin sunlight.

The beast roared, revealing a layer of dripping teeth.

Trapped between two monsters.

A plume of green fog burst from the dragon's mouth, jetting through the broken glass towards the intruder.

She lurched to her right; the spray hit the wall. It hissed and bubbled as it made contact with the plaster.

A caustic sting hit my nostrils, burning them.

"I don't have time for this," muttered the gray-skinned elf. She darted towards the door, glancing over her shoulder, grinning. "The message was simple, pretty Lyra: Welcome back."

Acknowledgements

To the many people who have kept me sane while writing this, thank you.

To my beta-reader Alicia: Thank you for your enthusiasm, your time and your theories. Thank you for being a fan when I needed one the most. Thank you for making the hours and effort of writing worth it.

To my cover artist and beta-reader, Alexis: Thank you for your infinite patience, incredible skill, and beautiful talent. I couldn't have chosen anyone better to make my world come to life. You're an amazing artist and an even better friend.

To Jessica, my line editor, sacrificer of time and sanity: I'm fortunate to know someone who is willing to read anything I put in their hands, regardless of quality. I'm more fortunate to have someone who helps to make it better. Even though we butt heads at times, I cannot express enough how incredibly grateful I am for your time, energy, and feedback. I couldn't have found someone better, even if I wanted *to*.

To Lynne, my mother & cheerleader: You have unwavering faith in this project, even when I don't. You've dropped everything on more than one occasion to listen to me rant and rave, to reassure me that everything is worth it, to metaphorically pat me on the head when things have gotten tough. I know I couldn't do this without you. I love and respect you more than you know, and appreciate everything you do and are.

To Darin, my husband, my love: You are the man with the incredible missing wife, the man who has put up with dirty dishes in the sink for an extra chapter, the man who has dealt with melt-downs and drama, the man who has seen my tears and frustration and somehow, through it all, still loves me. I don't know how you do it, but I'm grateful. I love you more than my inadequate words can say.

And finally, to my reader: thank you for taking a chance on this series. Thank you for reading it. I appreciate each and every one of you for breathing life into this story with your imaginations.

About the Author

We're not saying A.M. Hodgson is a deadly ninja by night. But we're not *not* saying that, either. When she's not making up fantastical plotlines and endearingly flawed characters, she's reading, playing video games, or being forced to socialize with real, living, breathing people.

She lives in Spokane, Washington with her husband, two cats and a rage-filled chihuahua. She enjoys long walks on the beach, daring adventures, and other activities she only frequents in her imagination.

Learn more about A.M. Hodgson at her website: http://www.amhodgson.com